Between the Shadow and the Soul

Ciara Blowers

DEDICATION

To my mom, who would always let me borrow her laptop to type away at my stories when I was younger.
To you, the reader, thank you so much for picking up my story. If my story allows you to get away from your hectic world—even for a moment—and find solace, then I have achieved my goal as an author.

CHAPTER ONE

Everything was gray and white as our car plunged through the blizzard in the early morning of Tuesday, December 15th. I distinctly remember it being a Tuesday. Typically, I would be in my nice, warm bed, still asleep until I had to wake up to go to school. So it was odd when my parents woke me with urgency and rushed me into the car. I was placed behind the driver's seat and buckled in tightly. They barely spoke or answered my questions, but even as a child, I knew something was wrong. I could sense the tension and see the worried looks my parents gave each other as our car barreled down the road.

"Mommy, where are we going?" My puffy winter jacket was starting to become uncomfortable, as my father always had the heat on high during the winter.

My mother looked back at me and gently placed a hand on my knee, "Don't worry, sweetie. The family is just going to take a little trip." She tried to give me a reassuring smile.

I clutched onto my stuffed animal, Piggy. Piggy was a baby

toy gifted to me when I was born. It wasn't until I was older that I realized that Piggy was not a pig, but an elephant. I carried Piggy with me everywhere. She was white with pink spots and had a little bell inside.

"Fuck!" my father screamed as our minivan made a violent jerk. My mother whipped her head around to the front of the car.

"John, what's happening?" Fear and panic drenched my mother's words.

Tires squealing, my father tried to wrangle the minivan back into control, but we slammed into something and were launched into the air and began to flip. For a moment it felt like we were flying—like everything was weightless. I didn't have time to react or feel scared, just a plummeting feeling in my stomach as gravity came into play. The car landed. Hard. Everything happened so quickly, and before I knew it, everything went black.

It was cold as I came to.

Everything was blurry and my head hurt. As my eyes started to focus, I saw my mother slumped over in her seat. Something warm was trickling down my forehead, but my puffy jacket prevented me from reaching up.

"Mommy," it sounded like a whisper, and I was not sure if I had spoken it out loud.

Why is Mommy sleeping? What is going on?

My mother began to stir.

"Mommy," I said louder this time, panic starting to set in.

Why isn't Mommy answering me?

My mother straightened up in her seat. She began to look frantically around and shake my father.

"John, John, wake up!" she cried out.

I began to cry.

"God dammit! Oh my god, my legs, my legs are crushed!" my mother screamed. I rarely ever heard my parents swear, and even at nine years old, I was proud to admit I knew most of the swear words. I had picked them up from various television shows or at school—from the cool kids.

My mother turned her attention to me now. She unbuckled her seat belt and struggled to get back to me. The roof had caved in, so she couldn't fully crawl into the back seat with me, but she fit her torso through. I could see blood running down her face and bruises starting to form.

"Shh, honey, it's okay. Mommy's got you. I've got you, sweetheart," she tried to console me as she fumbled to get to my seat belt.

"What's wrong wi-wi-with Daddy?" I asked through big sobs.

She ignored my question. "Mommy is going to get us out, okay? Mommy can only do so much right now. Her legs aren't working right now. But you're going to have to be a big girl and listen to her. Can you do that for Mommy?"

"I can be a big girl," I said as I gave one last big sniffle and held back the flooding tears as best I could.

"That's my Cassie," she smiled. "Okay, I need you to—" but her sentence was cut off by the awful sound of tires screeching toward us. A lot of tires.

My mother jerked her head up to look out the back window. If she wasn't already white enough, she went bone pale at the image she saw.

"Cassie, get out of the car, right now," she tried to stay calm to not alarm me. I shifted Piggy into one hand and tried to pull the lever to open the door.

"Cassie, honey, open the door," urgency leaked through. "Open the door NOW!"

I tried, but the door wouldn't budge. It was jammed and my little arms could only push so hard.

"I'm trying, Mommy!" I screamed.

The screeching got closer and a loud horn blared. My mother tried to squeeze herself further through the gap and started pounding against the door frantically, begging for it to open. I couldn't stop the tears from returning.

The door still wouldn't budge; she looked at me, "Hold onto Piggy tightly. I love you, Cassie." She sat back, outstretched her arms, and a gust of wind blew the door open. I was flung out along with it, being ripped out of my seat. My mother and the car became smaller as I was propelled further away from it. Just before I hit the ground, I saw a semi smash into the back end of the car, taking away everything I loved in my life, and causing flames to erupt. The flames reached out toward me to pull me back, but I escaped just barely and crashed to the cold, hard ground.

"NOOO!" I jolt awake in my seat on the airplane. Sweat coating every inch of me, my heart racing, my lungs desperately gasping for air.

"Are you all right, dear?" the startled, sweet old man sitting next to me asks. I look around at all the worried stares from the surrounding passengers as I try and steady myself.

"Yes," I reply as my breathing becomes more regulated. "Just a bad dream," I say, loud enough for the others to hear me.

I try and smile to reassure the others that I'm not some crazy lady freaking out on an airplane. I shift in my seat uncomfortably as I try to get resituated. I clutch the backpack in my lap and try to forget what just happened. You would think after fourteen years, several therapists, and loads of medication this nightmare would stop. That somehow, I'd be able to get over the death of my parents, but life's a bitch that way, and there are rarely true happy endings.

"This is your captain speaking. We are beginning our descent into Heathrow Airport. The weather is a brisk eight degrees centigrade, and the local time is 6:07 a.m."

It had been a long trip from the great state of Michigan, and I still have at least two hours of driving to some small town I've already forgotten the name of.

"This will be a good thing, Cassie," my grandmother's words echo in my mind as I direct my still-embarrassed gaze out the airplane window. It's raining, but I heard that is typical for most days in this area. I love the rain, so this is not the issue. The issue is that I'm 23 years old, travelling to a school for magically gifted witches, in a

country I have never been to, all alone. Well, almost all alone. I made sure to stash Piggy in my backpack.

Oh, yeah, I am a witch. That shocker was just the icing on the cake after my parents died. I had become angry one day and caused pictures to fling off the walls with a wave of my hand. Questions piled up over the years, but my grandmother, who had taken me in, told me as much as she could. Some things made sense, some didn't, but I knew there was information missing. Either she truly did not know everything, or she was purposely keeping things from me.

There is magic coursing through everyone's blood, some just have traces—like my grandmother, where it comes out as "gifts," like singing, dancing, public speaking—and some have blood that is overrun with magic. My parents and I fall into the latter category. The whole blowing open the car door made a lot more sense after learning this fact.

Technically, my grandmother could have sent me to this school whenever she wanted, but I think she knew I needed her. I needed some connection to the only family member I had left in the world. She and I would binge as many witchy shows as we could to take notes. *Charmed* became a staple of my childhood. Magic was an escape until I grew older, and then it became a tool I abused. Magic does not mix well with a hormonal teenager with anger management issues. But I am also still human, and human vices can work almost as well as magic.

This will be a good thing. I need some direction.

I did the whole college thing, but even then, I didn't know

what I wanted to do. I'm hoping this school can fill some of the missing gaps in my grandmother's stories and give me answers to some of the questions I've held onto all these years. Afterall, I am a legacy.

An older man in a driver's uniform with a sign reading, "Cassandra Rodden," in big, black letters is waiting for me when I walk off the plane. He greets me with the sweetest English accent, while also informing me his name is Walt. After claiming my baggage, I stop in the bathroom to relieve my full bladder before the long drive. For a busy airport, the bathroom is surprisingly empty.

The mirror is unforgiving as I gaze into it. One of the few things that really stuck out about my mother when she was still alive was that she always looked so well put together. She took pride in her appearance. That's something I've always tried to carry on, but no amount of makeup could cover the purple and blueish circles that had formed underneath my eyes on the plane. It also does not help that my black turtleneck, black and white plaid skirt, and black boots only accentuate those circles. I tuck my silver blonde hair behind my ear, adjust my skirt, and head back out to where Walt is waiting patiently.

"So, Miss Rodden," Walt tries to start a conversation as we pull out of the airport, "I see I'll be taking you to Kingshire Academy up in Northwood."

Ahh, that's the name.

"Guess so, Walt."

"Beautiful up there, it is. Oh, if you get too warm, just let me know and I'll adjust the heat." He gives me a smile in the mirror.

"Thank you. Will do," I say with a forced smile.

I'm not one to seek out conversations with others, but I have become a master in faking it and figuring out what is expected in a conversation, and that's not just because I'm a girl. We all live very superficial lives—the same conversations over and over again, the same stories told, the same lies perpetuated to make us all seem cooler than we actually are. No one ever gets down to raw emotions, so we just talk about the weather and our jobs—always giving people an edited version of who we are so that they accept us. In doing so, though, some of us never discover who we truly are.

Walt rambles off different facts about the area as we drive, and I feign interest, but the rain steals my attention like a mistress does a married man. The smell of rain is so alluring, the way the sound sooths and welcomes me. I am incredibly anxious to start this new journey, so I like to think of the rain as an old friend telling me it'll be all right.

Before I know it, we're pulling off the main road onto gravel, which we traverse for about a mile. I peek from the back seat through the windshield and see that the road stretches up to an enormous estate bordered with tall shrubbery. Never in my life have I seen something like this, but I guess when you grow up in a small town called Marshall, everything seems big. The estate looks so grandiose and proper.

Walt slows the car as we approach a large gate guarding the

entrance. The rain starts to let up, barely just a drizzle now.

He rolls the car window down and speaks into a small box, "Cassandra Rodden has arrived. Sorry we are a tad late."

I look at the time on my phone: 8:02 a.m. Check in ended at eight o'clock, but I am sure it will be fine.

A beep sounds, and the gates open slowly.

"Fancy," I say as Walt rolls up the window.

He chuckles.

We drive up to a large roundabout with a small fountain in the middle. Walt comes to a stop right in front of the old-but-elegant doors. As he gets out and walks around the car to my door, I clutch my backpack and prepare to step out.

"This will be a good thing," I repeat to myself quietly.

Walt is able to quickly gather my suitcases from the trunk after helping me out of the car.

"Welp, Miss Rodden, it has been a pleasure," he says, tipping his hat.

"Thank you, Walt. Drive safe."

"Always do, ma'am."

And with one last smile, he gets back into the car and makes the trek back down the long gravel road.

A small gust of wind passes right through me as I make it to the top of the stone steps, causing me to pause. I stare at the daunting doors, unsure if I want to commit.

There's still time to back out, right? No, I need this. I need to learn to control things better. I need answers.

9

With a heavy sigh and heaving my backpack onto my shoulder, I wrap my hand around the large door handle and give it a push. I have to give the door more of a push than originally expected due to underestimating its weight, but it finally *creaks* open.

The doors open to a main walk-in area. Everything inside is just as you would expect it—grand, extravagant, and sophisticated. High ceilings with elegant portraits hanging on every inch of wall. A girl with large, round glasses sits at a table just inside the entrance. There is a deep burgundy banner draped across the table that reads in gold letters, "Welcome to Kingshire Academy." She instantly notices me when I walk in and puts down the book that she's reading. Her hair is short and styled in a pixie cut. I notice as I walk closer, her name tag notifies that her name is Alice.

"Hello!" she says enthusiastically.

"Hi, um, Cassandra Rodden, checking in," I say, not sure what I'm supposed to do.

"Perfect. You are a tad late, but that is okay. Let me just find your name and get you checked in."

Goodness, I am only a few minutes late.

Alice lifts her clipboard and searches for my name. She hums softly to herself. I look around at several other people in the main entrance. There is a young boy with his two parents standing around. One of the two men is looking at the different cases with school trophies and pictures, the other is trying to console the young boy, whose face is red from crying.

"But I am going to miss my daddies. I want to go home with

you," he sobs in a thick Scottish accent.

"Time to be a strong lad, okay? We'll visit sometime soon. We promise."

My heart aches as I remember my mother and father.

"Time to be a big girl, Cassie."

I shake my head to clear my mother's words.

"Okay, so, it looks like your room will be in the west wing. Here is a map of the grounds, as well as your class schedule. Any books you'll need should be in your room already. Just go up the stairs behind me and there will be signs directing you to the different halls. Unfortunately, we do not have an elevator," Alice says as she hands me my map and schedule. She smiles and then motions to the grand staircase behind her.

"Thanks," I say, trying to match her smile.

I grab my suitcase and wheel it over to the stairs.

Note to self: maybe don't wear heels often here.

The stairs themselves are not too bad, as I use magic to make it easier to lift my suitcase, but my boots are pinching my toes with each step and are making them sore. I am relieved when I finally make it up them all and find the sign that signals where my hall is.

All the doors are adorned with numbers. I double check my sheet, which tells me that I will be staying in room 333. I walk slowly down the hall, looking at all the numbers. A couple people squeeze by me and mutter things under their breath, due to my suitcase taking up most of the hallway. I ignore them.

330...331...332...333, here it is.

The door to the room is slightly ajar. I try to control my labored breathing from all the stairs as I slowly push the door open. Immediately in the room to the left is the bathroom, which looks occupied at the moment, as the door is shut and the light is on. I close the door softly behind me and walk the rest of the way inside. The room isn't large, but it does not feel cramped. There are raised beds along the opposite walls. Small desks and chairs are placed at the foot of the beds.

Welcome home, I guess.

"Jesus Christ!" a voice shouts behind me.

I spin around to see a very petite girl clutching her chest.

"I am so sorry. I did not mean to scare you," I try and assure.

Her skin is a light brown and her dark hair falls just above her shoulders. She's wearing a pair of baggy jeans and a shirt that says, "Women do it better."

I think I am going to like her.

She chuckles. "You're good, babe. My name is Nora. You better be my new roommate Cassandra, or otherwise we might have some issues," she says in the cutest British accent, but she speaks quickly so I have to listen closely.

I smile. "Yep, that's me."

"Bitchin'. So, I already chose the left side of the room. Hope that's okay?"

Looks like I have no choice.

"Yeah, not a problem."

"Oh my god," Nora says as she suddenly gets very close to

my face. "Your eyes are so wicked!"

I blush. This is most people's reaction to my eyes, and it is understandable. It's not every day that you see someone with one blue eye and the other brown.

"Oh, yeah, thanks, I guess. It's called heterochromia. It's a condition that causes irises to be different colors."

Nora investigates my eyes for a moment more.

"Wicked. I love it. The only weird thing I have is that I was born with a third nipple. So, how do you like England so far? Have you ever been over here before?" Nora asks as she goes back to setting up her side of the room.

I try to suppress a laugh. I appreciate her bluntness and candor. I swing my suitcase and backpack onto my bed and start to unpack. There are dresser drawers underneath the raised beds, but no closet.

"Uh, no, I haven't ever been here before. It's very beautiful, from what I've seen so far. How about you?"

"Well, my family is from India, but I was born over this way. It's pretty boring sometimes here. I've been going to the Academy for a few years now. I'd love to go to the States though. I truly feel like New York calls to me, even though I have never been."

I let Nora take charge of the conversation while we both unpack and get our things around. Talking to new people gives me anxiety, because I never know if they'll get my humor or care about anything I have to say. Plus, I like listening to Nora. She's so passionate about everything. She gives me a rundown of our classes, and thankfully we have a similar schedule. She informs me that everyone that is a Level 6 will have tactical training together in the mornings.

As I settle more into the room, and as Nora keeps rambling on about this and that, I feel good. Something inside of me feels like I am exactly where I'm supposed to be.

CHAPTER TWO

"Crap! We've got to get to the ceremony!" Nora exclaims, looking at the time on her phone.

"Ceremony? What ceremony?"

"It's the welcoming ceremony. They do it every year, and we cannot be late. Let's go!"

Oh, joy...

Nora and I hurry out of our room and make our way down the stairs with the other students heading to the ceremony. We take a different staircase than the main one I took to get to the room. Nora says that it will be quicker, but she forgets to mention that it's going to be steeper.

The school holds students of all ages, but most of them range from 11-23, and in total there are only about a couple hundred current students. My grandmother told me that over the years, there are fewer people who have stronger traces of magic in their blood. Whether this is due to non-magical and magical people reproducing, or just that maybe magic has lost its hope in the world and humanity, no one can tell. Regardless of why, good magic is fading in the world and being replaced with something darker.

My heel does not make full contact with the last step as Nora and I scurry down them and I stumble. A set of strong arms flashes out to steady me before I make a complete embarrassment of myself.

"You all right there?" his melodic voice shows hints of concern.

My eyes travel to meet his.

"Yeah." My face instantly turns red as his forest green eyes stare back into mine. "Th-thank you," I stutter out.

I take a step back when I notice I'm still in his arms. His face warms into a smile. His golden-brown hair has a few curls. He's tall, but not too tall—and muscular, but lean at the same time.

"Anytime. I'm Henry, by the way. Interesting eyes."

It's like my brain is turning to mush. My skin feels hot and I open my mouth to speak, but nothing comes out. All I can really hear is my heart thudding in my ears.

"Henry, this is Cassie," Nora offers from behind me and gives me a slight nudge. "She's from the States. She's new."

I am now uncomfortably aware that I'm holding up the entire staircase. Others are huffing at the hold up.

"Yeah, um, Nora where do we go now?" I ask, trying to move out of the way so other students can pass.

"This way," she says, moving around me.

I follow behind her, trying not make this anymore awkward than it already is.

"Well, hey," Henry gently grabs my wrist and I turn back to face him. His hand on my skin causes my heart to flutter. "It was nice to meet you."

I nod. "Sounds good."

I turn and walk quickly to catch up with Nora. I hear him chuckle as I leave, but I do not dare turn back to look at him.

Sounds good? Really?

I catch up to Nora and she links arms with me, "Damn, not even hear twenty-four hours and you've already got the Headmistress's son drooling over you." She giggles and I ignore her.

We make our way into an auditorium. It is a simple room, not adorned with any grand artwork or fixtures like the rest of the estate. It looks like it had been an addition to the school at some point. A stage stands in the far back and there are folding chairs lined up in rows facing it. It's kind of nice to be around something so normal looking. Reminds me a lot of the small auditoriums back in my hometown.

"Oh, look! There's Yash," Nora exclaims as she points to a man with a thick beard surveying the incoming people, a few rows from the front.

"Who?" I ask curiously.

"Yash!" she shouts and gets all excited. She picks up her pace and unlinks from my arm to get to him quicker.

I join them at a row where Yash has saved three seats.

"Yash, Cassie, Cassie, Yash...my boyfriend," Nora says proudly.

"Hello," I say softly.

"Welcome, Yankee!" he responds enthusiastically with a laugh.

Nora slugs him in the arm.

"I'm sorry, what did you call me?" I ask, confused.

"You know…Yankee. Someone who lives in the US. I don't mean it as derogatory," he reassures me, clearly embarrassed I don't understand.

"Oh, cute." I laugh. "Thanks, erm…tea biscuit?"

This s me trying to make a joke. The two of them stare a moment, and then bust out laughing.

"I like her," Yash says to Nora. She nods in agreement. "Welp, I saved us all some seats, so shall we?" Yash presents the seats with a grand gesture.

"Oh, why thank you, darling." Nora giggles as she takes the seat in the middle.

I sit on the end and nonchalantly look around at the students. The younger students, or Level 1s and 2s, as Nora mentioned earlier when she broke everything down, take up the first couple rows. Slowly, the seats on the stage begin to fill and I assume they are faculty. Most of them look older, possibly in their late 40s to 50s.

A lean but muscular frame comes into view as he walks toward the stage. Jeans hugging his legs perfectly; not too tight. His burgundy shirt peeks out slightly from his oatmeal-colored sweater. His slight curls give away his identity, and I know it's Henry. He takes a seat with a couple other guys a few rows ahead of us.

"Can everyone please take their seats now." A middle-aged woman's voice pulls my attention as she comes to stand in front of a podium in the middle of the stage.

This must be the Headmistress.

Standing in front of the podium, much of her appearance is blocked from my view, but I can tell she is dressed very proper. Her dull brown hair is pulled up into a perfect bun—not a strand out of place. She's wearing a deep-forest-green velvet blazer and white blouse. I remember Nora's comment about Henry being her son. I can see the resemblance, but Henry's eyes are warm and hers seem hard and cold. Something inside me warns me to not cross her.

The room quiets down and she begins, "Welcome, witches, to another year. Let me introduce myself…I am Headmistress Ansley. Some of you are new, some of you have been with us for years, but I expect everyone to uphold themselves to the highest level while you are here. Not only are you here to learn control and knowledge, but skills that will help us fight against the Anarchy, if you choose to join the Protectors."

The Headmistress continues to talk, but all my senses suddenly pique as I feel myself being watched. I quickly scan the room until my focus lands on a set of piercing blue eyes. The man is far to the right in the row of faculty seated on the stage, but he looks much younger than the rest of them, late 20s to early 30s. His expression gives no hint as to what he's thinking, but he continues to stare. His dark brown, almost black hair is thinner on the sides than it is on the top of his head. His jawline, just like the color of his eyes, is very prominent. He's wearing a black V-neck sweater with a white collared shirt underneath and gray slacks.

Our eyes remain locked until he slowly looks away, relieving me from their hold. I hadn't realized I had been holding my breath, and I slowly let it out.

I nudge Nora's arm and whisper into her ear, "Who's the man on the far right, with the blue eyes?"

"That's Professor Cillian Morris. He teaches self-defense and tactical training. Super hot. Super mysterious. I think he's like thirty or something. He has taught at the school for a few years, but he is recently just getting back from an assignment that he's been on the past couple years. Why?" she whispers back.

"Oh, no reason," I say, and sit back into my seat.

Cillian Morris. Hmm…

I try to direct my attention back to the Headmistress, who is talking more about the Anarchy. My grandmother had talked about them a little when I was growing up. The Anarchy is a group of witches who like to cause chaos in the world. We try to keep the fact that there are indeed witches in the world away from the humans. Many witches hold influential positions around the world, but we are always at war with the Anarchy. Historically, it seems like they are always a few steps ahead of us. They cause chaos and we have to make it look like a natural gas explosion, or they start tension between two countries, and we have to intervene. The Anarchy works under the ideals that witches are better than humans, and they need to be submissive to us. That or eradicated altogether.

Kingshire Academy is well known for training witches to join the Protectors—not a particularly creative name, but I didn't pick it. The Protectors lead the charge in the fight against the Anarchy. They work solely to end them. Take our magic away, and we are mere humans, just like everyone else. The Protectors work under the ideals of peace and coexistence, so long as the humans never actually find out about us.

"Now please, take today to walk the grounds, make new friends, prepare yourselves for tomorrow," Headmistress Ansley encourages.

I notice Henry glance back over his shoulder at me. I drop my eyes and blush.

"You should all have received a book of rules. Please study and follow those rules, as we have zero-tolerance policies. This concludes the Welcoming Ceremony. We have set up refreshments in the Dining Hall for you all to go and enjoy. Thank you."

Everyone around us begins to stand and file out of the auditorium. I steal one more glance at Cillian before getting in line to head out of the room with Nora and Yash.

"God, I am so tired of listening to her chunter on about rules. I cannot wait to graduate this year and have the Joining Ceremony," Nora complains.

"Is she really that bad?" I ask.

Both Yash and Nora look at me and nod.

"She's worse than just bad—she's a total dictator," Yash clarifies.

Great.

"Hey, uh, what's the Joining Ceremony?"

"You don't know?" Nora asks, shocked.

I shake my head and begin to feel self-conscious.

"My parents died when I was young. They were the magical ones. My grandmother raised me, but she doesn't have magic."

I had wanted to save the whole my-parents-are-dead talk for later, but might I as well get it out there.

"Oh, Cassie, I am so sorry. We didn't know." Nora looks suddenly sad.

"It's fine. I actually came here hoping to learn more about them. They came here when they were about my age as well."

We make it out of the auditorium. I let Nora and Yash lead the way to the Dining Hall.

Moving on from the unexpected news, Nora explains, "Well, they'll tell more about the Joining in class, but basically, every witch has someone that their magic pairs with, kind of like two puzzle pieces. Joining with that person makes your powers stronger."

"Oh, okay, interesting."

We make it to the Dining Hall and stop just outside the entrance. It is a large room filled with rows of tables. The tables look like they fit about four people to them. It is crazy to me how big this place is.

"This is the Dining Hall. They typically have it open for breakfast from five to nine a.m., lunch from noon to two, and finally dinner starts at six p.m. The food is okay, if you have no taste buds,"

Nora snickers.

"Does everyone typically eat together?" I notice some of the younger students in here with the older students.

"Yes and no. Classes get out at different times and such. But we typically all just group by levels when we're all in here," Yash explains.

Nora wraps his arm around her shoulders.

"Ugh, I am starving. Can we please eat now and ask questions later?" Nora whines.

Yash and I chuckle at her. We begin to walk through the entrance when I feel someone shove me from behind. This time, Henry's arms aren't there to catch me, and I tumble to the floor. My knees fall hard against the stone tile floor. I know bruises are sure to follow.

"Lauren! What the hell?" Nora's voice screams behind me.

I turn around to see what is going on as Yash helps me up. My whole body is on fire with embarrassment, and I quickly adjust my skirt. I hope I hadn't accidentally flashed anymore on my tumble downward.

A tall, very slender girl is standing next to Nora. Her eyes are dark brown, and her long hair is pitch black. Her skin is so porcelain, it looks almost translucent. She wears a sick grin on her face, and holds her arms crossed.

"Sorry, must not have seen you there in my way." Her voice is shrill and full of sarcasm.

"Um, no worries," I say, trying to give her the benefit of the doubt.

Nora looks pissed.

"Why don't you watch where you're going next time, Lauren? Got your nose pointed to high? Can't see over it?"

Lauren huffs and saunters on her way further into the room. My knees ache from the fall, and we walk slowly up to get in line.

"So, who was that?" I whisper to Nora as we fall in line.

"Lauren Cole, or the devil herself, as I like to refer to her," Nora says sourly.

Yash chuckles as he listens in. I peek over my shoulder to see her still throwing daggers at me with her eyes.

"And why does she hate me?" I ask as I turn back around.

"Who knows, really? Lauren has always been very cold to everyone, ever since she's been here. Her dad is super rich and donates a lot of money to the school, so she gets away with a lot," Nora says, her tone hinting of past conflict with Lauren.

"She doesn't seem to have many friends around her..." I notice she's sitting at a table alone.

"Who needs friends when every guy is basically tripping over themselves for your attention? She's also pretty powerful, which she makes sure everyone knows."

I decide to drop the topic and try to forget it as we make it up to where the food is displayed. There are an assortment of soups, salads, and sandwiches. I opt for a small salad and chicken noodle soup. I'm exhausted from all the travelling and the severe time change. I check the clock hanging in the hall, and it's only 12:33 p.m.

Going to be a long day.

Yash and Nora find an empty table near some other Level 6s and we sit down. I suddenly notice Henry walk into the hall. It feels like my nerves come alive with electricity when he walks in. I watch him as he walks over to the display of food. Nora notices my attention pique and follows my eyes to discover what I'm staring at.

"Guess who Cassie already has a crush on?" Nora teases to Yash, but he's too focused on his ham sandwich to care. Nora stares at him until he realizes she's looking at him.

"You say something, babe?" Yash's mouth still full with his latest bite.

"Sometimes I truly wonder why I love you," Nora says, looking at him in disgust.

I laugh softly and play with the cherry tomato in my salad. Nora and Yash continue to bicker and I tune them out.

"Mind if I sit?" Henry's voice beckons from beside me.

I freeze with my fork in hand, and I slowly look up to Nora. Nora doesn't waste any time saying he's welcome to and beams at me. Henry sets down his tray of food and pulls out the chair next to mine.

"Oh, hey, mate, hope you don't mind, but I brought a mini fridge for us," Yash says.

"Not at all. I was just thinking that's what our room needed," Henry replies.

"So, Cassie, Yash and Henry are roommates. Have been for the past couple years." Nora moves her eyebrows up and down and smiles. I can feel my face turning red. I just want her to shut up.

"Oh, that's…cool," I croak pathetically.

"And loving every day of it. Rooming with the Headmistress's son has some major perks," Yash says, reaching over to high five Henry.

Henry and Yash laugh together as they smack hands.

"Oh my god, Henry, you have got to tell your mum to stop it with all the rules. I need to be free to do what I want," Nora states dramatically.

Henry chuckles. "I know, I know. I try to tell her, but it only goes so far."

"Anyone want to give me a rundown of these rules?"

Henry speaks, "They aren't too terrible, just no leaving the school grounds, no using magic maliciously against a student, no abusing magic. You can only use magic minimally outside of class as well."

"What he means to say is, no getting caught doing any of these things," Nora corrects with a laugh.

I try to take it all in and laugh with them.

"Don't like the food?" Henry says directly to me, as Nora is once again preoccupied with Yash and his eating habits.

I run my fingers through my hair and my heart begins to race.

"No, um, just travelled a lot and I'm tired. It's a lot to take in." I look around the large hall.

"You'll get used to it. I promise."

Henry's emerald eyes are beautiful and warm. I feel like I

could look at them forever and never get tired of it.

I clear my throat. "I think I am going to get another water. Anyone want anything?"

"If they have a rice pudding cup, can you snag me one?" Yash asks—of course his ears perk at more food.

"I can go if you want?" Henry offers.

"No worries, I got it." I try smile at him, but I feel like my face just turns out weirdly contorted. "Pudding cup coming right up!"

I go to stand, but am startled by Lauren appearing suddenly beside our table.

"Go away, Lauren," Nora growls.

I notice Lauren has an open bottle of milk in her hand. I decide to ignore her and begin to walk away when I feel like I am tripped. Thankfully, I'm able to catch myself in time. I find myself instantly enraged, as I know it's not a coincidence I tripped again. I spin around to face Lauren.

Benefit of the doubt, my ass.

"You really should be more careful," she sneers.

"Lauren, hello, you technically just broke rules. Stop using magic to harass others. I saw you wave your hand. Why can't you just leave us alone?" Nora protests, standing up. She places her hands on the table, looking as if she's ready to pounce over it, if need be.

"Rules broken? Why, whatever could you mean? I saw the poor girl trip again. She really needs to learn to be less clumsy."

"What is your problem with me?" I muster the courage to speak up.

"I don't like you," she says simply, locking eyes with me.

"You don't even know me. We are two grown adult women. Why are you behaving like a child?"

I try to settle the anger rising inside of me. I don't want to make a scene—especially on my first day here. This is supposed to be a clean slate and my new chance at gaining control.

"Because I can. Because I can tell when someone is weaker than me and doesn't belong. I know all about you, Cassandra Rodden. Poor little orphan witch who grew up with a grandmother who didn't have any magic. How pathetic. You're useless and just a waste of space here at the academy."

I am shocked by her words. My heart hurts; I know my grandmother did everything she could to teach me about my magic and the history of it all. My grandmother, who was always there for me when I lost control of my magic. The bit about being an orphan was not a new insult. Many of my tormentors growing up had used that.

I ball my fists and dig my nails deep into my palms. I can feel my magic increasing, stronger now, which surprises me. Normally, my magic is tied to my emotions, yes, but it seems like they have an extra jumper attached to them right now, giving them a boost—which is not a good thing.

"You know nothing about me. You may have read some file, but you don't know me and the things I have been through," I say through clenched teeth.

"Lauren, you have three seconds to piss off before I jump

over this table and beat your arse," Nora warns.

Lauren ignores her and leans in closer to my face. Her hot breath assaults my skin as she speaks, "Oh, you'd be surprised how much I know about you. No one wants you here. You probably don't have that much magic in the first place."

"I am not going anywhere," I say sternly.

"Prepare for hell then," she says with a smirk.

She raises her arm and dumps the cold milk over my head. I can feel it running down my body and spilling everywhere, seeping into my clothes and bra.

"Oh, hell no," Nora says as she walks around the table to Lauren. Yash attempts to hold her back, but Nora shakes him off.

I have tried to contain my magic, but this is the last straw. My body begins to shake as the floor tremors. Everyone whispers frantically and looks around to see what is going on.

Don't do it, Cassie. Contain it. Be strong.

I squeeze my eyes shut and take a step away from Lauren. The tremors are increasing, and whispers turn to shouting. A high-pitched ring overcomes my ears. I drop to my knees.

Stop, stop, stop. Contain it.

My head feels like it's going to burst as I try to hold everything back.

"Stop!" I scream out.

I slam my fist against the tile floor, causing it to crack. This is just the release I need though, and the anger begins to retreat. My breathing slows and the tremors settle. I slowly open my eyes to see everyone looking at me. Everyone looks scared—except Lauren, who looks pleased with herself. I hear people rush into the hall and look back to see various faculty members. Headmistress Ansley is among them and she is making a beeline toward us.

"What is going on in here?" she demands.

My throat tightens as I try to hold back my tears. There are some chunks of stone tile left clinging to my knuckles, which I try to brush off inconspicuously.

"I-I…" I try to speak, but no more words will come out. I am frozen with embarrassment and fear.

I hadn't noticed Henry stand up from the table during the commotion, and he is now stretching out his hand to help me to my feet. I take it, but keep my eyes away from his.

"It wasn't her fault, Mum," Henry offers in my defense.

"Yeah, looks like Cassandra just slipped," Lauren says innocently.

"Bullshit, Lauren. You know that's not what happened," Nora pipes up.

The Headmistress looks extremely annoyed. "And how do you explain the milk all over Miss Rodden then?" she asks Lauren.

I don't want to cause any more of a commotion on my first day. I just want to get the hell out of here.

"I slipped, and that caused the milk to spill as well," I say softly, staring at my feet in shame.

"And the tremors? The whole school was shaking." Headmistress Ansley does not seem convinced.

"I'm sorry," is all I can muster up to say.

"Very well. Because this is your first day here, Miss Rodden, I will be letting you off with a warning. Please get yourself cleaned up. Miss Malik, please escort your roommate back to your room and go over the rule book with her."

Nora lets out a scoff of frustration.

"And Miss Cole, let's not have any more slipping incidents, hmm?"

Lauren rolls her eyes and walks away. Nora comes to my side and we make our way out of the Dining Hall. Yash asks if he can come along, but Nora shakes her head. Once out of the Hall, I let the tears flow and pick up my pace. I'm not sure how to get back to our room, but I need to distance myself from that scene. Fast.

"Cassie, wait up! I can't walk as fast as you!" Nora shouts after me. Her short legs are working overtime to keep up with me.

"I'm sorry, I just want to be alone. I need to get away."

"Well, that's fine, but you aren't even going the right way!"

I stop walking and look around to see where I am. It looks like every other hallway I have been down so far at this Academy. I let out a frustrated sigh.

"Why does this place have to be so freaking big?"

Nora chuckles as she finally catches up to me.

"You'll get used to it. Come on, our room is back this way."

I follow Nora as we walk in silence. I can smell the milk slowly spoiling on my clothes and in my hair.

Bleh.

"Thanks…for sticking up for me back there. I am sorry about making a scene. Sometimes it's hard for me to control my emotions."

"You are perfectly fine. I got your back, as long as you've got mine. Plus, I royally hate that witch. Never seen a witch make tremors though…" she says curiously.

I'm not sure how to respond, so I don't. We finally make it back to our room and I am anxious to get in the shower. I just want to get cleaned up and relax.

"I'm going to go meet back up with Yash, if you don't mind? We have some plans, but I'll be back soon."

"Don't worry about me. I'm going to get cleaned up and finish unpacking." I reassure her, but I'm happy she's meeting Yash. I want to be alone.

She says goodbye and heads out of our room. I quickly find a towel in my suitcase and head into the bathroom. It's small—it has a toilet and a small sink, with a small standup shower directly across from the sink.

Hmmm, well, it's better than a communal shower.

Thankfully, when I had gone to college, I went to a community college nearby my grandmother's home. I was able to stay home and use everything I was already comfortable with.

I peel off my curdling turtleneck and try to run a brush through my hair. The milk has caused my hair to knot together and it's a struggle to get them out. My knees surprisingly do not look as bad as I expected. Normally, I would've had deep bruises by now, but my skin is only slightly discolored.

Wonder if they'll look worse tomorrow?

The standup shower has a glass door. I open it and turn on the water. The spout sputters and groans before fully turning on. I let the water run for a minute to warm up before stepping in. The water pressure is decent, as well as the temperature. I welcome the warmth as it cascades over my skin.

I go to reach for my shampoo, but realize I left it outside of the shower, on the sink. I can see its blurry blue shape through the shower door. I already feel the water running cooler and don't want to lose the heat that's already built up in the little shower. I use my magic to lift the bottle of shampoo up off the sink's counter and over the top of the shower.

The smell of vanilla and honey soon replace the smell of rancid milk. I try not to think about what happened as I wash my hair and lather my body with soap, but it consumes my thoughts.

Of course, that happened right in front of Henry. What was that chick's problem? Maybe I should just go home. Already made a mess here. Ugh, I could really use a drink. To hell with this school and these people. She's right. I don't fit in here.

My thoughts continue to sour, much like the milk I just washed off. The water is running colder still, and I know I have to get out soon. I do one last rinse of my hair and turn off the shower.

After getting out and drying off, I try to call my grandmother. The line rings several times as I get dressed, but then forwards to her voicemail. I panic and don't want to alert her, so I leave a quick message saying that I love her, and I made it safely to the Academy.

I shove my suitcases off my bed and bury myself into the comforter. I thank myself for having set it up first thing when I arrived. I scroll through different social media apps and see that I have a friend request from Nora Malik. I hold off on accepting it, because I am seriously contemplating just leaving and going back home.

My body feels drained and sluggish, so it isn't a surprise to me when my eyelids become heavy. I tuck my phone underneath my pillow and let the sleep consume me.

I wake to Nora opening the door, the light from the hallway piercing through our darkened room.

"Oh, sorry, didn't know you'd be sleeping," she whispers, tiptoeing into the room.

I pull my phone from beneath my pillow and look at the time. It is 6:52 p.m.

Goodness, I slept awhile.

I clear my throat and sit up, "No worries."

"Yash and I are going to go get some dinner now before the Hall closes. Do you want to come with?"

I think back to Lauren and the milk. My stomach turns with leftover embarrassment.

"Um, no, I think I'm good. I may actually go for a walk."

"It's dark out already. You sure?" she seems apprehensive.

"Uh, yeah, no, it's fine. I walk alone all the time at home."

"Well, how about you give me your number and text me if

you need anything, all right? We start training first thing tomorrow morning. I'll probably be getting to bed soon, myself."

"Yeah, that's fine," I say as we exchange phones. I quickly type my information and hand it back to her. She gives me one last friendly look before departing and I give her a wave.

I'll be going for a walk, but not around here. I open the PickMeUp app on my phone to see if any cars will come out this way. I'm able to find one, but to avoid suspicion, I direct the driver to wait on the other side of the gate. It's going to cost a pretty penny for the ride, but I want to find a bar to go to. The app says that the driver will be there in about 30 minutes. I swing my legs over the side of the bed and dress to go out. I grab an oversized emerald sweater, a pair of jeans, and my white high tops. I dash on some simple makeup and head out.

I know going through the main entrance is conspicuous, but I don't know any of the other entrances and exits yet. There are a few other students around, but for the most part, the school is quiet.

I slip out the front door and make my way down the steps. It is dark out and the only light comes from large flood lights attached to the school. The gravel crunches beneath my feet as I proceed toward the side of the gate. I assume there will be fencing or something in between the tall shrubbery I can scale.

While walking toward the gate, I notice a room off to the side with large windows. I see my reflection in them as I walk. I pick up my pace, because I can't see inside to know if anyone has noticed me.

After reaching the wall of shrubbery, I reach inside and am

relieved to find fencing. I use both the branches from the shrubbery and the bars from the fence to carefully make my way up to the top. I'm in luck, because the top is flat and lacks spikes. I straddle the peak while I take off my small crossbody purse and drop it to the ground. It had given me some issues on the way up, getting snagged and slowing me down.

Okay, awesome, see, I got this!

I feel accomplished, but my celebration comes prematurely. As I progress down the other side, my foot comes to rest on a branch that snaps when I shift my weight, and I'm left dangling. I try to gather my footing, but there isn't a branch that can help, and the fencing is only useful to hold onto.

Shit.

I try to peek down to see how far I am from the ground. I'm still several feet away, but it's the only choice I have. My hands are slipping, and my arms hurt from dangling.

Here goes nothing.

I release my hold on the bars and fall to the ground. My ankles give out and I fall back hard onto my butt.

"Shit, shit, shit, that hurts," I curse and begin to feel dizzy.

I take a couple deep breaths and hurry to my feet, as I hear a car approaching. I snatch up my purse and brush the dirt and grass off my pants. The car has a tell-tale PickMeUp sticker displayed on the front windshield.

Thank goodness it's my ride and not someone else.

I peek through the main entrance of the gate before climbing into the car just to make sure no one is coming after me. It is all clear. I open the door and slide in.

"Where to? You put the town, but I need to know a specific location," the driver explains. She seems to be about my age from the obscured glimpse I have from her backseat. She has dark hair that is wild with curls.

"Um, is there a bar in that town? It was the closest town to here, and I really just want to get a drink."

"Well, unfortunately there isn't much around here. The only place close by is the White Horse Pub, really."

"Works for me," I say as I lean back into the leather seat.

"Buckle up, and we'll be on our way, then. I am Kathleen, by the way."

I do as she asks, and we start to move. She has trouble getting the car turned around, but soon we are off, back down the long, dark road. Kathleen doesn't talk at all on our drive, which I am thankful for. I look out at the sea of darkness and relief saunters its way in the further we travel from the school. I tell myself I will go back soon, but I've never been good at listening to myself.

CHAPTER THREE

I step into the dimly lit pub they call the White Horse. Surprisingly, it looks just like the bars back home, except with English sports teams proudly displayed on the walls. I guess I don't know what I was expecting to be so different.

There is a pool table close to the entrance; booths line the left side, and the bar lines the right. There are only a few people inside, most likely the regulars—the drunk who never seems to go home until he can barely walk, the older lady who reminisces of her late husband while she drinks red wine, a couple of younger men playing pool with two underage-looking girls, and finally, the bartender, who has worked there forever and knows everyone's drinks by heart. Same stereotypes, different country.

I can still feel some leftover anger coursing through me from my earlier encounter with Lauren.

Not even here 24 hours and already have a rival.

I'm sure there's a story behind her hatred for me. That, or maybe she's just a mean girl who takes pride in being a bitch. Either way, I know who to look out for.

I slide into an open seat at the bar with my back to the door. The bar top in front of where I sit is a tad sticky, but I don't mind too much.

"What can I get you, lady?" I look up to see the bartender staring at me. Her dark curls are held back by a floral headband, tattoos are displayed up and down both of her arms. She is wearing a pair of clearly worn-out overalls with various stains on them, but she looks nice. She adjusts her septum piercing briefly as I peer behind her, looking at the specials. Nothing looks all that interesting.

"Um...can I just get a Malibu Rum and Coke?"

She seems almost insulted by my choice, but nods and begins to prepare the simple drink. I pull my phone out from my purse and look at my notifications.

(1) New Message:

Grandma: Hi Honey, you're going to do great. If your parents could see you now, they would be so happy. Remember to not be a smart ass. Love you.

I smile slightly. A twinge of guilt settles in my heart, though, after reading her message.

Would they be happy though? Already causing a scene on the first day, sneaking off grounds to go to a pub.

The bartender hands me my drink and I give a quick thank you. It tastes just like any other Malibu Rum and Coke I've had, and the familiarity sooths my anxious nerves. I am about halfway through the drink when I feel someone standing uncomfortably close to me. I look up to see a plump older man. His faded red flannel is wrinkled, and the stained-eggshell-colored shirt underneath barely covers his overflowing belly. He gives me a crooked smile and I instantly feel disgusted.

"Well, hey there, gorgeous." His breath reeks of stale beer and hot dogs. "Why don't you let me buy you a drink, eh?" He reaches out to brush my hair with his fingertips.

I lean away, "No, thanks."

"Oh, come on, gorgeous, just one drink won't hurt ya," he persists, this time getting even closer, pushing his bulging belly up against my thigh.

Thank god I changed into a pair of thicker jeans.

"I said no." I glare at him. I can feel the anger swelling the magic inside me.

"Now look, bitch," he grabs a chunk of my hair, "I offered you a drink. Take it."

Something inside of my brain snaps and I can't control myself. I turn my eyes to his chest and concentrate on his heartbeat. I imagine my magic sliding around his heart, and slowly squeezing tighter and tighter.

His expression quickly changes to confusion as he stumbles back.

Tighter.

Confusion soon turns to terror as his thick brain figures out

40

what is happening.

"I said no." My teeth are clenched. It feels as if something else has taken over my body and I'm okay with it. His terror seems to feed the demon inside of me. It makes me feel happy in a sick and twisted way. Schadenfreude like I have never felt. In this moment, I am okay with killing this man.

Who knows how many women he's abused or assaulted? I would be doing this world a favor.

Tighter.

His heart struggles against my magical vice grip. Truly, I am surprised it hasn't given in yet. His heart is stronger than I gave him credit for. The blood pumps slower and slower. His lungs begin to burn as they try to gasp for air. His lips turn a faint blue.

"Cassandra, stop," a sweet-but-stern, unfamiliar voice calls out to me, piercing through my trance.

I feel a warm hand on my shoulder. My connection is broken, and I look away, confused as to what just happened. Just as the anger had taken control, the unfamiliar voice slays it and it retreats deep inside me.

I look down at my drink as the man I almost killed gasps for air.

"The lady said no. Be on your way, sir," the sweet voice advises sternly.

"She-she-she almost killed me!" the old man tries to shout, but it comes out as a raspy wheeze.

I roll my eyes.

"I believe you are mistaken. What I did see, however, was you put your hands on this woman. Now, be on your way, or I will phone the authorities." The unfamiliar voice's tone stays calm and even. He has a beautiful English accent that lets loose a swarm of butterflies in my stomach.

Out of the corner of my eye, I see the old man start to protest more, but he gives up, frowns and walks away.

"May I sit?" the sweet voice asks.

The question catches me off guard, and I look to see who the unfamiliar voice might belong to. A set of piercing blue eyes gaze down at me. Eyes that I don't think I will ever forget.

Cillian Morris. I am so busted.

"Y-yeah, of course," I stammer, as so many thoughts rush through my head.

He takes off his dark blue peacoat and hangs it on the back of the chair. Underneath, he's wearing a thick maroon sweater.

"So, how much trouble am I in?" I ask, eyeing him with hesitation.

How did he know I was here? Coincidence? Ugh, I will probably be sent home now, for sure.

"Are you asking for leaving school grounds, or the fact you almost killed that poor man over there?" His voice is like silk.

Poor man? Oh, please...

"I have no sympathy for him," I say sourly. "He started it."

His eyes stay locked on mine. "Ah, yes, but you need to control yourself better. Humans tend to notice when odd things happen—especially odd deaths."

His poker face is amazing. No emotion bleeds through to give me any hint of what he's thinking. I finish my drink and motion to the bartender for another one.

"It's hard for me to control."

"Drinking causes us to lose our control with magic. Drugs and alcohol affect us the same way it does humans. I saw you in the Dining Hall earlier. You can barely keep your emotions and power in check when you're sober."

Ouch. You saw me but I didn't see you.

I look away and stare at the row of bottles lined behind the bar. "Yeah, well, maybe I like losing control. Maybe the world needs a little chaos. Plus, how do you know I was sober then?" I ask sarcastically.

The bartender drops off my second and I immediately start sucking it down in spite.

"Is that what you told the little girl whose arm you broke in middle school? Or the boy's jaw you broke in high school?"

I stop drinking and look at him. Anger issues have always plagued me, and his mention of those events launch me back into all the difficult memories.

"How do you—"

"How do I know? We screen all of our students prior to admission," he states simply with a shrug.

That makes sense.

I sheepishly go back to sipping on my drink. The warmth

from the liquor slowly spreads from my chest outward.

"Well, I'm old enough to drink in all countries, so why can't you just leave me alone? Maybe I should just go home. I don't belong here. I don't belong anywhere," I say, feeling defeated.

"You haven't even given yourself a chance yet." His words comfort me as I shift in my seat.

"Want anything, handsome?"

We both turn to the bartender standing in front of us. I hadn't even realized she had come over again.

"No, thanks, we need to get going anyway," Cillian replies.

"Wait!" I shout as the bartender starts to turn away. I look at Cillian, "Have one drink with me?" Yep, the liquor is definitely starting to have an effect.

He laughs softly. His smile sends ripples all over my body, making me shiver.

"And why would that be a good idea?"

"Have one drink with me, and then I'll go back with you, simple as that. But don't have a drink with me, and I stay here and get massively wasted. Who knows what will happen then? Deal?" Yeah, because that's a good ultimatum, right?

He stares at me, his eyes studying my intentions. My heart rate increases, and it seems like time stands still. Our lives coming to two diverged roads and everything hinges on this one answer.

"Deal."

I squeal internally with delight.

"Congratulations. Now, what do you guys want? I've got

other customers." The bartender is clearly getting annoyed.

"Beer will b—" Cillian begins, but I interject.

"Actually," I have an idea. I look deep into the bartender's eyes and decide to use a little bit more magic, "Can we please get two of the biggest, most expensive, extravagant drinks you can come up with?"

This is a little trick I picked up a few years ago. It rarely works, but it looks like it might now. The bartender's eyes glaze over as I speak. Her eyes stay locked on mine for a few seconds, then she shakes her head slightly to break the trance.

"Sure, I've got some pitchers. I'll make you something great and extravagant." She stays for a moment longer, then goes to work on the drinks.

"Well," Cillian shakes his head and chuckles, "Magic was not in the deal."

I smirk. "It was not *not* in the deal. Technically, you agreed to one drink, and that's what we are getting—one drink."

"You are a smart arse aren't you? Be careful when you influence others. That type of magic can be dangerous."

I'm a little embarrassed by his warning and I fiddle with the edge of the napkin in front of me.

"I know. It has never really worked like that before," I say quietly, in my own defense.

Silence falls over us as we wait for our "one drink." It doesn't take long, though, for the lovely bartender to drop off our pitchers of some mystical blue drink a few moments later. Both pitchers are topped with a few gently-floating maraschino cherries. She seems proud of her drink and waits eagerly for us to try it.

I excitedly slide the drink closer to my mouth and give a squeal. Cillian, on the other hand cautiously slides his closer to inspect it. The drink is deliciously sweat, with a hint of sour. It tastes almost exactly like a hard blue candy. I pluck a cherry out and pop it into my mouth.

"Oh my gosh, this is perfect! May I ask, what is your name?" I beam at the bartender, who looks relieved to hear I like it.

"My name is Mary, ma'am," she replies.

"Well, Mary, I love it! And what shall we call this concoction?" I continue to drink.

"Oh, well, um, how about Midnight Kiss? You two look cute together, and it's almost midnight, so? I don't know?" She looks a little uncomfortable being put on the spot.

"Perfect, Mary. Thank you, again."

She nods and makes her way to the other end of the bar to help a group of people who just came in. Surprisingly, the bar is filling up a little more.

I look at Cillian, still eyeing his drink. "So, what do you think?" I nudge his arm with my elbow.

He sighs, raises the pitcher, and takes a drink. He almost immediately begins to cough.

"Well, it's, um, certainly strong," he manages to get out, before coughing a few more times.

I laugh at his struggle.

"Hey now, I am used to beer, not these types of drinks," he tries to recover.

He was right about one thing though—they are incredibly strong.

"So, how did you know I was gone, by the way?" I decide to try and start a conversation, avoiding the awkward silence.

He smirks. "Well, I saw you climb over the front gate and go to the car waiting for you."

My cheeks flush.

So much for being stealthy. Wait...that means he must've seen me fall as well. Ugh. Hopefully the shrubbery obscured that view.

My eyes drop to my drink.

"I just wanted to make sure you were okay and to bring you back so you wouldn't get in worse trouble. You're lucky Night Watch hadn't started yet."

The door behind us slams shut as more people file into the small bar. I continue drinking as the awkward silence returns. I'm about halfway done and really feeling like myself when Journey's "Don't Stop Believin'" comes on throughout the bar. Now, I don't know about you, but when I've been drinking, and this song comes on, it's like an unwritten rule that you must sing along at the top of your lungs.

Not even caring if I look ridiculous, I sit my pitcher down and get my air microphone ready. I peek to my side and see Cillian looking at me curiously. I wink at him as the beginning notes rhythmically sound off. The piano causes some of the other pub goers to sway back and forth, their muscle memory activated.

I start off at a normal volume and some of the people around us turn to look as I finish the first verse.

Just do it. Go big, or go home.

I stand up and push my seat back.

If I'm going to do this, I am going to do it properly and give everyone a show.

"What are you doing?" Cillian looks as if I have grown a second head.

"This song is universal, Cillian. Just you wait."

I continue on with the song as it enters the second verse. More people turn to watch as I sing louder.

"Mary! Turn it up!" I yell to the bartender, who is swaying along behind the bar with everyone else.

She nods and turns the volume up slightly as I make my way into the middle of the room. I feel happiness and joy pouring out of me. I wink at a sweet older gentleman as my eyes meet his. He smiles bashfully and his wife smacks the back of his head. A giggle escapes me briefly as I move on from them.

People in the bar start to dance and sing along with me as I skip around. I feel all of our hearts beating together as one. I'm not trying to use magic right now, but I still feel it pouring out of me in waves. Waves that are washing over everyone and seeping into their pores, consuming them.

I jump on top of a table as I enter the chorus and prepare my lungs to take on the high note—the note where the excitement and happiness reaches its highest point. The note that is the most memorable.

Almost everyone is dancing and singing along. No one has a care in the world, and people are just happy. I look to Cillian, who is still seated at the bar. His poker face has returned, but I can tell in those blue eyes that even he feels the magic beckoning him to let loose. I feel a pull toward him that is almost irresistible. The lights surge as we lock eyes and several corked bottles pop. Maybe it's the alcohol, but my powers feel stronger now than they ever have. I don't think too much of it, though, as I continue with the song.

Here it comes—the climax.

I belt it out so loud, my imaginary microphone doing such a good job. The whole bar is roaring. It almost feels like everyone is floating, our bodies lighter than air. I am their heroin and every single one of them is high.

I reach down to the gentleman closest to the table I am standing on and he holds my hand as I jump down. I skip my way back over to Cillian, the song coming to an end. As it fades, I slowly sit back in my chair and look into Cillian's eyes. My breathing is heavy, and I feel like I am dreaming. Everything is so intoxicating.

"Told you it was universal," I say with a smirk.

I slowly drop my imaginary microphone and pick up my pitcher. The song is over, but everything stills feels so alive. Everyone cheers and laughs, looking at each other. I nod my head toward Cillian, give him a smile, and proceed to finish my one drink.

A deal is a deal, so I pay for the drinks and we head out, leaving the roaring pub behind us. I should not have finished the rest of the pitcher, as I am very wobbly on my feet and words are a tad harder to enunciate, but it's too late now. The deed has been done. The alcohol consumed.

As we head to Cillian's car a few blocks away, I try my best to walk in a straight line. It is a tad past 1:00 a.m. at this point, and the streets have settled down. As we round off the main street, the few people that linger disappear behind us.

"Thank you," I say softly, breaking the silence, "for earlier, I mean, with that guy." I look down at my feet, sheepishly trying to avoid looking at him, but also so I don't stumble.

"Not a problem," he says after a few seconds.

"It's just...I know I probably haven't made the greatest first impression. I know I have made horrible decisions in the past, but I've come here to try and gain control. I am more than what you've read in my file," I drunkenly babble on.

He clears his throat. "I know you are. You are just very powerful, Cassandra. More powerful than you even realize."

I stumble just the slightest as I take my eyes off my feet. His hand gently grabs my arm to steady me, and there his eyes are again, staring straight into mine as we stop for a moment. My heart slams into my throat.

Holy hell, is he a gorgeous man. How can someone be this beautiful?

Light from a streetlamp casts down onto his face accentuating his jawline—even though it begins to flicker. His lips look so soft and supple.

"Well, Cassandra," he smirks. I don't know if it's the alcohol or the lack of action I've had the past few months, but the way my name seductively slips out of his mouth is almost orgasmic. I bite the inside of my cheek to suppress a moan as my heartbeat pounds in my ears. "You are very powerful. The things I have seen you do tonight are very impressive, but can also be very dangerous."

He lets go of my arm and we start walking again. Cillian keeps a smaller gap between us now, in case I stumble again.

"It's not that impressive." Let's just ignore the dangerous part for a minute. "Typically, I can influence a few people's moods. It was nothing. Yeah, there were a few new things that I noticed happen, but I don't know..." I try to brush it all off. I am not in the most coherent state to be the center of the conversation.

"There were more than just a few people in that bar tonight. There is so much for you to learn, and you are starting way behind the others at the Academy."

We finally arrive at his car, which is a beautiful silver Stingray.

Of course, a sexy man would have a sexy car.

As soon as I open the door, he speaks across the car.

"Cassandra, I mean it. You need to learn control. While impressive, you could have killed that man today. This cannot happen again. Do you understand me?"

This time my heart plummets straight into my stomach, smashing all the butterflies. The disappointment in his voice affects me more than it should.

"I understand." My eyes sting as they begin to fill with tears.

We ride most of the way in silence, but I can feel the energy between us. It's almost suffocating being in this small space with him. I let out a sigh of relief when we pull up to the school.

Cillian parks his car in the faculty lot behind the main building. I don't wait for him, even though I see him walking around the car to open my door. I jump out too quickly and am hit with a bad case of the spins. My stomach lurches and I feel like I am going to vomit everywhere. Cillian appears and takes me softly into his arms.

"I've got you, steady now. Can you walk?"

I try to make sense of his words, but my brain feels like mush and my mouth is dry.

"Um…yeah, I can make it," I say, feeling my knees give out from underneath me.

I hear Cillian sigh before he picks me up into him arms. I struggle a bit, but he holds onto me firmly.

"No, I can do it. I can walk," I protest.

"Close your eyes, okay?" he quietly directs.

I do as he says and hold onto his jacket. He smells like black pepper and patchouli. It comforts me, and I find myself pressing my face deep into his chest. I feel a tingling and pulling sensation all over me. Before I know it, Cillian is setting me down softly in my bed.

"You walk really fast. Like…really fast. How did you know…where I am—where I…? I'm so thirsty," I mumble.

"Shh, get some rest," Cillian whispers.

My eyelids are so heavy, I can't keep them open. I roll over and fall asleep instantly, before my brain can question anything more.

CHAPTER FOUR

It seems like my eyes are only closed for a minute when Nora's voice pierces the darkness.

"Cassie," she starts off in a whisper.

I try to snuff her voice out by throwing my pillow over my ears, but it gets louder and I'm pulled from my slumber.

"Cassie, you're going to be late for Tactical. Cassie, wake up!" She shakes my shoulder.

I groan. Sleep will have to wait. With consciousness comes a pounding headache and I feel greasy all over. Not to mention my stomach is also sore from Mary's sugary Midnight Kiss.

I open one eye to see Nora's face uncomfortably close to mine.

"Oh, good, so you aren't dead! I hope you know that you smell like a dump truck filled with rancid alcohol. I mean, bloody hell, Cassie, where did you even go last night?"

"It's a long story," I manage to croak out.

"Well, you need to get up. It's almost 7:00 a.m. Being late on your first day will not look good. Professor Morris is going to be sooooo pissed."

Cillian? Oh my god, I am so pathetic.

Last night's adventure resurfaces with the mention of his name. I sit up abruptly and opened both eyes.

"Cillian teaches Tactical?" I feel suddenly frantic. I search for my phone to check the time, to see just how screwed I am, but I can't find it.

"Cillian, huh?" she pauses, "Yes, remember? I told you that yesterday when you asked about him. And he is a stickler for being on time." She stands up and grabs a bottle of water off her bed. She's wearing a sleek pair of black leggings and a white tank top.

"Here," she tosses the water bottle onto my bed. "Drink that. It'll help. I got up early and made it for you after I woke up to your...smell."

I open the container and give it a quick sniff. It makes my stomach turn; the vinegar aroma is very powerful. I give Nora an unsure look.

She rolls her eyes. "It's a family recipe, you'll be fine. I'm gonna get going so I'm not punished, but you clean yourself up and get to class as soon as you can. And don't think you are getting out of telling me everything, especially who the guy was that dropped you off in your bed. I gotta say, I am a little mad you didn't invite me to come along."

I chuckle nervously. "Um, yeah, I'll be there as soon as I can. I'll tell you about it later."

Nora gives me a, "you better, bitch" look before heading out of the room. I groan as sheer panic settles in.

How could I mess up so badly already?

I take another sniff of the wicked-smelling concoction and decide it will be best just to chug it.

"Here goes nothing, then." I plug my nose and feel the burn of the vinegar as I pour it down my throat.

I run down the hall after getting dressed as quickly as I could. I had used a wet wipe to clean my face and armpits, practically ripped some of my hair out trying to brush the matts out, all in an effort to not look like a complete mess in front of Cillian. Thankfully, I had been able to quickly find a cute set of workout clothes—a baby blue sports bra underneath a black zip-up jacket, and black cutout leggings.

Nora's witchy juice slowly starts to help with the pounding, but I still feel disgusting. I pull my hair back into a ponytail as I run down different halls. I slowly make the realization that I have absolutely no idea where the Tactical room is.

Fuck.

I frantically try to remember the map from yesterday that had everything laid out on it. It isn't until I see the naked lady that I know I am close. I remember thinking the naked lady statue was a tad much, as it was used as a marker on the map, but I remember it being in a hallway just a few feet down from the Tactical room.

I bust through the doors and into a large room lined with an indoor track. I see Nora and the others on the other end of the room, all standing around Cillian. I slow my pace to try and not seem as frantic and embarrass myself even more. The students' attention pings on me as they notice me approach the group. The hangover sweats start to ramp up and I can feel the nauseousness make a comeback.

Cillian stops whatever he's talking about and turns to see what the others are looking at. I advert my gaze to the floor. I don't want to face him. Sheepishly, I make my way to Nora's side.

"Ahh, Miss Rodden, thank you so much for finally joining us." I can hear the disappointment dripping off his words.

"Yeah, no problem, wouldn't miss it," I reply back without even thinking.

"Care to explain to the class—who were all on time, might I add—and myself why you are late? Why you felt the need to waste everyone's time right now by not taking things seriously?"

My eyes shoot up to meet his and I am annoyed that he doesn't just drop it. I am a tad shocked by his behavior toward me, and how cold he's being.

Don't do it, Cassie, just let it go.

The angel on my shoulder pleads, but the devil always wins.

"I think you know why," I say, holding his gaze, not wanting to back down. The other students look back and forth between us with confusion.

He smirks and his eyes tighten. My heart is pounding, and I can't tell if it's from all this tension or because my organs desperately need water.

"Take two laps, and during those two laps, please think about why you are here, and understand that I do not tolerate tardiness. You are better than what you have presented so far."

Last night floods my memory and almost stopping that guy's heart. The air in the room becomes uncomfortable and tears sting my eyes. I bite my lip to prevent the waterworks from spilling out.

"Professor," Henry takes a step forward toward us, "if you don't mind, I'll run the two laps as well."

I shoot him a questioning look, and he quickly glances at me, but then back to Cillian. Henry's wearing a grey exercise shirt and black shorts. My imagination starts to drift. The muscles are more noticeable in his outfit today.

"And why, Mr. Ansley, would you want to do that?" Cillian asks.

I snap back to the present and watch as Cillian turns to face Henry directly. Henry stands up a little straighter.

"Because we are a team, and when one of us faulters, the rest must be able to step in and help," he says boldly.

Cillian looks as if he's trying to find a way around what Henry said, but instead stares at him for a moment. "Very well. Students," Cillian turns to address the whole group, "let this be an example of what a team should and should not do. Yes, Mr. Ansley is correct, you are all a team—especially when fighting against the Anarchy— and you must lean on each other for help. However," his eyes fall back onto me, "one must realize when hope has been lost and someone has become dead weight."

Feel like that might have been a tad harsh.

My heart breaks without me even realizing I had given him the power to do so. I bite my lip harder until I taste blood. I turn on my heel and begin to jog on the track, trying not to think about what just happened.

My organs are pleading for water as I struggle with my laps. I'm sweating so much and the pounding in my head only intensifies. I truly don't know how I am going to make it through this whole class without throwing up.

Henry quickly catches up to me and matches my pace.

"Hey, don't worry about Professor Morris. He's a hard arse, but he means well."

I just nod my head and continue. I'm not really in the mood to chat.

"So, uh, why were you late?" Henry asks curiously.

I shoot a glance at him. He jogs effortlessly, keeping my stride—his skin is lightly tanned and his soft curls bounce ever so slightly.

Talk to him. Maybe it'll distract you.

"Um," I start off slowly, even though I am already struggling with controlling my breathing, "I went out last night to a pub. Cillian busted me, but I was already pretty wasted. Overslept."

Just play it cool.

I want to watch his reaction, but decide to keep my focus forward.

"No way! That is so cool." He chuckles. His reaction makes me feel better and I smile.

"Yeah, I guess. I feel like utter garbage now, though."

We're making our round back toward the group and I try to pick up my pace a tad to not give Cillian the satisfaction of watching me struggle.

"Hey, well, you still look great." I see him blush a little out of the corner of my eye.

We make small talk as we round the final curve and rejoin the group. Talking with Henry has made me feel better overall. Cillian is finishing up whatever speech he was giving as I give Nora an exasperated look. I take my spot by her side and listen to what Cillian has to say.

"For a warmup, I want everyone to do five laps and meet me back here, where we will start sparring," Cillian directs.

Oh great, more laps.

People disperse and make their way onto the track. I am already drenched in sweat, so I unzip my jacket and toss it onto the ground by the water station. I can't grab and fill the small paper cup fast enough. The cold water is so relieving as it seeps into my thirsty organs, and quenches my dry throat.

"Damn, Yankee, looking good!" an unfamiliar voice comes from beside Nora.

I look up and see a brute-looking guy with dark curls and olive skin. I notice his hazel eyes and that he gives off a very sleezy aura. I become self-conscious and my cheeks flush.

"Uh, thanks?" I fill my cup again, not knowing what more to say.

"Knock it off, Nick," Henry says beside me.

Nick moves closer to us and I instinctively take a step back.

"What? Can't I appreciate a sexy woman?" he asks, raising his hands in defense.

My stomach turns again, but this time I know it isn't from the hangover.

"Hey! Let's get moving! I want everyone on that track now!" Cillian yells.

I crumple up my cup and throw it in the small garbage next to the water jug. Nora grabs my arm and pulls me back onto the track. I am thankful for the rescue and look back to see Cillian still watching me. We begin to run, but this time I match Nora's pace, thankful for her small stride.

"Don't worry about Nick. He's a creep, but he's harmless," she reassures me. I know all too well about harmless creeps and just how deceiving they can be.

The five laps are literal hell, but I keep up as best as I can. I feel bad for Nora; I can tell she feels obligated to stay with me. Henry also stays nearby, but keeps enough distance to where it isn't obvious. As for Cillian, I can tell he is watching me. He's studying me. I just don't know why. He watches everyone in class, so it's not like I'm special, but something feels different when I catch his eyes on me. Even though they never betray him, it seems he is waiting for something to happen.

As we all make our way back to the center of the room, I am not the only person struggling to control their breath. Thankfully, however, I am feeling better overall. I can feel my magic strengthening and my body recovering.

A couple of the guys have taken off their shirts and I am impressed by how built they all are—every single one has six-pack abs. I am lean and muscular, but you can tell I prefer pizza to salad.

Cillian directs us to get into pairs to spar. We are to switch every 15 minutes. The class has an even number of ten people, so everyone has a partner.

"Now, I don't want you to go easy on your opponent, but there are rules. Rule number one: No magic. I know, you're all looking at me like I am crazy, because this is a school for the magically gifted. But trust me, you must not become reliant on magic. When the enemy is up close and personal, sometimes you must resort to hand-to-hand combat, especially if your power is drained. Magic works like a rechargeable battery. If you expend it, you must wait for it to recharge. We will, of course, be using magic in this class as well, so we will build your magics' stamina, as well as eventually adding weapons, but not today. Rule number two: No maliciously hurting your opponent. They tap out, you stop. I will not tolerate malice. And finally, rule number three: Everyone fights everyone. Got it?"

We all nod in unison.

"Good. Get to it. Spread out, and good luck. I will be walking around and observing."

Nora and I walk over to an area not yet claimed by a pair.

"I don't know about this, Nora." I say, a little nervous. I look around at the other pairs already starting.

A punch suddenly lands in my stomach and forces all the air out of my lungs. I double over as I desperately gasp for air. I look up at Nora, who is smirking.

"What…the…fuck, dude?!" I say between gasps.

"Come on, Cassie. He said not to go easy, and just because I'm your roommate doesn't mean I'm not going to show you what I got. Plus, I am still a little pissed about you going out without me."

Fair enough.

I suck in a couple more breaths and stand up straight. If this is how it's going to be, then I'm going to show everyone what I am capable of. No more being weak.

I take my stance and hold up my fists.

"Come on, then." I give her a devious smile, and she lunges forward.

She is scrappy and fast, but she's trying too hard. She goes for the obvious blows, which makes her actions predictable. It isn't long before I have her pinned and Cillian blows his whistle, signaling us to switch. We untangle ourselves, laughing as we get up.

"Well, Yankee, there might just be some fight in you yet, eh?" she laughs.

I give her a playful shove and move on to my next partner. He is beautifully dark skinned, and his dreads are neatly pulled back into a large ponytail. A sheen of sweat glistens on his arms. He is very tall, though, and I know he has the physical advantage.

"Hi, I'm Cassie." I outreach my hand and he gently shakes it.

"Caleb," he replies.

The whistle signals us to begin. I can tell his punches are dialed back, which I am thankful for, but he knows not to be obvious like Nora.

Every now and then I see Cillian walk around the pairs to observe our fighting. I try not to get distracted, but I constantly have to keep refocusing myself.

Both Caleb and I work up a sweat, but neither of us end up winning before time is up. He gives me a small bow and I do the same.

"Okay, class, circle up," Cillian directs.

"But we haven't made it through everyone yet!" Lauren whines. Something tells me she wants a chance to lay some blows into me. She is next in my rotation.

I roll my eyes and join the circle.

"Yes, thank you, Miss Cole, for the obvious," Cillian says sarcastically. Lauren crosses her arms and pouts. "I've changed my mind, because I am the professor. Walking around, I saw some excellent examples of fighting styles that some of you could take note of. Here is what we are going to do now: I call your name, you come to the middle of the circle. You will have ten minutes to fight the other person. The same three rules still apply."

We all look around at each other, waiting for him to say someone's name.

Please don't be me.

Even though I'm feeling better, I am almost scared of my powers. I don't want to accidentally hurt someone.

"Henry and Cassie, come to the center."

My brain takes a moment to process, and Nora has to nudge me forward. I look at Henry as he steps into the center with me. He looks cautious as well. Henry had taken his shirt off since we ran our opening laps, and his body looks even better. He is muscular, but not bulky, which I had known already, but his shirtless appearance causes a bit of a distraction. I try to swallow—my mouth suddenly very dry.

"Are you sure about this? I mean, I'm not feeling the greatest," I try to persuade Cillian.

"Everyone fights," Cillian says sternly. "Now, at my signal, you will begin."

Henry and I face each other and get into our stances.

"You ready for this?" Henry questions.

"Yeah, of course." *Lies.* "Just don't hold back, okay?" I use flirting as a defense mechanism to shroud my nervousness.

"Not in my nature, love." Henry smirks.

Fuck, I am done for.

"Begin," Cillian says softly.

It is only a second, but everything seems to slow down as I shift my weight slightly on the balls of my feet, waiting for Henry to make the first move. The room is silent, everyone holding their breath to see who will strike first.

Henry advances forward and throws a bolo punch to catch me off guard, but I counteract by taking a step back with a check hook. The circle around us gets bigger as the others realize we need more space.

"Class, pay attention, please, to their styles. How they move together. How they anticipate and respond," Cillian commentates.

Henry advances hard and fast, which makes it difficult to keep up with his combinations. To give myself a few seconds to recover, I complete a roundoff back handspring, aiming to clip his jaw with my foot.

Thank you, gymnastics lessons.

This move, however, only gives me maybe two seconds to process my next one. I jab, but Henry is quick and ducks out of the way. He uses this missed blow to sweep my legs out from underneath me, and I come crashing hard onto the mat below.

I'm really getting tired of getting the wind knocked out of me, but I use this to my advantage. Some of the other students cheer for Henry, but I exaggerate wheezing for air. It doesn't take long for Henry to come to my aid, thinking he has actually hurt me. As he reaches down, I grab his arm and flip him into an armbar.

Got you now.

Henry struggles as he tries to get out of my hold, but I' in control now. The whistle blows, signaling the end. I quickly release Henry, adrenaline coursing through me, charging up my magic like a battery. Nora cheers loudly, and Henry hops up with a smile on his face.

"Not bad, Cassie. Nice round," he says, outstretching his hand. I shake it, but I can't hide my joy.

"Right back at ya." I give him a flirty wink and smile back.

Cillian steps toward Henry and me, "Okay class, perfect example of 'never let your enemy fool you.' Always expect the worst." He leans close to me and in a hushed tone says, "Good job, Cassandra."

Here come the butterflies again.

A few more pairs spar, and it's interesting to watch the others fight without having to worry about defending myself. I catch Henry looking at me every now and then, as the other rounds go on. His sweet face never ceases to make me blush whenever our eyes meet.

"Okay, class, one more for the day. All of you have done wonderful. Cassie, Lauren, to the center please."

Crap.

Hearing mine and Lauren's name in the same sentence makes bile run into the back of my throat.

Lauren steps to the center of the circle and offers a sickening sneer. I have watched Lauren fight other rounds, and she is good. She toes the line of what could be considered fighting dirty, and for whatever reason, this girl has it out for me.

It's fine. You got this.

My mental pep talk fails as I reluctantly step back into the circle. The whistle hasn't even been blown yet, and Lauren is already on the attack. I look to Cillian for interference, but he just stands and watches. I grit my teeth and know I have to grow some balls sometime. The real world isn't fair. It isn't going to give you a warning saying, "Hey, I'm going to start attacking you now. Be ready!".

I try to keep up, but Lauren is strong, even without magic—like she's been training her whole life for this exact moment. I misjudge a blow and it lands directly into my chest. I am flung back a few feet with great force; I feel a rib crack. My lungs deflate like a popped balloon and they burn as I desperately try to fill them with air.

She must be using magic at this point. There is no way she could have flung me as far back as she did without it.

I look up at Lauren with confusion and worry.

Why isn't Cillian stopping this fight?

I have no time to process before Lauren is on top of me. I frantically try to wriggle my way out of her hold. We are outside the circle now, on the track.

"Lauren, stop, please," I beg. I cannot breathe; my whole body hurts.

Lauren does not relent as I crawl away. She quickly catches up and slams her foot into my side. This time I am flung even further and crash into the wall.

"Lauren, ENOUGH!" Cillian's voice is fuzzy and faded. I lay on the ground, writhing in pain.

Lauren does not heed his command and walks over to me. She grabs my arm and twists it behind my back. I am in shock. I can't even try to fight back. I can hear and feel the tendons being stretched to their limits and tearing in my shoulder, snapping back like broken rubber bands.

"No one wants you here, you bitch!" Lauren hisses into my ear.

I scream out in agony, pain radiating throughout my entire body. I feel Lauren's weight lift off me abruptly and see that Cillian has flung her off me with his magic. She lands to the side, and Nora and Henry rush to me. Henry touches my back with concern.

Pain soon turns to anger, and I have had more than my fill of it. The anger spills over, and I can no longer control it. Henry's hand feels warm on my back and I can feel my magic getting stronger with my anger.

I slowly stand up, my left arm hanging limp at my side.

"Cassie, are you okay?" Nora asks with concern.

I ignore her, and my eyes lock onto Lauren, who is slowly getting up as well. Cillian steps between us to block my view of her.

"Cassandra, calm down. You're hurt. You need to go to the Infirmary," Cillian says.

His words do not faze me. I look down at my limp arm and focus my magic to travel to the ripped tendons and to the ribs that are surely broken. I feel the fibers slowly weaving together, repairing the tendons; magic fills the fractures in my ribs and hardens. My arm slowly shrinks back into place and everyone around me gasps.

"H-how did you do that?" Henry asks, eyes wide with disbelief. Even Cillian seems taken aback by this.

But I do not answer. I lock my focus back onto Lauren, who looks nervous now. My body is on fire with magic and anger. The room begins to shake, and everyone becomes frantic. There are several people between Lauren and me, so getting to her is not going to be the easiest.

I close my eyes for a brief second and my body tingles. It is not until I open my eyes that I realize I have somehow transported myself to directly in front of Lauren. She stumbles back in shock. I would have too, but something else is in control now.

I lift her up by the throat and squeeze as hard as I can. She fights against my grasp, but to no avail. Her legs flail about as I slowly begin to suffocate her, crushing her windpipe.

I do not feel like myself. I do not feel anything.

"Cassie, stop! You're killing her!" Nora runs toward me, but I raise my other arm and create a forcefield, preventing anyone from coming closer to us.

Lauren is barely struggling against me now. Her lips turn a faint blue and all the color fades from her face. Her eyes roll back in her head.

"Cassandra, stop. Stop, this is not you."

Cillian?

Cillian's voice somehow penetrates my thoughts, but it is just enough of a distraction to bring me back to my senses. I drop the forcefield and feel myself being flung abruptly away from Lauren.

Tears begin to fall as regret floods through me and I realize what I have done. I get up quickly and rush back to Lauren. Everyone takes several steps away from me as I pass. Thankfully, Lauren is coughing, and the color is returning to her face.

Henry grabs me and holds on as I get closer to her.

"Lauren, Lauren, I'm sorry. I didn't mean it. I'm so sorry," I sob, as Cillian leans down to check on her.

"You crazy, bitch! You could have killed me!" Lauren manages to spout between coughs.

The room has stopped shaking and it is deathly quiet—the only noise coming from my sobs and Lauren's coughing. I can feel everyone's eyes on me.

Cillian stands up and addresses the students, "Class, rules are put into place so these exact instances can be avoided. Miss Cole, you used your magic and actively attacked Miss Rodden. You broke the rules first. Ho—"

"Are you freaking kidding me!" Lauren interjects, jumping to her feet. "She almost killed me!"

Cillian looks at her, "If you would let me finish, Miss Cole, Miss Rodden's behavior was unacceptable as well. Both of you took things too far, and it will not be tolerated. Both of you will be on Night Watch for the rest of the week."

"But Lauren started it!" Nora chimes in, "Lauren *did* seriously injury Cassie."

"Yeah, Professor, Cassie was just defending herself," Henry says hesitantly.

I hang my head in embarrassment, Henry still holding onto me. I feel so weak, if he was there, I might collapse. I do not want others defending my behavior. I lost control again, and once again someone's life was almost the price.

"Fine. Miss Malik, Mr. Ansley, you get Night Watch duty as

well. You do not question my judgment," Cillian says sternly.

Nora looks as if she wants to say more but holds back.

"Class is dismissed. Lauren, head to the Infirmary to get checked out. I will make sure you are excused from your next class. Cassandra, stay with me."

Henry slowly releases his hold on me and turns me around to look at him, "Are you sure you are okay?" The concern in his voice hugs my heart.

"Yeah," I sniffle and nod. I try to give a reassuring smile, but I know it is not convincing. "Thanks."

"I'll see you back at the room, Cassie." Nora stays for a moment longer than everyone else, but soon leaves as well.

I am apprehensive to look at Cillian, and I shift my weight back and forth nervously. He steps close to me—closer than I would have thought he would step. He gently grabs my chin and lifts my eyes to meet his.

"Are you okay, really? What happened there?" He searches my eyes for the truth.

I want to fall apart in his arms. I want to tell him every emotion I felt and how scared I was. The lights in the room flicker, which cause him to drop his hand and take a step back.

"No," I whisper, "I am not okay. I lost control again. I made an embarrassment of myself again. I almost *killed* someone again." I bite my lip in an effort to stop the tears.

"The only thing we can do now is learn from this. I am partially to blame. I did not know Lauren would attack you like that.

You expended a great deal of magic and energy today. You'll most likely feel drained for a few hours. Have you ever done those things before that you did?"

"What do you mean?" He knows I have trouble containing my anger.

"Shifting, forcefield, and self-healing? Many witches never learn those skills. They take years to learn and master. We teach some of these skills during the second half of Level 6 year, but what you did was on a different level." The way he speaks makes it seem like he doesn't believe that I haven't done them before.

I shake my head. "No, I didn't even really know what was going on. It felt like something else had taken control. Sometimes I do things and I don't know how I do them. I am not able to recreate them." I hang my head again.

"You really do have so much to learn," he whispers.

I see Cillian begin to reach out toward me again, but he stops himself.

"Can I go?" I just want to get out of here.

"Get some rest and eat something. I'll make sure you are excused the rest of the day."

I nod and head toward the exit.

Nora is waiting for me when I get back to our room. I throw myself onto my bed and bury my head in the sheets.

"Cassie?" She gently touches my shoulder.

I sigh. Nora has been nothing but warm and welcoming to

me since I arrived—probably the only person I would qualify as a friend—so I know I should push myself to open up to her. I do not want to push her away.

I pull my head from the covers and look at her. Her expression is not filled with fear of me, but rather genuine concern.

"I don't know what happened back there, Nora. Sometimes I lose control over my anger and bad things happen. I know what I did was awful, and I hate myself for it." I would make a horrible accomplice. If I were to ever get caught, my face would easily give me away.

She sits beside me on the bed. "It's not all your fault. Lauren was way out of line. I know she is a bitch, but I have never seen her act that way. Well, before you got here." I look at her. "But either way, I think it's incredibly cool—all the magic you did—so I am just deciding to overlook the part where you two almost killed each other." She smiles.

"I honestly don't know how I did it all."

"But you *did* do it! That's the main point I am trying to make here. You are very powerful, Cassie. You know, there is a bedtime story based off a prophecy that has been passed down through history of a witch who was so powerful that she was able to unite the two sides. The good, the evil."

"There's always a bedtime story prophesizing that exact thing. You do realize that, right?"

She playfully pushes me and we laugh together.

"Well, I think you, Cassandra Rodden, are extremely badass

and I am so happy you are my roommate."

"Same, Nora. Thank you for sticking up for me back there, by the way." I'll never forget how she had.

"Anytime, babe. But as much as I want to stay and chat, I've got to get to Herbology."

Strangely, I don't want her to go. I don't want to be alone.

"But don't worry, I'll make sure to bring us some food later, okay?" she says as she hops off my bed and changes out of her workout gear.

"Yeah, sounds good to me. Cillian excused me for the rest of the day, and I am exhausted. I may visit the infirmary, though, just to make sure I'm okay. That is, if I can find it."

"Hmm, do all Americans call their professors by their first names?"

Oh shit.

"Oh, did I? I guess I didn't even realize. Uh, yeah, some teachers prefer that. Silly me, you know, still trying to get accustomed here," I try to be convincing.

She eyes me suspiciously. "You Americans sure are…interesting."

"We sure are," I say with a nervous laugh.

She pulls on a pair of boyfriend jeans and a long-sleeved green shirt. She kisses my cheek and heads off to Herbology. I stare around the room for a few minutes, trying to see what I can occupy my time with. I feel fine, but part of me wants to go get checked out. I'll wait a little while to avoid running into Lauren again. I check my phone for any new notifications.

Henry Ansley followed you on Instagram

I smile and click on his profile. He is sweet and athletic, which his pictures convey, as I scroll through them for a few minutes. I decide to follow him back. Part of me feels a little giddy. I also go in and accept Nora's follow request as well.

Might as well try this whole making friends thing.

I spend the next couple of hours visiting the Infirmary and getting examined. Everything comes back perfectly normal. I roam the halls to try and get a better feel of where everything is, but end up making my way outside to walk the grounds. The fresh air feels nice, and what I come to find is that the countryside has a relaxing atmosphere. It allows me time to think about everything that has happened in the last 24 hours and self-reflect. I feel different here, but I can't tell if it as a bad different or a good different.

Nora brings salads and sandwiches in for lunch, and I am starving. While we eat, she tells me more about what Night Watch entails. Basically, it is the school's way of providing extra security without having to pay an outside contractor for it. We'll start at 10:00 p.m., and walk the perimeter until 4:00 a.m., with a professor to keep an eye on us. Nora mentions that most people who are stuck with it usually go to sleep right after dinner, get up for the shift, and then crash from 4:00 a.m. to 7:00 a.m. Nora, and her witchy-herb intuition, makes a concoction in Herbology to help us stay awake.

"So, once we get out there, I'll give you one of these," she holds up a capsule with ground-up herbs inside it.

"Are there any side effects?" I ask, taking the pill from her to examine it.

"Nothing really," she says with a shrug.

I roll the capsule between two fingers.

"And they were fine with you making these?" I inquire skeptically.

"Well, you see, I could basically teach the classes they give us here about herbology. Mrs. Alberts knows this, so she just leaves me be and lets me do my own thing."

Fair enough.

Nora reaches out for the capsule and I drop it into her palm. I swallow my last bite of food and lean my head back against the drawers. Nora and I had decided sitting on the floor would be best while we ate.

"Hey, why wasn't Yash in Tactical this morning? I thought he was a Level Six just like us?"

"He is, but sometimes he gets pulled for technical stuff. He has an affinity for all that stuff and the Headmistress pulls him out when she needs his help."

"Oh, okay. I've heard the word affinity a few times around here. What does it mean?"

She gives me a look.

"You have to remember, I didn't grow up around all of this," I remind her, waving my arm around.

"True, okay, so, affinities are just when your magic leans more toward a certain skill or power. For me, my affinity is for plants and physical spells. For Yash, it's technology and being able to use his magic to break codes or increase security. I think that's the case, anyway. I don't really know. Every time he talks about it my brain hurts, so I just nod along."

"Okay, makes sense," I say, trying to grasp it all.

"Do you know what yours might be?"

"No, not at all." I kind of feel ashamed I don't. Cillian was right about me starting way behind the others.

I sigh heavily as silence falls around us.

"Still thinking about earlier?" Nora peeks up at me.

"Yeah, I don't know…I just hope Lauren is okay. Sometimes I let my emotions get the best of me, and then something else takes control and someone else ends up paying the price."

"Yeah, you were definitely scary, that's for sure. It looked like your eyes were glowing."

I jerk my head up, "What do you mean they were glowing?"

Nora stops mid-bite, "I just thought they looked extra…vibrant. Let's go with vibrant. Either way, I am sure that witch is fine. It was scary—but amazing to see you in action. I overheard people talking about how powerful you were before you arrived. I mean, hell, you were doing things that we haven't even learned yet."

I scoff. "I am not that powerful, and I don't know. Stuff just happens sometimes."

"Yeah, we'll see, I guess. I've got a good feeling about you though, Cassie."

I roll my eyes and smile.

"So, erm, you ever going to tell me about last night?" she asks impatiently, but I am grateful for the change in subject.

Welp, might as well be honest.

"I snuck out to go to a pub and Cillian caught me. I was pretty drunk, so he helped me inside."

Nora's jaw drops to the floor.

"No way!" she screams. "Oh my God, Cassie. I don't even know what to say right now. I am never speechless."

I giggle and blush. "It's nothing, though, really. Do not make a big deal out of this."

Nora licks her lips and shakes her head.

"They really did pick the best roommate for me. Here I was, thinking that I would corrupt you! I am so happy you are here. Plus, who knew how much of a degenerate you'd be?!"

I throw my crumbled napkin at her and erupt into laughter. I hold onto this moment. This is the moment I know I have found my best friend and I will remember this moment forever.

CHAPTER FIVE

Nora skips off to her last class, History of Witchcraft, while I put the finishing touches on my half of the room. Nora had asked if I wanted to eat dinner in the Dining Hall, but I held off. Instead, she and Yash bring food and we eat on the floor again. It's nice learning about Yash and Nora's lives. Both of their families are originally from India, but moved to England just before they were born. Only Nora's family is magical, and they all have affinities for herbs. Yash, on the other hand, is the first witch in his family. Their families lived next door to each other, and Yash explains that Nora and her parents had helped his parents more than words could describe while they were growing up, with handling the whole magic situation. They had both been taught from a young age all about magic and its history. Yash's family had to travel back to India for work, and they had moved there permanently a few years ago.

Yash and Nora both came to the Academy when they turned thirteen. As they grew older, friendship turned into love, which brings us up to date. I can't help but look at them both adoringly as they talk about each other. They work so well together, even when they're arguing.

"Well, you delinquents better try and get a nap in before Night Watch. Headmistress needs my help again, anyway," Yash says, clapping his hands together.

"She should really pay you for all you do for her. If I didn't know better, I'd think you two were off having an affair!" Nora jokes.

Yash stands and leans down to kiss Nora on her forehead.

"Nah, could never cheat on you, my love. You'd chop my balls off if I did."

"Damn right, I would," Nora says, jumping up and pretending to punch Yash in the stomach.

"See you both tomorrow morning," Yash says as he departs our room.

"Later, hot stuff!" Nora calls after him.

Yash closes the door behind him. I smile and chuckle to myself as I gather up all the trash from dinner.

"You two are adorable."

"Yeah, I really do love that stinky man. I'd give my life for him."

My mood turns somber as I think about my love interests over the years. Or should I say, failed love interests. But I guess that's one of the risks you run when you push people away and don't let them get too close. My thoughts soon drift to my parents and the love they had. It has been so long that my memories of them are harder and harder to remember, like the exact way their laughs sounded, or how tight my father would always squeeze me with his hugs.

"What's the matter, Cassie?" Nora asks, concerned. My face has given away my change in mood.

"Nothing. Just taking everything in. Yours and Yash's relationship reminds me a lot of my parents. They had a love that was immeasurable."

"You said they went here, right?"

I nod. "Yeah, they did."

"Do you have any pictures of them?"

"Uh, yeah, hold up," I say, grabbing my purse and digging through it. "Most of my photos are still at my grandmother's house, but I always keep this one with me."

I find the picture neatly tucked away in the fold of my wallet. It is well-worn from age and frequently being pulled out of its pocket, as well as from too many tears staining it. I hop onto my bed and slide back so my back presses against the wall. Nora does the same beside me.

"This was taken the day before the accident," I say, my voice cracking slightly. I try and clear my throat to prevent it from tightening as I show the photo to Nora.

The photo shows young me loaded up with winter gear from head to toe. I could barely move my arms and legs with it all on. Everything I have on is a bright pink that stands out vibrantly against the snow. I'm standing next to a very lumpy snowman, smiling as wide as I could at the camera. I had named the snowman Bob. Bob had borrowed one of my mother's scarves and my father's pipe. I had used rocks for his eyes and the buttons down his front.

My father stands on the other side of the snowman. He's wearing a red cap with a heavy, matching plaid coat. His rounded glasses are slightly foggy from his breath, but his vibrant green eyes are happy, his cheeks rosy from the cold. He was the one holding the camera up for us all and you can see his outstretched arm in the picture. My mother stands behind me, with her hands on my shoulders. Her beautiful skin rivals the snow's beauty. Her blue knit hat makes her blue eyes pop. She's wearing a black vest with a thick white sweater underneath. We all look so happy.

"That is my father. His name was Johnathan. My mother hated that coat, by the way," I say pointing to him and chuckling. "And that's my mother behind me. Her name was Elizabeth."

I don't realize I am crying until a tear drips down my cheek.

"Oh, Cassie, you don't have to talk about them. I don't want to upset you," Nora says, concerned. She wraps her arm around my shoulders.

"No, it's fine," I say, hurrying to wipe away my tears. "I don't talk about them enough. I remember being so happy here. I loved building snowmen. After the first real snow in Michigan, my father would run around the house getting me ready, and we'd spend hours outside building them. My mom would have to bribe us inside with hot cocoa."

"That sounds so wonderful, Cassie. You look exactly like your mother."

I smile. "My grandmother tells me that a lot. Nothing could compare to her though. She always looked so well put together. The day after this was taken, we were in a very bad accident and they were gone. Everything I loved just ripped away from me. Sometimes it's hard remembering everything about them. What's worse is that sometimes it doesn't even feel real."

"Well, hey, thank you for sharing this with me. I have open ears if you ever want to talk about it, okay?"

Nora's kind words help me more than I can realize. It's nice having everything out in the open. My grandmother was always there to listen, but I know thinking of my mother, her daughter, saddens her.

"Thanks, Nora." I try to smile as she squeezes my shoulders. "Well, enough tears for one day. How about let's try and nap before Night Watch?"

"Let's!" she says and releases my shoulders. Instead of getting off my bed, she just catapults herself to hers. I look at her like she is crazy, but a good crazy.

We both set alarms and snuggle into our beds. I use my magic to flip off the light switch. I hold the picture against my chest as I close my eyes. I also grab Piggy and tuck her underneath my arm. I lay there and wonder if the pain I feel deep inside my chest will ever fully go away.

I'm not able to nap like Nora is. My mind keeps me preoccupied, as if I am missing something, but I cannot figure out what that something is. The alarms sound and we both unwillingly get up and around for the night.

I slip on a thick sweater and black high tops, while Nora dons much the same. We make our way out of our room and to the front of the building. The night air washes over me and gives me a slight chill. Henry and Nick are standing at the bottom of the steps, and Lauren is off to the side, on her phone. I am nervous. I do not know what to expect from her reaction-wise after this morning. Henry turns and smiles at me as Nora and I descend the steps. It's hard to swallow and I feel my cheeks go warm, smiling back.

"Hey, how are you?" Henry asks as Nora and I join him.

"Better. Thank you," I sheepishly look down at my feet.

"Well, you look absolutely hot, no matter what. Especially when you rage." Nick's disgusting comment makes everything uncomfortable.

"Nick, why are you even here?" Nora sneers.

"Hey, Henry, be right back," I tell him as I step away to confront Lauren. Nora and Nick bicker back and forth about why he's there. Lauren hears me approach and looks up from her phone.

"Stay away from me, creep," she says and takes a step back.

I raise my hands to show I mean no harm. "Look, Lauren, I'm sorry for what happened. Are you okay?"

She studies me for a second to see if I'm being sincere. "Well, my throat does hurt a tad." She touches her neck dramatically. "But just know that I had you if Professor Morris hadn't intervened. I won."

"I agree," not wanting to start more drama, I am willing to inflate her ego, "You won that round."

She flashes a fake smile. "This doesn't mean I like you. Stay away from me, okay?"

"Not a problem."

She looks back at her phone and walks away. I sigh in relief.

Thank God.

"Cassie?" Henry's sweet voice comes from behind me.

I turn to look at him. He looks nervous and I wonder what for.

"Yeah?" His eyes are somehow brighter in the moonlight. My breathing quickens.

He shoves his hands deep into the pockets of his dark blue jeans. "Well, so, it's a couple weeks out, and I know you just got here and everything, and we don't really know each other, but I was wondering if you'd like to go to the All Hallows dance with me?"

My heart pounds in my chest so hard, I swear it's audible.

"Um, what's the All Hallows dance?" Growing up, I never went to school dances. Not because I didn't want to, but because my classmates had known something was different about me. They knew I had anger management issues and stayed clear, unless they were tormenting me.

"It's this dance that takes place in October on Halloween. It's a witch thing. It's a tradition at the school."

"Well, October is more than just a couple weeks away, you know?" I tease.

"Well, yeah, I know, but I know my mind won't change about wanting to go with you."

His words are sincere, and they make me feel all warm inside.

"Well, uh—" I am interrupted by Cillian clearing his throat at the bottom of the stairs. We all turn to him. He is looking directly at me.

How much of that did he just hear?

"Okay, students, welcome to Night Watch. I am the professor on duty to chaperone you all. For some of you, this is not your first time." He gives Nick a side glance and Nick puffs up his chest. "But if this is your first time, here is how it will go. You will walk the perimeter until four o'clock a.m. You will not speak; you will not be on your phones. This is a punishment. If you see anything alarming, please notify me immediately. I will be walking along with you all, but I will stay toward the back. Also, no magic—unless absolutely necessary—will be used."

"I thought Professor Abram was on Night Watch this term?" Henry questions.

Cillian looks at him emotionless, "You are incorrect."

"But my mum said—" Henry tries to protest.

"That's enough," Cillian cuts him off. "Just because you are the Headmistress's son does not mean you may question me."

Henry shrinks a little at Cillian's words, but I see his jaw clench. "Sorry, Professor."

"Now, everyone come get a flashlight out of the bag, and let's get to walking." Cillian holds up a large burlap bag.

The few of us get in line to pick one out. I am last one in line, and I keep my eyes down as I reach into the bag. The others turn theirs on and begin walking down the path. The flashlight is big and bulky, but I like how its size makes it useful as a weapon. I turn mine on and jog to catch up to the others.

"Cassandra?" Cillian says my name softly. The difference between now and the tone he took with Henry is so drastic, it catches me off guard.

I stop in my tracks and slowly turn back around. His eyes soften as I look into them.

"Yes?" I ask nervously.

"Cassandra." Him just saying my name makes me start to tingle. "Don't get involved with Henry." His statement seems to be more of like a command than a suggestion.

So, he had heard the dance conversation…

Part of me is a little offended and the tingling instantly ceases.

What gives him the right to tell me who and who not to get involved with? I am a grown woman.

"Excuse me? What makes you think you can decide that?" my tone coming out a little ruder than I intend.

His eyes go hard again, and his lips purse into a tight line. "Just don't. He is not good for you."

I am really peeved off now. I turn on my heel and walk to catch up with the others, leaving Cillian behind.

"I am speaking to you. Do not just walk away," he says sternly after me.

Without looking back or stopping I say, "I'm sorry, professor, but we aren't supposed to talk. This is a punishment after all." I smirk to myself for that comeback.

The rest of the students had stopped a few feet ahead when they noticed Cillian and I were not with them. I jog the few feet to catch up to them.

Nora is handing out her energy pills. "They are like caffeine pills, but better," she explains as she dumps one into each outstretched hand.

"Can I get one?" I ask, joining her.

"Of course, babe!" she replies.

"What did Professor Morris want?" Henry asks, still a little butthurt about being called out.

"It was nothing. Just giving me a hard time about earlier." I shrug it off as no big deal. "Let's get walking, shall we?"

We all pop a not-caffeine pill and start our long walk around the perimeter.

The hours drag by and my feet are killing me, but Nora's herbs definitely help to stay awake—even though they tasted like dirt. Lauren has trouble staying off her phone, and Nick often finds it hard to not talk, especially about himself. But part of me is thankful for the required quiet throughout our shift. Sometimes I fall behind and walk alone, taking in all the stars and wildlife noises. Cillian hangs far back from the group, but we are never out of his sight. I can tell Henry is anxious for me to give him an answer about the dance, but I don't mind letting him sweat it out before I accept or decline. He occasionally looks back at me and makes funny faces. I giggle and shift my eyes to my feet or to the side of the path.

My favorite part of the whole night is getting to watch the sun slowly rise. Since Watch ends at 4:00, we don't see the sunrise break the skyline, but we can see the sky getting brighter. The pitch black and deep blues slowly fade from the sky; the stars blend in and become lost in the impending daylight.

As we approach the front doors, everyone lets out a collective sigh of relief.

"Bloody hell, mate. Thank god this is over with. That was awful," Nick complains as we make our way up the steps.

Cillian goes to the front of the group and stands at the top of the stairs. "Okay, students, very nicely done. Thank you for mostly behaving on this little punishment. Be prepared, though, to spend the rest of the week doing this exact same thing. Return your flashlight, and then go get some rest. I'll see you all in class in a few hours."

Henry is in front of me and just about to hand his flashlight to Cillian when I decide to give him my answer.

"Hey, Henry?" He turns around in front of Cillian and looks down at me. "Yes." I say simply.

He seems a little confused at first, and then it all clicks.

"Really?" His face lights up. "Awesome that-um th-that's so cool." He trips through his words, trying to conceal his excitement. "I'll see you in class, okay?"

I smile and nod. Henry drops his flashlight in the bag and continues into the school. I walk up the next couple of steps to face

Cillian. He looks straight ahead, over the top of my head and his face remains expressionless. I put the flashlight in the bag slowly, watching to see if he'll say anything.

Standing on the top step, I get on my tip toes and whisper sternly, "Don't ever tell me what to do again."

The corner of his mouth raises slightly, but only for a second. If I had blinked, I might have missed it.

Take that.

I continue on into the school, where Nora is waiting for me, all the while grinning to myself.

CHAPTER SIX

The next couple of weeks run smoother as I adjust. Nora and I have all the same classes, which is nice. She is able to walk with me everywhere to help me learn the layout. It doesn't take me long to get familiar with it. Henry and I continue our flirtatious friendship, neither one making a real first move. Henry, Nora, Yash, and I slowly become a tight-knit group. Cillian iced me out the rest of the week we had Night Watch, but I know he always has an eye or ear focused on me. Nick continues his unwanted advances and comments, but I ignore him as much as I can.

Classes are enjoyable as everyone gets settled into the year. As days carry on without me losing control of my powers, fewer people are scared to go up against me in Tactical. Cillian never pairs me and Lauren again, and for that I am thankful. Lauren has reeled back her open hatred toward me since the incident, but every now and then, I can feel her eyes burning holes into the back of my head like her life depends on it.

Herbology is interesting, but not nearly one of my strong suits. There are myriad different concoctions you can put together to create different spells. Spells range from euphoric to lethal, protection to offense. Class is held in a large greenhouse behind the school. Plants drape every inch of the room of every color. While it is not my favorite class, it is refreshing being around all the beautiful plants.

History of Witchcraft class holds my attention faithfully. I want to know anything and everything about the history of witches and the Anarchy. We also learn more about the prophecy that Nora mentioned on our second day. Turns out it is more than just a bedtime story. Many witches believe it to be true. They believe that one day, a witch will come along with immeasurable power and unite all sides. The Prophecy is displayed in almost every textbook we use, as far as I can tell.

Good and Evil
Two sides that have fought against each other
Since the Dawn of Time
Battles raged in the Shadows
And prices Paid by lives lost

But Legend speaks of a Witch
With a Lost Soul
There will come a time
From a decision made
That will open a Pathway
For Good and Evil to be born

For she who carries the weight of Both
Shall give way to the Chosen One
Two paths will lie before her
One that will lead to her Salvation
The other to Damnation

I have never been one to believe in prophecies. Prophecies give hope and, while hope is a good thing, it can also be poisonous. It leaves room for disappointment and sadness, two things that I already have plenty of in my life.

The Anarchy, on the other hand, is your typical terrorist group—except for the fact that their members are witches. Their thirst for power is expressed by intimidation and chaos. They strive to show the world just how capable witches are of taking over and causing terror. Their stretch is far and wide. In class, I sometimes think of the darkness I have felt inside me when I have lost control. I wonder what it might take to turn a person evil. What excuse do they give to warrant all this chaos?

Summer quickly comes to an end and transitions to fall, even though it hadn't felt like much of a summer, with all the rain and clouds. As each day passes, I can feel myself growing stronger. The more I train my magic, the more confidence I have in using it. I am able to work with it instead of it working against me. Everything feels good for once as I settle in.

History is over for the day, but I have more I need to do. I tell Nora to save me some dinner and that I'm heading to Herbology to touch up on some spells before our quiz. I know Mrs. Alberts will be there late tending to all the plants. She is delighted when I stop by to study and ask her questions. She is such an interesting lady with a thick Scottish accent. Her red hair is always frizzled and untamed. Her pale skin always has some traces of dirt on it. She wears an apron every day that is covered in fertilizer or soil, pockets filled with different dried herbs. She talks about the plants as if they are alive, and to an extent, they are. But she gives them names and creates personalities for them. It's amusing and makes things more fun.

Hours have passed without me realizing, as I look up from my book to stretch. The sun has set, and the greenhouse is surrounded by darkness. I am so consumed with my readings that I don't realize Nick has come into the room as well and is sitting behind me, fiddling with several different ingredients.

Mrs. Alberts comes over to where I'm seated, taking off her worn gardening gloves and shoving them into her apron.

"I think I am about to get going. Hubby and I are going to have a little anniversary dinner. Will you two be fine here alone? You'll just have to shut the lights off when you leave," Mrs. Alberts asks.

I assure her that I won't be too much longer and start to pack my things.

"Hey, Mrs. Alberts, can you actually get me the hibiscus you were showing us earlier?" Nick asks.

I can see Mrs. Alberts wants to get out of there for her dinner. I think it was rude of Nick to even ask her, knowing she has already stayed much later than normal for us.

"Actually, Mrs. Alberts, I can help him, if you want to get going," I offer with a smile.

I can feel her relief but hesitation, "Are you sure?"

"Of course. Go have fun."

She gives me a warm smile and mouths, "thank you," before heading out. I spin around in my chair to look at Nick.

"What was it you needed? You know she wanted to get out of here," I say with a hint of annoyance.

"Hibiscus. I believe she said she had some dried over in the cabinets in the back of the greenhouse," Nick says in an even tone through a crooked smile.

"And why can't you just get it for yourself?"

I know I said I would help him, but I really do not want to.

"Please? I am almost done with this and it's one of the last things I need," he pleads, jutting his bottom lip out into a pout.

I groan and roll my eyes.

"Fine. Better not be for some stupid potion to make girls fawn over you," I say, passing him to go to the back cabinets.

"Why would I need that when they already do?" he says pompously.

I make my way to the back of the greenhouse to the cabinets behind some rows of assorted flowers. There is a special section where all the dried herbs and ingredients are kept. They are supposed to be kept in alphabetical order, but most students never take the time to put them away properly.

It is not that hard, people. We should all know the alphabet by now.

I look through all the ingredients, but cannot find the hibiscus. I know we have the living plant, but spells can be very picky. I sigh with frustration as I take one more look through all the little jars before giving up. I weave my way through the rows of plants back up to where Nick is waiting.

"Hey, I couldn't find the dried hibiscus."

"Oh, no worries," Nick smiles. "Thanks for looking. I appreciate it."

"Sure…I guess," I say, looking at him warily. Even if Nick is being nice, he still gives me a bad vibe.

Goodness, he gives me the creeps.

I walk over to where my stuff is and take a drink of water. After several gulps, I put the lid back on and gather my things. I can feel his eyes on me still.

"I'm finishing up as well, if you want to walk back together?" Nick says as he packs up his things, leaving the mixture he was making just sitting out on the table.

Ugh, be more open to people, Cassie.

I look outside at how dark it is and weigh my options. The greenhouse isn't far from the school, so it will be a quick walk back. Plus, I guess it wouldn't be complete torture to try and get to know Nick better.

"Erm…sure," I say reluctantly. I am becoming increasingly sleepy and just want to get back to my room. I hope Nora remembered to save me some dinner. I want to eat and go to bed.

I wait for Nick to grab the rest of his things and we head out. I make sure to shut the lights off as Mrs. Alberts requested.

It is chillier than I expected outside. A stiff breeze blows through us as we make our way up the hill. Thankfully, I'm wearing a pair of thick brown tights underneath my brown plaid skirt. I hug my arms against my body, even though my chunky sweater is doing a decent job keeping my torso warm.

My head slowly begins to hurt as Nick and I walk quietly up to the school. The pain starts deep inside my temples and grows outward. My legs feel heavier with each step, and my stomach turns.

Ugh, what is going on? Is it the salmon salad I had for lunch? I wonder how long it takes for food poisoning to settle in...

My skin feels clammy underneath my clothes and my breathing becomes shallow.

"You feeling okay, Cassie?" Nick asks. He's right next to me, but his voice sounds a little fuzzy.

"Um, yeah, I don't know. I am not feeling the greatest. I had the salmon salad for lunch. Maybe that's it."

We are just about to round the corner to the front of the school when I stop for a second to lean against the cool stone wall. The coolness of the stone helps keep the dizziness at bay.

"You know, I don't think I am doing so well." I can barely stand straight up. Every part of me feels weak. "Can you go get a nurse or something?"

After not hearing Nick reply, I look around to see where he went. I'm still dizzy, so looking around makes my stomach lurch. Nick is standing silently slightly behind me. His eyes are wide and frenzied. They are locked onto me like an animal locks theirs onto their prey.

"Nick, what's going on?" I'm getting scared. I look around quickly to see if there is anyone nearby, but make sure Nick is still in my line of sight.

Dammit. No one is out here. Why do I feel so dizzy and weak? Did he do something? Oh god…

Suddenly it becomes clear. "My water? What did you do to my water?" My words slowly begin to slur.

He takes a step closer. "You think you're some hot shit, don't you, Cassie, with your powers? Like you're better than me. Won't even give me the time of day. But without your powers, you're just like every other slut out there."

Another step.

"What are you talking about, Nick?" Tears turn my vision blurry and I try to blink them away quickly. "I do not think I'm better than anyone here."

Another step.

I try to move backward, but my ankle twists, and I almost fall.

"Stop, Nick. Whatever this is, just stop." I throw my hand up to use my powers, but nothing happens. Terror sets in and I pray that someone will see what is happening.

Nick lets out a roar of laughter. "I may have been a tad off on the proportions when making the Diminish potion, so that may be why you're having all these side effects." He slowly contorts his face into a sickening grin and laughs slightly. "But you'd think that the professors would be smarter about teaching us such a…" he ponders for a second on what his next word should be, "such a useful spell."

We just learned about the Diminish potion last week in class. It is potion that can strip a witch of their magic momentarily. It has to be consumed to work, and it is supposed to go unnoticed by the affected. But clearly, Nick did something wrong with the ingredients.

Should I try and run? Can I make it?

I have flats on, but with how dizzy I am, I doubt I would make it far. Plus, I have seen how fast Nick can run.

"And come on, babe, the way you dress," he moans, and my skin crawls. "You dress so seductively. It's basically an invitation."

Okay, Cassie, you're going to have to fight. Scream, punch, scratch.

"Why are you doing this?" The panic is evident in my voice, even though I'm trying to suppress it.

"Why, you ask? Because I can. Because you have no idea just how special you are. Don't worry though, I can't kill you. We are just going to have a little fun."

I try to prepare myself—and my lungs—but Nick can sense it and lunges for me. My limbs are so heavy, and I don't have time to even try and react. He pushes me up against the wall firmly.

I scream as loud as I can, but he squishes my face against the bricks with one hand. I can feel the skin on my check being ripped open against the wall as I struggle. His other arm grips onto mine and forces it behind my back. He is pressing me so hard against the wall, I can barely breathe.

"Nick, stop! Please, stop it. Please—don't do this to me." I try to speak as he continues pressing my face against the wall. My sobbing is uncontrollable. I use my free hand to try and grab him, but my efforts are futile. My lungs strain to pull in air.

He takes away the hand against my face and uses it to grab at my tights and skirt instead.

Scream, Cassie! Do something!

But I can't. It isn't hard for him to shred my tights. Time seems to slow and I brace for what is coming next. My muscles tense and I close my eyes. I force my mind to go somewhere else, anywhere else.

Please just let me die. I don't want to go through this again.

"Cassie!" Henry's voice shouts out to me.

I slowly open my eyes.

Henry? Was that real?

"Get away from her!" Henry's voice sounds like it's getting closer.

My face is pointing away from the school and I can't see anyone. The pressure against me lifts quickly and I drop to the ground. My vision is still blurry and I scramble backwards. I run into someone's legs and I scream as loud as I can, fearing they are Nick's.

"Cassandra, it's me! It's me, you're okay! I've got you."

Cillian.

He kneels and takes me in his arms. I hold onto him tightly, not wanting him to let go. I'm still sobbing and screaming as Cillian tries to calm me.

I'm safe. I'm safe. But where's Henry? Where's Nick?

I blink more, trying to see where Nick had gone, in case he is still in attack mode.

"Nick, Nick! He attacked me!" I sob.

"Shh, you're okay. You're okay, Cassandra. I'm here," Cillian consoles me.

Finally, I see Nick on the ground. Henry and another boy are on top of him, pinning him down.

The Headmistress comes into view and she scurries over to us. "Cassie, good heavens! Are you okay?" Her voice is frantic as she leans down to inspect me.

I'm still so dizzy, but I try to control my breathing and stop sobbing. I take a deep breath in; my ribs are sore and my lungs ache as I attempt to fill them.

"Nick," I have to stop and swallow; my saliva feels thick, "Nick, he drugged my water. He said something about a Diminishing potion."

Her dark brown eyes go hard, turning a deep black from anger. She stands up and looks over to where Henry and the other boy have apprehended Nick. They are all on their feet now, Nick still sneering at me.

I cringe and turn into Cillian, his warmth giving me more comfort than I can describe. I can feel his heart beating almost as fast as mine; his muscles tighten slightly as I move closer.

I slowly begin to regain my motor functions and my vision becomes clearer. The fog disperses, and my brain is able to process things better. Terror and fear are replaced with anger. I can barely feel my magic, if at all, but my physical strength is increasing.

"And what do you have to say for yourself, Mr. Galloway?" Headmistress Ansley asks sternly.

I motion to Cillian I want to stand, and we do slowly, my eyes never leaving Nick. He gives an evil chuckle as Cillian steadies me. Henry jabs Nick in his ribs. Nick winces and coughs a few times, but never breaks his lock on me.

"I said, Mr. Galloway, what do you have to say yourself?" The Headmistress's tone sends a chill up my spine.

Nick is silent for a moment and then speaks, "I did nothing that she didn't already have comin' to her." He laughs again, louder this time.

I lose it and run toward him; my legs find their way without faltering. I crash into him hard enough to send him flying backward to the ground. I scream violently and hit him in the face as hard as I can over and over again.

"FUCK YOU! FUCK YOU!" I scream at him with every ounce of air in my lungs.

He just lays there and laughs as I proceed to smash his nose into pieces, blood splattering all over. I can feel my knuckles fracturing as they slam against the bones in his face.

Henry bear-hugs me off Nick and doesn't let me go.

"Let me go! I want to kill him!" I protest. I feel like the animal now. I want to rip him to pieces and watch the life drain from his eyes. I want to hear him take in his last breath and listen to the life slowly wheeze out of him.

He deserves to die. Let me kill him! I will kill him!

"Enough!" The Headmistress comes to stand between us. The boy I don't know helps Nick to his feet, but keeps him restrained. Blood is gushing out of his nose and into his mouth. It makes him look sinister, as he continues to smile. I notice some of his teeth are bashed in.

"I will watch you die one day," I warn Nick.

"Charlie, take Nick to the holding cells. Cillian, come with me, and Henry, escort Cassandra to the Infirmary and stay with her until I come back," she directs.

I stop struggling against Henry and look at Cillian, not wanting him to leave me. Cillian's face is hard, much like it normally is, but there is an anger inside him that is leaking out.

"And as far as I am concerned, Mr. Galloway, you are hereby expelled from the Academy immediately. I will be sending in a formal request to have you stripped of your magic. Now, get out of my site."

Nick takes a mouthful of blood and spits it at the Headmistress, nearly missing her shoe. Headmistress marches right up to him and pulls a leather strap from her pocket. She wraps it tightly around Nick's neck.

"No more magic for you," she says.

Charlie struggles to direct Nick off to the cells, but the Headmistress is right behind him. Cillian stares at me and stands very still, as if he can't move. I can feel him restraining himself.

"Come, Cillian," Headmistress Ansley calls after him as she passes by Henry and me.

He waivers for a few seconds, but then turns and follows the others. I watch them all disappear out of sight.

Henry releases his hold, but soon realizes that I will need his support. I suddenly become aware of the fact that my tights and skirt are ripped and I am freezing. My hands and eyes frantically scan over my legs and ripped clothing, but my skin is numb from the cold. I touch my cheek and find blood. My body begins to shake uncontrollably, and the sobs return.

"I can't go through this again, Henry, I can't."

Hearing the panic rise in my voice, Henry, while still holding me up, moves around to face me. "Shh, Cassie it's okay, it's okay. Look at me. I've got you. You are safe with me."

This calms me some, and he places his hand gently on the cheek that isn't bleeding, although it is still sore from Nick's hand. I flinch without thinking and he freezes. I nod at him, though, to continue and I lean into his warm palm.

"Cassie," he says softly. I squeeze my eyes shut, not wanting to see him. I am embarrassed for being so weak. "Cassie, please look at me."

I reluctantly open my eyes. His face is soft and full of concern.

"I'm so sorry, Henry."

His face turns confused and angry. "What in the bloody hell do you have to be sorry for right now, Cassie? This is not your fault. Not at all. Come here."

My shaking worsens and he pulls me into him. He's wearing a thick leather jacket, and I bury my arms deep inside it.

"Let's get you inside, okay?"

I nod my head against his chest. His shirt smells of a mix of cinnamon and old books. Two of my favorite smells.

"Do you think you can stand on your own for a moment?"

I clench my teeth and will my body to steady itself as I let go of Henry. "I think so."

He proceeds to take off his jacket and drape it over my shoulders. I welcome the warmth and quickly stick my arms through the sleeves. His skin instantly raises up in little bumps, the cool night air surrounding us. I feel bad. I don't want him to be cold just so I won't be.

He sticks his arm out and I loop mine through it. We walk slowly to the front door. Just being close to Henry makes me feel better—both physically and emotionally. I know I am safe with him. My stomach settles and my headache subsides.

We make it up the front stairs and I stop Henry before he opens the door.

"Henry?" my voice just barely above a whisper.

"Yes, Cassie?" His eyes are so soft and patient.

"Thank you. I don't know what I would have done." I dig my nails into my palms, not wanting to cry more.

He smiles and squeezes my arm softly. "You have no idea the things I would do to keep you safe, Cassie."

We head inside and make our way to the Infirmary. The night nurse rushes to me when she sees us slowly enter.

"Oh, my goodness. What happened to her?" She is a sweet older lady with round glasses. Her scrubs fit a tad snug, but her oversized cardigan looks as if it is drowning her. Her nametag notifies me that her name is Margaret.

Henry clears his throat, not sure on how to describe what happened.

"I was drugged and assaulted by another student...by a male student." I try to hide my shame by being strong, but all I want is to crawl into a very dark hole and disappear.

Her face goes pale with shock and horror as she looks me up and down.

"Oh, my dear...I am so sorry. Come here, please, we will get you taken care of."

She helps me over to a bed with a large curtain around it. She pushes the curtain back and motions for me to join her.

"Okay, my dear, I need you to—"

"I know how it goes. I'll undress for the exam," I say quietly. I'm not trying to be rude when I interrupt her, it's just that everything feels like déjà vu.

Her mouth opens slightly with pity, which only makes me feel more embarrassed.

Poor girl, I know. How could this happen to someone multiple times?

I am sure those thoughts are running through her head. She composes herself and motions for Henry to give us some privacy as she pulls the curtain.

"Well, Mr. Ansley, you'll have to excuse yourself during the exam, please."

"Wait, Henry," Margaret stops pulling the curtain and they both turn to look at me. "Please don't leave, Henry." I don't want him to leave me.

"I'm not going anywhere, love," he assures.

"Can you please text Nora as well? I don't know where my phone is, and I am sure she's worried."

He nods.

Margaret closes the curtain and retrieves different sized towels from a cabinet. I slowly peel off what remains of my clothing. Blood has dripped down onto my sweater, ruining it. I lay Henry's jacket on the bed softly. The adrenaline has worn off and the pain is increasing. All I want is Henry to come back and help me feel better.

I take a deep breath and turn to Margaret, who is waiting for me to finish undressing. She has a gown in her hand for me to wear. I take it from her and slip it on. The stiff fabric feels rough against my skin and I somehow feel more exposed with it on.

I take another deep breath, "Okay, I am ready."

Margaret examines every inch and notates every bruise and scratch, takes blood samples, and uses her magic to examine the details of it. Even though Nick hadn't been able to go all the way through with his assault, he had left many scratches and bruises.

I feel so dirty, even as Margaret uses a damp towel to clean off some of the blood and dirt. I just want to take a boiling hot shower to burn away any trace of Nick still left on me, but that will to have to wait.

After she is done examining my legs, I put Henry's jacket back on over my gown. It is very cold in the room and I begin to shiver. I sit on the bed as Margaret cleans up my face as much as she can.

"Can you open the curtain please? I want to see Henry."

"Are you sure you're okay with that? We are almost done." Margaret looks apprehensive of my request.

"Please, thank you."

Margaret opens the curtain and I see Henry sitting in a chair against a nearby wall. He jumps up and comes over when he sees me.

"I texted Nora. How are you?" His eyes full of concern as they search me. "Also, I had one of my boys go out and find your phone and gather the bookbag that you dropped." He holds up my things.

Part of me wants to start crying again as Margaret places a brown, earthy-smelling mud paste on my cuts.

"I know the paste doesn't smell the greatest, but it'll help heal the scratches faster. I keep telling the Headmistress we need a Healer on staff, but they are hard to come by," she explains, as she adorns my face with a sterile patch and tapes the edges. "There, all done now, deary." She gives me a warm smile.

"WHERE THE BLOODY HELL IS HE? IMMA KILL HIM!" Nora's voice travels up the hallway and into the Infirmary. It isn't long after hearing her that her short stature comes into frame. She looks heated, even in her bunny pajama pants and T-shirt.

"Nora!" I sit up straighter and peer around Henry.

"Oh my god, Cassie! Where is the tosser? I swear to God, Imma give him a piece of mind. And by mind, I mean a foot so far down his throat, he chokes," She continues, louder as she gets closer. She comes right up between Margaret and Henry and hugs me a little too hard.

I wince.

"Oh my, I am so sorry! I am such a git. Are you okay?" She turns to Margaret. "Is she okay?"

"I can answer, you know. I am right here."

"Shut up, I know you are." We giggle and smile for a moment, but her face quickly turns serious again. "Are you okay, though?"

"I will be. Hopefully, I can leave here soon. I think the exam is over with," I hint. Margaret pats my shoulder.

"I would like to speak with you first," the Headmistress's voice commands. I hadn't heard her approach.

Everyone turns to look at her. Cillian, unfortunately, is not with her. I can't help but feel a tad disappointed.

Why isn't he here with the Headmistress?

"Henry, Nora, please go wait in the hallway." They nod and follow her directions. The Headmistress looks tired, as it is late now, but she is still dressed in her heels and blazer. Regardless, she looks intimidating. She takes the chart Margaret offers her and looks it over.

"How are you doing, Miss Rodden?" she asks, still looking over my paperwork.

I am getting really tired of everyone asking that. "Better. If it wasn't for you all..." my voice trails off.

"Yes, well, Professor Morris and I were just getting back from a meeting out of town. Henry and Charlie were meeting us at the front of the school when we heard your screams. I am very sorry for what happened. Rest assured, though, that Nick has been expelled from the Academy and I have submitted a request for him to be stripped."

"What does that mean?"

The Headmistress looks up from the paperwork, confused by my question, "Sometimes, when witches commit unforgivable acts, a request can be sent to the Protectors for them to strip away the offender's magic—to make them human."

"Oh, okay," I reply. There is still so much I have to learn.

She sits down at the foot of the bed, which surprises me, "But please do not worry, Cassie," She looks deep into my eyes, "Nick will not set foot on these grounds again, I can promise you that."

Maybe he should—when my powers come back.

"When can I expect to have my powers back?" I feel so defenseless, so normal. It scares me. From what I've learned in class, the Diminish potion should have worn off by now, and my powers should be restored.

She becomes a little frantic and looks at Margaret, "Her powers haven't returned yet?"

What do you mean haven't returned yet?

"I ran her blood. It looks like Mr. Galloway did not measure properly when making the Diminish potion—part of the reason why she was so debilitated. We will have to wait for her body to metabolize the ingredients before we will start to see them return.

She should be good by morning," Margaret estimates.

God dammit.

"Well," the Headmistress stands, "you are free to go back to your room now, but I want Henry to escort you."

"That's fine. Thank you, again, both of you." I swing my legs over the side of the bed and stand up, a little too quicky. Margaret has to catch and steady me.

"Are you sure you don't want to stay a tad longer, dear?" Margaret asks, concerned.

"I just stood up too quickly. I'll be okay." I know Nora and Henry have been listening the whole time, so I speak up a little louder. "I'm sure Henry and Nora will be able to help me."

They immediately come back into the room. "I've got her, Margaret," Henry says gently.

"Oh, such a sweet boy," she gushes over him.

Henry blushes and fidgets awkwardly.

I wrap Henry's jacket tighter around myself, as the hospital gown is paper thin, and I don't want to be any more exposed than I already am. Margaret has bagged what was left of my ripped clothing and is disposing of it as we leave.

"Wait, can I have that?"

Margaret looks at me like I'm mad for wanting the clothes.

"If you want, sure." She hands me the bag and I clutch it close. I have my own plans for the clothing.

Henry and Nora match my slow pace as we walk back to our room. They both keep their eyes glued to me, worried that I may need their assistance at any moment. Part of me wants to be thankful for having people who care, but it is hard right now, in this moment. I hate myself.

Fortunately, everyone is asleep in their rooms, and we do not run into anyone else. We finally make it back to the room in unbearable silence.

"Thank you, Henry, for walking me back. Nora, you can go inside, I'll be in there in just a second." Nora nods and proceeds into our room without a fuss, but makes sure to leave the door open a crack.

I go to take off his jacket, but he stops me. "Please, keep it for now."

I nod. He hands me my book bag and I ease it onto my shoulder.

"If you don't mind," he looks nervous as he speaks, "I'd really like to stay with you tonight, just in case you need me."

I am a little caught off guard by him offering. "Oh, um, it's fine, really. I'll be okay. Nora's here."

"I can sleep on the floor, I just…" he struggles to find the right words, "I just, I want to make sure nothing ever hurts you again. I really care about you, Cassie."

My heart skips a beat.

Nora comes back to the door. "Henry, I mean this in the nicest possible way, but piss off. You will never know what it's like to go through this experience as a woman. I'll look after her."

"Yeah," he clears his throat and looks sad, "okay, sorry. I'll see you tomorrow." I feel bad for Nora's bluntness, but I'm also thankful. I want Henry to stay, but at the same time, I know I need to process this on my own.

"Yeah, sounds good." I try to offer a reassuring smile, but I'm sure it's easy to see through it.

I watch him walk slowly back down the hall before I enter my room and close the door behind me.

"I'm here if you want to talk, Cassie, but I understand if not. I swear, if I had been there... Not to mention the arsehole spiking your drink. I mean, what sort of low life does that?" Nora gets heated again.

"Nora," I say softly. I don't want to talk about it anymore. I want to shower and sleep."

"Sorry, I'm not helping at all." She hangs her head.

"No, you're fine. I think I'm just going to get cleaned up and then go to bed, though. I'm exhausted."

"Of course. I'm going to lie down too, so I may fall asleep, but wake me if you need anything."

"Of course."

I shut myself into our small bathroom and look around. I welcome how small the room feels in this moment—small enough to know nothing is hiding here.

The shower handle *squeaks* as I turn it to hot. The water shoots out of the showerhead with more force than I am expecting, causing me to jump a little.

Get it together. You're fine.

But he still touched you. Attacked you. Took advantage of you. You were weak.

But he had spiked my water.

Doesn't matter. You're disgusting. It was your fault.

"Argh!" My internal monologue is arguing with itself. I slam my fist down on the sink and look at my reflection. My hair is untamed and matted with blood. My cheek is swollen and I see the bruises are starting to form as I peel off the gauze. I slip Henry's jacket off and hang it gently on the doorknob. The hospital gown slides off with the undoing of two strings. I wad it into a ball and stuff it into the wastebasket next to the sink.

My body looks like how I remember my body looking. I know this is my body, but it isn't at the same time. My collarbone and ribs hurt from being slammed up against the wall. I have a few scratches on the side of my thigh where he shredded my tights. The hot water from the shower steams up the confined space.

I sigh and know I should probably get in soon if I want warm water for the length of my shower. I open the glass door, and a cloud of steam ambushes my senses. I blindly step in and pull it closed behind me. It takes a minute for my eyes to adjust to all the steam. The water that trickles down my body carries hints of blood and dirt. Margaret hadn't been able to get all of the blood off—mine or Nick's.

My body feels foreign as my hands gently lather soap onto every inch of my skin. The memory plays over and over in my head. I can't tell if I am crying, or if it is just water from the shower running down my face. It feels like tears, though. I start to hyperventilate. It does not help that all the steam has made the air so thin. Darkness slowly creeps into the corners of my vision. I reach out to find the wall and slowly slide down, in case I pass out.

Worthless. Disgusting!

But it wasn't my fault. I can do this. I am okay.

You won't ever be okay again.

"Shut up, shut up, shut up, shut up!" I bang my hands against my head.

"Cassie, are you okay?" Nora's muffled voice sounds like she's right up against the door.

Get it together.

"Yea-h," my voice cracks, "I'll be out soon."

"Okay, I'm here if you need me."

I steady my breathing. The water starts to run cooler, and I know I only have a few precious moments before it turns ice cold.

A man and his actions do not define me. I am strong.

I repeat that a few times to myself, and it helps enough to stand back up. I am not okay, but I will be with time. I've made it through this once, I can do it again.

During one of my low points in high school, and in a bid to make friends, I showed up at a popular girl's party. I hadn't realized how many drinks I had, and a senior boy took advantage of me. I thought he was truly interested in the things I was saying, but he was only interested in getting into my pants—by any means necessary. The whole school found out about it and called me all sorts of names. I had been the bad person in that situation, not him. I couldn't control my magic, so I broke his jaw and almost killed him. I wonder if Cillian knows that backstory from my file. My grandmother had tried to help me press charges, but the boy was the police chief's son, so things didn't go far. It was interesting when the boy disappeared one day, and suspicion was cast onto me, but I truly have no idea what happened to him. I learned to cope by closing myself off from everything.

I dry off and dress in some comfy sweats and an oversized sweatshirt. Nora is already half asleep in her bed, and it is obvious she's only staying up for me. I grab Henry's jacket from the bathroom doorknob and crawl into bed. I snuggle up to it, inhaling the delicious cinnamon smell, still so aromatic.

"I love you, Cassie. I truly do. You're my best mate. I am so sorry if I fall asleep." Nora yawns and keeps nodding off.

"You're fine, Nora. Get some rest. I'll be okay," I say softly. "I love you, too."

She's already snoring quietly, and I smile to myself.

You're my best mate, too, Nora.

CHAPTER SEVEN

For the next couple of hours, I plead for sleep to come, but to no avail. My body is exhausted, but my mind is wired. Everything that has happened floods my thoughts—Cillian, Henry, Nick, Nora, life in general. I finally decide I need to get outside and go for a walk. Maybe some exercise and fresh air will help. It always did for me back home. Plus, I want to take the clothes and find somewhere discrete to burn them.

I quietly slip on some athletic shoes and slowly open our door. I hear Nora turn slightly in her sleep, but keeps snoring. I am still sore, but my physical strength is returning. I can sense my magic again, but it is faint. I do not want to push things right now.

I almost trip on Henry, who has apparently decided to sleep outside of my room tonight. He looks so uncomfortable, with a tiny pillow and thin blanket. It is quite drafty in the old hallway, so I sneak back into the room and pull a thicker blanket off my bed for him. Thankfully, he seems like a heavy sleeper, and doesn't even move when I drape the blanket over him.

Does everyone in this country sleep hard? Lucky bastards. I can't believe he is actually sleeping out here.

The hallways stay dimly lit during the night, otherwise I'd be walking around blind. I make my way outside and across the grounds to an area with walking paths. One looks to lead just around to the front of the grounds, the other looks like it travels deeper behind the school, into a small, wooded area. I do not know where it goes, but all paths lead somewhere, I tell myself. I am drawn to the more scenic path and continue to it. It will offer me more seclusion to burn my clothes.

The moon is bright, and stars litter the sky. I hear my shoes crunch against the gravel and fallen leaves as I walk. Leaves have started to turn beautiful shades of red and orange, as the days grow shorter. The plastic bag containing my clothes keeps *swishing* and bumping into my leg.

Not too terribly far ahead, the path circles by a small pond. The water is so still, it reflects a clear image of the sky above. There is a small birch tree sitting near the water's edge on top of a small hill.

Perfect.

I make my way underneath the tree and set the bag of clothes down.

Crap, kind of need a lighter if I want to burn it. I suppose I can try to see if my magic is back enough? I've never used magic to burn something before. Hmm…

I feel my magic intensify as the minutes pass, but it can't be even close to usable.

I have to try. I need to try.

I take a few steps and raise my hand toward the bag.

Please work, fire. Light this bag and consume it.

Nothing.

I concentrate harder and imagine the bag bursting into flames.

Nothing.

I squeeze my eyes shut and focus all my energy on the bag. My arm starts to shake.

"Come on!" I scream through gritted teeth.

I drop to my knees, my body weak again.

"Please, please, just work," I beg my magic.

"Try again," Cillian's soft voice whispers into my ear. I feel his warm breath on my sore cheek.

My head snaps up to see him kneeling beside me.

"I can't do it," I say, defeated.

His eyes are set, but they are soft.

"Try again," he repeats softly.

I reluctantly stand and hold my arm out once more. It's useless. I know it isn't going to work. I know my magic isn't strong enough yet.

A few seconds pass and still nothing happens. I groan in frustration. I want to go over to the bag and just fling it into the pond. I want to cry and scream into the night sky.

Just then, I feel Cillian gently place his hand on my shoulder. Even through my clothing, I feel Cillian's warmth. My magic spikes ever so slightly when he touches me.

"Again," Cillian encourages.

I am almost too distracted by the unusual warmth from his hand to notice that the bag of clothes has burst into flames. I jump up and down in my momentary happiness.

Fuck you, Nick!

But as I break Cillian's connection with my shoulder, I feel my magic decrease again slightly. I feel the need to twirl around, so I do. It is such a release to burn those clothes. I stop and look at Cillian, now standing there with his hands in his pockets, watching me with a slight smile on his face.

"Thank you, Cillian."

He tilts his head forward slightly. "No need to thank me."

"How did you know I was out here?" I ask.

"I couldn't sleep," he says simply. "I usually come out here for a run when I can't sleep. It allows my brain to process through things, and I have a lot to process right now."

I notice now that he's wearing athletic clothes.

"I never want to feel this weak again, Cillian. I feel so helpless," I confide in him.

"That's one of the reasons why I stress the importance of hand-to-hand combat. There are many ways a witch can be rendered powerless. We cannot always rely on our magic."

An idea pops into my head.

"Fight me. Right now," I blurt out.

Cillian looks confused. "You are not in the right mindset

right now."

"No, Cillian, I am in the perfect mindset right now. I literally cannot rely on my powers, even if I wanted to. Please...I need this right now. I need to not feel so weak," I beg him.

He looks at me, debating what he should do.

"Well, I guess if you won't do it by choice," I say, inching closer to him, "I will just have to give you a reason."

I throw a punch at him, but he quickly dodges it. He gives me a look that says, "Are you really going to do this?"

We circle around each other. both of us trying to predicate what is coming next.

"I won't hold back if we do this," Cillian warns.

"Good. I don't want you to."

I lunge at him with a combination of jabs, each one he is able to deflect. I'm not fighting Cillian to win; I am fighting him to learn. Cillian is amazing at hand-to-hand combat. His body moves effortlessly, avoiding my advances. I feel the electricity between us heighten every time we get close. This electricity makes me feel more alive, and my powers are feeding off it—growing stronger the longer we continue.

I see a blind spot open for Cillian as he anticipates me throwing another jab, but instead I drop to the ground and sweep his legs out from under him. I waste no time climbing on top of him to pin him down.

I am out of breath as I hold his shoulders down and look at him. He stares back into my eyes and doesn't struggle against me.

The moonlight bounces off his beautiful blue eyes and makes them glow.

"Very well done," he says.

I am giddy inside, and I smile at him.

"But you did one thing wrong," his voice grows quieter.

I look at him, perplexed. I lean forward toward him, alleviating some of my weight off his chest. I wait for him to tell me what I had done wrong. Cillian uses this to his advantage and is able to easily shift my weight off him. He holds onto me as we switch positions, and he pins me down.

Dammit.

Cillian smirks and lets out a small laugh.

"Oh, Cillian, my, was that a laugh I heard from you?" I tease.

"I do indeed laugh sometimes, I will have you know."

"Well, it looks to me as if you've done something wrong as well."

He doesn't have time to react before my magic *whooshes* him off me. Instead of hearing a thud, I hear a splash. I scramble quickly to my feet and see that Cillian has landed a few feet into the pond.

Laughter erupts from my lungs as Cillian bursts through the surface of the water. The pond is deeper than I had originally guessed, and Cillian has to tread water to stay afloat.

"I-I am soooo sorry." I can barely get the words out as the laughter takes over.

"Well, don't just stand there. How about giving me a hand up?" He is smiling and I feel my face going red from laughter.

I make my way carefully to the edge of the water. There is a steep slope you can't see from the top of the hill, up by the tree. Mud and pond water seep into my athletic shoes, causing my socks to go squishy. I ease my way carefully down the slope so I don't fall. I lean down and reach out to Cillian, who has made it over to the edge.

His smile turns from innocent to devious as soon as we lock hands.

I pause, and my tone turns serious, "Don't you dare."

He wouldn't.

"Oh, but I would," he says as he tugs just hard enough for me to fall into the water. I don't even have time to question how he heard my thoughts as the cold water shocks my senses. But I welcome it. It's refreshing. I feel weightless as I float just below the surface, not wanting to depart the water just yet. I look up to see the moon's light penetrating the top layers of darkness. Ripples from my impact still expand out, becoming bigger and further apart. I feel at peace in the water until my lungs beg me for air, so I reach toward the bright moon to guide myself back to the surface.

Cillian is laughing as I emerge, clearly amused with himself. I swim over to him and we tread water together. His drenched hair hangs in a small curl, resting between his eyes.

"I see your powers are coming back."

I tread closer.

"I guess they are." I smile coyly.

"I would've had you, if you hadn't have cheated." Cillian's laughter softens until he is just smiling at me. His smile is invigorating.

It feels like the moon is putting me into a trance, and I'm losing my self-control. The outside world does not matter in this moment. Everything fades away except him and me. Right here. Right now. The moonlight shines brighter, as if a spotlight has been placed on us.

"Maybe you still can," my face only inches away from his.

His smile disappears and his expression goes still once more. But I see something new in his eyes—almost as if the moon is helping me see deeper into them, the rigid curtains parting slightly.

"Cassandra…" his voice sounds soft and almost strained.

I get closer.

I feel his warm breath on my cheeks as it skims over the top of the water. I stop treading and just float. The electricity between us is intoxicating as our magic swirls together between us. I have never felt so alive in my life. My body aches to feel his lips against mine. We are the moon's puppets now; my lips part slightly. He grabs my waist with one arm and treads with the other.

I close my eyes as our lips are about to touch. I feel his upper lip barely brush mine.

"Arh-wooo!" A wolf's howl in the distance breaks the spell, and the veil is lifted.

My eyes flutter open to see Cillian a few feet away already. I start treading again to stay afloat without his support.

Oh no. What did I just almost do? Why did I do that?

"It's getting late. We should head back," he says, his eyes

avoiding mine.

I nod and stay silent.

"But first, since your magic is back, a training exercise."

Cillian closes his eyes and vanishes. I look around the empty water frantically.

"Cillian!" I scream. I swim around in a quick circle, trying to see where he had gone.

"Up here," his voice calls from the top of the hill, water dripping from his clothes.

"That is called shifting. You did it once earlier, with Lauren, remember? Only advanced witches can access this portion of their magic, and even then, some never achieve the skill. Now, you do it."

My arms are tired from the constant treading, and it becomes harder to keep the pond water out of my mouth.

"Cillian, I don't think I can do this. I don't even know how. When I did it the other day, I wasn't aware of what my powers were doing. It just happened."

"You could find yourself in a situation where you have to shift quickly or die. You will not always have a classroom setting where that is the only thing you must concentrate on. Cassandra, I must know if you are serious about going down this path. You said you never wanted to feel weak again. I believe that you hold power inside of you that could rival some of the best witches out there. We just have to push and train you and your magic."

Pond water rushes into my mouth as I struggle to keep my head above the surface. I gag from the bitter, fishy taste.

I will not be weak.

"Close your eyes and focus on where you want to go. Picture yourself in that setting."

I close my eyes as he directs, and I picture the spot next to him on the hill.

"Feel your magic guiding you where you want to go. Will yourself to where you want to be. Feel your body begin to pull." Cillian's voice is distant as I let my head slip under the water.

Cillian. I want to be where he is.

I picture his face, his eyes. My fingertips begin to tingle. The sensation slowly travels throughout my body. I feel myself being pulled through the water abruptly, and I land hard on my hands and knees. Water goes up my nose, causing me to have a coughing fit. I open my eyes to see muddy grass below.

"I did it!" Joy revels through me. "I did it!"

Coughing turns to laughter as I sit back onto my heels.

"Very good," Cillian nods his head in satisfaction.

I stand up and run my hand through my wet hair, wringing it out. My clothes are saturated with pond water.

"I am very serious about this, Cillian. You make me feel like I could literally conquer the world. I want you to teach me everything." Confidence exudes from my pores.

"Very well, then. We will meet here every night for training at midnight. Do not let anyone else know about this. I will show you things I have not taught in class yet."

"You got it, professor. Deal?" I outstretch my hand to seal

the deal.

He looks at my hand skeptically and smirks.

"Deal."

As we shake hands, his feels so comfortable in mine. I turn away when I feel my cheeks go warm. Even in the moonlight, I'm sure he can see my color change.

"Shall we try shifting inside?" I ask, eager for more.

Cillian chuckles. "No, that will be all for tonight. Shifting can be dangerous, especially if your magic is low. Never try and shift to a place you have never been either, or can't see. Too many things could go wrong," he warns.

I think briefly about pushing him to try again, but I know he is right. Even just that little amount wiped out the magic I had restored. We finish ringing out our clothes before head up the path back to the school. Neither of us talk about what did or did not happen in the pond. Part of this night seems like a dream.

Cillian and I go our separate ways once we enter the building. Henry is still snuggled up against my door. I feel a twinge of guilt as I listen to him snore softly. I tiptoe around him as quietly as I can, but my shoes are still squishy and filled with water.

Definitely need to shower again.

I smell of a disgusting mix of stale pond water and dirt. A quick shower fixes that, and as I lay in my bed, I feel anxious and excited for tomorrow. There will be questions about Nick and what happened, but I am no longer scared. I am determined. I feel like I have the power to never let someone hurt me like that again.

CHAPTER EIGHT

The attack happened on Monday. Headmistress Ansley told me I could take a day or two off if I needed to, but when I wake up on Tuesday, I don't feel weighed down by the attack. My scratches and bruises are almost completely gone, and I want to carry on. If I miss classes again, more speculation will ensue. Whispers carry on throughout the next couple of days, but surprisingly, people do not miss Nick. Gossip doesn't carry here like it does other places. Maybe it's because most of the Level 6s are in their early twenties, but there are heavier things that weigh down on others. There is an Anarchy attack back in the States that overshadows Nick's absence—the explosion at a major natural gas plant was on every news channel. Authorities say it was due to faulty equipment, which could totally have been the case, but that is exactly what the Protectors want the world to think. Try telling a bunch of humans there are witches out there trying to destroy them and their lives, and just watch the panic that follows. But between the explosion, and the fact that the All Hallows Dance is this coming Saturday, I am able to pretend like nothing happened, and that is exactly what I do.

Henry and Nora seem very suspicious of how well I am handling things, but I can't explain it. It is like I am looking at the world through a different pair of glasses. I welcome my emotions and try to open myself up instead of shutting myself down and closing everyone else out. I am hungry for more knowledge and more training. Being around Henry and Cillian makes me feel better, and the more I am with them in class, the more confident I become. It is a sort of high for me.

Cillian and I meet every night at midnight to train. I find myself being able to operate with less sleep and I feel stronger every day. Cillian had commented on my scratches and bruises being almost completely healed.

Cillian teaches me about all different kinds of magic and combat training during our time together. He pushes me to be better, and I like that. He makes me challenge myself and believes in me and my magic. I am learning to do things I never even thought were possible. The more time we spend together, the more I find myself falling for him. I think about him when I close my eyes to go to sleep, and I am excited to see him in class when I wake up. I can't explain it. The way we train together, the magic I feel between us, it is undeniable. But Cillian always seems to keep me at arm's length—never getting too close. He does such a good job keeping his thoughts and emotions hidden away behind those icy blue eyes.

It has just barely turned Friday morning as Cillian and I stop our training for a water break. We had been trying to strengthen my self-healing powers by purposely cutting my hand to see how quickly it would heal. It is painful and makes me nauseated, but my magic is getting better at it. Cillian says that there are two types of healing magic—the ability to heal yourself and the ability to heal others. Both are very uncommon nowadays. Healers are hunted and held captive by the Anarchy to abuse.

"How's the hand?" Cillian asks as he takes a seat beside me on the hill. I have a cloth pressed to it so blood doesn't get everywhere.

I remove the cloth to show him the cut. The skin is visibly injured, but slowly coming together to seal the wound.

"Very good," he says, taking a sip of water.

"Doesn't hurt any less each time, though," I say, examining the wound healing. I feel the hairs on my arms stand up through my jacket with how close Cillian is to me.

"Hmm…well, I suppose it doesn't."

Silence falls between us and I decide to break it.

"How come we never talk about you?" I ask, curious of him and his life.

"Not much to talk about," he says, his eyes straight forward to the pond.

"Well, I'd like to know more about you." My stomach is jam-packed with butterflies.

Cillian sighs. "Come on, let's get back to work."

I groan, knowing our conversation has ended. Cillian gets to his feet and walks over to his equipment bag. He pulls out two fighting sticks and tosses one toward me. I catch it as I stand. The wound on my hand is completely closed now, leaving behind a small pink line.

"It's not fair. You know so much about me and I know next to nothing about you," I continue, twirling the stick in my hands.

"Do you know everything about any of your other professors?" I see him smirk slightly through the dark.

Okay, smart ass.

"I don't want to know about them. I want to know about you. Plus, are you out late at night with your other students training them?"

Cillian chuckles as we circle up, each twirling our fighting sticks.

"Fine. Win this match and you can ask me three questions of your choosing, and I will answer them to the best of my ability."

This causes my heart to skip and I try to contain my smile. I am determined now.

"Let's get going, then," I say as I swipe the stick at him.

The fighting stick is new to me, so it takes some time to get used to it. Cillian takes great pleasure in whacking me with his during this adjustment period. It doesn't take him long to sweep out my legs and I land hard on my tailbone.

I groan in frustration.

"You know, it's not really fair, since I don't know how to use this really," I say getting back on my feet.

"Okay then, let's add some magic." Cillian shifts out of view.

"Still not fair!" I shout into the darkness. "You know more magic than I do!" I stand still and listen for him.

"You may always be at a disadvantage, Cassandra," his silky voice tickles in my ear. It sends a shiver up and down my spine. He touches my shoulder with his hand, which makes me weak in the knees. "Anticipate and execute. You let your emotions cloud you, sometimes leaving you open to blind spots."

He's doing this on purpose. Two can play at this game.

I spin around with my stick outstretched, but Cillian shifts away.

"On the contrary, Cillian, I believe fighting with emotion makes you more powerful. I've come to find out recently that emotions can make you determined."

I hear his stick swinging through the air and turn around to block it just as he is about to whack my arm. We continue our little game of shift-and-go-seek as the night moves on around us. I can tell he is determined not to answer any questions, which only makes me want to know more. I shift away to just inside of the edge of the tree line across from the pond. Cillian scans the surroundings, listening for me.

I wonder what's hiding behind those eyes.

"Your magic is learning quickly," he says. "I have to say, I am very impressed."

I shift to right behind him. I stand on my tiptoes to get closer to his ear.

"Careful, Cillian," I whisper into his ear, "your emotions are showing."

He doesn't turn around. "We should call it here soon. We've been at this for a while."

The clouds part around the moon and its light glows down onto us. We are both breathing heavily as I lower myself from my tiptoes, but I stay close to him.

"Scared you're going to lose?" I tease. I feel a pull toward him, even though I am already close to him.

He turns around slowly to face me. I look up into his eyes and grip onto my stick tighter. My breath catches in my throat. My body tingles as my magic courses through me.

"Not at all, but we should both get some sleep," he says simply.

I raise one of my hands to Cillian face, lowering my fighting stick in the other, and gently lay it on his cheek. I feel him tremble slightly under my hand. His jaw clenches, but he doesn't move away.

All the fallen leaves on the ground lift and swirl around us. I know our magic is causing this to happen.

"Cassandra…" Cillian whispers, looking around at all the leaves.

"I have never felt more powerful than I do with you. This past week, training with you, you can't tell me you don't feel something as well."

He closes his eyes and uses his stick to move my hand away from his face. All the leaves around us fall back to the ground. My heart sinks with the leaves as Cillian begins to walk away from me. The clouds rush to cover up the moonlight.

"I am sorry if I gave you any mixed signals. I know that sometimes tragic events can bring two people together, but you are my student, and I am your professor. Training is over for the night. I'll see you back in class."

I feel foolish and exposed. My eyes sting with tears.

"Yes, but, Cillian, I am not some young naïve schoolgirl. You and I are both adults. Our magic speaks for itself," I try to explain where I'm coming from.

Cillian uses his magic to pull my fighting stick from my hand. He catches it as it flies to him and he puts it in his equipment bag. He keeps his eyes away from me, which only makes me feel worse.

Thunder forms in the distance. Cillian looks to the sky as he heaves the bag onto his shoulder.

"So, you just aren't even going to talk to me now?"

He looks at me, "Cassa—I mean Miss Rodden, again, I apologize if I gave you any indication—"

Of course, he doesn't like me. I begged him to help me and he's just being nice. Oh my god, how could I be so stupid?

"Nope, you know what, my bad. My fault. I am sorry. See you in class," I say, begging my tears to hold off for just a moment more.

The storm rolls in quickly and the wind picks up. Small droplets of cold rain begin to fall. Cillian looks to the sky again and back to me. He takes a step toward me, but I take a step back. He looks like he is about to say something, but I shift away, back into my room. I have embarrassed myself enough already. No reason to stick around and endure more.

Nora is snoring away as the storm rolls over the school. I slide into bed and listen to the thunder and rain as my heart breaks. Sleep eventually finds its way to me, but it is certainly not restful sleep. I toss and turn until my alarm sounds to get up for the day.

I roll over and click it off with a groan.

God dammit.

CHAPTER NINE

Nora notices I am quieter today as we dress for class.

"Are you excited for the dance tomorrow? Did the dress you ordered come in?" I know she is probing. While Nora has slept through all of my nightly endeavors, I know she's suspicious.

"Mhmm."

I throw on a ratty old crew neck over my sports bra and lean on the bathroom door, waiting for Nora to finish.

"Did you not sleep well? What's going on, Cassie?" Nora is worried. Maybe she thinks I'm finally breaking down about the attack.

"It's nothing. Just drop it," I say, a little too harshly.

"Woah, okay, babe, maybe you need to check yourself. I am not the enemy here," she says, raising her hands in defense.

I feel bad for snapping at her.

"I'm sorry, Nora. I've got a lot on my mind, is all."

"Well, what's going on? Maybe I can help?" she offers.

Friends share their struggles.

I word vomit everything about Cillian and our overnight trainings. I tell her everything I'm feeling and how he had rejected me. She listens to every word and doesn't interrupt once, but I can tell she is upset.

"So that's why you've been kicking my arse in Tactical recently! I knew you had been training more."

I give her a look that screams, "Not the point."

"Men, I tell you. I've seen the way he looks at you, Cassie. You weren't wrong to think there was something. He and Henry constantly have their eyes on you."

I groan.

Ugh, Henry.

"And that's another thing…Part of me likes Henry as well. He's handsome and funny, plus I know he likes me. Things with Henry are easy but…" I trail off, not really having a good excuse.

Nora smiles and chuckles at my dilemma.

"Well, my dear, best advice I can give you is fuck 'em. You are one badass witch, plus you are hot. Let's just get through classes today and then enjoy our weekend. The dance is going to be so awesome. We'll clean you up nice so every guy there will trip over each other to get to you, okay?"

"You are something," I say to Nora as I roll my eyes and laugh.

"I know." She gestures dramatically. "It's hard being this amazing. Amazing friend, amazing witch, amazing girlfriend, amazing roommate. You'd be lost without me! I mean, who else would be this helpful for a friend who has two insanely gorgeous men staring at her constantly?"

We chuckle as Nora slips on her shoes.

"Welp, let's go, I guess," I say reluctantly and open the door.

We make our way slowly to Tactical. Henry and Yash's faces light up when they see us walk in.

"See? Look, utterly smitten. What fools," Nora whispers to me. We giggle as we approach them.

Once we reach them, we all stand around and wait for Cillian to begin class. I look around the room and don't see him. Henry brings up the dance and that there will be a pre-party celebration in his and Yash's room. Nora squeals with excitement.

Why isn't Cillian here yet?

I check the clock in the room, and it shows that he is five minutes late.

Oh god, is he that mortified of me, he's late to class?

I want to shrink away just as I hear the door open and see him walk in.

Okay, good. He is here.

He walks over to where we are gathered, and I notice Nora giving him a death glare. I nudge her softly as the class forms a half circle around Cillian.

"Okay, class, today is going to be a little different. I want to begin with talking about the Joining Ceremony that will take place later this year, before graduation. Most of you are aware of what it entails, but I want to go over it all with you, since some of our training will start to relate to it. Now, the Joining Ceremony is where you will be joined with your magical pair. Each witch has one other person out in the world that their magic can join with—one person whose magic complements theirs completely. Typically, the witch you are destined to join with is around your own age, which is why we hold the ceremony for the graduating class."

"But that's not always the case, right, Professor?" Nora speaks up. I side-eye her as I become uncomfortable.

"Correct. We will not know who you are meant to paired with until the ceremony, and even then, we might not know. We will run tests throughout the rest of the year for you to gain a better idea. You will be able to feel your magic reaching out to this person. You will join hands and present yourself in front of the Serpent, who will mark you, if you have found your match."

A serpent? What does a serpent have to do with all of this?

I am uncomfortably aware of my magic reaching out toward both Cillian and Henry. I think back to Cillian's arms last night, when he rolled up his sleeves. He doesn't have any markings from what I remember.

"Can you choose who you are joined with?" a voice asks from the back.

"No, you cannot," Cillian replies.

"So, technically, that means a student could join with a professor? If that is what is destined?" Nora asks.

My palms perspire with anxiety.

Oh my god, Nora, why did I tell you everything? Please just let it go.

Cillian stares at Nora for a moment and then answers, "Yes, technically, that could happen, but I have not seen it in my time here. Joining also does not mean that you will be linked emotionally or romantically. I have seen best friends joined, siblings—people who have never met before, and they come across each other one day and it happens."

"So that means you can be joined with someone outside of the ceremony?" Lauren asks.

"Yes, there are times where outside of the ceremony two can be joined. Our magic has a mind of its own, and sometimes you may have the person you are meant to be joined with, but at that particular point in time, you—and your magic—may not be ready to be joined. When diving into it all, it can become complex. Even still, after thousands of years, witches are trying to figure things out."

"Can a joined pair ever be broken?" Yash asks.

"No, it cannot. Once you have joined with a person, you cannot join with another, or break your current bond. Even if the other person passes, you will never be able to join with another. Once joined, your magic will become stronger. You may even find that as a pair, you can do magic you cannot do separately."

"Are you joined, Professor?" Nora asks. This time I jab her ribs harder. She winces and glares at me.

Cillian looks uncomfortable. "No, I have not. I do not bare the markings, and have yet to come across my magical pair."

My stomach turns inside with his words.

"My mum has the markings," Henry speaks up. "She and my

dad were joined. The markings are beautiful."

I search my memory to see if I can recall an example of the markings they're talking about, but most people here wear long sleeves due to the cold weather. I distantly remember gold vines that wrapped around my mother's and father's arms, but never questioned them until now. My mother had told me they were matching tattoos, the one time I asked.

"Anyway, enough of this for now. You will learn more soon."

I am thankful for the change in topic. I don't want to think about joining with someone right now, when my heart aches, and everything is so confusing. I shift my weight uncomfortably.

"Today, we will be strengthening our minds. There are many ways an enemy can come at you. You may be physically strong, but if you are not mentally prepared as well, the enemy could find a way in. There are certain spells that allow one to be taken over and controlled without realizing it. So, one thing we can do to build our mental strength is an exercise called Resolve. What will happen is everyone will take turns lying down as the rest of the class forms a circle around them. The person lying in the middle will be put into a sort of trance. There are a lot of things that we hold onto mentally, whether it be fear, anxiety, an unresolved issue in your past. Your goal during this exercise is to resolve it—to work through it. Whatever makes you the most mentally weak and vulnerable will be projected above you."

Are you serious?

"So that means everyone will see it?" Lauren askes nervously.

I have never seen her nervous before. She catches me glancing at her and her face turns mean again, her brow furrowing with a scowl.

I roll my eyes.

"Yes, everyone will see. Exposing ourselves in front of the group will bring everyone closer as a team. Look at your classmates around you. One day, you may have to give your life to save them, or vice versa. Everyone in this room right now has secrets, things they do not want others to know—for fear of judgment—but the people next to you right now are your family."

I feel everyone's energies become anxious and uncomfortable. There is a lot I hold inside, and the last thing I want is to have it displayed for everyone to see.

"How do we resolve it though?" Damon asks. Damon is quiet for the most part. I've seen him hanging out with Henry every now and then. Damon is on the shorter side, but he made up for it with speed. His long dark curls fall to his shoulders and beard. When he speaks, hints of an Italian accent shine through.

"That is something only you will be able to answer. Maybe it will be admitting something that is weighing heavily, overcoming a fear by facing that fear," Cillian says ominously.

"Cill—I mean, Professor, can you go first to show us what to expect? I think that would make everyone feel more comfortable and willing," I ask.

Cillian doesn't look at me, but I see his jaw tense. A few other students murmur in agreement.

"Sure, I suppose. Miss Malik, I believe you are versed in the usage of sage?"

Nora nods.

"Good, well, everyone, please form a circle. Miss Malik, come here for a moment."

Nora walks over to Cillian and they discuss what she needs to do. Henry, Yash, and I join the circle, each exchanging nervous glances. We all lower ourselves to the floor and sit with our legs underneath us.

"You have to repeat the verse exactly, otherwise it won't work, okay?" Cillian warns Nora. She looks nervous holding the sage smudge stick in her hands.

Cillian lays down on his back, his arms to his sides, palms open to the ceiling.

"You must try and relax yourself. Take in deep breaths. Mister Patel, please light the smudge stick." Yash shrugs, emptyhanded.

Nora sits directly above Cillian's head. She looks around frantically for something to light the smudge stick with.

"I haven't got a light, Professor."

I waive my hand toward Nora without thinking and light the smudge stick for her. She looks at me wide-eyed, just like everyone else in the circle. I shrink into myself a little and drop my eyes, the smudge stick burning.

"Thanks, Cassie," Nora says. I see the corner of Cillian's mouth turn into a smirk, but it disappears quickly.

With his eyes still closed, Cillian directs Nora to begin.

"Non temete l'oscurita—acetate il suo abbraccio. Et lux in tenebris lucet. Fear not the darkness—but welcome its embrace. And light shines in the darkness," Nora chants. It is evident that she is unsure about reciting the phrases, but the longer she chants, the more confident she becomes. The smoke fills our circle, but does not drift outside of it. The smoke burns my nose and makes my eyes water. I suppress the urge to cough.

Cillian's muscles relax as he falls into his trance. An image forms in the smoke above him. It is very distorted and dark, as if we are looking through a frosted windshield on a cold, dark morning.

"No! You must not go back!" Cillian's voice shouts in the distance, coming from the distorted images, instead of Cillian's mouth. "Sophia, please don't!"

Sophia? Who is Sophia?

An image comes into view of a young woman. She is beautiful. Her skin is pale, and she has beautiful auburn hair. Her eyes are wide with fear and determination. She has bruises and scrapes on her face.

"Goodbye, Cillian," she says as she charges toward the men advancing toward them.

The image swirls abruptly to show Cillian limping toward a body on a stone beach, lying lifeless at the edge of the water. He turns the body over to reveal the young woman he called Sophia. Her eyes are open, but their color is faded, turned murky from lack of life. Her lips have turned blue, her body cold and stiff. Cillian collapses and sobs as he holds her body in his arms. His screams echo through the room, sending chills through me. I feel the love that he holds for her, and his pain as it rips through him.

The image fades to darkness. Voices are still audible, but we can no longer tell who they belong to.

"You must protect her. She is important," a woman's voice says.

"Tell me you don't feel something between us?" My own voice surprises me. I look around at the others to see if they could make out who it is, but no one seems to notice.

Why is this bringing up our conversation?

"Enough! Break the spell, Nora," Cillian's voice demands clearly through the smoke.

Nora stops chanting and swirls her arms around to clear the smoke. Everyone lets out a breath, as if we had all been collectively holding it in.

So many questions plague me as Cillian sits up.

"This is just one example of what this exercise could bring up," Cillian says, looking around at us. I look at him with confusion, but his eyes are cold.

"But you didn't resolve anything, did you?" Yash asks.

"And that is what may happen, Mister Patel. This is merely an exercise to try and strengthen you mentally. Even sometimes just highlighting an issue can strengthen you."

What if I am a bad issue to him? Oh great.

"Okay, who is next?"

Everyone shrinks back, not wanting to go first. Cillian calls on Damon and takes the smudge stick from Nora. She crawls toward me and situates herself between Yash and me. She looks at me to gauge my reaction on what had just happened, but I keep myself composed.

Damon's resolve is almost as bad as Cillian's. He is afraid of being buried alive. Images of a confined space are displayed in the smoke. I feel myself suffocating with Damon and the panic rises inside. Damon tries to use his magic to burst through and up to the surface, but his panic causes his magic to be unsteady. He manages to get through the wooden coffin, but the dirt collapses on top of him, filling his lungs and mouth as he tries to scream.

Cillian ends the trance and Damon shoots up. He's sweating profusely and coughing.

"Dealing with ourselves is one of the most challenging things we can do," Cillian reiterates.

Nora is next. Her Resolve displays the one thing Nora dreads most in the world. We see Yash dying in different ways, not much older than he is right now. Each time Nora tries to prevent it and save him. First is sickness—she tries to heal him with her herbs. Next, he trips down the stairs and she tries to catch him. She panics, as her efforts every time are futile. But then something changes. Nora stops panicking and closes her eyes.

"This isn't real," she says. "I can change this."

The image swirls to reveal Nora and Yash together. They are sitting on a porch swing, both very old in age. They are laughing and smiling as the sun sets. Both have gray hair, and their faces are filled with wrinkles.

"Told you you weren't going to be able to get rid of me," Nora says to Yash.

Yash pulls her close and kisses her cheek. "I would never want to, my love."

Cillian disperses the smoke and Nora's Resolve fades. Cillian claps his hands to wake Nora.

"Very well done, Miss Malik."

Nora looks at Yash and smiles. My heart feels so warm for them. I feel Cillian's eyes on me, but I don't look.

"Please take note of what you all just saw Nora do. She was able to change her fear and conquer it. She changed the narrative. All right, up next…Lauren."

This should be interesting.

"I don't want to do this," Lauren says adamantly.

"Too bad, Miss Cole. We must all participate. Get over here."

Lauren pouts, but reluctantly makes her way to the middle. She lays down and the trance begins. I feel the rage oozing from her as images of mirrors and shadows form. They only appear for a brief second, my face taking their place, forming clearly in the smoke.

What the hell?

Lauren's sick laughter echoes throughout the room, coming from her mouth and not the smoke. She moves around on the floor in the middle of the circle.

Cillian puts out the smudge stick and looks at Lauren with annoyance. She sits up and looks at him.

"You need to take this seriously, Miss Cole. Night Watch, tonight."

This turns Lauren's mood sour. "Are you serious?"

"Yes, yes, I am. Keep protesting and I'll give you Watch tomorrow as well."

"But the dance is tomorrow!"

"Exactly. So, I suggest you start taking this seriously. Now, get back into the rim of the circle. Cassandra, you are up next."

Lauren pouts her way back to her spot at the edge of the circle. My throat tightens as I slowly make my way to the middle.

Please, please, please do not show Cillian. Please do not show any of the times I've almost killed someone.

There are so many things I plead my subconsciousness not to show as I lay down and look up at Cillian. My palms shake as I turn them upward.

"You'll be okay. Are you ready?" Cillian asks.

Not in the slightest.

"Yes," I say, my voice shaking slightly.

I close my eyes and anxiously wait for what will come next. I try my best to relax my muscles, but every one feels tense. The smoke infiltrates my nasal passages as Cillian relights the smudge with his magic. It burns and I am uncomfortable, but I try to keep still.

"Non temete l'oscurita—acetate il suo abbraccio. Et lux in tenebris lucet. Fear not the darkness—but welcome its embrace. And light shines in the darkness," Cillian softly chants the phrase over and over until he sounds very far away. It feels like I am falling asleep.

Please not Cillian.

I open my eyes to see that everything is blindingly white and cold. I find myself lying on my back. I shiver in my ratty crewneck and yoga pants as I slowly stand and look around.

What the hell?

I get to my feet and take a few steps forward, the snow crunching and compacting beneath my feet. A warm substance drips from my nose. I reach up and touch it. It is sticky. I pull my hand down to reveal blood coating my fingertips.

My footsteps no longer crunch in snow, there is now hard ground below me, so I stop and look down. I am on a road. I can barely see the black pavement under the slick snow coating it. Lights flash on me as a van comes barreling toward me. I have no time to react. I throw up my hands and try to shift away, but I cannot sense my magic. I close my eyes and brace myself for the impact.

The van whooshes right through me, as if I am only a ghost. I watch the car continue past me and that's when I realize what is happening. I can barely see it through the blinding snow—a weathered bumper sticker that reads, "Hughes Elementary."

I know that van.

My feet run after the car before I have a chance to think about what I'm doing.

"Stop! Stop! There's going to be an accident!" I scream, chasing after the car. My throat strains against my screams. My legs carry me so quickly, it feels like I barely touch the ground.

But it's no use. The car flips up into the air and crashes down hard onto the ground, rolling several times before coming to a stop. My legs slow as I make my way closer to the car.

"Get out of the car! Get out!" I scream as I watch my mother struggle inside the car. I move closer, but something prevents me from interfering. All I can do is stand off to the side and watch.

"Cillian, get me out! I don't want to be here! Please don't make me watch this!"

The sound of tires screeching erupts through the falling snow. I look to my side to see the semi sliding, the driver trying to regain control. I look back to my parent's car—it will only be a matter of seconds now. The van door flings open and I see my younger self being ejected out, just as the semi smashes into the van, causing an eruption of smoke and fire.

I drop to my knees, unable to breathe.

Please get me out of this. This isn't real. This is just a memory. Please get me out.

I see my younger self lying a few feet away in a snowbank. I hear myself sobbing and screaming. It all feels so real. But I see something I don't remember being there before. A dark, ghostly apparition appears next to younger me, laying in the snowbank.

"Hey!" I call after it.

This part didn't happen.

I stand, but still can't move closer.

"Get away from her! Hey!" I try to get its attention.

The black apparition turns to my voice, exposing deep-red glowing eyes. The hairs on the back of my neck raise.

This isn't real. This part didn't happen.

Horns form on the creature as it moves closer to me. I sense the evil seeping out of it and poisoning the surrounding area.

"Cillian, get me out of here!" I scream.

Still nothing.

The apparition is almost to me now. I take a few steps backward and stumble as it leans down toward my face. It smells awful, like rancid garbage. I hear it let lose a deep, sinister growl.

My heart races.

"W-what are you?" my voice shaky from terror.

"I am coming for you, Cassandra." The tone is so low and menacing. It doesn't sound human.

"No, please! Stop!" I scream. I throw up my arm to put something—anything—between the apparition and myself as it reaches out for me.

It grips onto my arm hard and I scream in pain. It feels like it is on fire, and its handprint sears into my skin. I squeeze my eyes shut and thrash around, trying to break its hold on me.

"Let me go! Let me go! Let me go!"

"Cassandra, stop, it's okay. You're back! I've got you!" Cillian voice is frantic. My whole body is freezing, so I don't believe it's really his voice. I still feel the monster's hold on me.

Maybe it is a trick.

I sob. "Please, let me go."

"Open your eyes, Cassandra," Cillian's voice urges.

I'm still shaking, but I open my eyes and see my classmates

staring at me with concern.

"What the hell was that? Why didn't you pull me out?" I sob. Cillian is at a loss for words.

"Her skin is ice cold, it's turning blue. We need to get her warmed up," Henry says, leaning down next to me. He unzips his jacket and drapes it over my arms.

"Class is dismissed. Henry, help me get her to your mum's office. She needs to hear what has happened."

Everyone stands still around me, unmoving. People look scared and have pity written all over their faces. Even Lauren's eyes are wide.

"Class is dismissed, now!" Cillian shouts.

"Professor, her arm…" Henry says.

The crowd disperses as I shiver. I raise my arm to see that I have a perfect handprint seared into the skin. My stomach lurches and I want to vomit. The burn bubbles up with fresh blisters.

"Cillian, why am I not healing? Why am I not healing?"

Henry and Cillian help me to my feet slowly, but frustration builds inside of me. I shake off their helping hands.

"You told us we would be safe. Why didn't you pull me out?!" I scream at Cillian. "The last thing I wanted was to relive my parent's deaths. I begged for you to make it stop! Do I disgust you that much that you would torture me like this?" I'm being a little overdramatic, but I am pissed.

Cillian stands there, jaw clenched, eyes hard as I yell at him.

"We tried to get you out, Cassie," Henry says softly. "We

couldn't though. It was like some other force was keeping you in there. You were convulsing and turning blue. We tried everything. Professor Morris had to—"

"Enough, Henry. She's right. I put her in danger with this exercise. This was not supposed to be able to happen. But right now, we need to get to the Headmistress. The apparition you saw belongs to the Anarchy. If they have found a way into the school, we need to be prepared."

Cillian looks disappointed and angry with himself, which subdues my own anger toward him.

Of course, he tried to get me out.

"Cillian…I'm sorry," I say, but he won't look at me.

"We need to get going. Come on."

The three of us make our way to the Headmistress's office. I'm still shivering from the cold as we enter her office. My magic feels drained and my wound is still not healing.

Headmistress Ansley looks alarmed at my state as we walk in.

"Oh, heavens, what's happened now? Sit down, sit down," she says, coming around her desk.

I sit in the leather chair she has positioned in front of her desk. I try to stop my teeth from chattering, but it only strains my jaw.

"We were doing the Resolve exercise in class today. Something disrupted Miss Rodden's exercise," Cillian explains.

"Disrupted how?" she demands.

"We do not know, but it prevented us from pulling her out.

There was also a dark figure from the Anarchy that made its way into her Resolve. It…it attacked her." I can see it is difficult for Cillian to admit the last part.

The Headmistress notices my arm now and the burn. Bruises are forming around the edges of the handprint, tracing the blisters. She turns bone white.

"Impossible," she says breathlessly.

"I was there, Mum, we could see it projected onto the smoke during the exercise."

"We are going to have to cancel the dance tomorrow. We can't risk anything happening."

"No!" I shout. "Please don't do that. I don't need everyone blaming me. I remember Yash telling me that the school is protected, right?"

They all turn to look at me as if I'm crazy.

"Well, yes, it is, but if they managed to get to you already, then we cannot risk it," the Headmistress says.

"I agree," Cillian offers.

"It would be stupid of them to try and attack again. They must know that we know they were able to do this one thing. So, let's bring in some reinforcements. If they see us cancelling things, they will know we are scared."

She thinks about my words for a moment. My shivering subsides as my body finally starts to warm.

"Cassie does have a point, Mum," Henry speaks up.

Headmistress Ansley sighs.

"Please, I need this dance—as I am sure many other students do. A break from the madness of it all," I plead.

I can see Cillian is growing upset.

"Very well," the Headmistress says, "I will make a few phone calls and bring some reinforcements in. I will also be putting in place a curfew, and restricting students from venturing off too far into the school grounds."

I am relieved.

"Thank you, Headmistress, truly."

"Henry, see to it that Miss Rodden gets back to her room in one piece. Cillian, a word…"

"Actually, may I speak with Professor Morris for a moment, please?"

"Very well. You may speak outside. Henry, there is something I want to discuss with you anyway."

I slip off Henry's jacket and hand it to him before I make my way out of her office. Cillian closes the door behind him, but he won't look at me. His jaw is clenched, and I can see he is upset.

"Cillian, I am sorry for getting so upset with you earlier. I know you tried to bring me out."

"You are my student, and I put you in danger. Of course, I did everything I could to pull you out."

Back to this again, I see.

"That apparition in my memory, it wasn't there when the accident happened. Something felt very off about it all—I just can't put my finger on what else specifically. The apparition, he…he told me that he was coming for me. Do you know what he meant by that? Why would they be coming after me? Why do my powers feel so drained, and why isn't this wound healing?"

Cillian is concerned. "I hadn't heard that part in your Resolve." Cillian lets out a frustrated sigh. "There is a lot you still need to learn, Cassandra. There are theories out there, but you don't need to worry yourself about it."

He is avoiding my questions.

"If it has to do with me—which it clearly does," I hold up my arm, "then I want to know, Cillian." He paces around in a small circle. He runs his hands through his hair with frustration. "Unless you want to tell me about Sophia instead?"

Cillian stops in his tracks and turns to me. I regret bringing her up immediately.

"You will never bring her up again, do you understand me?" He has never taken this tone with me before. Something tragic had happened and I clearly struck the wrong chord.

"I'm sorry." I feel so small.

Cillian sighs. "No, you're fine. I am sorry for my tone. You are curious, which is to be expected—but please, do not bring her up again. Okay?"

I nod. My cheeks warm with regret.

"Do I know why that *thing* said he was coming for you? Yes, yes, I do know something. There is a theory out there that you may be the Chosen One."

I feel the urge to laugh. "From the Prophecy?" I say,

skeptical.

Cillian doesn't respond.

"Wait, are you serious? You actually believe this?"

"Doesn't matter what I believe. What matters is that the Anarchy believes you might be, and that puts you in a very dangerous situation."

"How long has this been the case?" I ask, crossing my arms. I'm frustrated again.

How could I not have been told anything about this?

The door to the Headmistress's office opens and Henry pokes his head out shyly.

"She wants to speak with you, Professor."

Cillian nods at Henry and turns back to me. "I promise we will talk more about this later."

"Yes, we will," I say, and he disappears into the Headmistress's office.

Henry looks at me nervously as we stand outside the office door.

"What were you and Professor Morris talking about?" he asks.

"To be honest, Henry, I have absolutely no idea. Everything is so confusing." My legs are suddenly weak with Cillian's departure.

"Well, let's get you back to your room."

Henry and I make our way back to my room, where Nora and Yash are waiting impatiently. I keep mine and Cillian's conversation to myself. Mostly because I don't believe in prophecies—life never has happy endings like everyone is so indulged into thinking they do—and because the last thing I want is to draw more attention to myself.

Nora is excited the dance is still on, and I am too, honestly. I meant what I said about just wanting to feel normal for a night. Henry examines my arm and I feel it slowly begin to heal, which provides some relief. The blisters heal, but the bruises remain.

The rest of the day carries on as if almost nothing had happened, but I am plagued with questions about the prophecy and the apparition. It ends with me lying awake in bed, listening to Nora snore softly, thinking about tomorrow. I try to ignore all the bad things and focus on the fact that I have never been to a dance before, never had an event I needed to dress up fancy for. I am nervous and excited. A small pit forms in my stomach when I think about tomorrow, but I blame it on Cillian's rejection and everything else. I mean, if you had a menacing monster tell you that they were coming for you, you'd probably have a small pit as well, right? But for one whole day and night, I want to be normal. I close my eyes and prepare myself for tomorrow.

CHAPTER TEN

I look into the mirror and study my dress, running my hands over the soft velvet. The color is one of my favorites—a beautiful, deep and iridescent teal. It has a draped neckline with thin shoulder straps and a slit up the side of my right leg. The hem of the dress plays at my ankles as I shift my weight back and forth. I debate on whether the dress is too much for the occasion, but Nora says that the ladies here love to go all out for any occasion.

My wavy hair is held back on one side by a few bobby pins. I smooth out a wrinkle and adjust my strap. I tried covering the bruise on my arm with some make up, but it still shows through slightly. I'm worried as to why it hasn't healed all the way yet.

I take a deep breath. I am nervous.

"Cassie, you ready yet?" Nora calls from the other side of the door. I hear a slight annoyance in her tone. To be fair, I have been hogging the bathroom for a solid 15 minutes, just staring at myself.

I shake the thoughts away and open the door.

"Ready as I'll ever be." I smile to prove I am not nervous.

Nora's jaw drops. "Oh my god! Babe! You look fabulous!" she squeals.

"Oh, stop it. You look amazing as well."

Nora chose a beautiful olive-green dress. The length, and how it accentuates her features, make her look taller than she normally is. Well, that and the five-inch heels she's wearing, so the dress doesn't drag on the floor.

"Why, thank you. I know I do. Okay, so, we are stopping by Henry and Yash's room first and then the dance, okay?" Nora says, grabbing a small clutch.

"You got it, boss," I say with a giggle.

Nora gives me a look as we head out the room. My palms get sweaty as we near Henry and Yash's room. My skin feels warm and my heart rate increases.

I hope he likes the dress. Do I look stupid? Ugh, is there still time to go and change? Oh crap, my thong feels weird.

Nora knocks softly on the door and I am surprised when Lauren opens it. Lauren's smile quickly turns into a frown.

"Lauren, what the bloody hell are you doing here?" Nora seems just as surprised as I am.

Lauren huffs. Her dress is black and so plunging, I truly do not know how her boobs are staying in it. The color makes her look much more intimidating, but it does suit her. "Damon and I are going to the dance together. He said pregame was here."

Nora and I exchange a brief side-eye conversation. Yash opens the door all the way behind Lauren.

"Nora! Oh, my love, you look amazing!" Yash gushes over Nora in her dress.

She blushes, but gives Yash a look regarding Lauren's presence. Yash quickly picks up on it.

"Eh, Lauren, erm, can you move so they can come in?" he asks.

Lauren rolls her eyes, but reluctantly moves out of the way. We enter and I quickly survey the room to find Henry. I am impressed with the size of the room. It's at least double the size of mine and Nora's, but I guess Yash was correct when he said that rooming with Henry comes with perks.

There are a few other people that I know from classes gathered around one of the beds, drinking from red cups, but no Henry. I sense that he is close by, though, as my magic begins to surge.

"Yash, where's He—"

I can't even finish my statement when a door opens on the side of the room. It looks to be their bathroom, from the small view I have.

Out steps Henry and time slows. I suck in a sharp breath as my eyes slowly travel down Henry's body. He's wearing a slim-fitted charcoal grey suit with a teal tie and white undershirt. The suit is tailored perfectly to his body. The material hugs his muscles just right. His curls appear more defined with some product, but this just adds more perfection to his overall look. Butterflies fill my stomach and I feel tingly down below. I know Henry is very handsome on an average day, but he is drop-dead gorgeous in his suit.

And then his eyes land on me, and a smile spreads across his face.

"Drool much?" Nora whispers as she jabs me in my side.

I close my mouth, which had dropped open, and clear my throat. My cheeks flush with embarrassment.

"Cassie, you're here!" He sounds so happy, and he quickly walks over to me.

"Y-yeah," my voice cracks, and I clear my throat again. Nora snickers and I shoot her a glare. "I wouldn't miss it."

"You look so beautiful. I am speechless, I really am," Henry gushes as he looks me up and down.

Blushing intensifies. "You look gorgeous as well."

I am an idiot. Gorgeous really? You couldn't have said handsome?

Henry chuckles and stuffs his hands into the pockets of his pants. His cheeks blush, which makes me feel better about embarrassing myself.

"Thank you. Well, um, we've got some liquor on the back table if either of you want any." He motions toward where the drinks are, and it makes sense now why people are congregating over there.

"Yash, babe, can you make me something I'll like?" Nora directs toward Yash. "Oh, and make one for Cassie as well?"

Yash nods and follows Nora's orders, but he grabs something she doesn't want. Yash picks up a yellow bottle, which causes Nora to yell at him.

"Not that one, you plonker!"

Nora walks over to Yash, leaving Henry and me standing alone in awkward silence.

"So, um, nice room," I try to make conversation as I walk further into the room. It feels like first time meeting jitters all over again. I catch a brief whiff of someone's perfume that smells sweet and cinnamon-y. It reminds me how the candle aisles smell during Christmas time.

"Uh, yeah." He tousles his curls slightly.

Oh god, he is so hot. Why do I feel so awkward right now? Ugh, hopefully Nora hurries up with those drinks.

I notice Lauren sipping from a cup and glaring at me. I roll my eyes and ignore her. I feel Henry's strong hand at my elbow. He turns me to look at him.

"Cassie, you have no idea how lucky I feel right now to be here with you. You make me realize just how much I was missing in my life," he says sweetly.

My heart skips in my chest and I bite my lip.

He brushes a stray strand of hair behind my ear. His fingertips send ripples of electricity across my cheek as they lightly touch my skin.

"Drink time, bitches!" Nora yells with drinks in both hands.

God, the timing in this place.

Only Henry does not back away. He stays close, with his fingertips on my cheek, his eyes locked onto mine.

"Break it up, you two. You guys can have your movie moment some other time." Nora's tone is drenched with annoyance.

She pouts like a three-year-old.

"Until later then?" Henry whispers.

Is it hot in here, or is it just me?

I nod and he steps away. Nora shoves a drink into my hand and Yash hands Henry one as well. I investigate the concoction and gave it a sniff.

It smells sickly sweet and the dark purple liquid has a slight shimmer to it. It looks tantalizing.

"What is it?" I question.

Nora acts offended by my inquiry. "That, my dear, is what I like to call A Witch's Bleeding Heart."

Hmm, how fitting.

"Ahh, I see," I say, swirling the pretty mixture around.

"It's a mix of vodka, grenadine, apple syrup, and some of my witchy herb collection to add the shimmer and color." Nora beams at her creation.

I take a sip and find it is actually pretty good. I take a more fulfilled drink. I also want to tame my nerves.

We all hang out for the next half hour. A few more people trickle in, once they hear Yash and Henry have liquor. I sit by Henry on his bed and it is nice to see peoples' nerves and awkwardness slip away as the liquor is consumed. Soon everyone is laughing and having a good time. I even see Lauren smile, sitting on Damon's lap.

"Okay, my darlings, how about we take this up a notch?" Nora looks devious, holding up a small baggie of capsules.

Where has she been keeping those?

"Oh, babe, you know how I was last time." Yash seems to be transported back into an unpleasant memory as he looks at the bag.

"What is it?" Lauren asks.

"So, it's basically a homemade witchy herb concoction that's similar to MDMA," Nora explains. "I modified the recipe so that it will affect your senses more."

We all look at each other apprehensively.

"But in a good way!" Nora quickly adds. "Fabrics will feel extra nice, lights will be way cooler, that kind of stuff. Plus, it only lasts about two hours, that way you aren't trippin' for very long."

"Fuck it," I say, after no one else speaks up. "I need to escape a little bit. Gimme."

I hold my hand out and she shakes a pill out from the baggie into it. That is all the motivation everyone else needs and soon they all have their hands out.

"Yash, babe, how about you?" Nora coaxes.

"Ugh, sure, fine," he says reluctantly.

"Peer pressure at its finest!" Nora squeals in delight.

"But promise me—everyone—to try and not be obvious. Okay? And no one snitches. You get caught, that is your own fault then." Yash looks us all in our eyes as we nod in agreement.

I stand up and raise my pill, "Well, cheers!"

We all clink our pills together and place them in our mouths.

I give Henry a stealthy wink as he swallows his and he smiles.

"Cheers, Cassie," he says with a wink back.

My nerves have vanished completely, and I am excited for the rest of the night. I'm almost impatient for the drug to start working and to slip into a different view of the world. Tonight is going to be important. I can feel it in the air.

We finish our drinks and get around to head down to the dance. Henry holds out his arm for me to loop mine through and I take it without hesitation. Henry makes me happy. There is no denying the feelings I am forming for him, but there is also no denying the feelings I have for Cillian as well. Unfortunately, with Cillian they are unrequited. I force those thoughts out of my mind. In this moment, I am with Henry, and I want to have an amazing night.

Nora had said that they normally go all out with decorations and glamour in the Grand Hall, but I am not prepared for just how amazing it looks. There is a live band called Royal Blood playing at the far end. There are multi-colored lights flashing and bouncing around the walls. Tables and chairs are set up for people to sit and eat. Snacks and beverages are on the left side of the hall, all beautifully displayed. But the thing I love the most is the dance floor. Large white-and-black-checkered squares display out into a larger square.

I squeeze Henry's arm tighter at the entrance. The drugs have started to kick in and make me slightly lightheaded.

Henry stops and looks at me. "Is something wrong?"

"Just a tad lightheaded. I think Nora's witchy drugs are kicking in." I smile.

The outline of Henry's curls waver slightly, and I feel the urge to giggle for no reason.

"Definitely kicking in," I correct, letting it out.

"You sure are something, Cassie," Henry says with a giggle himself. "You ready for all this?"

I look around the hall at everything going on. I am blissfully happy.

"You know, this is my first official dance," I say sheepishly.

"You joking me?" He sounds like he doesn't believe me. He steps in front of me, letting go of my arm.

"I'm serious," I say, feeling a tad embarrassed now.

Henry takes my hand in his and gives it a gentle kiss, taking a bow. "Well, Miss Rodden, I am honored to be escorting you."

I playfully shove him and laugh.

"My, what a gentleman." I roll my eyes.

"Come on," Henry says, looping my arm back around his. "I'll show you how we do things on this side of the pond."

Our little group from the room makes our way to the edge of the dance floor. Some of them are staring at the dancing lights with their mouths open, others are giggling incessantly with each other. Nora comes up and whisks me away from Henry. We twirl together in a circle and laugh like two giddy schoolgirls.

"Oh, my goodness, Cassie, I am so happy I met you." Nora gushes as she hugs me.

Nora's silk dress feels so nice and smooth under my fingertips.

"Your hair! I love it! It's so soft and beautiful," Nora says, stroking my locks.

The band begins an upbeat song and Nora's attention is immediately drawn away.

"Ah! I love this song! Dance! Everyone, dance!" she shouts and starts jumping around.

I step back and watch her flail across the dance floor. She is incredibly off beat, but she owns it.

Yash comes up beside me. "She's amazing, isn't she?"

I look at Yash, who can't take his eyes off Nora. His smile is so wide, he looks like he'll break his face from grinning so big. He is absolutely smitten.

"Yeah, she truly is," I agree.

"You know, she loves you, Cassie. She can't stop talking about you." His eyes are still locked on Nora as she attempts the lawnmower dance move.

My heart has never felt such love before. Tears well up in the corners of my eyes, and I try to blink them away.

Yash looks at me as I sniffle to prevent my makeup from being ruined.

"Sorry, love, I didn't intend for you to cry."

"No, you're fine. I just, I love her, too, Yash."

"Yash! Join me, lover!" Nora calls to him.

"Welp, I'll see you out there?" Yash asks as he moonwalks toward Nora.

"Yeah, I'll be there soon. I just don't think y'all are ready for my dance moves yet!" I yell after him.

The music gets louder and drowns out my words. I look around and see Henry conversing with Damon, Lauren seething next to them.

Goodness, you'd think happy drugs would, you know, make her happier.

I continue to look around the hall. Mostly, I am trying to enjoy all of the pretty lights, but a part of me does want to see if Cillian is around.

No luck.

My mouth is dry, so I decide to go grab some punch. My body is so loose, and I can't help but sway to the music as I move toward the punch bowl. The music washes over me, consuming me—the musical notes dancing around me.

The drink and snack tables are plentiful, filled with a beautiful array of little desserts and sandwiches. The punch is held in beautiful crystal bowls

I keep giggling to myself for no reason as I slowly fill a glass with the red liquid. The ruby color of the punch is so vibrant. I study it longer than a non-intoxicated person would. I play with the liquid, stirring the ladle around the bowl.

"Cassandra," Cillian's voice is soft, just above a whisper.

My body freezes for a moment.

Cillian.

I hurry to fill my cup and set the ladle down. I feel the warmth of his body close to mine, my nerves coming alive with electricity.

Okay, act sober. You can do this. Act sober.

I turn to face him, but I don't want him to see my pupils, so I keep my head down. I sneak glances up through my eyelashes at him.

"Cillian," I manage to whisper back.

"How are you?"

"Fine," I reply quickly.

Keep it short and simple.

I take a sip of the punch and have to refrain myself from instantly spitting it out. It tastes like 99% cheap vodka, with a splash of fruit punch for color. It is bitter and does not taste good. I suppress a cough and choke a little, forcing myself to swallow the nasty liquid.

"Everything all right?" Cillian asks, concerned.

"Like you care?" the words spill out of me before I have a chance to reign them in.

I look up at him now. He is stunning. He's wearing an all-black suit that complements every aspect of his gloomy and serious persona.

"Are you high right now?" his tone angry, as he looks more intently into my eyes.

I drop my eyes to the cup I am still holding.

"It's none of your business." I'm embarrassed now.

Is he disappointed in me?

He shakes his head and sighs as I sneak a peek.

"How many times do I have to tell you that things like this leave you vulnerable? Your magic won't be as well controlled," he says sternly.

My trip turns bad as the negative energy messes with my thoughts. My body starts to panic. I need to get out of the situation. I shift my weight uncomfortably from side to side.

"And after what happened yesterday—"

I cut him off, "Stop acting like you care, Cillian," I look into his eyes, "you made it clear the other night that you don't. So please, just leave me alone. It's too hard, and I am not in the right headspace to be talking about this with you. And you continue to keep things from me, which is a whole other conversation we need to have."

I try to be strong, but part of me feels like it is breaking. He looks hurt for a second, but then his stone face returns.

Cillian steps closer to me. "You think I don't care about you?" His voice is reserved and quiet.

"M' lady, care to dance?" Henry's sweet voice catches my attention.

Henry is next to us and has his hand extended toward me. He has taken his suit jacket off and unbuttoned the top button of his shirt, his tie hanging loose now. Henry looks slightly concerned and Cillian takes a step back.

"Yes, Henry, I would love to dance with you." I make the poor choice to gulp down the rest of my drink and look at Cillian again. The liquid is already trying to find a way back out, but I hold it down. "By the way, the punch is spiked. So, if you are going to criticize me, you better include everyone in this room."

I shove the cup into Cillian's chest, and he takes it softly. Our hands touch for an instant, causing a small burst of electricity to shock between us. I quickly drop my hand when he has a grasp on the cup.

"Let's go, Henry." I eagerly grab Henry's hand and drag him onto the dance floor.

We maneuver our way to the heart of the checkerboard, where Nora and Yash are dancing. Even Damon and Lauren have made their way to the dance floor as well.

"Cassie!" I can barely hear Nora scream my name over the music.

I smile at her, but focus on Henry. I pull him close to my body, and we move as one to the beat of the music. He holds my waist more aggressively, and I welcome it. I run my fingers through his curls and the sensation is instantly addictive. My thoughts are carried away with fantasies and I grab onto his hair a little bit harder.

The music drowns out all other sounds, so it is easy to forget about the world. We are all mesmerized by the beat—moving, dancing, laughing. I turn around and give him my back. I guide his hands to each side of my hips. The negative thoughts are gone now, and I am able to focus on the trip taking control once again. Henry and my bodies are in tune as we continue dancing. It is almost as if our heartbeats have synced together.

The band plays a few more songs, and I am out of breath and sweaty at the end of them. We all are. My hair is sticking to the back of my neck. Henry and I separate at some point and I dance with Nora. She, of course, has to point out that Cillian's eyes haven't left me all night.

A slower, more melodic song begins to play now. Everyone gets closer to their dates and begins to dance all at once. Slightly confused, I move back over to Henry and he slowly draws me close to him. He places one hand in mine, and the other falls above the dimples in my back. His hold is firm.

"Is this some sort of dance everyone knows?" I say into his ear, stepping closer into him.

He chuckles. "Just follow my lead. Trust me?" He stares into my eyes. His pupils are still dilated, hiding his emerald irises.

I giggle. "Always."

Henry smiles and we flow into the rhythm with the others. It is just like how it is in the movies—dresses twirling around in unison, steps together and apart. Henry is an amazing dancer; he never misses a beat. I don't even have to worry about accidentally stepping on his toes.

Heather and Abigail, next to us, have had a little too much punch, and their dancing is slightly off. But they are laughing and enjoying each other.

The tempo quickens and so do our steps. I giggle more with glee. My cheeks hurt from smiling so much. Part of me wishes I had made more of an effort to go to dances growing up.

The quicker the tempo, the quicker the spins, and I soon feel like a feather in the wind. I am being swept away and consumed. I close my eyes and let Henry guide me.

"Get ready," Henry advises, as his hands grab my waist. "Hands on my shoulders.

My eyes flutter open. "Ready for what?" I ask, placing my hands on his broad shoulders as directed. But before he can answer, the music reaches a climax, and I am lifted into the air and spun 90 degrees.

I let out a squeal of happiness as Henry bring me back down.

"That was so fun!" I exclaim.

Henry chuckles as the tempo descends and everyone slows again. I look up at Henry in admiration. Every part of me feels happy and warm.

"Henry, thank you. I—"

Before I can finish, Henry pulls me in and kisses me hard. My lips go tingly with desire and hunger for more. I kiss him back with passion and pull him even closer. My body feels weightless and on fire. My magic roars through me like a wild animal on a rampage. I feel like I might burst. I stop moving my feet, but it feels like we are still spinning.

As our lips melt into each other's, I hear the song start to end. Henry groans softly and I feel him become greedy. He doesn't want it to end either.

The song is coming to its finale, and I know we will have to pull away soon. We part our lips, but lean our foreheads together. I giggle softly and smile.

I hear people gasp and murmur together when the music does not start up again. I slowly open my eyes to see what is going on. I begin to feel the sensation of descending and make the realization that Henry and I are floating above the crowd.

The music has stopped, because everyone is turning to watch us make our way back down to the ground. Everyone is wide eyed with mouths agape.

"What the hell?" I say as I look back at Henry, while clutching him tighter, afraid that we might suddenly drop.

He seems just as surprised as I am.

"Cassie, I think it's us doing this—together," he says bashfully.

I laugh and smile as my feet make contact with the dance floor.

"Goodness, they act as if they've never seen two people floating before," I joke.

Everyone starts to get over their shock and the music starts back up.

Henry leans into my ear, "Do you want to get out of here?"

I feel my heartbeat pounding throughout my body, especially in my fingertips. My lips still tingle from his touch. I want more. I want Henry. I notice my panties becoming wet with desire.

I nod and we make our way out of the throng of people on the dance floor. Most of the people we pass stop and stare, but I keep my eyes down. I don't see Nora or Yash, but I assume they are somewhere in the crowd.

Henry grips my hand with determination and part of me is really turned on by this side of him. Another part of me hopes that Cillian doesn't see us leave, but at the same time, I hope that he does. I notice the clock on the wall as we leave. It reads nearly 11:30 p.m.

The air is cooler when we exit the Grand Hall. The coolness sobers me up a little, but I am still just as determined. The music fades as we make our way down the corridor. None of the other students are out this far that I can see. We round another corner into a dimly lit hallway. I can't tell where we are, but I'm not too worried about it. I notice different-sized mirrors hanging on the walls as we scurry by them.

Henry stops abruptly and I accidentally run into his back.

"Sorry!" I laugh.

Henry takes this moment to pin me against the wall. His weight and body heat feel satisfying against me.

"Oh, you think that's funny, now, do you, love?" he lowers his tone seductively and my body aches for him.

I lick and bite my lip to suppress another giggle.

He rests his forehead against mine and places his hands on either side of my head and leans deeper into me. Almost like he is trying to resist his urges.

"Cassie, I-I think I—"

But I don't let him finish. I grab his shirt and pull him in to kiss me. I see the lights flicker and surge beneath my eyelids.

His lips are so soft and luscious. We continue kissing as he gently thrusts his hips into me.

"Is there somewhere more private we can go?" I barely manage to get out as I break from his lips for a moment.

I open my eyes and scream. Nora is standing directly behind Henry.

"Nora! You scared me. What are you doing?!" I am not expecting to see her here.

I quickly push Henry away, but just slightly. Nora is staring blankly at me, not saying anything. I'm a little concerned when she still doesn't answer me. Her eyes are glazed over and emotionless.

"Nora, what's wrong? Where's Yash?" I ask, quickly looking down the corridor to see if he is nearby.

I go to take a step toward her, but Henry holds me back.

"Cassie, look…" He nods his head toward her hand.

My eyes travel downward to her hand, which is holding a large knife. Blood slowly drips off the tip into a little puddle on the ground. The hem of her dress is soaked in blood, and it is slowly creeping its way up.

"Nora," I say cautiously, "what happened? Where's Yash?"

Panic rises inside me, and Henry steps between Nora and me. Nora squeezes her eyes shut tightly and brings her hands to her head. She lets out a blood-curdling scream.

"Nora!" Henry says sternly. "It's okay, just tell us what happened."

Our heads snap in the direction of the Grand Hall as we hear screams coming from there.

"Henry, she's not herself. Something is very wrong," I say, taking a step closer to him.

Nora stops screaming and opens her eyes. They are filled with rage and menace. They go black as she lunges at us with the knife.

Henry tries to grab her, but she is quick, and plunges the knife deep into his chest.

"NO!" I scream as I watch in horror.

Henry drops to his knees in shock and clutches his chest. Blood slowly seeps out from the wound onto his white shirt.

No, this can't be real.

Nora's attention quickly turns to me, and she does not hesitate, lunging again. We tumble to the floor as I try to hold her off.

"Nora! Nora, it's me! It's Cassie. Why are you doing this?" I plead.

Nora hisses and scratches at me like a rabid animal.

"Nora, I don't want to hurt you!"

I use my magic to fling her off of me, giving me time to get back onto my feet. I quickly rip my dress so it won't get in the way.

Nora bounces back to her feet quickly and circles me. A predator and its prey.

I look briefly toward Henry and see that he is slumped over, propped lifelessly against the wall.

I can feel him dying slowly.

My attention returns to Nora, and she comes at me again. Cillian's training has prepared me for defensive moves, and I am able to get ahold of her. She lets out another scream as I trap and hold her in a headlock.

"Nora, please, stop!" I beg her.

She bites onto my arm hard, causing me to release my hold

on her. Her teeth puncture my skin and blood pools in her teeth marks. This is all the distraction she needs to get on top of me and wrap her hands around my throat. She squeezes as hard as she can, and I feel my windpipe collapse. I try to breathe or make a sound, but her grip is too tight. My head feels like it is going to burst, and black dots speckle my vision. I try to grab at her face and her eyes.

Focus, Cassandra.

Cillian's words penetrate my thoughts.

You won't always be able to have the time to react. Focus and concentrate on where you want to go.

I close my eyes and stop struggling against Nora. I picture the empty spaces in the hallway.

Come on. Come on. Come on!

My body goes tingly and I feel myself being pulled into the unknown. I land hard on my back and my head smacks against the tiled hallway.

Get up, get up!

I kip myself up onto my feet and steady myself. I am dizzy from hitting my head. I am behind Nora and I see her looking around, confused. It doesn't take her long to figure out I am behind her and she scrambles toward me like a demon crawling out of hell.

"Enough, Nora. This ends now."

I raise my hand and use my magic to lift her up into the air. She struggles against my magical hold, but she cannot escape. I fling her far down the hallway and she crashes into a wall. Her head hits first, and she is knocked unconscious.

I waste no time running over to where Henry is and turn him onto his back. I still feel him slipping away; his magic and his lifeforce are barely there.

"Henry, open your eyes. Henry, look at me."

I don't realize I am crying until I see my tears stain Henry's shirt, mixing in as the blood spreads all over his chest, the knife still protruding.

"Henry, please wake up," I beg him and gently slap his face.

His eyes barely open, and I feel him try to take a deep breath.

"Cassie?" His voice is weak.

I hold his head in my arms.

"I'm here, Henry, I'm here. It'll be okay."

But it isn't going to be okay. The wound is fatal, and Henry slips back into unconsciousness. His face has gone pale and his head weighs heavier in my arms. More screams erupt in the distance.

What the hell is going on?

"Cassandra!" Cillian's voice screams down the hallway.

Through tear-blurred eyes I look up and see Cillian running toward me. He closes the distance quicker by shifting to us. Henry's blood covers my hands and arms, and I feel it seeping into my dress.

"Cillian! Help me, please!" I am sobbing.

Cillian slides down on the other side of Henry.

"We have to do something!" I beg Cillian.

Cillian's face is pale, and I have never seen him look so scared.

"I will not let him die. He was trying to protect me. I have to save him."

I know what I have to do. Cillian and I are powerful together, and even though he will try to deny it, I know we can do this.

I pull the knife out of Henry's chest and blood gushes out. The noise the knife makes as I pull it out is sickening.

"Cassandra, he's too far gone. What are you doing?" Cillian whispers so Henry can't hear.

I don't listen to him. I throw the knife to the side and it lands with a loud clank.

"Give me your hands!" I demand.

"Cassandra—"

"Give me your fucking hands, Cillian!" I stare at him with determination.

Cillian complies and places his hands in mine. I place our hands on Henry's chest.

"We can do this, Cillian. We can bring him back. Please, just trust me."

I close my eyes and will my magic to flow into Henry to repair the damage. Cillian does the same.

The building begins to shake, the mirrors along the hallway fall and shatter.

"I will not let you die on me, Henry!"

I grit my teeth and press harder into his chest. Cillian's magic flows together with mine and we grow stronger by the second. Henry's magic has disappeared now, his lifeforce gone as well.

"Come on!" I scream. "Focus on directing our magic to

repair."

The lightbulbs around us in the hallway explode and the building shakes more violently.

I concentrate our magic on pulling the pooled blood back into Henry's veins and restoring the sliced muscle and tendons.

The air swirls around us.

I can feel our effort start to work. I open my eyes and see the blood retreating back into the wound.

I let out a nervous laugh of relief.

"Yes! Yes! It's working!" I scream.

Cillian opens his eyes and watches in shock.

"Keep going!" I urge.

It is like our magic is radiating out of us. It is beautiful. We are glowing.

I feel our magic continue getting stronger. Henry's magic starts to come back as well, and soon it joins with Cillian's and my own. There is an explosion of light as Henry's magic flows into the mix and it blinds me. All I see now is pure white.

The tremors begin to subside and become less intense as the blinding light dims, and my vision is restored.

I can hear and feel Henry's heart beating faintly. He gasps and jolts up into a sitting position. He clutches his chest as he sucks in deep breaths.

"Henry!" I can't hold back my happiness and wrap my arms around him.

Tears of joy begin to flow.

"We did it," I whisper.

"Oh my god," Cillian says breathlessly, sitting back.

"Henry?" the Headmistress's voice is scared and frantic as she rushes up to us. "Oh my god, Henry, my boy, my boy, are you okay? There was an attack."

I have never seen this side of the Headmistress. Her hair is a mess and blood stains her cheek. She looks as if she, too, is holding back tears.

Henry's breathing steadies, and I sit back to give him some space. His shirt is still stained with blood, but it is no longer soaked. He is shaking slightly, but I see him start to process it all.

"Cillian, what happened?" Headmistress Ansley demands.

Cillian looks up at her, but he is at a loss for words.

"Mum, I think I am okay," Henry says, looking at me.

I smile and let the tears flow freely. Other professors and the medical team circle us. Cillian and I help Henry to his feet, and the medics take over. Henry can't support his full weight, so he relies on the others.

"They saved me, Mum."

"Nora attacked Henry and me." I motion to Nora, who is being helped to her feet. She seems confused and does not appear to know what is going on. "But I don't think it was really her. She seemed possessed. Something else was in control of her."

"Yes, it seems that a few students were taken control over and used to attack others," the Headmistress says softly.

"But I thought there were spells in place to protect against this kind of thing? Is everyone okay? Who all was taken over?" I am severely confused and questions spill out. Adrenaline still courses through me, but I am beginning to feel weak.

"Yes, there are, but there are also wards up to prevent what happened to you yesterday as well," she says sternly. "It is clear now that there is someone on the inside. As far as the numbers of injured and deceased, we are unsure."

I step back in shock.

Deceased?

"What do you mean deceased? Is this because of me? Is this because of the Anarchy?" My questions go unanswered. The Headmistress has instead directed her attention to a guard and is talking about what to do next.

"Answer me, dammit!" I scream.

"Enough!" she yells at me. "We need to figure things out still. Yes, some students did not make it, as well as one staff member, but we do not know the full extent yet." She turns to address Cillian and the security team, "Get my son to the Infirmary immediately. Shut this school down and get everyone to their rooms. Cillian, do not take your eyes off Miss Rodden again. Understood?"

"Understood." Cillian moves to where I am and stands behind me.

"Also, take the affected students down to the holding cells until we get this shit show figured out." The Headmistress smooths her hair.

Everything is happening all at once and I can't control all the emotions rushing through me. I am exhausted, and my legs are still shaking slightly.

"I don't want to leave Cassie, though, Mum," Henry says as the medical team goes to take him away.

"I'll be fine, Henry," I speak up before the Headmistress has a chance to argue. I know Henry will fight with the little strength he has left, but he needs to be assessed to make sure he is okay. He did die, afterall

I walk up to him and place a hand softly on his cheek.

"You saved me," Henry whispers, "and for that, I will be forever in your debt."

"I'll see you soon, Henry. Okay?" I reassure him.

He looks like he wants to protest more, but then nods. He lets the medics lead him away and out of my sight.

I look around to find Nora again, but she has already been whisked away.

"Please don't hurt Nora. If it's true her mind was taken over, she didn't even know what she was doing," I beg the Headmistress.

"Miss Malik will be handled. Unfortunately, it looks like she slit Mister Patel's throat, and that will need to be addressed with their families."

This information sends me into another spiral downward and I become dizzy.

The bloody knife.

"Yash? Yash is dead?" The words come out as a whisper, for fear that if I say them any louder, they might actually be true.

"Miss Rodden, are you aware of any students being under the influence at this dance tonight?" the Headmistress asks sternly.

I gulp.

"Um…"

"If you know something, then tell me." Her eyes are hard. I can sense she will know if I am lying.

"Yes. A few of us took a pill before the dance. Nora made a witchy form of MDMA, she said."

"Hmm…Interesting."

"Why? What's going on?"

Shit. I didn't mean to get Nora in more trouble.

"And who all took these pills?" she continues without answering me.

"But I did also notice the punch was spiked, as well. Ask Cillian, he knows about the punch."

The Headmistress sighs aggressively. "The names, Miss Rodden."

"Well, myself, Nora, Yash, Lauren, Damon, Henry, and maybe a couple other people, but that's all I remember right now."

"Certain drugs, Miss Rodden make it easier for your mind to be taken control over, as I am sure you have already been taught in class."

"Well, yes, we have been taught that, but—"

"I will not tolerate any excuses from you right now, Miss Rodden. You were warned and yet you still felt the need to participate in an act that put not only you, but other students at risk.

You helped put my own son at risk."

I retreat a step back and bump into Cillian. "No, I would never put Henry in harm's way."

"How do we know you, Miss Rodden, were not taken control over and manipulated Henry away to attack him?" the Headmistress starts toward me.

"No! I told you the truth. Nora attacked us. Henry and I, we were just...talking."

"Tabitha, enough." Cillian steps in to prevent her further advancement toward me.

Tabitha? I hadn't realized I didn't know her first name.

"What she is saying is true. I saw the tail end of the altercation. Nora was the one attacking, and Cassandra was defending Henry and herself. Nora had fatally stabbed Henry, but...Cassandra and I were able to bring him back."

The Headmistress's jaw drops.

"Impossible," she whispers.

"It's true. Ask Henry yourself."

Cillian and Tabitha stare at each other for a few moments—their eyes exchanging unspoken words.

"Very well. Cillian, please escort Miss Rodden to a safe place for the evening and get her cleaned up. There will be a mandatory school meeting tomorrow to discuss what has happened, and that the Joining Ceremony will be pushed up. We cannot have our students weak. Especially now."

Cillian nods and gently takes my arm to lead me away. My

head is spinning as Cillian lead me quickly down the corridor.
Yash is dead? People are dead? What have I done?

CHAPTER ELEVEN

I take off my heels and throw them away in a nearby trashcan. They are bloody and broken and I don't care about them anymore.

Cillian directs me to a door that leads down a set of stairs, which I have never seen. It is cold in the stairwell, and my legs feel like gelatin as he pulls me along. It is hard for me to keep up with his stride.

The stairwell leads to a single door at the bottom. Cillian pulls a key out of his pocket and unlocks it. It *creaks* open with a loud whine. It looks to be an underground tunnel system. The flood lights flicker on as the door closes behind us with a loud thud.

"What is this?" I am paranoid now.

But Cillian doesn't answer. We plunge deeper into the tunnel and the ground becomes uneven.

Cillian's pace only increases. The lighting is so poor, I can barely even see my feet.

"Cillian, slow down, please," my plea echoes through the tunnel.

"We are almost there."

"Cillian, please!"

I trip over something in the darkness and I tumble to the ground, my arms not reaching out fast enough to catch myself.

I feel the harsh ground tear open the skin on my knees and warm blood trickles out from the wounds. Instead of getting back on my feet, I sit on the ground sobbing. I pull my knees up to my chest; I am shaking from the cold. My body feels like it is going into shock and shutting down.

"This is all my fault. I am so sorry, Cillian," I sob as I rock back and forth.

Cillian paces in front of me and starts to get angry. He screams in frustration and punches the side of the tunnel.

"Oh, great, now you're mad at me. I can't do anything right!"

His demeanor instantly changes, and he rushes to kneel at my side.

"Shh, no, not at all, Cassandra. I am not mad at you."

I have never seen Cillian show this much emotion. Maybe it is the lack of light in the tunnel, but I swear I see tears welling up in his eyes.

"Then why are you so mad?"

"Because that's twice now I was supposed to be protecting you here. Twice now where I wasn't there to help you. Cassandra,

I—" He bites his lip to prevent himself from saying more.

My sobbing subsides and I lean closer to him.

"What? It's not your job to protect me, Cillian," I say, trying to coax more out of him.

He hangs his head in his hands and sighs. He raises his head after a moment and runs his fingers through his hair, his jaw clenched.

"When I saw you in that hallway tonight, covered in blood, I-I thought that you were injured. I was not worried about Henry. I was worried about you." He can't look at me. "It has been my job for so long to look after you, and now, in the times you've needed me the most, I've failed you."

"I've only been here a few months, Cillian, you can't expect to be everywhere I am," I reassure him.

He gives a halfhearted laugh. "Yeah, months..." he trails off, lost in thought.

"Give yourself a break, Cillian." I go to take his hand in mine, but whatever moment we were having has ended and he pulls his hand away.

"Sorry," I say as I retreat.

"We must get going. These tunnels lead to various spots within the school. This specific tunnel will lead us directly to my room, where you'll stay for the evening. I am not letting you out of my sight."

I ignore everything else he says except for the part about me staying in his room.

"I need to get clean clothes from my room though." I am suddenly uncomfortably aware of how much of a hot mess I am right now. My dress is shredded and caked with dried blood. My hair is going all sorts of directions. My hands are still sticky from all the blood.

"I'll send another professor to grab an overnight bag from your room. A female professor," he assures me, sensing my hesitation.

Cillian takes off his suit jacket and drapes it around my shoulders. I am grateful for the warmth it provides.

"Let's get going," he says, standing. "Can you walk, or do you need me to carry you? I promise I won't go as quickly."

To be in your arms is all I want right now.

"I think I can walk," I say instead.

"Do you trust me?" He extends his hand to help me get up.

More than you know.

I nod and take his hand. My head starts to pound as I stand, and I feel a hangover already starting to settle in.

As soon as I am vertical again, he tries to let go of my hand, but I hold on tight.

"Please?" I whisper.

He doesn't pull away this time, and we continue down the tunnel. My knees ache, as the wounds on them stretch with every step. I feel warm blood slowly creeping down to one ankle.

But Cillian is right. It is only a few more yards before we encounter another locked door. He retrieves the key from his pocket and unlocks it. Once through, there are a few steps up that lead into a large room with a wall of windows to the outside. Through the windows lies the front area of the school.

So that's how he saw me sneak out on my first night.

I stand at the top of the stairs, taking the room in. Cillian steps around me to turn on some lights. The room is open and unobstructed by any dividing walls. On the left, there is a small kitchen and a door, which I assume leads back into the school. Directly across the kitchen, down a few steps, is a bed shoved against the wall of windows. Everything looks organized and simple.

Cillian is already in the kitchen, retrieving two bottles from the refrigerator.

"The windows are only one way," he mumbles.

Cillian rummages through the cabinets now and pulls out a few things. He brings everything to the small table next to the kitchen.

"Sit," he orders softly.

I follow the order without protest and slump into one of the chairs, my body instantly starting to relax. I can now feel how exhausted I am as I investigate the objects he has brought to the table—a medical kit, a bottle of ibuprofen, and two beers.

Cillian retrieves a bottle opener from a drawer and opens the beers. He sits in the chair next to mine.

"Beer?" he asks, extending one of the open bottles toward me.

I look at him as if he is confused. "But—"

"Might as well, after the night we've had," he states, understanding my hesitation.

I take it and fiddle with the bottle in my hands. Cillian takes a long pull from his bottle and then opens the medical kit to attend to my knees.

"You don't have to do that. I can try and heal myself," I protest. I don't want him to feel like he has to take care of me just because my dumb self fell.

Cillian scoffs. "Most of our magic is drained from what we did back there. So, for now, we will do it the human way."

His touch is so gentle and warm as he cleans the lacerations.

I sigh and decide to chug the beer in my hand.

"Best way to get over a hangover is to never stop drinking, so you don't get one."

My grandmother's words drift through my mind. Even in her old age, she could drink anyone under the table.

The carbonation burns my throat, and the cold liquid gives me a brain freeze, but it is the only thing I can control in this moment. My face contorts as I coax the brain freeze to stop.

"Ow," I say, pushing my tongue to the roof of my mouth.

Cillian chuckles.

"What's going to happen to Nora?" I ask hesitantly.

"I am not sure. The affected students will be screened, and until we find the insider, everything will be on strict lockdown. It is going to be a long night for her and the others."

"I wonder if she even knows about Yash."

"I am sure she'll be informed. It will have to be brought up in her questioning."

"You know, all the training you've been giving me saved me back there. I shifted all by myself while Nora was actively attacking."

Cillian's mood appears to improve. "Very good."

"You make me better," I say quietly.

Cillian ignores my last comment and the conversation fizzles, the room now silent. I look around at the minimal decorations that adorn Cillian's living space. There are a lot of old books scattered about, but that is about it. The room looks as if it could belong to anyone, or be left at just a moment's notice.

"So, the Joining Ceremony..." I try to start back up conversation.

"What about it?" Cillian says quietly as he works.

"Why haven't you ever joined with someone before?" I probe.

Cillian sighs. "It's not like you can force a join. Every witch has someone that their magic complements—someone that makes their magic stronger. A lot of different pairings can either weaken your magic or make it better, but there's only one pairing that results in its full potential. It's a lot like puzzle pieces. There are some that can work, some that can't, but only one piece that completes the picture."

Cillian moves on to clean the scratches on my face. The alcohol wipe stings as it touches the open wounds, but Cillian proceeds with caution.

"Has a professor every joined with a student before?" I keep my eyes on the empty bottle in my hand.

Cillian's hand wavers for a moment.

"No, but we've already gone over this," he says plainly.

"I know," my tone drops, and my shoulders slump forward.

"Not that I know of, anyway," he adds.

"Oh?" My tone perks back up. "So, it's not like it's against any rules. I mean, if you can't control who your magic is meant to pair with?" I peek up at him.

He gives me an agitated look.

"So that means you could technically pair with me, right?" I whisper the words, afraid of the response.

Cillian sighs heavily and tosses the alcohol wipe onto the table. He takes another long pull from his beer as I anticipate his reply.

"Yes, technically, you could, if that's what's meant to be. There are trials we will run before the ceremony to try and narrow down who your magical partner could be, but only the ceremony will show who it truly is, and even then, we may not know. Both you and your magic have to be ready." I smile to myself at the thought. "But you will not be pairing with me," he says as he finishes his beer.

I stand up and knock his jacket off from my shoulders. "And why not? You just said technically I could. There is a possibility. You've seen what our magic does together, Cillian."

He stares off into space, avoiding eye contact with me.

"Yeah, and we've seen what yours and Henry's does together

as well," he says sternly.

It's like a punch to the gut, and I bite the inside of my cheek.

"That's not fair, Cillian. Why can't you just admit it?! You and me, we work together! We brought someone back from the dead!" I raise my voice and I get heated.

"Admit what, Cassandra?" He turns to look at me. His eyes are hard, but I see it again—I can see his internal conflict.

I am so angry that I step away and turn my back to him.

"I have feelings for you, Cillian. I am drawn to you. You make me feel things I have never felt before."

My nose stings as tears threaten to form. I wiggle my nose to prevent them as I hear Cillian get up and walk back into the kitchen. The refrigerator door opens, and I hear a clink of another beer bottle being opened.

"But you have feelings for Henry as well," he finally says. "You are drawn to him as well, and Henry is your most logical choice. You're powerful, he's powerful. You both are around the same age. I have seen many joined pairs over the years to know what patterns to look for."

I turn back around and walk up to him. He leans back against the counter and sips his beer nonchalantly.

"But he is not you. Look me in the eye right now and tell me you don't have feelings for me. Tell me you don't, and I'll drop this, but I know I am not crazy."

I search his eyes for something—anything. Any clue as to what he is thinking.

"You should get cleaned up. The bathroom is that way." He points behind me. "Towels are in there. I'll set the couch up. You can take the bed."

And with those words, the final blow is dealt and my heart shatters.

"Fine."

I turn and head toward the bathroom. I make sure to slam the door behind me.

Not even the warm water from the shower eases my tense muscles. My mind is spinning with everything that has happened. I quickly clean myself, making sure to get all the blood off my skin. I wonder how many more times I will have to wash away someone else's blood from my hands.

I hope Henry is okay. Ugh, and Nora. What's going to happen to her?

I think about everyone who was in the room with us when we took those pills, or who may have seemed off during the dance.

Smash!

The sound of glass shattering outside startles me, even though the shower muffles it slightly. I quickly finish getting the soap out of my hair and rush out of the shower. I fling a towel around my body and pause at the bathroom door.

Please no. Not another attack.

My heart is racing.

"Cillian, what was that?" I ask hesitantly as I turn the doorknob.

I swing the door open and step out, nearly running into

Cillian. I take a step backward and into the wall next to the bathroom door.

"Oh, goodness, what was that noise? Is everything okay?" I peer around him to see what has happened.

Cillian steps forward, closing the space between us. He says nothing, but I can see in his eyes that he is struggling internally. He places a hand beside my head up against the wall, and leans his body softly into mine. My heart is beating so fast, I think it's going to burst out of my chest at any moment. I try to swallow, but my throat is tight.

"Cillian," I whisper, his eyes locked onto mine. The struggle is no longer visible in his eyes. A decision has been made.

Cillian uses his other hand, although shaking slightly, to softly cup my cheek. His thumb slowly traces the outline of my lips. Cillian groans in frustration, dropping his gaze and his head, but his hands remain. He leans his forehead to mine and I breathe heavier. We are caught in a standstill.

Even though he is pressing my body up against the wall gently, I release the hold I have on my towel. I push my hips into him to give myself a little room from the wall. I unwrap the towel slowly and let it fall to the floor. His thumb, still resting on my lips, I draw into my mouth and suck on it sensually for a moment before I pull back to look at him. I press myself back up against the wall and wait.

"Your move," I whisper breathlessly.

Cillian breathes heavily as he pulls his head back, his gaze meeting mine once more.

Come on, Cillian. Meet me halfway, here.

Cillian maneuvers his hand from my cheek to the nape of my neck, holding it securely while also lifting my head upward. He inches his lips closer to mine. My body aches for his with impatience and desire. I move my hands to his chest.

His lips still hesitate as they brush against mine, but I already feel the little magic I have left and my nerves going crazy. Slowly, his lips melt into mine. He kisses me deeply and passionately. His lips are so soft and delectable. I want more.

I am surprised when he pulls back slightly.

"Cassandra, I—"

But it is not the time to talk. I grab the back of his neck and pull his lips back to mine. This must be all he needs to let loose, because I suddenly feel a new sense of urgency in his kisses. I move my hands to his shirt and hastily work to unbutton it. His hands move to undo his pants, our lips never parting. I have trouble with a couple of the buttons so I just rip his shirt open.

Electricity courses through me. After his clothes are off, he picks me up and pins me against the wall, both hands cupping my ass, my legs wrapping around his lower torso. His skin feels amazing against mine. My hands travel up and down the muscles in his back. I can feel that he is hungry for more.

I need a second to breathe, so I stretch out my neck. He happily makes his way down it as I try to control my breathing. I am slightly dizzy from it all. I moan into his ear as I feel a pleasurable pain form where he is gently sucking at my neck. I grab onto his hair and entangle it between my fingers. His aroma overwhelms my senses. I am completely his.

I giggle as his five o'clock shadow tickles my neck. He stops and looks at me.

"Is everything all right?" He looks concerned.

"Mhmm," I mumble and nod as I try to kiss him again.

He pulls away and smiles.

"Can we take this slow?" He breathes heavily.

How slow are we talking here? We are already naked.

"Of course," I say. My lips are tingling and swollen slightly from our kisses.

Cillian pulls me away from the wall, my full weight still in his arms, and he carries me to his bed. The moon is shining brightly through the windows. Cillian lays me down gently at the foot of the bed. I scoot myself up to the head of it and admire Cillian's body in the moonlight. The light reflects off his skin, causing it to glow. I have never realized how defined and muscular he is.

Cillian crawls up the bed to meet me. I part my legs and let his pelvis sink further into me as he lays on top of me. I feel myself swell with pleasure and become wet as I yearn for him to enter me.

Cillian kisses me more gently now, each kiss satisfying and well executed. He puts one hand underneath my head, the other slowly travels down to my breasts, and then traces the outline of my side until he reaches my thigh. His fingertips grip slightly to encourage my leg to bend.

I arch my back to stretch, but to also push my hips into him more. I want him so badly.

He chuckles. "Patience now," he says, his lips still against mine.

I groan in playful frustration. But I can feel that Cillian is just as eager as I am. He guides himself slowly into me, my body quivers beneath him, and I moan in pleasure. It is euphoric. My magic explodes throughout me as Cillian and I become one. I have never experienced this sensation before. He moves himself in and out of me slowly, but this just amplifies everything. My fingertips throb with pleasure, and my toes curl as we continue this rhythm for a few minutes.

"Let me get on top," I whisper into his ear.

Without breaking apart, Cillian flips me over on top of him. I giggle with the quick motion. Being on top of him now, I feel powerful. I feel him pulsating inside of me as I to move my hips forward and backward, his hands gripped onto my hips. He moans in pleasure beneath me.

Cillian sits up and our arms wrap around each other as I continue moving my hips. I hold onto him tighter, feeling myself coming to climax. I feel the bed begin to tremor, but I pay no attention to it, until everything in the room raises up, stopping suspended in the air. I feel the magic pouring out of us both into the surrounding space.

"I'm going to cum," my voice trembles into his ear.

The lights flicker as I throw back my head to moan in pleasure. I dig my nails into his back as my body explodes in climax.

The lights surge and explode around the room. My body collapses into his arms as I finish my release. Everything that hangs suspended in the air comes crashing to the floor.

"Oh, I'm not done with you yet," Cillian growls into my ear as I breathe heavily. Both of our bodies glitter with a sheen of sweat.

Holy shit.

"I'm taking back over," Cillian says as we change positions. He twirls my body around so I am laying on my stomach. He spreads my legs with his and shoves his way back into me. He pins me down, laying on top of me as I grip at the bed sheets. His hands make their way underneath my shoulders, and he holds onto my breasts to get better leverage, pounding into me.

From his moans, I can tell he is getting close. I hold my breath, as I, too, feel myself coming close again already. He thrusts several more times before letting out one final moan. His body quivers against me before he rolls off me, onto his back. We are both breathing heavily and sweating as I turn over onto my back as well.

I still feel our magic intertwining as we both try to catch our breath. My body feels alive with electricity.

"Holy shit," I say as I turn my head to look at Cillian.

He chuckles. Cillian turns to face me and lifts his head up. He rests his check on his fist as he looks at me. I turn onto my side and do the same. Our breathing settles as he continues staring at me, not saying anything. Just taking me in.

"Sorry about your room," I say with a chuckle.

"I don't even care," he says, his eyes never leaving mine.

I blush as he reaches out to tuck a strand of damp hair behind my ear. I can't even begin to describe how I feel in this moment.

"I'll be right back, okay?" I say as I get up quickly to use the bathroom.

"I'll be right here," Cillian says and I stop on the threshold. I look at him for a moment more, taking him in.

I smile and shut the bathroom door behind me. Part of me feels a little sad and worried. Worried that this is all just a dream, and when I go back out, he'll have disappeared.

I hurry to use the toilet and clean myself up before rushing back out. Cillian is still there, only he has pulled the blankets up. I make my way over to the side of the bed and slip under the covers. Cillian holds out his arm for me to snuggle into. I nuzzle into him and lay my head on his chest. I feel at peace in his arms, in the midst of all this chaos.

I move my left hand to his chest and draw circles with my fingertips. I feel my scrapes and scratches beginning to heal.

"More powerful than we even know," I hear Cillian barely whisper.

"What was that?" I ask, in case I heard him wrong.

He leans down and places a gentle kiss at the top of my head.

"Nothing. You just never cease to impress me," he says into my hair. "Let's get some sleep, for tomorrow…everything changes. You may need to step into the role of the Chosen One. After what I witnessed you accomplish tonight, though, there's no doubt in my mind." I hear a hint of worry in his tone.

My eyelids are heavy, and I know I need to sleep. Cillian is right. Everything will change tomorrow. I sigh deeply as he caresses my arm with his thumb. There is nothing more we can do tonight to fix things. I accept the situation and brace myself for tomorrow. The thought of Cillian being by my side makes everything seem slightly less scary.

I surrender my body to the exhaustion and let myself slip into unconsciousness. Tomorrow will be its own battle, but for tonight—tonight I am his and nothing more.

CHAPTER TWELVE

The sun beams through the windows and onto my skin. It's warm and inviting. It holds onto me tightly and begs for me not to wake just yet as I slowly stir. The tragedies from yesterday pester away at my thoughts, but so does the euphoria from Cillian.

Cillian and I wake in the same position we fell asleep. I lift my head and look to see if he is awake or not. He is.

"I was trying not to wake you. You looked so peaceful," he says softly. His eyes are so soft as he looks at me.

"It seemed like I only just closed my eyes," I say as I stretch and sit up. Cillian sits up with me.

"You know, you remind me so much of a mourning dove."

"Is that a good thing or a bad thing?" I ask, running my fingers through my tangled hair.

Cillian cups my cheek. "You have been through so much, Cassandra. So much pain and sorrow, but I see you every day trying to be better. I've watched you grow so much over these past few months. You give me hope."

I sit in silence and absorb his words. I don't think he knows how much they mean to me. I hold onto his hand, still against my cheek.

"Thank you, Cillian."

He brings my hand to his lips and kisses it softly, causing my heart to flutter.

"We should probably get up and around now, though. Tabitha is holding a mandatory meeting this morning to go over everything."

I groan and fall back onto the bed, taking the blankets with me and covering my head.

"I'm not ready, Cillian. I'm scared," I confide through the bedding.

Cillian pulls back the blanket, exposing my face. He leans close and kisses my cheek.

"It's okay to be scared, Little Dove, but sometimes we need to be strong for others. Make decisions that put us in momentary situations of discomfort for the greater good."

Little Dove? I have a nickname now. Jesus, this man is handsome AND poetic.

I squeal with delight internally.

"I know," I say and try to keep my cool about the nickname.

"Let's get dressed then, okay?"

"Okay," I say and we both climb out of bed.

I rummage through the bag of clothes that was brought to me last night and pull out a grey turtleneck sweater and pair of blue jeans. I sneak extra peaks at Cillian as he dresses and he does the same to me. He dresses in a thick, charcoal grey sweater and dark pants. I notice as he pulls the sweater on over his head, that he has a tattoo near the V section of his pelvis. I don't get a good look at it before it's covered with his sweater.

"Ready?" he asks, fixing his sweater.

I sigh. "No, but like you said, momentary discomfort."

He smiles, and we make our way out of his room and down the long hall. We don't have to take the tunnels, because our magic is restored, and we can shift if needed.

The mood in the Academy is sullen and heavy. I feel it all around as we walk. I see more and more guards dressed in all black as we get closer to the auditorium. We pass the Grand Hall and I try not to look its way. The Headmistress is waiting outside her office, her eyes narrow as we approach. I become increasingly uncomfortable as we get closer.

She looks like she is on a war path.

We come to a stop in front of her as others file past us to get to the meeting. I notice Henry up ahead, waiting at the entrance, his eyes searching for me.

"Go on ahead, Miss Rodden. Professor Morris and I need to have a little chat." Her tone is deadly, and it sent chills throughout me.

I look to Cillian, who motions with his head for me to go. His demeanor has gone rigid in the Headmistress's presence. I give him a small smile and see the faintest upturn of the corner of his mouth in response.

There we go.

I say goodbye and make my way toward Henry. His face lights up when his eyes meet me. He hugs me tightly, and his arms are warm. He's wearing a deep forest green sweater that complements his eyes.

"How are you, Henry?" I ask as I pull away. He looks completely normal, which makes me happy.

"Better than ever! I cannot even describe it," he boasts. "I feel like I've been given a second chance because of you."

"Oh Henry, I was so afraid." I shake my head to try and get the thoughts of all the blood and screams out of my mind.

"I truly am so lucky to have met you."

Henry grabs my hand and holds it. I am uncomfortable, but do not want to pull away. Even after being with Cillian last night, I still can't deny that Henry means something to me. What that something is, I am not yet sure, but I know I never want to hurt him. I feel like I have betrayed him.

"We should probably go get our seats now, though. I think the assembly is starting soon."

"Okay, sure," I nod with a smile.

As Henry leads me away, I peek back over my shoulder to see Cillian disappearing into the Headmistress's office.

I bite the inside of my cheek, but put it out of my mind as Henry and I walk into the auditorium. Everyone is quieter than usual. Fear of the unknown displays on all the faces. Paranoia and rumors are spreading of what happened. There are familiar faces missing from the crowd, and I feel guilty. I don't know who all was affected and who all had been killed. All of those deaths fall on me, though. I had told the Headmistress to keep the dance scheduled, that everything would be fine.

I drop my eyes. I don't want the others to see my guilt in them.

Henry and I find seats near front of the room. Henry, sensing my change in mood, squeezes my hand gently. I look up at him and try to give him a reassuring smile, but fail.

"What's the matter?" he asks, concerned.

"People died last night, Henry. Some of our friends died last night. You, yourself almost died. All their blood is on my hands. Seeing everyone now…it's making it all real. I can't ignore it. Your mom wanted to cancel the dance, but I was the one who told her not to." My throat tightens, and it's hard to swallow.

Henry wraps his arm around my shoulder and pulls me into his chest. I don't resist.

"Cassie, it's okay. This is all on the Anarchy. They did this, not you," he tries to comfort me.

I dig my nails into the palms of my hands and sit up straight. I hear a commotion happening on the stage.

"Thanks, Henry," I say, and I sit further back in my chair.

Henry takes back his arm and we turn our attention to the professors gathering on the stage. The Headmistress approaches the podium, Cillian standing to her side.

Something is off.

Cillian stares straight ahead, above the crowd. A gnawing feeling starts in the pit of my stomach, but I tell myself I'm overreacting.

Cillian always looks that way.

The other professors on stage look just as fearful as the students. Professor Marian's eyes are puffy and red—a bruise darkens the left one. Professor Alberts is missing.

Oh no, not her…

Headmistress Ansley clears her throat from the podium. "Students, as you all know, last night, there was an attack on the Academy. Several students and professors, unfortunately, did not make it."

I feel like I am going to throw up—the bile rising into the back of my mouth. The sour, hot liquid tests my gag reflex.

"Now is the time to be strong. We will not let another attack blindside us like it did last night. Level Six students, the Joining Ceremony will take place next Saturday. Professor Morris will be training you this week to prepare you, and to test out potential matches. We need everyone at their peak strength right now. Levels One through Four are being sent home. Levels Five and Six, you will be staying to train."

My eyes dart back to Cillian, who hasn't moved. Several students in the crowd begin to murmur about the news.

"Headmistress Ansley, why did the Anarchy attack us like this? What happened to the students who were taken over? How was it even possible?" Catherine's small voice pipes up from off to the side. I don't know much about her. I believe she is a Level 5.

Several other students verbally agree with her questions.

The Headmistress looks annoyed. "The attack is still under investigation, but I can assure you that you are safe."

"But there has to be a reason why," Catherine protests, standing up from her seat.

"Yeah, we need answers!" a boy I do not know stands now as well.

I squirm in my seat uncomfortably.

"Enough, students!" the Headmistress booms into the microphone.

I stand even before I know what I am doing. I walk to the middle aisle and look out at all the faces. Some are angry, some are scared, others are sad. They all deserve to know the truth.

"Sit down, Miss Rodden!" Headmistress Ansley demands.

I ignore her.

Momentary discomfort. Momentary discomfort.

I stand up tall and take a deep breath before I begin.

"It's because of me," I project, so my voice is loud enough for everyone to hear.

Catherine sneers as several others laugh.

"Oh, really? You expect us to believe that? Come on, Cassie, you are not that special. We all know you have anger issues, but so do half the students here."

She doesn't believe me—none of them do, which is

understandable. What would an international, centuries-old terror group want with a 23-year-old Michigan girl like me?

"It's true. The Headmistress won't tell you, but I believe you all deserve to know the truth. The Anarchy did this because of me. They did this because they think I am the Chosen One from the Prophecy—the one with unmatchable power; the one that could tip the scales. I never meant for any of this to happen." I can't hold back my emotions any longer, and I let the tears fall. "I don't know why I am this person or how, or even if I truly am, but I can tell you this, I will fight for all of you. I will make sure nothing like this ever happens again."

"How can we trust you? How can we even know if you might be the Chosen One?" the boy I do not know asks, his glasses sliding down his nose. He pushes them back up as he waits for my response.

I search for the right words. Something, anything to help my case.

I close my eyes and take a deep breath. I turn my palms outward at my sides, and I picture my magic flowing out of my hands like water, spreading and expanding across the floor—reaching out to everyone, row by row. My power syncs with Henry and Cillian's quickly, which boosts signals for mine. I hear oohs and ahhs as I push my magic further. I open my eyes to see the lights have all dimmed and are flickering, the crowd is responding to the visuals of my magic reaching out and spreading. It is a beautiful gold, and it glows and shimmers as it vines out from my palms, wrapping itself around people's legs, their chairs, their arms.

The air begins to swirl around in the room, causing my hair to dance around my face. I feel us all becoming connected. I feel everything, all their worries and their pain. I feel myself lift slowly into the air. I don't even know what I'm doing. Cillian always says our magic works as a separate entity sometimes, so I guess I'm giving my magic time to speak for itself. It is like we are all becoming one, breathing together, our hearts beating in sync.

My magic slowly loses its strength the longer I hold the connection between everyone. I lower myself back to the floor as my magic retreats back to me. After my magic releases everyone, my knees give out, but Henry is there to catch me and keep me upright. Everyone chatters excitedly to each other, causing a hum to echo throughout the room.

"Silence! Everyone, silence!" the Headmistress shouts.

The buzz of excitement and curiosity dies as the Headmistress takes back control over the meeting. Henry and I make our way back to our seats. I search Cillian's face for any hint of what he's thinking, but he continues to stare off into the distance.

"Now, as I was saying, Levels One through Four will be sent home. You guardians have been notified. We will be increasing our security for the remaining students. A curfew will be enacted and strictly enforced. Students who remain will stay within the Academy's walls at all times. Trails will be closed. Of course, if you wish to leave, no one will stop you, but need I remind you that this is what we all have been working toward? We must raise up our arms to defend ourselves and the greater good. Now, please make your way back to your rooms to wait for further instruction. Levels One through Four, begin packing. You are all dismissed."

The students slowly funnel out of the auditorium. The gnawing feeling has only gotten worse, and I can tell something happened in Cillian's meeting with the Headmistress.

Did she find out about last night? How could she have? No, there must be something else going on.

Cillian descends from the stage and waits off to the side with his hands shoved deep into his pockets. I motion for Henry to go on without me and that I will join him shortly. Henry thinks nothing of it and heads out.

The air is heavy as the last remaining students file out and the room falls silent. I hate how good Cillian is at not letting his emotions spill through.

I walk up to him timidly, the invisible pull I feel between us growing stronger.

"Is everything okay?" I muster up.

"Professor," the Headmistress calls from behind me.

I look over my shoulder to see her holding the door open slightly. She is watching the two of us. She and Cillian exchange another silent conversation with their eyes.

Cillian nods his head slightly and the Headmistress leaves.

"What was all that about?" I ask, feeling out of the loop.

Cillian sighs. "We think there may be a lead on where the head of the Anarchy is."

"That's great!" Relief floods me.

"Yes, well, I will be leaving after the Joining Ceremony to investigate it."

Oh, that's not great.

"Oh, well, I mean, that's okay. I don't really see the point in sending you alone, when we'll most likely join the fight, but you are the man for the job."

I reach for his hand, but he pulls it away. I am confused and a little hurt.

"What's wrong, Cillian? You know you can talk to me."

He finally looks into my eyes and my heart knows.

"Last night was a mistake. It should have never happened."

"But it did happen." I take a step closer and he responds by taking a step back.

"Well, it shouldn't have. It was a very emotional evening, and you were there. You were basically throwing yourself at me, anyway. You told me to tell you last night if I did not have any feelings for you, so this is me doing what you asked."

My stomach drops. I open my mouth to say something, but not even a squeak escapes.

Thunder roars above the school and rain begins to pound against the roof. I feel exposed, and all I want to do is retreat into myself.

"I don't understand," I'm barely able to whisper.

"You never do. I say one thing, and you do the opposite. You are maddening. If that attack had not happened, you would have been with Henry anyway, so it does not matter what you and I did.

You got your rocks off either way."

I feel like I am drifting above my body, just watching what is going on.

How can he say these things to me right now?

"It wasn't like that…" I finally say softly.

"Well, I am tired of your little schoolgirl crush. It is pathetic."

Using my own words against me.

I stare down at my feet. The rain pounds harder on the roof of the school. I want to cry; I want to feel something other than the gaping hole inside my chest.

He continues, "I will work with you and Henry this next week on training. Our afterhours training cannot happen anymore. It is clear to me now that those sessions are giving you false hope. I do apologize if I have given you any indication that there was something between us."

"Does this have something to do with the Headmistress?"

"I have been put on your guard detail, so I will still be around, but please do not try and interact more than necessary. Cassandra, do you understand me?"

I feel his eyes on my face, but I can't look at him yet. I can't bring myself to face him. I'm afraid he will see the wound he's ripped open inside of me through my eyes.

"Cassandra, this is important. Do you understand me?" he repeats slowly.

"And what if Henry and I don't join? What if he's not the person my magic is meant to be joined with? And even if he is, you said a joined bond doesn't have to be intimate." I look back into his eyes now.

"Do you understand me?" I see the muscles in his jaw set.

Anger finds a home in my heart, filling the hole.

If he can be cold, so can I.

The lights in the room flicker as the storm roars outside.

"Yes, I understand you, Cillian." I spin around, leaving him behind.

"You need to control your magic, now more than ever," he yells after me.

His words only feed the darkness inside.

"Your parents worked hard to keep you safe, Cassandra. Do not let their deaths be in vain because you lose control."

I spin back around and fling Cillian across the room. He lands hard on the floor and comes sliding to a stop before hitting the wall. I don't care if he is injured. I can feel that he is alive, and that is good enough.

"Don't you dare bring my parents into this," I say sternly as he coughs on the ground.

"You can't even see how far your magic reaches," he says quietly, but I don't stick around to hear more.

"Asshole," I mutter to myself as the door closes behind me.

How could he do this? How could he say that it was nothing?

So many questions run through my head as I blindly walk to my room. I have completely forgotten about Henry until I hear a soft knock at my door a few moments after arriving.

"Come in," I say, wiping the residual tears from my eyes and sitting up straighter in bed.

Henry enters with caution, and I put on a tough face for him.

"Cassie, what is going on, other than the obvious? I can feel something is off with you."

Henry sits on my bed and looks at me with concerned eyes.

My defenses fall and I begin to sob. "I am such an awful person, Henry." I feel like I can tell Henry anything, and he deserves to know it all. "I just feel like nothing I do is ever good enough. All of a sudden, I am meant to be this 'Chosen One' that is supposed to unite everyone, but how am I supposed to do that when I can't even figure out my own feelings? Half the time I can barely even control my magic and I am scared. I'm scared because I can feel them growing stronger and because of the attacks that happened. Oh my god, and Yash and Nora and you." I hang my head into my hands and sob. "All I do is bring pain and suffering to the ones that love me."

Henry sits beside me patiently, listening to everything.

"Cassie—"

"And, to make things worse, you are one of the most amazing men I have ever met in my life and I have feelings for you, but…" I bite my lip, deliberating on what to say next.

"But you also have feelings for Cillian as well," Henry says softly.

I look at Henry and see only sadness displayed on his face.

"You know?"

"Of course, I do, Cassie. I'm not blind. I see the way you light up around him. It isn't hard to put two and two together, love. But that doesn't change the fact that I think I'm in love with you. Doesn't change the fact that when you and I are together, I feel like I can tackle the world. We are stronger together—that is undeniable. I meant what I said the other day. You make me realize I have not been whole my whole life. You saved me, Cassie, in more ways than one. I would not be here if it weren't for you. I believe in us. Maybe I am a fool, but at least I am fool that tries." He shrugs. I try to process everything he's just said.

Ugh, why does he have to be such a decent guy?

"Oh, Henry," I say, still sobbing.

"But you don't have to say anything. This is not about me. You are going through something right now that I cannot even possibly imagine. I'm not going anywhere, unless you want me to." He twiddles his thumbs in his lap as he finishes.

I throw my arms around him and hug him tightly.

"Thank you, Henry."

I let go of him after a moment and sit back.

"Would you mind staying with me tonight? I just don't want to be alone, especially with Nora still gone."

"Of course," he says eagerly. "I didn't want to sleep alone tonight either. It's eerie with Yash gone."

"I just want to know what's going to happen with Nora."

"Hopefully, we will know soon," he says.

I pat the space beside me on my small, twin-size bed. He

climbs up and gets underneath my heavy comforter. I nuzzle up to his chest and feel instantly more relaxed. I want to give Henry a chance, because even though I know my feelings for Cillian are true, Henry has always been there for me. I know now that I love both of them, just in different ways. It would be a disservice to my heart and Henry's, if I don't even consider him.

"But don't think I won't give Cillian a run for his money," Henry jokes.

"I don't think you have to worry about him, Henry. He has made it clear that I am not good enough."

"Bollocks. You're more than good enough," Henry says into my hair.

My eyes are so tired from all the crying I've done the past several days. The rain outside is calming and the sun peeks through the clouds. A brave ray maneuvers its way through my curtain and onto my shoulder. It feels nice.

"I want to know everything about you, Cassie. When you're ready, that is."

"Maybe in a little bit, but for now, I kind of just want to lay here with you, if that's all right?"

"Of course it is," Henry says as he gives me a light squeeze.

CHAPTER THIRTEEN

Henry and I lay in my bed for hours. Most of the time is spent in silence, just enjoying each other, but the other half is me telling him everything and anything about myself. He, in return, tells me anything I want to know about him. Henry has a way of making everything brighter. I feel like I have known him for years. We laugh so much that my sides hurt. It is easy being with him.

"Oh my god, it's dark out now!" Henry exclaims as we get over a laughing fit.

I don't believe him, so I look out the window.

"Holy crap! You're right!" My stomach starts to growl, and I make the realization that dinner is probably over already.

How have I gone all day without eating?

"I don't know about you, but I am absolutely starving." Henry pats his stomach.

Oh no, did he hear my stomach? That would be so embarrassing.

"I think we might have missed dinner already. I am so sorry. I hadn't realized how much time we wasted."

"Don't worry, love, I know where they keep the good stuff. And this time was not wasted," he says with a wink.

Two soft knocks come at my door. Henry and I look at each other, confused.

"Cassandra," Cillian's voice echoes through the door.

Henry gets upset and he gets off my bed. My palms are instantly sweaty and my pulse quickens. My leg gets tangled in the sheets, and I trip getting off my bed. Henry tries to catch me, but I tumble to the ground with a loud thud.

The commotion causes Cillian to burst through the door.

"Cassandra!" Cillian's voice is frantic.

I look up at Cillian, Henry already helping me to my feet.

Cillian clears his throat and places his hands together behind his back. "I apologize, I thought you were in danger."

I roll my eyes.

"Don't worry, mate. *I've* got her," contempt is wrapped around Henry's words.

Cillian ignores Henry. "Are you all right?"

"Yes, I am fine. What do you want, Cillian? Why are you here?"

The tension in my small room is overwhelming.

"Well, other than the fact that I am still supposed to be watching over you, I have some news for you about Nora."

My mood instantly changes, and I become impatient that he hasn't already blurted out the information.

"What is it? Is she okay? Where is she? Can I see her?" I can't get the questions out fast enough.

"She's okay. She is traumatized over it all. She is aware that Mister Patel is deceased, but we withheld the information that she caused it. She, like the others, does not remember much from the whole ordeal. The affected students will be back in class tomorrow and be able to return to their rooms tomorrow evening. We need everyone training right now."

"And anything more on the possible insider?" Henry interjects. I notice he's standing taller and puffing out his chest a tad.

Men…

Cillian turns his body slightly toward Henry to address his question, but he keeps his eyes on me.

"No, nothing yet." I hear the frustration in Cillian's tone.

My stomach gurgles loudly in the silence.

"Erm, we were actually just about to go get some food. We did not realize how late it had gotten. We were…preoccupied," Henry says. I know he is trying to get rid of Cillian, while also making him jealous.

Cillian's eyes squint slightly. "Perfect, I am starving, and with Cassandra having twenty-four/seven guard duty now, I would be happy to accompany you both wherever you're going."

I groan. "What? You never said anything about that earlier." My mind goes back over our conversation from earlier, but so much of it has been eclipsed by my heartbreak.

"Well, if you had not flung me against a wall, I would have gotten to that bit," Cillian says coolly.

Henry suppresses a laugh, while I smile and scoff.

"Some would say it was well deserved," I say, staring into his eyes.

I feel a twinge of pain in my heart as he stands there in front of me. My lips tingle with the memories of last night.

"Hmm, well… I will oversee most of the guard duties. At night, though, a guard will be posted at your door. So, shall we *all* go get some food, then?" Cillian looks at the both of us.

Henry and I exchange glances, but this is a fight I am not going to win.

With another groan, I slip on some moccasins and we file out of my room.

The awkward silence as we walk down the hall is almost unbearable. Cillian and Henry sandwich me in between them. Cillian on my right, Henry on my left.

Our footsteps are the only sounds that echo down the deserted hallway. No one dares to be caught outside of their rooms right now. We pass several guards, but that is it. I don't like how quiet things are. It only magnifies everything—every awkward moment, every sad thought, every growl and grumble of my stomach.

The outsides of my arms tingle with electricity as my magic reaches outward to both of them, and my hands feel unusually warm.

I cross my arms as we walk to avoid an accidental hitting of hands. Cillian notices this immediately.

"Are you cold?" he asks.

"No," I say, with a little too much venom.

Henry muffles a laugh again.

We make our way to the Dining Hall and back into the preparation area. Henry flicks on the lights and investigates the fridge. I hang back by one of the counters and Cillian stands by the door.

"Hmmm... looks like we've got shepherd's pie or bangers and mash," Henry lists off.

"I thought you said you knew where the good stuff was, Henry?" I tease.

Henry chuckles and pulls out a few containers of food.

To be honest, I'm not really all that hungry anymore. I feel slightly nauseated from all the negative energy between the three of us, but I don't want Cillian to see how much of a mess I am beneath my façade. It is physically painful to be around him right now. I never knew my heart could break into as many pieces as it has. Every word, every look from Cillian causes another piece to break off. And then there is Henry, slowly trying to put all the pieces back together again.

We eat in silence, and it is actually pretty delicious. Warm comfort food sure does have a way of making things suck just the tiniest bit less. Cillian barely touches his food, which makes me think he was lying when he said he was hungry as well.

We don't stay for long and are soon headed back to my room. We pass a few more guards on our way, and each one is a brutal reminder of what all is going on. The whole school feels like the life and air has been sucked out of it.

"Well, Mister Ansley, I've got it from here. Have a good

night."

"Um, excuse me, no. I told him he could actually spend the night since Nora is gone. I don't really want to be alone right now," I interject.

"Sorry, but the Headmistress wants everyone in their own rooms," Cillian replies, unfazed.

"Mum didn't mention anything about that to me earlier." Henry challenges, glaring at Cillian.

"Are you disobeying school orders right now, Mister Ansley?"

"Okay, put 'em away, lads." I am tired and don't want to deal with either of them anymore. "Henry, I'll see you tomorrow. Stop by my room and walk me to class?"

"Of course," Henry replies, breaking away from his glare.

I give Henry a long hug and snuggle my head into his soft, but firm chest. The hug probably lasts a little longer than it should, but I can tell it makes Cillian uncomfortable, and I enjoy every second of it.

"You sure you'll be okay?" Henry asks as he releases me.

"Yeah, I mean, what's the worst that can happen in a night?" I joke to try and disguise my anxiety. For the first time in my life, I don't want to be alone. Being alone is no longer my safe haven. Being alone means having to face my demons on my own, and I am afraid of them now.

"You sure do have an interesting sense of humor, don't you, Cassie?" Henry smiles.

Henry gives Cillian one last glare before departing slowly down the hallway. I watch him go until he rounds a corner and can no longer be seen.

My smile slowly fades, and then it is just Cillian and me standing there. My eyes have recovered enough to once again start forming tears. They sting, and I can't bear to look at him.

"Cassandra," Cillian says softly.

But I don't want to hear anything he has to say.

"Sorry, but don't you remember? No fraternization," I say as I hurry into my room and slam the door in his face.

Once inside, I slump down to the floor and sit with my back against the door. I pull my knees to my chest, bury my head in my arms, and let the tears flow. I try to be quiet, for fear of Cillian hearing me.

I contemplate shifting into Henry's room, but a part of me—which I am trying desperately to drown deep inside of me—wants to stay, because I know Cillian is still outside my door. I still feel my magic beckoning to him through the door. I am alone, but alone with him, which provides some comfort.

Just a pathetic schoolgirl. How is it so easy for him to be so cruel?

I use my magic to pull my pillow and blanket off my bed. I set my pillow up and drape the blanket over me as I lay down on the hard, carpeted floor. Even if Cillian doesn't have feelings for me, I want to be close to him, which makes me hate myself even more.

Stupid, stupid heart.

I cry myself to sleep. Something I haven't really done since my parents passed. I spent years building up walls to seal my heart away. Not letting anyone in. I did all of that, just to have Cillian destroy it in a matter of seconds. I know it is better to feel, though, because it reminds me that I'm real. Sometimes it feels like I have lost myself behind all those walls. Feeling like something else was taking my place. I have to keep everything together now, though. No more losing control. It is not just my life that depends on me getting my shit together, but everyone else's at this school. It is time to start embracing this whole prophecy. Time to start accepting that I am the Chosen One.

CHAPTER FOURTEEN

I am awoken by a few knocks at my door. I feel extremely confused as I look around my room, not remembering why I'm on the floor, and I have no idea what time it is. Light shines in through my window. I sit for a second and everything comes back to me.

Crap! Class!

I jolt up and hurry into the bathroom to look at myself in the mirror.

Hair? A mess. Makeup? Smeared. Body odor? Most likely.

"Cassie?" Henry calls from outside.

I am too busy frantically washing my face to answer him. I hear him speaking with someone else, but their voices are too muffled to tell who.

As I finish scrubbing my face, Cillian and Henry barge into my room.

I groan in frustration. "People have to stop doing that!"

I'm not necessarily frustrated with them; I'm frustrated that I overslept on the floor and am now running late. That both of them were witnessing me being a hot mess is just a bonus.

"Sorry," Henry apologizes immediately.

Cillian observes my sleeping arrangements on the floor and I grow embarrassed. I begin to strip down to my bra and underwear so I can change into fresh gym clothes. I'm so flustered, I don't even think about them being in the room.

Henry clears his throat. "Erm, Cassie,"

I'm putting an old long-sleeved top on over my head and I freeze. My cheeks burn with the realization that I am practically naked in front of them. In front of both of them.

Cillian chuckles softly.

"Shit, sorry. Can you both just wait outside please? I just need a moment. Clearly, I am fine. I am not in danger at this moment in time."

They shuffle out of my room, and I finish getting dressed. I run my brush through my knotted hair and tie it into a high ponytail.

"Did she sleep on the floor last night?" I hear Henry ask Cillian through the door.

Oh, great.

I take one final look in the mirror before I head out.

Ugh, it will have to do.

My worn top and plain black leggings will suffice. I normally just wear this as pajamas, but I didn't want to waste more time putting together something cute. Besides, I have a sports bra on underneath. Don't have the time to be cute anymore.

It will all be just fine. Just keep telling yourself that.

Cillian and Henry are waiting patiently outside my door. They're both wearing black joggers, but Henry dons a blue shirt, while Cillian's is dark grey.

As we make our way to training, I feel a kink in my neck from sleeping on the floor. I rub it as inconspicuously as possible while we walk, because both of them are keeping me under a microscope.

"So, Nora will be back today, right? And the others?"

Yes, distract them with conversation.

Cillian nods, but keeps his eyes forward.

I sigh as we round the corner and I push open the doors to the Training Room. Just beyond them, the other students are waiting in the center of the room. It doesn't take me long to spot her short stature off to the side of the group.

Nora.

She looks run down and tired. Her face is paler than normal. Her shoulders slump forward, and her arms are crossed. She and the other affected students wear plain gray sweatsuit ensembles.

I sprint toward her. "Nora!"

My voice causes her to whip her head in my direction. She immediately uncrosses her arms and runs toward me. We meet each other halfway and I hug her as tightly as I can. Her body collapses into my arms, but I hold her with ease.

Her body starts to shake, and I feel her tears seep into my shirt.

"He's gone, Cassie. He's gone. They wouldn't let me see you. They-they think I did something to cause it all. I-I would never hurt a-anyone," she sobs into my shoulder.

"Shh, I know. I know, Nora. It's okay," I try to comfort her.

Be a leader, Cassie. Be strong.

She pulls away from me slightly, but I keep her in the embrace. "They say I attacked you. Is that true? They say I attacked both you and Henry."

I look around and find everyone watching us. Henry has come to stand beside me, but gives Nora and me space.

I deliberate on what my next words should be. "Yes, Nora, you did."

I feel her knees give out slightly. Her eyes look like she has been rubbing them raw from all her crying.

"Henry, I am so sorry. I didn't hurt either of you, though, did I?" Nora searches my face for the answer. She takes a step back from my embrace to stare at us both.

I look at Henry and he tilts his head forward slightly, giving me the go ahead.

I clear my throat. "You stabbed Henry…in the heart."

I wait anxiously for her reaction. Confusion spreads across her face.

"But how-how is he alive? How are you alive, Henry?" Her eyes bounce between us.

"Um, well, Cillian and I brought him back," I say softly.

Her next reaction is not one I expect.

"I bloody knew it. You are the Chosen One. I called it!" Her sobs turn into laughter and a smile spreads across her face. "No witch has ever been able to do that before. Oh my god, there is a light in all of this darkness."

A few of the others shift uncomfortably and I hear Lauren scoff to the side of me. She too is wearing the unflattering ensemble. I hadn't realized she had also been one of the students affected in the attack.

"Well, I don't know if there's a way to confirm it, but the Anarchy thinks I am, so…" I trail off, not knowing what more to say.

Nora is about to say more when Cillian starts class.

"Okay, everyone, now I know some of you may be wondering why I have asked Level Fives to join us," I look around now to see unfamiliar faces. "Well, the simple answer is that we need them. We need everyone we can gather right now, and having them train with you will make them stronger. These next few days, I will be pushing you all and your magic to limits we have not seen yet.

That and the fact that we are no longer an even number.

I quickly count the remaining Level 6s and it looks like we are down to only seven. My heart aches, as I know Yash had been killed, but it appears Abigail and Caleb are also no longer with us. But with the Level 5s, we are an even fourteen.

As Cillian continues to speak, I notice other professors and guards are wheeling in boards holding an assortment of weapons— knives, swords, spears, all sorts of weapons other than guns. In History, I learned that witches are above guns. Guns make things too easy and never show true power and strength.

"It will be trying, and it will be strenuous, but this is the time where we need to figure out if you are cut out for this. So, for our first exercise this morning, I need everyone to form a line, please," Cillian directs.

We all murmur to each other as we shuffle to form a line. Cillian walks to the opposite side of the room. We all watch him curiously to try and figure out what the exercise will entail. A guard has wheeled over a board full of assorted knives to where Cillian is headed.

I gulp as I take my place in line behind Henry. Nora stands behind me. She makes small talk with the person behind her. I believe she told me a while ago the girl's name is Sarah. She and Nora roomed together Sarah's first year here. She is a Level 5, but she too enjoys herbs, like Nora. Sarah has strawberry blonde hair pulled into two braids.

I shift my weight from side to side as my anxiety builds. There are only two people in front of Henry, one of them being Lauren.

"Okay, everyone, listen up," Cillian shouts from the other side of the track. He isn't too far away, probably only 25 yards. "You will each take turns. You will step up and face me. The object of this exercise is to simply stop the blade."

Is he really about to throw knives at us? Thank goodness I am not first up.

I notice a few medical personnel walk into the room and stand on the sidelines.

"Okay, first up, let's go."

Damon is up first. He doesn't seem nervous as he steps away from the line and toward Cillian.

"Oh joy, a game my father and I used to play. This should be fun," I hear Lauren say under her breath.

Jesus, that explains so much.

Cillian picks up a knife, and without warning, sends it flying toward Damon's face. Damon panics and before he has time to react, the blade slices the side of his ear. Damon collapses to the ground screaming as blood pours from the side of his head. A medic rushes to Damon and helps him to the sideline.

Cillian is visibly disappointed.

"I told you all that things are going to become more difficult. I expect better of you all. Next!" he yells.

Lauren eagerly steps up and places a hand over her eyes.

"She has got to be kidding." Nora says behind me.

I am a little nervous for Lauren. Cillian doesn't let it faze him, and he sends one soaring toward her. The blade whines as it pierces through the air.

Lauren holds up her other hand just in time and stops the blade from hitting her. She keeps the blade suspended in the air as she uncovers her eyes. She smiles and lets the knife fall to the ground.

"Very well done, Lauren, but cockiness will not always play out in your favor," Cillian warns.

Lauren rolls her eyes and makes her way to the end of the line. She stops briefly as she passes me, "Don't choke, *Chosen One*," she sneers and cackles before continuing.

I brush off her words as Henry steps up for his turn. My palms perspire in anticipation. Cillian eyes Henry up and down and then selects the knife he wants to send Henry's way. His hand hovers over a few different ones, but he ends up picking one of the larger ones. I sense Henry's anxiety as Cillian toys with the knife in his hands. It isn't long before he sends it flying, only this time it has more speed than the others he's thrown.

I almost can't bear to watch as it barrels toward Henry. Everything slows and I see that it is going to hit Henry dead on. I open my mouth to shout, as Henry hadn't thrown his hand up yet, but just as it is about to pierce his face, the knife abruptly stops. It comes within a centimeter of his eye.

I close my mouth and clap excitedly with the rest of the class as Henry smirks at Cillian. Henry reaches up and grabs the knife from the air, looks at it, and then tosses it aside.

Atta boy.

Cillian smirks back. "Very well done, Mr. Ansley. I see you've gotten better at your telekinesis." I hear the animosity hidden in Cillian's praise. "Next!"

Oh crap, my turn.

"You got this, Cassie," Nora encourages from behind me.

Henry turns, walks up to me, and whispers into my ear, "You've got this, okay, love?"

"We do not have all day," Cillian says, annoyed.

Henry looks into my eyes and I nod. He makes his way to the

back of the line as I step before Cillian. Damon's blood has begun to dry on the floor. I try not to focus on that.

I can do this. It's just a knife. I've brought someone back from the dead. I can stop a silly little knife.

Cillian picks out another large knife.

Oh, come on.

I frown at him as he settles into his stance.

Concentrate. Concentrate.

Cillian pulls back his arm to prepare to throw the knife.

"Watch her choke," I hear Lauren say, just barely loud enough for me to hear.

Lauren's shrill voice leaks into my thoughts, disrupting my concentration as Cillian lets the knife loose toward me. I panic and duck out of the way before it can hit me.

Lauren lets out a cackle behind me. "See! I told everyone she'd choke. Some Chosen One. We are all doomed."

"Shut the hell up, Lauren! You did that on purpose!" Nora defends me.

I stand up and look at Cillian. He shakes his head in disappointment. I let out a groan of frustration.

"Again!" I yell at Cillian, taking my stance again.

"You failed, get to the back of the line," Cillian says.

"Again," I demand. I will not back down from this. I need to prove to the others that I can be the Chosen One they need.

Cillian sees my determination. "Very well, then."

He uses his magic to lift another knife from the board and

sends it soaring. This time, I am ready. I steady my breathing, focus on slowing everything down. Light gleams off the knife as it twirls through the air. I see the tip racing toward me. I picture the tip disintegrating just as it is about to hit me.

From the tip, down the blade, to the hilt. Disintegrate.

And sure enough, that is what happens. The blade disintegrates just before it collides with me. I hear the ash fall to a pile before me, the room silent. I smirk when I see Cillian. He tilts his head forward slightly in approval.

I hear a couple of my classmates clap for me, most likely Nora and Henry.

"Next!" Cillian yells.

I can't help but smile as I turn around to head to the back of the line. Nora reaches out for a high five as I pass by. I slap her hand and continue on. Others look at me cautiously as I pass, but I keep my head held high, especially when passing Lauren. She has her arms crossed and is glaring at me, so nothing out of the ordinary.

We all take a few more turns, but it seems like Cillian is growing bored, as we all end up passing eventually. Damon has returned after receiving aid from the medic. His left ear is wrapped and bandaged, but he perseveres. Even with all the reinforcements brought in, we still do not have a witch with an affinity for healing others. A part of me wanted to try to heal Damon but I needed to be careful now with my magic.

"Let's ramp this up, shall we?" Cillian boasts. "Multiple knives at once."

Seriously?!

Everyone in line lets out a groan.

"But I'll let you have an advantage. Pair up with the person you think your magic pairs well with best and reform the line," Cillian finishes.

I keep my eyes on Cillian as he looks everywhere but at me. Naturally, Henry and I pair up, and we're the first ones in the new line.

"Cassandra, Henry, step up," Cillian says as he uses his magic to lift about 20 knives into the air. They all hover around him; their tips pointing toward us.

Henry and I exchange nervous glances.

A handful come at the both of us and we dodge, each using our magic to fling knives away from the other at the same time. Henry trips, though and crashes to the floor defeated, but Cillian keeps hurdling knives at us. I sprint to where Henry is and stand in front of him as the next wave of knives heads our way. I use my magic to pull a spear off one of the boards and into my hands. I spin the spear around, deflecting the knives, giving Henry time to recover.

The attack stops after Cillian runs out of knives on the board.

I am out of breath, but delighted with myself.

"She cheated! No one said we could use the other weapons!" Lauren complains from the side.

"Oh my god, Lauren! Do you ever stop complaining?" I retort. I have had enough of her constant whining.

"No one ever said you couldn't use the other weapons,"

Cillian says. "Do you think the weapons were just there for decoration? Use your surroundings and take advantage of them. You will be put into situations where you have very few or no weapons, so you have to be smart and use what is available to you."

I scowl at Lauren, but then I hear it—the high pitch whine of a knife soaring through the air. Pain rips across my cheek as the sharp blade slices through my skin and muscle. I drop to my knees and hold my hand to my cheek. I feel skin dangling off and blood filling my hand.

"Cassie!" Henry yells as he and a medic hurry to my side.

"Don't touch me!"

They both back off.

Anger roars through me.

Really? A cheap shot?

I feel bad for yelling at Henry, but I also need people to know that I am not weak.

"Don't ever assume your opponent is done," Cillian says calmly.

I look up at him from where I am on the ground. I know this is a test, but at the same time, how can he treat me this way?

"Was that absolutely necessary?!" I scream as I make my way to my feet.

"I know you can handle it," he says sternly.

Doesn't mean I should have to put up with it.

"Come on, Cassandra, focus. If you're meant to be the Chosen One, there is a lot more you're going to have to learn. You cannot for one second turn your back."

I withdraw my hand from my cheek and let the blood run down freely. Several others gasp at the sight.

I feel my magic pounding through my veins, begging to be unleashed. I concentrate on using the magic to repair my cheek. I feel the fibers pulling back together. It doesn't take long for the wound to seal itself.

I ignore the various reactions from the others and look at all of the knives scattered around the floor. There are about 70 or so various knives strewn about the ground from the day so far.

Perfect.

"Henry, I am going to need you to move to the side, okay?" I ask him in a much nicer tone.

He complies. He and the medic retreat to the side, where the others are standing.

The lights flicker as I stretch my hands out to the sides and lift them up slowly. The knives quiver for a few seconds on the ground, but all slowly rise and point toward Cillian.

"So, Professor, what was it you were saying about knowing you can handle something?" I smirk deviously.

I send the knives soaring toward him without giving him the chance to prepare himself. He uses his magic to pull another spear off the wall like I had done. I use the knives as a front and quickly sprint behind them.

Cillian effortlessly deflects the knives. The last row is just about to reach him, so I jump into the air. I shift midair without hesitation to drop on top of him.

He anticipates this move.

He shifts out of my way and my knee falls hard onto the floor. I don't see where he went, but I feel that he is close. I look around frantically, but I am soon sent flying across the room. As soon as I land on the floor, I am up in the air again, incapacitated. His magic has its hold on me, squeezing my body tighter, and I see him now.

I can barely breathe as I struggle against his hold.

"Now, class, there are a few ways to get out of hold I'm using here." Cillian uses this as a teaching moment.

Use your surroundings.

I see that I am near the empty cart that had held all the knives. I will my magic to grab onto the cart. I suppress my smile when I know I have it.

I fling it as hard as I can at Cillian before he has a chance to say more. The cart crashes into him, breaking his hold on me. I fall to the ground, and as soon as my feet touch, I sprint toward him.

Cillian is already bouncing back to his feet as I try to land a blow, but his reflexes are quick.

We fight together, neither one giving the other a chance at cessation. We flow together so effortlessly, it is like we are fighting ourselves—consistently knowing what the other will do next.

I am extremely frustrated by this. I am still angry at Cillian. I know he isn't being truthful with me, I just don't know why. So many questions are mounting with no leads on answers. But there is one thing he cannot deny, and that is how powerful our magic is together.

I want this to be over with already. I sweep his legs out from underneath him and use my hands to push him down faster.

Once on his back, I climb on top of his chest and pin down his arms with my legs. I beckon one of the smaller knives to my open hand and it comes willingly. I press the cool blade against his throat.

Checkmate.

Everyone watches and waits from the side to see what will happen next. Instead of struggling, Cillian finally looks at me. We are both breathing heavily, and I'm still sitting on top of him, frozen.

"Class, sometimes in battle, you'll never know who you might have to sacrifice, or go up against." He keeps his eyes on me as he addresses the class. "The Anarchy gains new supporters every day. I have seen friends go up against friends. I've even seen joined pairs have to kill each other. All because one side wants to cause chaos in our world. You'll be put into tough situations. So, Cassandra," he addresses me directly now, "do you have what it takes? Do it, do it right now. Press the blade deeper and win."

Is he serious?

"I-I—"

"You have gotten stronger, Cassandra. Do it," he eggs me on.

The hand holding the knife begins to shake and my mind races.

"What are you doing, Cillian? Is this some sort of test?" my voice trembles.

"Do it!" he screams at me now.

I lift the knife above my head as the ground begins to shake.

"Just shut up!" I scream back at him.

"Do it! Prove to me and everyone that you can be strong! That you can kill for what's right!"

I think he is serious. How can he be serious? I'm not actually going to kill him.

The lights in the gym surge and flicker.

"Do it!"

"SHUT UP!" My scream echoes throughout the room, causing some of the lightbulbs to burst. But I know I can't do it. I drop the knife and roll off him. The rumblings slow and subside.

"But not strong enough," Cillian mutters under his breath in disappointment.

He hops back up to his feet as if nothing happened.

"Next pair, let's go. Henry, Cassandra, go run some laps." Cillian stops as he passes Henry, "Oh, and Henry, never leave your partner to fight on their own."

"Professor, when can we learn the things that you were doing with her? You two seem very *in sync*." Lauren's emphasis catches my attention.

God, I hate this bitch.

"We will run through this a couple more times, break for lunch, and then I will show you how to do some of the things that Cassandra and I did. Next pair."

I groan and Henry comes over to help me up. He gently examines where my cheek had been spliced earlier.

"Jesus, Cassie, it's as if it never happened," Henry says in disbelief.

I ignore him though, and shake my chin from his grasp. "Come on, let's get these laps over with."

I'm not mad at Henry, but I don't want any more attention on me.

Henry and I run our laps silently as the others rotate through the exercise. Nora and her friend Sam actually do a good job working together. Certainty not as well and she and Yash worked together, but I am thankful for this.

After about an hour, we break for lunch. It is quiet the whole time. Some people are already tired from the training. I eat my cold ham sandwich quickly, and tell Henry and Nora I need to step outside and get some fresh air.

"The guards won't allow you to go off on your own," Nora warns.

"Yeah, plus Cillian is watching us all still," Henry says with a hint of sour.

Cillian had seated himself a few tables away with a couple of other professors who joined him in training.

"I'll be quick. I just need to get away for a moment. I have a plan," I reassure them.

I get up and tell one of the guards that I need to use the restroom. He nods and tells me that he'll have to follow me. I tell him that is fine, but that he'll have to wait outside the door for privacy.

Once inside the bathroom, I close my eyes and concentrate on shifting outside. I picture the still pond where Cillian and I used to train. It doesn't take long for the tingling to come and I feel the cool breeze of the wind on my face.

I am really getting the hang of this.

I smile to myself as I open my eyes and see the pond. It is very gray and gloomy outside. All the grass has turned different shades of tan and brown as it slowly dies for the season. Most of the leaves have fallen by now.

I sit down by the tree and breathe in the fresh air. Everything just feels so heavy inside the school. I need to have some of the weight lifted off my shoulders. I shiver, as my still damp, long-sleeved shirt doesn't offer much defense against the wind. But it is also refreshing. I close my eyes and rest my chin on my knees.

Birds sing in the distance, and the therapeutic rustling of fallen leaves on the ground calms me. Winter is approaching. It will be here any day now.

I feel his magic before I hear him speak.

"Cassandra."

Cillian.

My heart decides to drop and hide deep inside my stomach. His sweet voice causes my mind to revisit the other night. His touch and his kiss. I shake away the thoughts and clear my throat.

"I'll come back soon. I just needed a break." I say, still staring at the pond.

"You're getting really good at shifting."

Oh, wow, a compliment? How nice of him. I roll my eyes.

I don't respond.

"Cassandra, I, um, I'm..." he struggles with himself, "I'm sorry."

I hear that his words are genuine. It makes me feel bad for acting rude to him, but I can't just act like my pain isn't valid. He broke me first.

"Sorry for what exactly?" I finally say as I stand and turn to face him.

I want to hear him say it.

He looks worn down in the natural light. More so than he did inside the school. He has light blue circles under his eyes, and his face is paler than normal. I try not to let his appearance deter me from being strong.

He ignores me and steps toward me, which catches me off guard. He reaches for my cheek, where he had cut me in training. I hold my breath as the back of his fingers brush my jawline. The butterflies return and my heart peeks out from its hiding place. The butterflies beckon my heart to come out and play with them.

I start to lean into his touch and I snap myself back.

"I'm fine," I say curtly.

Cillian chuckles slightly and I see the corner of his mouth turn upward into a smirk.

Stay strong. Stay strong.

He withdraws his hand and he seems to flip a switch in his eyes, shutting off his emotions.

"You can't sneak off like this again, do you understand me?"

"How did you even know I was gone?" I deflect.

"I told you I'd be watching you. It is my duty to make sure that you are safe, Cassandra."

"But I had gone into the bathroom. Did the guard tell you? Did you break into the bathroom?"

Come on, say it. You could feel me get further away, couldn't you? Because your magic reaches out for me just like mine does to you.

He shakes his head, frustrated.

That's what I thought.

"Why can't you just be honest with me?! Once, Cillian, just for once, be honest with me and be honest with yourself."

I wait for a response that I know will never come.

"It's not that easy, Cassandra."

"Welp, I came out here to get some peace of mind, and since I can't even do that, I will be going back. Happy?"

I start to storm past him, but I his hand catches my arm. The sun breaks through the clouds and shines down on us. I am surprised by the sudden warmth.

He acts like he is going to say something, but just as quickly as he grabbed my arm, he releases it. The sun tucks behind another cloud, and the sky returns to the gray it was before.

"Don't let the others know about the weather manipulation yet. It's something that no one else has ever been able to do. Sometimes it's best not to show our hand, and we don't know if someone here could be testing what powers you have," Cillian says cryptically.

"What do you mean, 'weather manipulation'?"

He looks at me shocked. "Do you really not notice?"

"Obviously not, if I just asked you what you meant by it."

"When you are angry, sad, or nervous, it storms. When you're happy, it's nice out."

Cillian calling attention to this makes me think back to the recent times it had stormed here and it starts to make sense. But I am still angry and, weather manipulation or not, I want to go back inside and away from him.

"K," I say and shift back into the bathroom I had left.

I open the door to see the guard still standing there.

Knew it.

I think about what Cillian said as I make my way back to Nora and Henry, who are now waiting by the entrance to the Dining Hall.

"We saw Cillian leave; did he catch you?" Nora questions as I approach.

Henry is brooding behind Nora and I try to not make the situation more awkward.

"Yeah, um, no, he didn't catch me," I lie.

This seems to make Henry feel better.

The guards have started to corral students back toward the Training Room. Nora looks exhausted, and I feel bad for her.

"Don't worry, Nora, just a few more hours, then we can go back to our room," I do my best to comfort her as we head back.

She looks up and smiles briefly, but drops her eyes back to her feet. "It just still doesn't feel real. I keep looking to my side expecting him to be there."

I can hear the pain in her words. I wrap my arm around her shoulders and hold her close as we walk with the others.

"I know, Nora."

We are just about to reach the entrance when Henry stops me. Nora notices and turns back. I nod for her to go on and we will catch up.

I am nervous in front of him right now.

"What's up?" I ask.

"You okay?"

"Yep. I am as okay as I can be right now."

"I'm so sorry for you having to go it alone with Cillian in there earlier." He hangs his head.

"Henry, you have nothing to be sorry for. Cillian is just being a hard ass. I made it so, it was only me. Don't worry." I place my hand on his cheek for reassurance without thinking.

Henry gently takes my waist and pulls me closer.

Cillian walks by us and clears his throat. "Come on, we're getting started."

Part of me is thankful for Cillian's interruption. I hear Henry groan slightly in frustration, but we quickly follow after him.

We all gather in the middle of the room as Cillian begins to explain shifting to the group.

"The more you train yourself in shifting, the further you'll be able to travel. At most, you can hope to shift a couple miles, but there have been some witches known to shift countries."

"Can we shift with someone? Like, if we touch someone, or something while we are shifting, will they shift too?" Nora questions.

"Yes, but it takes training. Just like the distance you can travel, you will be able to shift with small objects at first, and then bigger ones as your ability grows."

The class nods in unison.

"For this exercise though, I want us all to venture outside to the courtyard. So, if you please, everyone, let us head out there."

We all shuffle our way back out of the Training Room and into the courtyard. It is still gloomy, and the wind has picked up. Nora's tiny frame shivers in her sweatshirt, so I go over and wrap my arm around her shoulders. We all form a line horizontal to Cillian.

The wind keeps nipping at my nose and fingertips. I try to ignore it, but my teeth begin to chatter. Cillian continues to explain shifting, just like he had with me weeks ago. I can't help my mind from wandering back to the night Cillian first taught me—the pond and the moonlight. It seems so long ago.

A strong gust blows, and I shiver hard against Nora. I decide I have had enough and want to go grab a jacket. Cillian is explaining about the tingling sensation and how we should all shoot for shifting a few feet in front of us first, or at least to where he is standing. I let go of Nora as everyone closes their eyes to try to shift. I take this moment to picture my room, but even before the picture comes into view, I am greeted with the warm, stuffy air that always encompasses our room.

Hell yes.

I quickly look for a jacket for myself and one for Nora. I grab a black and a blue one that are lying on a chair and shift back outside. The cold air shocks my skin, so I quickly put on my jacket. Cillian gives me a look of disapproval, but I just smile back deviously and give him a wink.

Nora hears the crunch of my shoes come and go on the gravel, so she opens her eyes. She is surprised when I toss her the other jacket, but she is grateful. I motion for her to go back to practicing. I quickly shift to where Cillian is standing and wait for the others. Henry is not long behind me, except he looks a little pale after shifting.

I reach for his hand and squeeze it gently. "Good job," I whisper.

This seems to help the color return to his face.

"How are you so good at this already?" Henry asks.

"Oh, you know, just a natural, I guess," I say, not wanting to let anyone know that I have already received training on shifting.

Cillian chuckles as he overhears my lie and I shoot him a glare.

Lauren seems to have no trouble with this exercise as well. I didn't even noticed that she is on the other side already, looking bored out of her mind. She examines her nails as she waits, cocking her hip to the side.

A few minutes go by, and almost everyone shifts their way

over to the other side, everyone except Nora. Frustration is written all over her forehead as she struggles to execute a shift. Cillian is beside her, trying to help her, but it is to no avail. Some of the others have grown impatient, especially Lauren.

"It's okay, Nora," Cillian says to her. "Some witches never learn to shift, and that's okay. We cannot all have the same level of power in each task." His words are kind, but I can tell she isn't listening. Nora is stubborn, which is one of the many things I love about her.

"Or maybe she's just not that magical after all?" Lauren sneers. "Probably shouldn't have ever let her in, if you ask me."

My blood begins to boil, and I step toward her. "Shut up, Lauren. Nora is one of the most talented herbologists this Academy has ever seen. How dare you say that about her?"

Lauren counters by taking a step closer to me. "Well, if she's so great at herbology, maybe she's the one who took control of all our minds. Maybe it was that witchy MDMA she gave us. If she's so great, you know?"

"Lauren, enough!" Cillian yells. I hear Nora start to sniffle beside him.

But Lauren is relentless, "Hell, I saw the dirty witch kill her own boyfriend, for god's sake. Slit his throat ear-to-ear as he begged her not to."

"That's a lie! I would never have done that!" Nora says in her own defense.

"Oh, but, honey, you did," Lauren continues condescendingly

at Nora.

Thunder starts to roll and the sky darkens. I can almost hear Nora's heart break as the air rushes from her lungs. She collapses, but Cillian catches her before she hits the ground. Anger clouds my thinking, but as Lauren laughs, something clicks and doesn't make sense.

"How do you know that? I thought everyone affected by the mind control can't remember anything?"

Lauren stops laughing abruptly, thinking on her feet. "Well, obviously, my mind was taken over after that."

The wind picks up as everyone now casts suspicious glares on Lauren. The gusts swirl my hair back and forth. Lauren looks up to the sky and then back at me. A nasty smile spreads slowly across her face. She sashays her way up to me and leans her face in close to mine.

"Are you accusing me of something?" she asks as she licks her obnoxiously white teeth.

"Cassie, did you know?" Nora whimpers.

I look over my shoulder to Nora. She looks so betrayed and lost. My face says all she needs to know, because she hangs her head and starts to sob.

"Well, Cassie, aren't you going to go console your dirty witch?"

I don't need magic in this moment. I pull my fist back and punch Lauren in the face as hard as I can. I feel her nose shatter beneath my knuckles, and her teeth crack inside her mouth. She drops hard to the ground as she lets out a wail that could rival a banshee.

A couple of guards step in between us, but I have already done all that I needed to do. I take a few steps back and watch Lauren wither in pain on the ground. It surprisingly doesn't take her long to shoot up like a feral cat and start to claw at me. She howls as the guards pick her up and restrain her. Blood pours out of her nose and mouth.

To not be suspicious of my powers, I try to keep the weather looking like a storm is incoming, but I focus on slowing the wind. Hopefully the climate will take over and the storm will roll in naturally.

"Henry, get over here." Cillian motions for Henry to move and help him with Nora, who is lying collapsed on the ground. Henry quickly jogs over and attends to her.

"Enough!" Cillian's voice booms and echoes down the courtyard as he steps in between Lauren and me.

"Look what you did to me!" Lauren continues to screech. "How dare you!"

"Shh, Lauren, please, this can be fixed," Cillian intervenes and I look at him with confusion.

How are you going to fix this now, Cillian?

This seems to cool Lauren off slightly. As she struggles less, I swear I see her wound start to heal, ever so slightly—that, or her blood coagulates very quickly.

"Now, Cassandra, Lauren was screened by multiple

professors on her series of events that night. Truth spells were even used in questioning. So, if Lauren was able to somehow foresee all that happening, she would have been smart enough to consume cinnamon in some form, at some point before questioning. Cinnamon is the most common ingredient that can allow one to be protected from a Truth spell. Unfortunately, we did not find any cinnamon in anyone's blood when it was tested." Lauren beams with satisfaction as Cillian speaks. "However, Lauren, I don't remember you saying you saw Nora specifically in any of your interviews."

Lauren's smile fades.

"Well, I-I passed everything, so why don't you talk to Headmistress Ansley? My father is one of the biggest donors to this school. He would be flying off the handle if he knew how I was being treated right now. Plus, I didn't have cinnamon in my blood, you said so yourself."

"Yes, of course, see? Mystery solved." Something about Cillian's tone makes me suspicious. "While extremely inappropriate, Lauren, Cassandra, you are at fault here."

To be honest, I'm not even that mad. She deserved it, and I will accept the consequences. But really, though, it's not like they can expel me right now.

"So, Cassandra, please, come here." Cillian motions for me to come closer. Lauren's eye is starting to swell and bruise.

Hmm, maybe I was wrong about her healing herself.

Lauren flinches and whimpers as I move closer. I roll my eyes over her drama-queen behavior.

"What do you want, Cillian?"

"I want you to heal her."

I furrow my brow and I have to blink a few times for my brain to process this, the most asinine string of words I have ever heard before.

"I-I'm sorry, what did you just say to me?"

"You heard me. Heal her. I know you can do it." He stares at me as if I am supposed to be reading between lines that I cannot see.

"Um, but I've only ever healed in a tense situation. I don't know if I can."

Don't know if I want to...

Lauren stands up straighter and purses her lips as she waits. Raindrops start to fall sporadically.

"Looks like a storm is rolling in. Better do this *quickly,*" Cillian advises.

I sigh and give up on trying to figure out Cillian's unspoken words. I hate reading between the lines.

I reach up to Lauren's face and she flinches away.

"Will you stop moving? I am not going to hurt you. I have to be touching you to do this. Do you want a fucked-up nose or not?" I am so close to just walking away and not helping her.

She weighs her options for a moment and nods for me to continue. Her skin is very smooth, and between the contrasting sky and her pitch-black hair, her face looks as if it's made of porcelain. I never realized how pale she is, but then again, I never venture close to her unless forced to do so. I can see the outline of a contact in her right eye, but none in her left, which is starting to fill with blood.

Maybe my hit knocked it out?

"Will you just get on with it!" she orders, annoyed at my hesitation.

"Be quiet!" I remind her.

I use my other hand to maneuver my magic into squeezing her vocal cords together slightly, so she can't talk anymore.

Just in case.

I smile to myself as I close my eyes. I picture my magic slowly seeping into her skin and pouring into her arteries, spreading out from my touch and repairing. It starts to work, but something seems to be blocking my powers. I struggle to move past it, but I can feel my efforts failing.

I squeeze my eyes shut harder, but my powers slowly begin to retreat. Trying to concentrate on the storm and everything else is proving to be more than I expected on the power expenditure meter. Cillian senses my struggle. He gently places a hand on my shoulder and that is all I need. Together with his, my magic makes quick work of repairing all that was broken. I open my eyes to see Lauren's nose moving back into place.

She whimpers slightly as the bones reset with a few cracks and pops, and her swollen eye deflates. Soon, all that is left of our tussle is the dried blood on her face and sweatshirt.

Cillian's hand drops and he steps away. He acts as if nothing happened, which I am grateful for. I don't need Lauren to catch onto anything more. I do not trust her. I didn't before, but now I am suspicious of her intentions.

I back away from her and the rain picks up, turning into a steady drizzle. Her eyes lock with mine and something is so familiar about her in that moment. I cock my head to the side slightly as I try to figure out what it is, but Lauren averts her eyes, clears her throat, and shakes the guards off.

"Okay, class, that's it for the day. We will resume bright and early tomorrow. The guards will escort you back inside."

I turn back to face Nora. Henry is still holding her in his arms, but she no longer looks mad. I rush to her, "Nora, I am so sorry. I didn't want to tell you. I thought it was better if you didn't know."

Tears still flow down her cheeks freely, but the sobs have gone away. Her chin quivers as she speaks, "Cassie, it's okay. I know your heart was in the right place. Can we go back to our room now?" She seems in shock.

"Of course we can. Come on, let's go."

Henry starts to pass her over into my arms, but Cillian calls from behind us, "Actually, Cassandra, a moment alone, please?"

I see Henry's muscles tense and his jaw tighten. I sigh, but reassure Nora I won't be but a moment. Henry and Nora slowly walk back inside.

"Please tell me you don't actually believe all that bullshit Lauren said. Also, do we have to be out here in the rain?" I say, when they are out of earshot. The rain is starting to penetrate my layers and reach my no-longer-warm skin.

Cillian smirks and shoves his hands into his pockets. He takes several steps toward me and lowers his voice, "You could always make it stop."

"Try not to be obvious, remember?" I retort. "Now answer me."

"No, I do not believe her. But at least out here, she cannot hear us. Something is not sitting right with me about Lauren. Throughout the whole interview process after the attack, she was very calm. Coming out of a mind control spell like that, it's more likely for one to be disoriented and confused."

The hair on my arms starts to prickle with suspicion. "So, what do we do?"

"Nothing, as of right now. I'll have the guards keep an eye on her, but it is true that she didn't have cinnamon in her system."

"There has to be another way. Something we are missing or overlooking."

"Hmm, well, let us continue going about business, but keep your guard up with her."

"Always do with her. Hey, um, do you know if Lauren wears contacts?" Cillian looks perplexed by the question. "Like, would a record of that be kept somewhere?"

"I'm sure it's in her student file, or the Infirmary would have record. Why do you ask?" He seems interested in my suspicion.

"No reason in particular." I try to shrug it off, but I have to ask one more question. "Do you guys teach healing at lower levels?"

"No, that's something not everyone is able to do. I am

astonished at how well you have been able to adopt that skill with no formal training. Why all these questions?"

I deflect with a joke, "Well, I have had to utilize it a lot so far since I've been here."

This seems to rub Cillian the wrong way and his posture becomes stiff. "And for that, I am terribly sorry, Cassandra."

"I shouldn't be gone from Nora long. I'm really worried about her."

"Yes, of course. After you."

We walk silently back into the school. My hair is fairly wet now, so I try to wring it out. I thought that Nora and Henry would be waiting just inside, but it looks like he took her all the way back to our room.

Cillian continues to walk behind me silently, and I become very self-conscious about how I am walking.

Am I walking weird? Is he staring at my butt? Is my stride too fast?

These ridiculous thoughts run through my head as we walk down the hallway.

I just want to know what he is thinking. Things have been happening so quickly, and he may be leaving soon? One minute he is hot, the next he is cold with me.

Henry is waiting outside my room when Cillian and I arrive.

"Does he have to follow you around everywhere you go?" Henry asks quietly. "Why can't he get another guard to do it?"

"I'm sorry," I mouth.

Cillian clears his throat behind me, and I can tell he

overheard Henry.

"I put her to bed. I think she's asleep."

Henry is always so considerate, and I truly wonder if he has any flaws.

"Thank you, Henry. I don't know what I would do without you."

"I should probably head back to my room. Meet you for dinner?"

"Erm, let me text you after I see how everything is. I think that maybe we'll have to eat in our room tonight, if Nora even eats at all."

"Settled. I'll make sure you two get food," Henry says as he gives me a departing kiss on the cheek. I blush. It is unexpected, but not unwelcome.

I hold my cheek as he saunters down the hallway. I smile to myself as his kiss lingers.

"I have to go for a few hours, but I will return soon." Cillian's voice pulls me out of the moment I'm having. "I'll wait here until the new guard arrives."

I turn around and cannot ignore the small panic forming inside of me. "But you'll come back though, right?"

"I thought you didn't like me guarding you all the time?" I can tell he is baiting me. I instantly turn flustered.

"I-I don't. I mean, I don't like being guarded, in general," I stumble over my words, and my face flushes a deep shade of red.

Smooth.

"Ahh, makes sense," he says, obviously not believing me.

"I better go inside and get to Nora," I say as I go to open the door behind me. "But you'll be back though?" I repeat to ease my already forming nerves.

Cillian smirks and nods.

"Okay, bye."

I scurry in and close the door behind me quickly. I take a deep breath and try to settle my emotions before I go over to Nora's bed. She has her comforter completely covering her, head and all.

I sit on the edge and place my hand on the comforter. "Nora, I'm here."

She stirs a tad. I can tell she is not asleep under there. I am about to get up when I finally hear her muffled voice.

"Cassie, I feel so numb." She slowly uncovers her head. "I just want to feel something, but I can't. Why couldn't you save him too?"

Her words stab into my chest. "I didn't know until it was too late."

"Oh, okay, then." Her eyes make it seem like she is miles away.

"But if I had known, I would've tried, Nora. I swear, I would've tried."

But she doesn't respond. She lies there, staring blankly at the wall. I don't know what to do. Nora has always been there for me when I've needed her, but I feel like I am failing her right now, when she needs me.

"Do you ever think about death?" she whispers.

"Yeah, Nora, I do." I think back to my parents. Their death left me with so many questions and feeling lost. I was at my lowest in school when my tormentors had locked me in the school bathroom, where I was left crying for hours.

"Do you think it hurts? Do you think that there is a beyond?"

I have never been a religious person, but I hope there is. I hope there is something after we pass to make all the suffering worth it. Her questions are starting to scare me, so I grab onto her hand, resting outside the comforter. I will my magic to do anything to help her.

"Nora, you're scaring me right now. We can get through this. I promise."

She withdraws her hand from my grip and turns onto her side. "I just want to see him again. I think I'll go to sleep now."

I hesitate on what to do. "Okay, Nora. I will be right over here if you need me, okay? I think Henry is going to bring us some dinner later. Do you want me to see if they have your favorite butternut squash soup?"

Silence.

I pat her back gently; her clothes are still damp from the rain. I sit there for a few moments and decide to let her sleep. I slide off her bed and quickly change into dry clothing myself. I retrieve my phone from the desk and crawl into bed. I scroll through my contacts, stopping first at Cillian. I want to text him so badly, but I also know it is not appropriate. I rely on him too much.

I scroll down to Henry. My thumb hovers over the Chat option. I finally click it and type a message.

Me: Nora isn't doing so well. Can you see if they have her favorite soup?

I hit Send. I don't have to wait long for Henry's reply.

Henry: Of course. What does she like? I'll see if Tommy can make it for her.

Damn, he is wonderful.

Me: Butternut squash is her favorite
Me: She also likes extra croutons

Henry: Consider it done. I'll drop food off in a couple hours if that's all right?

Me: That's perfect
Me: Thank you, Henry. Sorry for it all.

I click out of my messages and start to scroll through social media. I am curious about my questions about Lauren from earlier, so I look her up. Someone as vain as her must have an account somewhere.

It doesn't take long to find her Instagram account. Half-naked bikini pictures of herself from around the world fill her page. Something about them looks altered, as if they are staged, but who doesn't alter their pictures in some way these days? We all try to make our lives look perfect and flawless online.

Perfection equals happiness, right?

Henry: don't worry your pretty little head, love

Henry's notification flashes across the top of my screen. I smile as I bite the edge of my lip.

Cillian: New guard is here. Be back soon. Be safe. Text if you need anything, and I will shift to you right away.

Cillian's notification replaces Henry's and I decide to just shut off my phone screen. For someone who said they don't have feelings for me, he sure is making things a hell of a lot harder all around. But Henry. Oh Henry. It is effortless to be with him. It's like a freefall.

I groan quietly in frustration.

Maybe a nap will help.

I am still tired from sleeping on the floor, plus Henry did say it would be a couple hours before he'd be able to get us food.

I can nap for an hour.

I set an alarm and look over at Nora one more time—she has not moved an inch. I close my eyes and let myself drift off into unconsciousness. Sleep welcomes me like an old friend, but I feel a disturbance.

I am walking blindly through a cave. The crevices are tight and jagged. I have difficulty squeezing my body through them. My hands scour the sides to guide me forward. I don't know how I ended up here, or where I am going, just that I need to keep moving forward.

It is cold in this cave. Several times, my skin catches and tears on pieces of jagged rock. But I persist. Light starts to penetrate the darkness as I make my way deeper into the cave. Muffled voices travel their way to me as well. I quicken my pace.

"Hello?" I call out to the voices, but they don't hear me.

More jagged edges slice through my skin as I push ahead. I start to panic, as it feels like the crevice is growing even smaller.

"Hello?! Can anyone hear me?" I call out once more. The voices get louder and the cave, more illuminated.

I squeeze through one last tight spot and fall into an open area. There are lights on either side of the opening. The voices are audible now, and I can make out one of them.

Lauren?

I cautiously make my way down the lit path, which leads to a corner.

"I am trying!" Lauren's voice screams.

"You need to be more careful," a deep voice growls.

I slowly peek around the corner to find Lauren looking into a large mirror. The mirror seems out of place, as it's hanging on the cave wall in another small opening. Lauren is looking into it and messing with one of her eyes. My gaze travels to the other side of the opening to see the dark apparition I had seen in my Resolve. My blood runs cold, and I gasp. My hand shoots up to cover my mouth as I duck back around the corner.

Did they see me? Did they hear me?

"Well, you need to let me in on more of your plan," Lauren continues.

My muscles relax slightly, and I remove my hand from my mouth. I muster up the courage to peek back around the corner, but Lauren has shifted and is standing directly in front of me.

"Ahh!" I scream and try to back away, but Lauren's claws grab onto my arm and we shift together to in front of the mirror. My heart races as I peer into the reflection, but I do not see my own. Instead, Lauren's evil grin is reflected.

I look to my side and no longer see Lauren there. I turn my attention back to the mirror.

"What the hell?" I say as I reach out to the mirror. Lauren cackles maniacally and shakes her head back and forth. She raises her hand to point behind me.

I freeze in horror. I feel hot breath on the back of my neck. I'm trembling as I force my head to slowly spin around. The demon's eyes glow bright red. I open my mouth to scream, but it is drowned out by the creature's snarling.

I jolt awake to the alarm blaring on my phone. I struggle with it as I try to make the noise stop and process everything that just happened. I am sweating profusely under my comforter.

Where am I? Where am I? Why am I sweating so much? Eww. Okay, breathe, breathe, breathe.

I throw my comforter back and look around the room. Everything is how I remember it.

Just a dream.

The hair on my neck feels prickled still, and I rub it tame with one of my hands. My breathing settles as I look at the time. It is only 6:00 p.m. I notice I have a couple new messages, so I open them up.

Received at 5:20 p.m.

Cillian: Is everything okay? Something feels off with your magic.

Received at 5:47 p.m.

Henry: Hey I'll be over soon with food.

Received at 5:57 p.m.

Henry: Grabbing food now.

I will have to revisit Cillian's text later. I don't know if things are okay or not.

I jump out of bed and change my sweat-drenched shirt quickly. I throw the soaked shirt in a clump on the floor and throw my comforter back over the mattress. I examine Nora's bed as I pull a clean shirt over my head.

"Nora, Henry will be here soon with food," I whisper.

No movement.

I walk over to her bed and shake her slightly. After that doesn't do it, I pull back her comforter gently. She opens her eyes slowly, but just stares blankly at the wall.

Thank goodness.

"Nora, I think you should eat something. Henry had the chef make you your favorite soup. Yum!"

Nora sighs, but starts to sit up slowly.

Knock, knock

"Okay, that must be Henry."

I walk over and open the door to see Henry's smiling face.

"I bring thy ladies sustenance," he says in an even more exaggerated British accent than his normal one.

"You are so lame." I laugh quietly at him as I shut the door behind him. I catch a glimpse of the interim guard—he looks very solider-like. He's wearing all black, and his hair is slicked back. He stands rigid and still.

"So, uh, Cillian isn't here?" Henry fishes.

Don't get your hopes up too much.

"He said he had to leave for a few hours. He'll be back soon."

Henry's disappointment displays on his face as he furrows his brow. He sets the bag of food on my bed and begins to pull out our dinner.

"Butternut squash for Nora, and lemon-baked salmon for Cassie."

I drag over my desk chair for him to sit on as I open Nora's soup for her.

"Nora, this soup smells delicious. I think it'll help you feel a little better."

The steaming soup is portioned into a round Styrofoam container. Thankfully, Henry remembered silverware. I open one of the spoons and stick it into her soup. Nora has her back pressed up against the wall, with her knees pulled to her chest.

I hand her the soup, and she takes it in both hands. I watch her stir it a couple times and then bring a small spoonful up to her mouth.

"Careful, it looks hot," I try to warn her, but she doesn't hesitate.

Okay then.

Henry has already dug into his lasagna and garlic bread. It smells amazing. Garlic bread is one of my favorites.

"Hey, Henry, do you want to go halfsies?" I offer. The salmon looks and smells delicious, but I have my eyes on that bread. Henry deliberates for a moment, looking down at his mostly-consumed container. I can tell he is struggling, so I make it easier for him. "Actually, I really only care about half of your garlic bread."

"Oh, yeah, of course, ha." He looks relieved, as he hasn't touched the bread yet.

Henry tosses me half and I eat it standing up. I inhale the salmon and garlic bread, and wash it down with the sweet tea Henry also brought.

"Thanks for the soup, Henry," Nora says, after only eating a few bites and setting the bowl off to her side.

"No worries. I asked Chef Tommy to include extra croutons. Cassie said you liked those." He smiles at her, but she keeps her eyes focused on her knees.

Ding.

My phone goes off as I'm throwing away the containers. I hurry over to see what it is.

Cillian: I am assuming you are all right. I'm headed back now. Can we talk when I get back?

I ponder on how to reply, or if I should even reply at all. But I do want to tell him about my dream. Maybe he can help me figure it all out.

Me: Sure

I toss the phone back onto my bed and Henry eyes me. I can tell he wants to ask who it was, but he refrains.

"Nora, do you want me to cover your soup up and save it for later?" I ask.

She nods slightly. I retrieve it and place it on my desk.

Henry clears his throat. "I'll have to get going here soon."

"Why?" I say quickly.

"Um, my mum wants to see me."

"Oh, okay. Thank you again for bringing us food."

"It was my pleasure. You two mean a lot to me. Nobody blames you, Nora. You didn't know what you were doing. It wasn't you." Henry glances over at Nora, but I can see he's just making her sadder.

I motion with my hand for him to cut it out. He means well. I can see he is hurting too. Yash was one of his best friends.

"Oh, uh, before I forget," Henry grabs a dark sweatshirt from the floor. I hadn't seen him bring it in. "I brought this for you, Nora. It was Yash's. I figured it might help you to have something of his. His things are being packed up and shipped back to his family in India tomorrow."

Nora's attention is piqued at the mention of Yash. She scrambles to the edge of her bed and gratefully takes it from Henry's outstretched hand. Her tears return as she holds the sweatshirt tightly. She takes a big whiff of it, but coughs.

"He always did smell of cheap cologne and strong deodorant." She laughs to herself for a second and then returns to crying quietly.

I place my hand on Henry's shoulder to comfort him. A tear forms in the corner of his eye.

"Well, um, I best be going." He sniffles and turns toward the door.

"Okay. I will see you tomorrow. Will you walk with us again to training?"

"Wouldn't miss it, love," Henry says as he opens the door and steps out.

We both hesitate at the threshold. I debate on whether I want to kiss his cheek goodbye, and I can tell he is debating something in the same vein.

"Oh, Cassie, you're bleeding." Henry reaches for my upper arm. I look down to see that I am, indeed, bleeding. A shallow cut runs across my arm, and blood is dripping down from it. I instantly think back to my dream and the cave—the jagged edges that pulled at my skin.

How have I not noticed this?

"Oh, um, weird, I must've cut it on something." I shrug it off. It's not that I don't trust Henry—I trust Henry with my life—but Cillian knows more about everything.

"Speak of the devil," Henry says curtly under his breath.

I look to see Cillian striding down the hallway. Henry still has his hand on my arm, which Cillian notices as he comes closer.

"Did something happen? Is everything all right?" Cillian exchanges glances between me and the guard. The guard looks frightened that he has missed something.

"I am so sorry, sir. I didn't hear anything going on," he rattles off quickly.

"Cillian, I am fine. It's a scratch," I try to defuse the nonexistent situation.

"I wouldn't let anything hurt her while I am around," Henry challenges Cillian.

"Sure," Cillian says sarcastically.

Henry steps up close to Cillian, their chests almost touching. "I've already proven that I would give my life to protect her."

Welp.

"Stop it! Both of you! You treat me like I am this fragile person. This is not an argument you need to be having right now. It's a scratch. I am fine. The guard did a fine job, so don't blame him." I have had enough of this constant measuring contest between the two of them. The lights in the hallway begin to flicker. I feel our magic building and it has to be defused soon.

Cillian and Henry continue to stare each other down for a few moments.

"She is the most important person in my life right now. I would give my life again for her in a heartbeat," Henry says sternly.

"So would I," Cillian retorts.

I have had enough of both of them, so I go back into my room and close the door. They can handle themselves. I go into the bathroom to clean my cut and heal it. Thankfully, the scratch has already closed. Only the dried blood remains.

Knock, knock

I groan in frustration.

Can I please just be left alone for a moment!

I swing open the door to see Cillian's piercing blue eyes.

"What?" I say, annoyed.

"I believe you said that we could talk when I got back?"

I look around him to make sure Henry is gone.

"I see you two finished your little tiff?"

Cillian settles his hands back into his front pockets. He is dressed in all black, like the other guards. Black blazer, black slacks, and a black button up. But it all suits him very nicely.

"Cassandra—"

"Fine, fine, yes we can talk. I want to tell you something anyway." I look back at Nora, who looks as if she has fallen back asleep. She had put on Yash's sweatshirt and is snuggled under her comforter.

"What's going on? Also, I double checked. Lauren did not have cinnamon in her system at all that night to alter the truth spell." He seems concerned.

My shoulders slump forward in disappointment. I know our voices will echo down the hallway, so I am concerned if anyone might be listening. Cillian senses my hesitation.

"Shall we go for a walk?" he offers.

"I don't know if I should leave Nora alone right now."

"I'll be okay, Cassie," Nora's voice says softly behind me.

I whip my head around to her. "Nora, I am so sorry, I thought you were sleeping."

Her eyes remain closed. "I'll be okay. I won't do anything bad. I heard you in your sleep earlier, you need to tell Cillian."

What did she hear?

"I'll be right back, okay?"

"Oh, and Cassie?"

"Yeah?"

"Cloves." She rolls onto her side and doesn't say anything more.

"Cloves? Nora what do you mean by cloves?"

She doesn't respond, so I shrug it off. I grab the first jacket I find, not realizing it's Henry's until we are already walking down the hall. I didn't realized that I never gave it back to him after the night Nick attacked me.

It is dark outside. The rain has stopped, and the sky is clear. The moon is full tonight, and it is slowly making its way to its peak. The moonlight dances across the path as we walk in silence.

"What was Nora talking about in there?" Cillian finally breaks the silence.

I stop on the trail and look around. I don't really know where to begin, so I start with what I first remember. I tell him absolutely everything—the cave, the scratches from the jagged edges, Lauren, the mirror, and the dark apparition. He listens intently and doesn't interrupt once. I constantly sneak glances at him to gauge his reaction, but his expression never changes.

"And then I somehow have a scratch on my arm. You know the rest." I am almost out of breath after explaining everything. I stand back and wait for his response.

"Interesting."

"Interesting? That's all you have to say?" Embarrassment floods me, and I pull Henry's jacket around me tighter.

"Sorry, I just—it's just, something is very off. I left earlier to do some digging on Lauren and her family. Everything either seems fabricated or absent. Typically, we keep extensive files on all of the students at the Academy, but…I am not sure yet."

I throw my arms up in frustration. "She has had it out for me since the moment I stepped into this school. And Cillian, seeing her in that mirror, something looked so familiar about her, I just can't put my finger on it. She was there in class when I first saw the apparition, she was with Nora and us all when we were drinking before the dance, and she's tested me and provoked my powers repeatedly, just like you said someone might try to.

Cillian rubs his chin in frustration. As he pulls on his chin, it only accentuates his jawline. I notice that more stubble has formed on his face than he usually allows.

Concentrate, woman.

"Cillian, I think Lauren is the inside person. I think she orchestrated the attack."

"There are still some things that just don't make sense, Cassandra."

Cloves.

"Cloves," I whisper. Everything clicks. "Cloves," I repeat.

Cillian looks at me as if I am having a stroke.

"What about cloves?"

"Can cloves alter a truth spell?" My body begins to shake. "Nora said something about cloves before we left. She must've heard you when you got there."

"Okay, but I don't see where you are going with this, though."

I begin to have a panic attack as all of my emotions go haywire. My breathing is shallow and quick. "The night of the dance, in Yash and Henry's room, it smelled like Christmas. It all makes sense. All she would've had to do was rub some clove oil onto her skin, and that would've been enough! Nora, you are brilliant."

I start to get lightheaded and sit down on the ground. Cillian sinks down and sits beside me. My body is still shaking as I try to control my breathing.

"I never asked for any of this. I don't want any of it. How many people will die because of me?"

Cillian places his arm around my shoulders for comfort. It only makes things worse, because that's exactly what I want him to do. I want him to console me and tell me that everything is going to be okay.

I shrug his arm off and stand up. "And then you go and do shit like this that makes everything so much harder." I start to pace back and forth.

"Cassandra, I'm sorry, I just wanted—" Cillian starts as he stands back up.

"I love you, Cillian. I love you with my entire existence. But if you don't love me, I can live with that. I have lived with so much pain in my life. But seeing you every day, feeling you close to me, it is killing me slowly inside. I can go on and pretend it doesn't, but then whenever something bad happens, I want to run to you. I want you, but you don't want me."

Everything is overflowing inside of me and it is difficult to process all the emotions I am feeling.

Cillian's eyes are fixated off somewhere in the distance. I don't want to be here anymore. I turn and start heading back to the school.

"Cassandra, please don't go," he whispers.

"I have to get back to Nora. She needs me right now," I say simply, and shift back to my room, leaving Cillian behind.

I can hear Nora snoring softly, which I am thankful for. She needs the rest. I bite my lip and try to muffle my sobs.

Ding

My phone goes off on my bed. I hurry over to silence it, so it does not disturb Nora. The text preview pops up onto the screen.

1 New Message

Cillian: I will speak with Tabitha about Lauren. In the mean...

The rest is cut off, so I open the complete message.

Cillian: I will speak with Tabitha about Lauren. In the meantime, do not let her know we are suspicious. I will also have another guard assigned to your protection detail from here on out.

Cillian: I never wanted to hurt you, Cassandra.

I throw my phone back onto my bed a little harder than I should have, and it bounces up and collides with the wall.

Nora stirs.

Shit!

Nora's snoring continues. I let out a sigh of relief. I strip off my clothes and take a hot shower to try and calm down. I stay in long after the water runs cold.

How can someone's heart break this much? Why can't I be good enough for him?

I don't sleep. I lay awake in bed, staring at Cillian's message, to which I have not responded. I am also afraid of what I might dream. I used to enjoy dreaming and getting to escape, but now I feel like it is a weak spot.

I can't feel Cillian's magic outside the door anymore. I hug onto Piggy and try to prepare myself for a new dawn.

CHAPTER FIFTEEN

Cillian keeps his word and an additional guard is assigned to me. I still see him in training, but things aren't the same. Henry is delighted about the change, but he doesn't press me as to why it happened. The next couple of days string together in a training-and-sleeping cycle. We repeat everything over and over.

Lauren is still in the training sessions. I can tell Cillian is keeping a stealthy eye on her, but I keep my distance.

Nora has become a shell of a person. She goes through the motions, but the light has been snuffed out inside of her. She wears Yash's sweatshirt every day and every night. I make sure she eats and bathes, but she has stopped all communication—a sullen expression permanently paints her face. Her hair is dull and unkept. I try to bring my concerns up to the Headmistress, but she assures me that Nora will be fine with time. She is existing, but nothing more.

"Okay, class, as you know, the Joining Ceremony will take place tomorrow evening. Outfits can be brought to your rooms if you do not already have anything appropriate to wear. After dressing, guards will escort you to the Grand Hall, where the Ceremony will take place. Any questions before we break?"

"Can I go to the loo?" Nora's voice asks softly.

I stare at her bewildered, as this is the first sentence Nora has spoken in days. Cillian is a little caught off guard as well.

"Uh, yes, Nora, of course you can."

Nora grabs my hand and squeezes it softly. "I love you, Cassandra."

Nora's behavior gives me cause for concern. "I love you too, Nora. What is this?"

She tries to smile and reaches to give me a hug. "I just want you to know that."

"Of course I do. I'll see you when you get back, okay?"

"Sure," she says as she pulls away from me.

The rest of the room is silent as Nora departs. Something in my gut tells me to follow her, but I also want to give her time alone if she needs it. I have been on her 24/7. I have not let her out of my sight at all, in case she needs me.

I look to Henry, who also looks concerned. He gives me a small shrug and a look that says, "Maybe she just has to pee?"

I ignore the others' questions. Instead, I focus on honing in on Nora's magic. It is another little trick I've picked up throughout the week. With Cillian not being my main guard anymore, I've wanted to check on him sometimes, to see how far away he was. I only do it when I'm anxious, being able to feel that he is close gives me some comfort.

I picture my magic following Nora and the path she would take. The bathrooms are just on the opposite side of the Training Room, along with showers and changing areas. But she feels further away. I try to push my magic farther into the school, but I can feel it losing strength. I grab onto Henry's hand to use his magic as an extra booster.

I close my eyes and picture my magic soaring down the hallways, searching for her unique output. It pings with a hit.

Found her.

Her magic is travelling further away from the Training Room. It appears as though she is heading back to our room.

There are plenty of closer bathrooms. Why is she going back to our room?

"Cassie?" Henry's voice causes me to lose my concentration, and my eyes flutter open. The Training Room is empty now, aside from Henry and Cillian looking at me. Everyone else has gone on to lunch.

"What were you doing?" Henry asks, looking at our joined hands. "I can feel you using our magic right now."

I release his hand. "Sorry, it's nothing. I think something might be wrong with Nora."

"And why do you think that?" Cillian asks. It is the first time he's spoken directly to me this week.

The pit in my stomach gnaws at my insides, growing bigger by the second.

What is she doing?

I try to concentrate again and grab Henry's hand once more. But this time, I can't ping her at all. An idea starts to form, and the blood drains from my face. My legs are running before I have time to process what's happening. I try to shift to our room, but can't for some reason. The tingling starts, but after that, it feels as if my path is blocked.

I hear Cillian and Henry close behind me, but I'm not worried about them. My feet pound on the floor as I will my legs to move faster. I run up the stairs two at a time and sprint to our hallway. I turn the corner and can finally see our door.

"Nora!" I scream.

I frantically try to open the door, but it is locked. I stand back and fling the door open with my magic.

"Nora, where are you?!" I scream, bursting into our room.

Henry and Cillian have caught up now. Once inside, I can hear the shower running in the bathroom. Condensation has started to form on the door from all the steam. The shower must be on full hot.

"Cassie, what is going on?" Henry asks, out of breath.

"I can't feel her magic anymore." Tears begin to fall as my body trembles in fear.

I try the bathroom door. It is also locked.

"Nora! Are you in there? Open the door!" I scream as I bang on the it.

No response.

"Maybe she just wanted to shower?" Henry inputs.

I ignore him. "Nora, I will bust down this goddamn door! Answer me!"

I try to shift into the bathroom, but I still can't.

"Cassie, calm down," Henry tries to ease my anxiety.

"I can't shift right now. Why can't I shift?" I am in full-on panic mode.

Cillian tries the door as well. "Nora, this is Cillian. Open the door."

"Fuck this. Cillian, move!"

Cillian moves out of the way and I bash open the door with my magic. A plume of steam rolls out into my face.

"Nora!" I scream as I plunge into the fog and blindly search for the shower door. Once I find the handle, I fling it open. Even with clouded vision, I can see Nora, fully dressed, slumped in the corner of the shower. The scolding hot water beats down on her relentlessly.

"Nora, no!" I scream.

I fumble to turn the water off, and it is only then that I see the blood pooling in the bottom of the shower.

"Cillian!" I shriek as I drop down to examine where the blood is coming from, hoping to try and stop it.

I can't feel her lifeforce anymore, and her magic is almost completely gone.

I grab her arms and pull up her sleeves to reveal huge gashes running from her wrists to her elbows—a small knife lying beside her.

"No, no, no, no, no, no! Nora no!" I wail.

I press down on her wounds to try and slow the bleeding. Cillian rushes into the bathroom and kneels down behind me.

"Oh my god. Henry, shift to the Infirmary now and grab a medic! Tell them to hurry," Cillian yells.

"I can't stop the bleeding," I wail as blood drenches my hands. "Cillian, give me your hand. We can save her. Just like Henry, we can save her!"

Cillian doesn't hesitate to put his hands on top of mine and I try to mimic exactly what I had done with Henry. But my magic is so weak, it feels blocked somehow.

"Come on! Why isn't this working! We did it before!"

We try for several minutes and nothing happens.

"Why isn't it working, Cillian?" I sob.

"I don't know," he says breathlessly.

Nora's face has gone pale. I don't hear Henry arrive with the medic, unaware of their presence until I someone drags me off of Nora.

"No, I can fix her. Just-just let me try!" I scream as I resist against the person.

They wrap their arms around me and restrain my hands. I don't realize it is Cillian pulling me off.

He carries me out into the room, and I collapse. Cillian holds onto me strongly, supporting my full weight. I watch in slow motion as the others rush into our tiny bathroom to help Nora.

Why couldn't I help her? I should have known. I shouldn't have let her out of my sight.

"We've got a pulse! It's weak, but we've got one!" one of the medics yells out. This makes everyone work even quicker.

Thank god.

They carry Nora out on a stretcher and rush her down the hall to the Infirmary, leaving Cillian, Henry, and me behind in the room. Henry has his hands interlocked on the back of his head.

"I should've known." I feel utterly defeated. "I knew I should've followed her." Anger begins to build within me. I feel something dark starting to consume me and I welcome it.

"None of us knew she would do this, Cassandra."

I stand up and break Cillian's hold on me. I turn around and get in his face.

"*I* knew! I knew she was hurting! I knew she was dying inside, and I tried to be there for her every moment. I failed her. I fail everyone!" I scream.

Cillian stands still in front of me as I scream at him. Henry has to pull my shoulder back for me to back up from Cillian's face.

"Cassie, calm down," Henry urges.

I turn my anger toward him. "Don't you fucking dare tell me to calm down right now. My best friend just tried to kill herself, and who knows?! She might end up succeeding. I saved *you*," I spew at him, pressing my pointer finger into his chest. "Why couldn't I save her?"

I feel Cillian walk up and stick his hand into my jacket pocket.

"Don't touch me right now!" I scream at him.

Cillian holds up a small bundle of herbs and twigs that he has retrieved from my pocket.

"What is that?" I demand.

Cillian examines it and takes a small sniff. "Well, looks to me like it is an Interference spell."

"What the hell is an Interference spell?" I hold the monster inside me at bay and let Cillian explain.

"This is very old magic, not really used anymore. It works as a signal jammer, basically. Witches stopped using it because it wasn't effective all the time. That and the fact that it has to be in very close contact to the person you want to affect."

"Hence, why I could still use some of my magic, but not all of it." I shake my head in disbelief. "She slipped it in my pocket when she hugged me."

If I wasn't so mad at her right now, I would be impressed. Nora is always so crafty that way.

"She knew you'd figure it out and come after her," Henry speaks up hesitantly.

The Headmistress appears in the doorway. She looks at Cillian and shakes her head ever so slightly, I almost don't catch it.

"No, she can't be—she can't be dead. Where is she? I can heal her now. Where is she?" I say through clenched teeth.

"Miss Rodden, there's nothing we can do now."

"Where is she?!" I demand.

With the Interference spell away from me now, I let the

monster inside me lose to rage about. Lights begin to flicker, and the room starts to shake. Wind rushes its way into the room and swirls about, picking up loose papers and flinging them around.

"Cassandra, enough! You cannot save her. She died before they could even get her to the Infirmary," she shouts above the wind.

This can't be happening. I need to get out of here. I need to get away.

All I can do is picture my grandmother's home. I long to be back with her. I wish I had never come to this school.

As the wind swirls and the tremors increase, I feel my fingers become tingly.

Take me home.

I feel myself being lifted into the air. The tingling sensation overtakes my whole body. I close my eyes and exhale one last breath.

Take me home.

And just like that, I feel myself being plunged into the unknown.

CHAPTER SIXTEEN

A couple birds sing a sweet tune as I feel myself being expelled from the unknown. My eyes are closed still, and I feel the chilly morning air kiss my cheeks.

"Cassandra?" my grandmother's sweet voice calls from behind me.

I open my eyes and turn around. I have shifted to the middle of her flower garden. I used to love coming out here as a kid to chase butterflies or play in the grass and create imaginary friends. It looks like the early morning frosts have killed most of her flowers.

My grandmother stands a few feet away. She has a shawl wrapped around her shoulders and looks to still be in her pajamas. Her long grey hair, though, is tucked into a perfect bun.

The monster inside of me dissipates at the sight of my her. Weight is lifted off my shoulders as I run to her.

"Grandma," I am barely able to mutter out as I sob.

She opens her arms and wraps them around me. Her fragile frame hugs me tight.

"Oh, Cassie, what happened? How did you get here?" Her voice is filled with concern. When I finally let her go, I notice I still have Nora's blood all over my hands.

"It's a long story, Grandma."

"How about we get you cleaned up, and then fix some yummy hot chocolate, hmm?" My grandmother's big chocolate-brown eyes are so warm and kind. The wrinkles around her eyes and mouth become more pronounced as she tries to smile at me.

I can't help but let out a laugh. I feel like a little kid again in my grandma's presence. She has been my protector for so long, always accepting of me, even when I had my anger phases. She always took my side and defended me, even if she knew I was wrong. Of course, she would help me learn from my mistakes, but if anyone else dared to tell her I was a bad kid, lord help that person.

"That sounds perfect, Grandma."

We walk along the cobblestone pathway up to her house. It is a big, old Victorian house with stained-glass windows and ornate trim. I had helped her paint it a beautiful teal a few summers ago.

I am immediately greeted by the familiar smells of vanilla and old books as we walk inside. Everywhere in sight is some sort of literature, laying out and about. My grandmother loves to read anything and everything she can get her hands on. She always says it was her parents that instilled the notion that books give you knowledge, and knowledge gives you power. Her parents loved reading so much, they ended up naming her Ophelia after one of their favorite characters from Shakespeare.

I always love to describe the inside of her home as beautiful chaos. Every inch of wall space has a picture or painting hanging on it. I used to love going through all of the floors and rearranging things to see if she'd notice. And she did, she noticed every time. My grandma is a person who barely has any magic in her blood, but with how beautifully she paints, I always thought she underestimated just how much she actually has.

The kitchen lies directly in the back of the house. I walk over to the sink and start scrubbing the blood away. My grandma pulls a scrub brush from underneath the sink and hands it to me for my nails.

We continue in silene as I scrub and she puts the kettle on for hot chocolate. There is a small table inside her kitchen that only seats two people. After setting the water to boil, she slowly sits down and waits for me to finish. The brush helps with most of it, but there are still a few stains underneath my nails. I give up and turn around to face her. I am ashamed of myself for everything that has happened, but what I am most ashamed of is running away.

"Come on, spit it out, girlie." My grandma always knows when I'm hiding something. I swear to she can read my innermost thoughts. That, or she is a human lie detector.

"Did my parents ever mention a Prophecy to you?"

"No, but I remember learning about several lores and prophecies during my studies when you were younger."

I lean against the counter and begin. The Prophecy, Henry, Cillian, Nora, Nick, Yash—I tell her absolutely everything. I glisten over the part about Cillian and I sleeping together, but I convey everything else as it happened.

My grandmother is a lot more expressive than Cillian, which I have missed. I hate constantly having to guess what someone is truly feeling. My grandmother lives through every emotion I've had the past few months. The kettle goes off as I finish telling her about Nora and finding out she is dead. It is perfect timing, because I see my grandmother tearing up.

She gets up slowly and removes the kettle from the heat. The cups *clink* together as she pulls my favorite one and her own from the cupboard. Mine is an old Eeyore mug that has big letters on it reading, "I feel blue." I just find it so funny every time.

I hear my grandmother sniffling as she pours the cocoa powder into the cups.

"And how did you get here? You shifted?"

"Yeah," I say, finally taking a seat at the table.

She brings my cup over and sets it down. Steam rolls off the top of the delicious liquid.

"Thank you."

My grandmother sighs heavily as she sits back down in her chair. I bring the cup up to my lips and blow on the top of the cocoa.

"Your mother always told me that you were special," she says quietly. "You look more like her every day."

I sip the liquid, not knowing what more to say at this moment. I feel so numb.

"Well, you're going to have to go back, my dear. Sounds like they really need you."

"I know, and I will, but I'm scared, Grandma."

She reaches over and grabs my hand. I want to collapse again and let the sadness overtake me.

"You are the strongest person I know, Cassie. You have been through hell and back. You have always just tried to bottle the pain away, but, honey, that bottle is full now. You can beat these horrible people. You are smart, and you are resilient. If you are this, Chosen One, then go be great. Hell, it's written you will be, so start owning that."

She always gives the best pep talks.

"Now, your friend, Nora, I am so sorry she did that. We all carry pain that others might not see. It sounds like she was amazing."

"But I wasn't there for her, Grandma. I couldn't save her. I failed her."

"My dear, you will not be able to save everyone. I am telling you that right now. I am sure you did all that you could for her. She knew you were going to try and save her, and that's why she put that spell in your pocket. She knew you loved her enough that you would come—that you would do everything you could to save her. She didn't want to be saved."

Everything makes so much sense when my grandmother breaks it down for me. She never tells me how to feel. Instead, she pulls it apart and explains it all for me, and then she lets me feel whatever I need to feel.

"Now, as far as the two men, that is something your heart,

and your brain are going to have to figure out. There's a reason they say 'mind, body, and soul.' Mind, for which type of person nurtures your intellect and who you logically think you should be with. Body, for whichever person satisfies your body and makes me you feel good. And finally, soul, for whoever makes you feel complete, like you have never felt before—that not being with them means you'd be living without a piece of yourself forever. Be true to your heart and soul, and your mind will figure the rest out."

"Thanks, Grandma," I say as I get up to hug her. I never want to let her go.

She pats my arm. "I wish you could stay. I miss you, but you probably shouldn't be gone too much longer."

"I know. I hope I can still shift back. Because I was in such close contact with Henry and Cillian, I'm not sure if I was using any of their power to help me shift." That realization had come to me halfway through my monologue.

"Well, before you go, I have something for you."

"For me?" I ask curiously.

Did she know I would be coming?

"Mhmm. Come on, let's go, and I will show you."

My grandmother stands up and I follow her into the living room. We walk across her plush carpet to the coffee table. On top of it is a beautiful eggshell-colored box with gold trim.

"What is it?" I say as I eye the box suspiciously.

"Well, go on and open it, and you'll find out," she says with a laugh. "Something told me you may stop by."

That's not cryptic.

I carefully pull the top off to reveal a beautiful silk gown. It is an exquisite white, with a lace panel inlet across the toro of the dress. I gently pull it out of the box to get a better look. The straps are thin, and buttons run from the bottom of the lace inlet all the way down to the floor. It looks like the A-line will flow freely as I walk in it.

"This was your mother's Joining Ceremony dress."

Goosebumps form on my arms as a shiver shoots through me with this news.

"She told me to give it to you when it was your time. It was like she knew she wouldn't be around to give it to you herself. I think they still wear all white to this thing. Seemed a little cult-ish back then, but your mother said it was the best day of her life. It was also the day she found out she was having you."

Really?

"I didn't know that."

"Yes, well, your mother waited to tell your father, but she called me that morning before the Ceremony to tell me. I think I was the only other person who knew."

"The day of the accident, did she tell you anything? I remember her and Dad being scared."

She sucks in a sharp breath. "She called me before you all left, saying that you guys were having to go somewhere for a little while."

Hmm… something is missing from this story.

I don't want to press my grandmother more—I can tell she is

getting sad. I stare back at the dress and fall in love with it. I gently place it back in the box so it won't wrinkle.

"Thank you so much, Grandma."

"It'll be all okay, Cassie. I know it will. Your mother wil- would be so proud. Now, let's see if we can get you back."

I hug my grandmother one more time and, with the dress in hand, I attempt to shift back to school. I know the shift here had used a great amount already, but the key question is, was it all my own magic that got me here?

Please work. Take me back to the Academy.

"Be strong, my dear…" my grandma's voice fades as the tingling sensation increases. I picture Cillian's and my spot by the pond. We all have anchor points throughout our lives—locations that mean a lot to us, or that we visit a lot. I remember vaguely Cillian saying that focusing on those can help one with shifting long distances. Wind starts to swirl around, and I feel the pulls and tugs.

Time to be the Chosen One.

My landing is a little bit harder than normal, as I can feel my magic start to sputter, like an old car dying out on the highway. I protect the box from the muddy ground as I drop to my knees.

Something feels different inside me now. Even though I didn't choose to take this all on, it is my responsibility now. I am not going to stand by and let another person I love die. I get to my feet, brush off the grass and mud stuck to my knees, and I begin to walk up toward the school. A new monster rages inside of me now, and it is hungry for revenge.

CHAPTER SEVENTEEN

Walking up the hill to the school, I see Cillian, Henry, and the Headmistress arguing outside. None of them have noticed me yet.

"Well, she has got to be bloody somewhere. She couldn't have just disappeared. Find her. Find both of them!" the Headmistress demands.

Who else is missing?

"I cannot believe both of you let all this shit happen," she continues.

"Actually, Headmistress, I cannot believe that *you* let this happen," I say as I make my way closer to them.

Relief floods all their faces.

"Excuse me? And where do you think you've been, Miss Rodden?" Her relief quickly turns to anger.

"I had to go home for a few minutes. Reset my head."

"Home? You mean back to America?" Henry says in

301

disbelief.

I see Cillian smirk. He is impressed.

"Yep, you got it. So, who else is missing?"

They all shift uncomfortably.

"Lauren. No one has been able to find her since training this morning," Henry finally says.

They all gauge my reaction to this news. A fire burns inside of me, but I know Lauren will pop up sooner or later.

"So, who is she, really?"

"We are still trying to figure that out, unfortunately," Headmistress Ansley admits.

"Tabitha, with all that's going on, maybe I shouldn't be following up on this tip and leaving."

The Headmistress snaps her head to Cillian. "You are going. You are lucky we haven't sent you already, but I want you around for the Ceremony."

I can see the anger building in Cillian, but he pushes it down.

"What's in the box?" Henry asks curiously, changing the subject.

"A dress," I say as I look down at it, "for the Joining Ceremony. It was my mother's. More important now, though, what's the game plan?"

The Headmistress begins to speak, "We've suspended the rest of training for the day. Students will remain under strict lockdown—"

"No," I interject.

She looks taken aback by my interjection. "No? And what do *you* think we should do?"

"What we came here to do. Train. And if the others don't want to, that's fine, but Cillian and Henry, I expect you to be in the Training Room in thirty minutes. I just need to change and drop this off in…" I trail off as I realize that even though I am trying to be strong right now, I don't know if I can go back into our room yet.

Henry and Cillian sense my hesitation. "You can drop it off in my room," they both of say in unison.

Awkwardness is sure to ensue. They both look at each other and then clear their throats.

The Headmistress steps forward. "She will stay with Cillian."

Henry groans and Cillian looks a little shocked by her decision.

"Besides, Henry, you will be staying with me tonight. With everything going on, and almost losing you once already, I am not letting you out of my sight."

"But, Mum, come on, are you serious?" Henry protests.

"I am. Now I must go meet with some of the other professors and reach out to Miss Malik's family. Henry, once you are done with training, come and find me." She starts to walk away, but catches herself. "Oh, and Cillian, remember, I will be keeping tabs."

Cillian's eyes narrow as the Headmistress departs.

"Welp, whatever is going on here, I am over it. So, I am going now as well," I say as I begin to walk towards the front door.

Cillian catches my arm as I walk past him. "Do you

remember how to get there?" he asks quietly.

"I am sure I can manage to find your room again," I say in an even tone.

"I'll shift in quickly and gather some things from your room, and then I'll be there. Henry, can you walk with her? I won't be long, but I don't want her to be alone."

"Of course," Henry says.

Cillian leans in close and whispers into my ear, "It is incredible how far you shifted, but please do not try that again. I do not want you getting hurt while doing that. Sometimes magic can fail during a shift."

I nod and head toward Cillian's room. Henry follows close behind. Once inside the school, I try to remember the route.

"So, um, when were you in Cillian's room?" Henry asks apprehensively.

I chew the inside of my cheek while I decide on how to respond. "Um, well, the night of the attack at the dance, your mom told him to stay with him in case more things went down."

I peek a glance at him, and I can see there is more he wants to ask. I quicken my pace to get to Cillian's room quicker.

"Did anything happen between you two?" he finally comes out with it.

I try to deflect his question, "Well, I don't think that's really any of your business."

"You're right. I am sorry. It was really inappropriate of me to ask."

He looks so defeated. I sigh and stop walking.

"Henry," I say, but he won't look at me.

"What?" he mumbles.

"Henry, look at me, please." He reluctantly turns his eyes to me. "I am sorry. I am sorry for not being more open about you and me. It is not fair to you. You are one of the most amazing people I have ever met, and I appreciate you so much, but with everything going on, I have barely had time to even breathe. Do I have feelings for you? Yes, Henry, I do, but I am realizing now that I can't keep letting my heart and my head get in the way of things." I'm not sure what to say next. He looks like a puppy who has just been kicked, and it hurts my heart.

"Do you have feelings for him?"

"Yes, I do. I can't just make them go away. Trust me, I've tried. But like I said, it is not the time to be starting a war between the three of us. Our hearts can wait. People are dying, Henry." My voice cracks as Nora infiltrates my thoughts again. I bite my lip to try and hold back the tears and continue walking.

Henry quickens his pace to catch up to me.

"Cassie, I am so sorry about all of this. I am being selfish, and that is not fair to you. I know you've been through hell."

"I just don't want all of their deaths to be in vain. If I'm meant to be this Chosen One, then I need to start being stronger. I need to start being a leader who people can have faith in." I clutch onto the box tighter in my arms.

"Well, I believe in you, Cassie. I have believed in you since the moment I saw you. I knew nothing would be the same," Henry says as we reach Cillian's door.

His words comfort me. "Thank you, Henry."

The door swings open. "Good, you made it," Cillian says as he moves out of the way for us to enter.

The room is no longer immaculate. Instead, books are strewn all over the floor, tables and chairs look out of place. The room appears as if it has been ransacked.

"Um, Cillian, what happened in here?" I say apprehensively, coming to a halt just inside the room. Henry takes in the distress of the room as well.

"Yeah, mate, did someone rob you?" Henry jokes.

Cillian surveys the room. He clears his throat. "Well, a mouse got in, and I had to find out where it was hiding."

"Oh, okay, that makes sense. Did you find it?" The last thing I want is a mouse running over me while I sleep.

"I believe I got all of its hiding spots," Cillian says proudly.

"Okay, well, um, where is my stuff? I want to change quickly before we go train." My jacket still has some of Nora's blood on it.

"It's in the bathroom for you."

"Thanks."

I head off to the bathroom and shut the door behind me softly. The atmosphere is getting a tad uncomfortable. I hear Henry and Cillian trying to converse as I change my clothes. There are several tote bags stuffed with various items. It looks like Cillian just grabbed everything he could.

I chuckle at the thought of him rummaging through my drawers, pulling out what he thought I might need. At least it looks like he was able to grab all the essentials for me.

I study my reflection in the mirror after getting changed. I see that I have changed since being here. We all look different, though. We have all been through so much, and there is still so much uncertainty with the future. We are no longer bright-eyed and innocent. Our trials all weigh on us differently.

I straighten my posture and take a deep breath. My mother's words drift to the front of my mind, *"Fear not the unknown. Embrace it and charge forward. For greatness was never achieved by standing in the shadows."*

"Time to go be great."

I am still in my own little world as I exit the bathroom.

"All set?" Cillian asks.

"Yep."

"Okay, let's get started then. First up, shift to the gym. I will see you both there." Cillian disappears.

"See you there," I say to Henry. All I have to do is blink and Cillian's room disappears, replaced with the gym. Henry isn't but a second behind.

"Not bad, you two. Now, let's get to work," Cillian says.

A few other students trickle in while we train. Damon and Sarah are among them. We all try to give reassuring smiles, but everyone is off. Cillian works us hard, and our magic is pushed further than it ever has been before. It becomes effortless, integrating magic into my fighting style. Everything is becoming one and it flows easily throughout me. It is almost like a dance that I did not need to be taught.

We train all evening, only stopping briefly to eat dinner. We are all getting stronger—I can feel it. I throw myself fully into the training to distract my mind from Nora. The one true friend I had in this world is gone now.

"Okay, let's call it a night, everyone. Big day tomorrow," Cillian announces as he runs a towel across his forehead.

"Henry and I will keep going," I say. We have been sparring. His shoulders slump from exhaustion.

"Cassie, it's getting late. We've been at this for hours," he protests.

Everyone else begins to pack up and head out of the Training Room, guards following them close behind.

"Fine. I'll train by myself then," I say simply as I use my magic to pull a spear toward me.

Cillian intercepts it and draws it to him. "Enough, Cassandra. You and Henry need your rest. Go along, Henry. I am sure you mum is waiting for you."

You are going to have to sleep at some point. Can't avoid it forever.

I sigh heavily and cross my arms in defeat.

"Very well. I'll see you tomorrow, Henry."

Henry walks over and takes me into his arms for a hug.

"It's going to be all right. Text me if you need anything,

okay?" Henry says as he lets go of me.

I nod and watch as he walks away. He takes a few steps and then shifts away to wherever his mother's room is.

And then it is just me and Cillian, standing there in the middle of the Training Room. So many emotions swirl around me as we stand in silence.

"I can see if you can stay somewhere else tonight?" he offers quietly. "I know you don't want me to be your guard anymore…"

I feel his eyes on me, waiting for my response.

"No, it's fine. I want to stay with you. If it were anyone else, it would be just as bad as being alone, and I don't want to be alone right now," I say softly.

"You can talk to me, you know?" Cillian says, taking a step toward me.

"I am just going to shift to your room, if that's all right?" My eyes avoid his.

"Of course, I'll be right behind you."

I shift to his room, but I am so tired and weak that I stumble. Cillian is there to gently grab my arm to steady me.

"Thanks," I mutter, and I pull my arm back.

"Cassandra, talk to me, please," he pleads. "You don't have to be afraid right now. I won't let anyone get to you."

I look up at him. I no longer have the strength to keep up my strong façade.

"I am afraid every waking minute now. I fear the thoughts that might infiltrate my mind about Nora and everyone else that has lost their life. I fear going to sleep, because not even that is an escape for me now. I fear that I will never be good enough, no matter how hard I try." I want to cry, but I don't even have the strength to do that. "And most of all, I fear that I will never be able to fill the hole you left inside of my heart."

Cillian begins to speak, but I hold up my hand to silence him.

"Please, not tonight. I want to shower and go to sleep. Afterall, tomorrow is a big day."

I can see Cillian's struggle spilling out. His cold composure is no longer one he can hide behind.

If he truly wanted to be with me, he would be. If he truly had feelings for me, it wouldn't be this hard to show them.

"Shower is all yours," he finally says.

"Exactly."

Showering is not relaxing. I have to cut it short, due to flashes of Nora in our own shower and everything else assaulting my thoughts. I begin to panic and hurry out quickly to get dressed. I exit to find Cillian settling onto the couch for the night. I keep quiet as I make my way under the covers of his bed. But even his bed holds memories I don't want to revisit.

Ugh.

I roll over to my side and stare at my mother's dress, which is hanging up in front of Cillian's closet doors. I try to focus on her and the memories I have of her. What her time here must have been like, especially when she met my father. I wonder what they could have been running from that day. Was it from the Anarchy? It isn't long before sleep takes me, and I drift off to memories of her.

CHAPTER EIGHTEEN

I put the dress on over my head and the material slithers down my body. It fits perfectly. The fabric hugs me ever so gently on the bodice. I picture my mother in this dress, trying to feel what she must've felt when she wore it. She must not have been terribly far along, but the material would have allowed her to conceal her secret with ease. I debate on what to do with my hair, and I end up just leaving it down and wavy.

Cillian appears in the doorway.

"You look beautiful," he says, leaning up against the doorjamb.

His attire consists of all black once again, but this time it is more formal. Black, shiny shoes accompany his black tux. His hair looks as if he put product in it to hold it in place.

"Thanks," I say softly.

"We should get going. The Ceremony will start soon."

I nod and turn toward him, but he doesn't move out of the way. Instead, he stares at me, taking me in as if this will be the last time he'll see me. His eyes are unrelenting, like normal. Sleep must have built back up his walls, but I can still see the slightest hint of sadness.

He reaches out and gently tucks my hair behind my left ear. I catch his hand before he can withdraw it and hold it against my cheek.

"The Serpent could still say Henry is not the person I am supposed to be joined with," I whisper.

He smirks and gives a small laugh. "There is so much I want to tell you, Cassandra, but…" He pulls in a deep breath and deliberates with himself for a moment.

"I am so tired of excuses," I say, tears threatening to ruin my makeup. I let go of his hand and push past him.

"Cassandra—"

"No, Cillian. Enough. I'm done. It shouldn't be this hard. It's time to go."

Cillian sets his jaw and shoves his hands into his pockets. "Very well, then, let's go."

The Ceremony is taking place in the Grand Hall. Some students' families have come in to watch, as well as some alumni from the school. Everyone who isn't participating in the ceremony dons all black, everyone that will be joined is wearing all white. A large, golden goblet is displayed in the center of the stage.

It is cooler in the Grand Hall today, as if it's still haunted from the lives that were lost. I shiver slightly as Cillian and I walk in.

I try not to think about the dance while we make our way onto the stage and I go to stand by Henry. Cillian takes his place beside the Headmistress. Henry's wearing a loose-fitting button-up shirt. He's left it untucked from his white pants, and the top three buttons are left undone. He's pushed up the sleeves to his elbows.

"Absolutely stunning, love," he whispers into my ear as he gives my cheek a soft kiss.

"Thank you."

I look around at the others, who are dressed in white, as we stand in a bowed line across the stage. Most of the women have gone with dresses, but Clara's wearing a beautiful suit with a lace corset underneath. Her auburn hair pairs well with the white. It highlights all the reds and oranges and makes it look like fire.

She notices me staring and waves. I return her wave and give her a smile.

"Are you ready for this?" Henry's voice whispers as he grabs and squeezes my hand.

I squeeze back. "As ready as I will ever be."

Headmistress Ansley walks to the center as the spectators gather around the stage. There are not any seats, but current students are in the front, and family members are toward the back. It looks as if all the students who had departed, Levels 1 through 4 have returned for the ceremony.

"Thank you, everyone, for joining us today on short notice. As you all know, the school has suffered great tragedy so far this year at the hands of the Anarchy. However, we believe that we may just have the upper hand on them now. Behind me stands a student whom we believe to be the Chosen One."

Oh, I see, we are just coming right out with it, then.

Several of the parents gasp and look between all of us on the stage. I am instantly nervous and can feel the other students' eyes on me. They already know from the other day, but the Headmistress is now making it official.

I shift uncomfortably. Henry squeezes my hand softly again to calm my nerves.

"We've thought we had the Chosen One before, so how do you know now?" one of the parents challenges.

"Yes, your skepticism is warranted, but I assure you that we have never seen power like this before." The Headmistress turns to look over her shoulder at me. She outstretches her arm toward me for me to step forward. "Come, Cassandra."

You have got to be kidding me.

I sigh and reluctantly step forward, leaving Henry behind me. The crowd whispers amongst themselves.

"Some of you may remember her parents, Johnathan and Elizabeth Rodden, who tragically passed away some time ago," Headmistress Ansley continues. "Cassandra, will you please give a demonstration?"

Something inside me tells me that despite her phrasing, this isn't a question. I look at the Headmistress and give her an 'are you serious?' look.

"Do what you did the other day," she whispers between

clenched teeth, her smile not leaving her face.

My palms begin to perspire, and I feel like I am going to throw up. I survey all the faces in the crowd. Some look annoyed, some hopeful, others look about as nervous as I feel.

"It issssssss time," a deep voice hisses from the goblet, and all the lights dim.

The voice startles everyone, and I take the few steps back to Henry.

"Does that always happen?" I whisper to him quickly.

"No," he says as he shakes his head slightly.

Even the Headmistress looks a caught off guard by the voice. Slowly, a Serpent dripping in gold raises out of the goblet. Even its tongue is gold as I see it flicker. I watch its deep-ruby red eyes raise about a foot into the air.

"Welcome to the Joining Ceremony. I am Eppla." The snake's mouth doesn't move, but I hear his hissed words vividly in my mind.

I feel myself falling into a trance as the snake sways back and forth. I shake my head and advert my gaze away from the Serpent.

The Headmistress bows her head slightly and speaks to the Serpent, "We were just about to have Cassandra complete a demonstration of her powers."

This seems to aggravate the Serpent, and he strikes toward the Headmistress. She jumps back.

"Begin," Eppla hisses.

"I apologize, Your Highness." The Headmistress stands up

straight, the room silent. "We are all gathered here today to witness the joining of a new generation of witches. Our students have worked hard over the past weeks to harness their powers, as well as get a sense of who their magic pairs with best. Being able to join with another is a great honor for us all, as it makes us stronger. Let us begin."

The Headmistress motions for Kathleen and Clara to step up first. They look at each other nervously as they approach the goblet. Kathleen and Clara are two of the sweetest people I have ever met. I remember them telling me that they have been together since high school. While in training, their magic did complement each other's, however, I do remember Clara's pairing better with Damon's magic.

"Now, intertwine your hands and reach toward the goblet," Headmistress Ansley directs them.

I see Clara mouth I love you to Kathleen as they extend their hands toward the Serpent. The Serpent's body shudders and writhes about as its head slowly begins to split into two.

My eyes widen as I watch the scene unfold. The new head looks the same, but this new head seems to be more temperamental. Both of their tongues flicker rapidly as they hover near the girls' hands.

The Serpents slither around their intertwined hands. One head goes up Kathleen's forearm, the other up Clara's. Clara whimpers at the snakes' touch. I lean forward to try and get a better view of what is happening, but it is hard to. Everyone is holding their breath in anticipation.

Suddenly, the Serpents strike the girls' forearms, their fangs plunging deep into their skin.

"Ahh!" Clara screams and tries to pull her hand away.

"Be still, Clara!" The Headmistress holds onto Clara's shoulders to prevent her from pulling away.

Um, no one said that the snake was going to bite us...

The Serpents' heads release the girls' arms and withdraw back into the goblet. The crowd lets out a collective sigh of relief, as gold marks display prominently on the girls' translucent skin, winding up their forearms.

"They are joined!" the Headmistress announces.

Everyone claps as Clara's arms fly around Kathleen. I can't help but smile at how happy they are. I sneak a glance at Cillian, and to my surprise, he is already looking at me. Anxiety begins to overflow within me, so I turn my focus back forward.

Kathleen and Clara make their way back into line, clutching each other. I can see the tiny fang marks now that causes their blood to form into little beads.

"Next pair, please," the Headmistress says as she motions toward Damon and Sarah.

Sarah is only a Level 5, but she and Damon have trained hard together this past week. Henry once told me it is extremely rare for Level 5s to be included in the ceremony.

They step up and extend their hands toward the waiting Serpents. The heads don't even travel up their forearms. With a few flicks of their tongues, they pull back and hiss.

The crowd lets out a collective sigh of disappointment. Damon and Sarah's hands drop to their sides.

"What happens now?" I whisper to Henry.

"Do not fear, young onessssss. Your matchesss are out there," the snake hisses. "You sssssshall find them one day."

Well, that's helpful.

The Headmistress nudges Damon and Sarah to move back to their positions on the stage. They retreat with their heads hung low. It isn't until they get back to their spots that I realize Henry and I are next.

I suddenly find it hard to swallow as my throat tightens. I see the Headmistress looking at us now, waiting for us to step forward. A loud ringing noise overtakes my hearing. Henry steps in front of me and I see his mouth moving, but I cannot hear his words. His face grows concerned as I look at him like a deer in headlights.

I feel a hand on the small of my back and realize Cillian has walked over to me. His cool hand feels nice against my back, as I can feel my body temperature has spiked. I look into his eyes and he nods slightly. The ringing fades and I am to regain my bearings.

"Cassie, are you okay?" Henry asks.

I take a deep breath and nod. The Headmistress is glaring at me for making a scene.

Cillian removes his hand and stands off to the side, near the Headmistress. Henry reaches out his hand, and I take it. The room is so silent, I can almost hear the crowd's lungs tighten with anticipation.

Henry and I take a few steps forward toward the goblet. Something in the Serpents' eyes changes and their attention is dead set on me. I thought the Headmistress had a soul-crushing glare, but this Serpent utterly terrifies me.

The goblet is beautiful. Rubies and emeralds adorn the rim of the it, as well as intricate designs I didn't see before. Etches of flowers and large trees bearing different fruit are inlaid on the main focal point of the goblet.

We take our stand before the Serpent and offer our hands. I can feel everyone's eyes on me, watching my every move.

"Ahh, Missss Rodden, finally. We have been waiting for you. We see the outcome of your mother'ssss decision hasss come now to fruition."

I am taken aback by this. "You knew my mother?"

"Of coursssssse. We overssee all of the joiningsss. Ever sssince the dawn of time," the Serpents hiss. They both sway back and forth so elegantly. It seems as if the heads take turns speaking.

"Cassie, who are you talking to?" Henry's voice whispers to me.

I look at him with confusion. "Don't you hear the Serpent?"

"I control who hearsss me and when," the Serpents hiss more aggressively now, as if I have offended them. "Wordsss do not always have to be sspoken."

I make the realization now that I'm not audibly hearing the Serpents' voice, but rather, inside my head.

"Never mind," I tell Henry, and concentrate back on the

Serpents.

What do you mean, my mother's decision? Can you tell me what they were running from the day of their accident?

"*Let us begin, shall we?*" the Serpents say as they slither up and around Henry's and my hands, ignoring my questions.

My Serpent feels very cold and wet. Its grasp on my forearm is uncomfortably tight.

The heads turn to look at me. "*Very interesting,*" one of the heads hisses as they both come to a rest just below our elbows.

What is interesting?

"*You have the ssssame decision to make asss your mother. Two pathss lay before you. One path will lead you to your damnation, the other to your sssalvation.*"

Well, that's not cryptic at all. What does that mean?

"*You have two paths that lay before you——*"

Yeah, yeah, yeah okay, I get it. Two paths. Do you mean Cillian and Henry?

"*Ahhh, yessss, Henry, the one who would sacrifice everything for you. And Cillian, the one who already hasss.*"

Don't you mean that Henry has already sacrificed everything? When he gave his life for me at the dance?

The Serpents shake their heads no.

Who should I join with then?

"*That isss a decision only you can make, but be wary, the Prophecy hinges on thisss.*"

No pressure then.

"Good and Evil will be born, balance mussst be found between the Shadow and the Soul."

I know the Prophecy, you don't have to recite it to me.

The snake hisses aggressively and continues, *"You may know sssome of the Prophecy, but you do not know all.*

> *Legend speaks of a Witch*
> *With a Lost Soul*
> *There will come a time*
> *From a decision made*
> *That will open a Pathway*
> *For Good and Evil to be born*
>
> *Two sides of the Same coin*
> *One side basked in Glorious Light*
> *One side drowned in the Darkest Night*
>
> *For she who carries the weight of Both*
> *Shall give way to the Chosen One*
> *Two paths will lie before her*
> *One that will lead to her Salvation*
> *The other to Damnation*
>
> *Challenges will arise*
> *Scales will be tipped*
> *And an Ultimate Sacrifice Reflected in Red*
> *For the Chosen One shall rise only when*
> *Balance is Found*
> *Between the Shadow and the Soul*

For she who carries the weight of both… What all does it mean? I would think they'd make prophecies more direct.

"Have you made your decision?" The Serpent ignores my questions.

Can't I be joined to both?

"No, you must choose one."

I can sense the crowd becoming uncomfortable with how long this is taking. Many begin to shift anxiously.

Everything is starting to overwhelm me, and I can't keep my thoughts straight. I think back to what my grandmother said about the heart and mind, but I need more time. I know Henry and I could be great together in time. Things with Henry are easy, and he makes me happy, but things with Cillian are unlike anything I have ever experienced before. Cillian though, is not a possibility. It is clear to me now that even if I could join with him, he doesn't want that. Cillian does not want to join with me. I have made up my mind.

Henry, I say quietly in my head.

"Interesting. Very well."

Interesting? How will I know if I made the right decision?

"In due time. Change is upon us all."

The Serpents twist further up and Henry's and my arms until they reach our shoulders. Everyone gasps. The heads bare their teeth and pull back. They strike, sending their fangs deep into our shoulders.

God dammit, this hurts!

The lights begin to flicker. I try to remain still, but my arm feels like it's on fire.

"Oh my God! Her dress!" I hear someone exclaim from the crowd.

I quickly look down at my dress to see what could be wrong. The dress is slowly turning a deep crimson red—the color spreading from my stomach outward.

The Serpents releases their bites from us and slither back down into the goblet. As they slowly retreat, I see beautiful gold designs laid precisely on my skin. The designs are vine-like, and they wrap around my whole arm.

"Oh, and Cassssandra, before I forget, tread carefully, asss things are never asss they ssseem. The answerssss that you ssseek can be found at the beginning."

The beginning? Please give me more.

The Serpents disappear completely back into the golden liquid.

"Look at their markings!" someone exclaims.

"No one has ever had markings like that before," says another.

The voices blend to create a hum of excitement. I feel so strong now. Stronger than I have ever felt before. I can feel the magic tingling throughout my body.

"It's her! She's the Chosen One!"

My dress is now completely saturated in the scarlet red. I release Henry's hand and raise my arm in front of me. I want to examine it fully. Gold vines wrap around my arm. Leaves branch out from the vines and spread out. It is beautiful.

Two little beads of blood form on my shoulder where the Serpent had struck me. I wipe away the blood to see a gold leaf forming on that skin.

Henry is in shock with it all. He stands there dumbfounded, looking at his arm.

"Non desistas, non exeris," the crowd begins to chant in unison.

What?

The chanting pulls my attention to the crowd. They are all staring at me wide-eyed, but I see hope in all their eyes.

"Non desistas, non exeris."

I step around the goblet and stand at the edge of the stage. I have never felt like I do right now. Every part of me feels alive with magic. I notice my skin begin to glow slightly with the magic that pulses through my veins.

"Non desistas, non exeris."

Wind finds its way into the Grand Hall and swirls around everyone. It causes a few strands of my hair to play around my face. I see everyone in the crowd has their left arm across their chests, their fists closed.

"Non desistas, non exeris,"

Non desistas, non exeris? Never give up, never surrender.

I raise up my left hand to signal the chanting to stop. The room dies down, as no one dares to speak in this moment.

"My fellow witches, the time has come for us to put an end to all of this violence for good. The Anarchy has taken so much from all of us, mothers, fathers, friends, the list goes on. I can feel all your pain and sadness. I know these times are very confusing, and it feels like it would be easier to just give up, but we can't. We cannot continue to allow evil to win. Darkness is absence of light, so one must search to find balance between the shadow and the soul. I will be that light in the darkness."

I take my raised arm and cross it over my chest. I close my fist and stand tall. The chanting resumes and I take my place as the Chosen One.

CHAPTER NINETEEN

The Ceremony begins to come to a conclusion. Three more pairs are joined, and the mood is lighter throughout the Grand Hall. But I am determined to get some answers. I wait patiently for the Headmistress to end the ceremony officially before I walk up to her and Cillian.

"We need to talk, now," I say sternly. I am no longer timid or scared of the Headmistress.

"Maybe later, hmm?" the Headmistress says, continuing to smile and say goodbye to the guests.

"I said now." The lights flicker slightly.

"Your powers are immeasurably stronger now, Cassandra," Cillian says.

"I know," I reply simply. With stronger magic comes stronger control. My powers no longer scare me. It is like my magic and I have an understanding of sorts now.

"Very well, Miss Rodden, we can all convene in my office. I have to say goodbye to a few more guests, but I will meet you there,"

Headmistress Ansley says through gritted teeth.

"Very well."

I head toward her office, Henry trailing behind me. I can hear from Henry's stride that he is walking differently now, with more confidence maybe. His steps are precise and thorough. I think we both walk more confidently now. We hold our heads a little higher, our shoulders less slumped forward.

It isn't very far to her office, but when we arrive, the door is locked. I look at the keyhole and imagine its inner workings. I picture my magic pushing the inner mechanism just right, and before I know it, I hear the lock click open. I smirk to myself at the ease.

Standing in the middle of the Headmistress's office, I try to formulate all the questions I want to ask her.

"Cassie, that was absolutely incredible. I knew it. I knew we were meant to be joined," Henry says. He picks me up into his arms and twirls me around. I can't help but laugh and feel giddy myself. I'm going to keep the whole two paths thing to myself for now.

"I know. It's all pretty crazy," I say as he sets me down.

"And not to mention your dress. Wonder why it turned red? And our arms! I can't stop looking at the markings!"

"Yeah, I can't stop either," I hold up my arm to examine the markings again. "They are gorgeous. As far as the dress, I have absolutely no idea."

"Maybe Mum will have some ideas?"

I don't respond, but he is too intoxicated with the markings to notice my silence. There are a lot of things I feel like his mother isn't letting on.

The door opens and the Headmistress walks in along with Cillian.

"How did you get in here? Did you shift? That will not be tolerated, both of you," the Headmistress scolds.

"I think you are mistaken, Headmistress. The door was unlocked when we got here."

She looks at me and I can tell she knows I am lying. She scoffs, but drops the subject. She walks over to her desk and leans on the front of it.

"So, what would you like to talk about?" she asks, clasping her hands together.

I figure it is better to not beat around the bush and just charge headfirst into my questions. I am tired of waiting for answers.

"Do you know what *really* happened to my parents?"

The room's energy drops and falls silent. The Headmistress glances quickly at Cillian, who is standing on the outskirts of the room, and then back to me. Cillian is leaning against one of the bookshelves, his eyes cast down toward his feet.

"I am not entirely sure what you mean by that, but your parents unfortunately passed in a traumatic accident. You know as much as I do about that situation."

"They were running from something the morning of our accident. I want to know why and what it was that they were running from."

"Well, I apologize, but I haven't the faintest idea."

Something inside of me calls bullshit.

"You went to school here with them, didn't you?"

"Yes, I did, but you are already aware of that. Your mother was a dear friend of mine..." she trails off as her mind conjures a memory.

"Did my mother ever mention someone else, or hang around someone else a lot, other than my father?"

She thinks about my question for a few moments. I can see her sifting through her memories.

"I do remember a man named Victor that your mother was friends with. He kept to himself most of the time, but you could always find them together. It is sad, really, I think your mother felt bad for him. He always followed her around like a love-struck puppy." The Headmistress laughs to herself softly.

My senses perk up and I can feel I am onto something.

"Did he and my mother ever become more than friends?"

"Oh, heavens, no. Your mother was completely smitten with Johnathan." She laughs more at this question.

"What ever happened to Victor?"

"Oh, well, after the Joining Ceremony, he wasn't able to find his match, so I believe he went to the front lines against the Anarchy. Last I knew, he had died in an attack somewhere in Ireland."

Damn, there goes that lead.

"Hmm, okay then." I feel a little defeated as I encounter another roadblock.

"Why are you bringing all of this up, Miss Rodden? Why the

sudden interest in everything?" She eyes me suspiciously.

I ignore her question. "Do you know there is more to the Prophecy than what you've taught us?"

Cillian clears his throat.

"The Prophecy, as you can imagine, is quite old. I have no doubt that some of the scripture has been lost over time. Now, what is this all about?"

I know I am pushing her too hard for answers.

"It's nothing," I try to play it off.

"Very well then, now, if you'll excuse us, I need to speak with Professor Morris here about his assignment. You and Henry go off and have some fun, okay?"

"You're still going to send him?" My tone is a little more frantic than I intend it to be.

"Of course I am. Nothing has changed to divert this mission," her tone serious.

My stomach begins to turn.

"But don't Henry and I need more training?"

"Yes, you do, but I will oversee your training now. Since you two are joined, you'll need someone who has been joined to help you navigate through new skills you may have acquired. Now, off you go."

Henry, who has been silent the whole time, now speaks up, "Come on Cassie, let's get some food?"

I chew the inside of my cheek, debating on whether I want to protest more.

"I'll touch base with you before I leave, Cassandra," Cillian's voice is soft.

I walk over to him, he looks defeated. His emotions are leaking through his normally cold and well-kept together exterior. There is something I want to try, but I don't know if it will work.

I place my hand softly against his cheek and look into his eyes, *"There is so much I need to tell you. Can we talk when you get back to your room?"* I try to concentrate hard and imagine my thoughts making their way into his mind.

Cillian glances at the markings on my arm and then moves his face away from my hand.

Oh no, did it not work?

"Not in my room," his voice infiltrates my thoughts.

I smile to myself, but he keeps his eyes adverted away from me.

"Our spot by the pond?"

"Sure," he whispers just loud enough for me to hear, but still keeps his eyes away from mine.

Yes!

I feel accomplished that it worked. I can't help but smile as Henry and I leave the room.

We grab food and are able to talk with the others who were also joined at the ceremony. Those who were not joined are sullen and keep to themselves, but I try to include them in our conversation as best I can. Everyone else is excited and anxious. They are biting at the chance to test out their powers now. But something inside of me feels like the worst is yet to come, and that our real fight is just beginning. Mystery now swirls around my parent's accident—too many questions and not enough answers. I am determined now more than ever to get to the bottom of it all.

CHAPTER TWENTY

After eating and changing, Henry and I spend some time together, talking about everything that has happened. I am lost in thought for the most part, and I can tell he senses it. I try to reassure him that I am happy, but that things are weighing heavily on me. I want to be enjoying this day with Nora and Yash as well. It's getting later, and I am getting antsier about meeting with Cillian. Henry asks if I want to go with him and some of his friends for a drink to celebrate, but I use the "I'm tired" excuse. Apparently, it is a tradition to sneak off grounds after the Ceremony to get drinks, but I need to speak with Cillian. Henry tries to persuade me to go, but he knows what boundaries to push. He departs with a swift kiss on my cheek and bounds down the hallway.

Because I hadn't exactly told Cillian a time, I decide after Henry leaves that I will go sit by the pond and wait. The fresh air will do me some good anyway, and give me time to think. I have on a simple pair of high-waisted blue jeans and a grey turtleneck. I decide to go with my forest green jacket. It is one of my heavier jackets and reaches down to my knees.

I notice Cillian has a bottle of rum on his counter. I open it and take a couple pulls. I am nervous. Nervous about seeing Cillian after pairing with Henry. Nervous about what the new knowledge of the Prophecy holds.

The liquor burns in my chest as it coats my throat. The rum has a very smokey taste with a harsh kick at the end. It causes an involuntary shiver to run up my spine. I feel the liquor's warmth spread throughout me and it calms my nerves.

With one last pull, I set the bottle down and make my way out of the room. I could just shift to the pond, but I want to walk. All the leaves have fallen, leaving the trees bare. The sun has almost set, with just the tiniest bit of light illuminating the sky.

I make it to our spot in no time. A sheen of ice coats the surface of the pond. I shove my hands deep into my jacket pockets as the wind picks up. I am frustrated with the wind, and before I know it, it stops.

Hmmm, did I do that?

I concentrate on there being wind and sure enough, wind begins to blow.

Okay, wind, stop.

And it does. I break out into a little happy dance as I play with the wind for a couple more minutes.

"You'll have to be extra careful with the weather stuff," Cillian's voice startles me from behind.

I spin around to face him, trying to compose myself. He has

changed from his Ceremony clothes as well. A burgundy sweater peeks out from behind his dark blue coat. He's wearing a pair of dark tan corduroy pants and brown shoes. I thought he'd be upset with me manipulating the elements, but instead, he looks amused.

"Sorry, I was just trying to see if I could control it easier now," I say sheepishly.

"And your findings?"

I smile and show him. The wind blows hard against him, causing him to stumble toward me a few steps. I dial it down as I giggle.

He chuckles as he finds his footing again. "Just don't make it snow in the dead of summer, okay?"

"Deal." I feel my cheeks blushing easier from the liquor. Memories of the very first deal we made drift forward. My heart gives a squeeze as I remember it fondly.

"So, it looks like you really are the Chosen One. How do you feel?" he asks.

"It feels good, but also scary. There's a lot going on. I am not sure what all I feel, really."

I reach up to move a strand of hair out of my face, causing my sleeve to raise slightly. I see the gold shimmering of my markings become exposed. Cillian's demeanor immediately changes. He becomes cold and looks disappointed.

He clears his throat and shoves his hands into his pockets.

"I knew Henry would be the person you were supposed to join with," he says. His voice is strained and low.

I drop my arm quickly, and things became awkward.

"Cillian—" I begin to explain.

"So, what did you need to talk about?"

I decide to not argue about Henry. "The Serpents, they spoke to me during the Ceremony. They told me about more of the Prophecy and my mother. I don't know, just, a lot isn't making sense right now. They told me I need to look to the beginning to find answers. The beginning of time? The beginning of me? I am tired of looking for answers and just coming up with more questions. And now I am questioning whether or not my parent's accident was actually an accident," I ramble everything off so quickly, I forget to breathe.

"Slow down, it's okay. Let's take this one thing at a time, okay?" Whether he intentionally does it or not, Cillian closes the space between us and he gently grabs onto my arm. Either way, he quickly realizes what he's doing and withdraws his hand from my arm.

My heart hurts slightly as I long for his touch.

"What did the Serpents say?" he asks.

I tell him all that I can remember of the new verses. I choose to leave out the bit about having two paths and an option for who to join with for now.

Cillian has a concentrated look on his face. "Hmm, unfortunately, prophecies aren't very specific. They can be left open to interpretation."

"I don't think my parent's crash was an accident anymore.

Something doesn't add up."

Cillian runs his fingers through his hair. "I don't think so either. A lot of things are not making sense anymore. I, too, am questioning a lot now…" he trails off, his tone ominous.

Silence falls upon us as the sky runs shades of blue. The moon is making an appearance behind some clouds.

"When do you leave?" I finally ask.

Cillian looks down at his watch. "In just a few minutes, actually. There is a car waiting for me back up at the school."

"Oh." Disappointment overcomes me. "Where are you going?"

Cillian lets out a heavy sigh. "Ireland. Intel suggests the headquarters may be there."

The cave from my dream flashes to the front of my mind.

"Well, maybe I should go with you?" I say, looking down at my shoes.

"You should stay with Henry, now more than ever. You two are joined. You should train more and prepare." I hear the sour laced in his words.

"But you'll come back though, right?"

When he doesn't answer I turn around to look at the frozen pond. Tears have filled my eyes, and I don't want him to see me cry again. I sniffle and wipe the tears away with the sleeve of my jacket.

"You have Henry. Don't worry about me," he finally says.

This just infuriates me, but I keep my back turned.

"Stop, please," I whisper.

"Besides, I am sure he will keep you satisfied," Cillian scoffs.

I lose it. I turn around and stomp right up to him. "Stop! You can't push me away and then make me feel bad about it. You know damn well I want you. I have always wanted you, Cillian. It is *you* who doesn't want *me*."

I look directly into his eyes as I shout. Without missing a beat, Cillian grabs my face and kisses me hard. My body wants to collapse into his arms, but I can't do this anymore. I shove him away. He looks surprised by this.

"No, you don't get to do this to me right now. Seriously?"

"I just don't think I could ever be the right person for you, Cassandra. There's too much you don't know," he says with his head hung low.

"Why couldn't you let me decide that? Why did you have to go and make that decision for me? Things could be so different right now! I have begged you to let me in!" I shout at him.

"How? How could they be different now, Cassandra?"

"Because I had a choice who I could join with!" The words spill out in the heat of the moment, before realize I'm saying them.

I throw my hand over my mouth, but it is already out there. Not wanting to deal with this situation, I try to run past Cillian, but he catches my arm.

"What do you mean, you had a choice?" he whispers. I can hear the pain in his voice.

Welp, I made my bed, now I have to lie in it.

I grit my teeth. "The Serpents said there were two people that

I could have joined with." I shake my arm out of his grip.

"So, you chose Henry, then." Cillian looks so angry. He shakes his head and he turns away from me.

"You gave me no choice, Cillian. You pushed me away."

"Fine then. We are done," he says harshly.

"We can't be done when we never even began. I am tired of being this bad habit that you just pick back up every now and then," I say back.

He keeps his back turned to me and remains silent. I finally have enough and shift away back to his room. I don't want to go through all this heartache again, and what's worse is that I still feel his kiss lingering on my lips.

I gaze out of the large glass windows at the car that is sitting idle in front of the school. I don't know why I am doing this to myself, but I have always been my best torturer.

Cillian's figure slowly comes into view as he walks up to the car from the side of the school. I hold my breath, hoping that he will glance over to the windows. Not that he could see me through the one-sided panes, but I hope that if he just looks, that maybe it means that he truly cares for me. But that isn't the case. Cillian quickly approaches the car and ducks inside of it. The car drives off down the long dirt path into the night. I can feel his magic getting further and further away.

I pull off my jacket and walk over to the liquor bottle, still on the counter from earlier. I swirl the liquid around in the bottle and determine that it will suffice. My phone begins to vibrate in my jacket pocket, where I had left it on the floor. I pull out my phone and see that I have several messages from Henry. I sigh heavily and slump down with my back against Cillian's bed. I know I should probably read what he has sent me.

(4) Missed Messages (1) Missed Phone Call

(7:02pm) **Henry:** are you sure you aren't up for some drinks? I can wait?

(7:30pm) **Henry:** we are leaving be back later

(7:50pm) **Henry:** Is it weird that I miss you right now?

(8:23pm) **Henry:** Everything okay?

I screw off the top of the liquor bottle and consume more of the smokey rum.

Ding

Henry: I think ur realy pretty

I take another, bigger pull this time. The effects of the alcohol start to come on stronger, and it is clearly the same for Henry. My whole body feels warm and fuzzy, and my lips are slightly numb. My sadness slowly starts to slip away. I figure I should text Henry before he gets too worried. I smile slightly at his latest message.

Me: I think you're really pretty too

I see three little dots pop up to signal that Henry is typing a reply. I stare at my phone, waiting for it. This helps keep my mind focused, instead of wandering off to think about you-know-who.

Henry: wish u were here

I ponder what to say back to him. Honestly, I wish I was there too, at the moment. I had let Cillian consume so much of me.

Me: me too
Me: are you staying with your mom still tonight?

Henry sends a picture of him and the boys. It is blurry, but they all look to be having a good time. They deserve to have a good time. After all the heaviness of everything, they deserve a normal night.

Henry: Nope
Henry: Want 2 come over when I get bakc?

Looks like alcohol has made him more confident. I chuckle as I pull myself up to use the restroom. I leave my phone open to Henry's messages on the edge of Cillian's bed. I stumble to the bathroom and flick on the light. I use the bathroom and proceed to wash my hands and stare at myself in the mirror—which, I will say, is never a good idea when you are under the influence. My cheeks are flushed, my eyes lack emotion. Everything outside of the room has melted away.

I glance down at the cool water as it runs over my warm hands. It feels nice, as it helps me feel at least a little more sober and in control.

I shut the water off and wipe my hands on a small hand towel nearby. My eyes travel slowly back up to the mirror, but the reflection I see staring back at me makes my blood run ice cold.

"AHHH!" I scream as I try to jump back, but Lauren's arm reaches out through the mirror and latches onto my own, digging her nails into my skin. She pulls her lips back and bares her teeth.

"Hello, Chosen One," she snarls.

I am frozen in horror as she slowly starts to pull me closer to the mirror.

"No! Stop!" I scream, struggling against her grip.

This isn't real. This isn't real.

As I struggle, I notice something about Lauren. Her eyes are just like mine—one blue, one brown.

"Your eyes…"

This catches her off guard and she stops pulling. I can see the rage building inside of her now. She lets out a screech and yanks hard with all her strength.

"NO!" I scream, as I use my other arm to smash the mirror. Shards fly everywhere and I tumble backward, hitting my head hard on the wall behind me.

My breathing is rapid as I frantically try to process what just happened. My head is pounding, and I quickly get up and run out of the bathroom. I snatch my phone off the bed and dial Cillian's number as quickly as I can.

It starts to ring as I work to steady my breathing. I see that my hand is bleeding where I had smashed it against the mirror, but it is already healing.

What am I doing? It's not like he can help right now. Why am I bothering him?

Two more rings.

"Cassandra? Is everything okay?" Cillian's voice is filled with concern.

Shit, what do I say?

"Cassandra I will turn back right now. What is going on?" Cillian demands.

"N-no it's fine." My voice is shaky. "It's nothing. Sorry I called."

"It doesn't sound like nothing. Driver, turn around."

"No! Cillian, it's fine. I meant to call Henry." I hope he believes my lie.

Cillian is silent on the other end and I imagine him working through my words to determine if they are true or not.

"Very well. Driver, continue on. Cassandra—"

"I gotta go. Bye." I hang up and begin to sob. I notice the bottle of liquor on the floor and take it to the kitchen sink, where I proceed to dump out the remaining liquid.

Ding.

The noise from my phone startles me and I jump.

Get it together.

I slide open my phone to another message from Henry.

Henry: Headd back. Be bck soon.

Thank goodness.

I find a small bag, stuff it with a few things, and head off to Henry's room. Part of me regrets nixing the guard detail but, dammit, I am the Chosen One. I need to start acting like it. I can't be protected at all times.

I contemplate finding the Headmistress and telling her what happened, but something about her bothers me, and I can't quite put my finger on it. Plus, to be honest, I'm not really sure where her room is, and I am not about to be stumbling drunk down random hallways, especially after what just happened.

Why are her eyes like mine? How can she go into a mirror? Ugh, what does this all mean?

I make it to Henry's room in no time and discover the door is locked. I could shift in or use my magic to unlock the door, but instead I sink down to the ground in front of it.

No mirrors in this hallway.

I lean my back up against the door and welcome the cooler temperature. My skin is on fire from the liquor and Lauren. I glance down and examine my arm where her nails had dug in. My markings glisten, and there is no trace of her nails on my skin anymore.

I hear commotion travelling down the hallway after several minutes.

Henry?

I sense him just before he and a few of his friends come into view, all stumbling down the hallway. They haven't noticed me yet. They're laughing and it looks like they had an amazing time.

I stand up with my bag in hand as they approach. When they notice me, I smile at Henry and give a small wave. Damon nudges Henry and taunts him.

"Oooooo, Henry, look who's waiting for youuu," Damon slurs his words slightly.

Henry's face blushes a deep red, and he jabs Damon in the side.

"Shut up, ya wanker," Henry replies.

Damon and Charlie snicker as they all come to a stop by Henry's door.

Damon grabs my hand and kisses it with a bow. "It's an honor, Chosen One."

I laugh uncomfortably. "You do not need to call me that."

"All right, we'll see ya tomorrow then, lads," Henry says to Damon and Charlie, encouraging them to disperse.

They thankfully take the hint and say their goodbyes. They continue to laugh and stumble down the hallway to their room.

Henry is still blushing as we stand there awkwardly.

"Hey," he says, running his hands through his hair. I can

smell the alcohol on his breath, but don't mind it.

"Hi," I say back, with a smile.

Henry rocks back onto his heels. "So, uh, why are you waiting out here?"

"Just wanted to wait for you out here. Figure I should start respecting locked doors."

"Okay, cool, cool. Shall we go in?"

"Lead the way," I say as I move away from the door so he can unlock it.

We walk in, and Henry flicks on the lights. I notice that all of Yash's stuff has been taken out of the room, even the bed. It has been replaced by a red velvet couch. My throat tightens, but I try not to concentrate on the sad thoughts.

I set my bag down on the couch and see that Henry is looking extra awkward standing in the middle of his room.

"You okay?"

"Uh, yeah, sorry, I am just a tad drunk right now, and I'm happy you're here."

"Well, I am happy I'm here as well, and I am a tad drunk myself. I may have gotten into a bottle of liquor in Cillian's room."

"Ugh, I cannot stand him." Henry shakes his head in frustration at the mention of Cillian's name.

"Don't worry, he left already on his assignment." I make sure to add that last part to soften the situation.

Henry seems relieved. "Well, I can't say that I will miss him."

"Yeah…" I'm not sure what else to say.

"Uh, hey, do you mind if I go shower and change quickly? I smell like the pub." Henry continues to rock back and forth on his heels.

"Yeah, sure, that'll give me time to change as well," I say, already sifting through my mind to remember if I had grabbed pajamas.

"Okay, cool."

Henry walks over to his desk beside the couch and empties his pockets before hurrying off to his shower. As I hear the water turn on, I search through my bag, only to come up empty. No pajamas. I look around Henry's room and find the dresser.

I am sure he won't mind if I borrow something.

I open the drawers and search through the assorted clothing. I find an old t-shirt and pull it out.

This'll do.

I change quickly. The t-shirt is big on me and falls past my butt, covering the lace panties I'm wearing. I am about to close the drawers when I spot a yearbook hidden within. I pull it out and began to thumb through the pages—looks like this one is from last year.

Maybe I can find something about Lauren in here.

I take the yearbook over to Henry's bed and sit down. It is leatherbound and heavy, with thick pages. It holds pictures divided into the different Levels. I search the pages for anything about Lauren.

Come on, where are you, Lauren?

I hear the water suddenly shut off in Henry's bathroom, and I quickly place the yearbook on the side of his desk and close his dresser drawers. I don't want him to think I was snooping.

The bathroom door swings open and Henry appears with only a pair of gray sweatpants on. There are some leftover water droplets still clinging to his beautiful abs. He rubs a towel through his hair as he steps further into the room. His joining markings look so beautiful running up his arm, accentuating his bicep. I have to remind myself to breathe as I look at him.

"I hope you don't mind…I forgot to bring my own pajamas," I say, pulling on his shirt that hangs loosely on me.

His smile grows wide as he takes me in.

"No, not at all. I gotta say, I like my clothes on you."

I feel my cheeks become warm and I look down at my feet. I hear Henry approach me. The lights flicker slightly in his room, and he chuckles softly. He places his hand under my chin and lifts my eyes to meet his. I can feel the heat from his shower rolling off him. Desire builds up in both of us as our lips gravitate toward each other. My breathing becomes shallow.

Henry's other hand finds its way to my waist and he guides me backwards. I stumble and flail my arm out, which causes me to knock down the yearbook I had put on Henry's desk. I would have ignored it, but the edge of the book stabs my foot and I wince in pain.

"Fuck, ouch, ouch, ouch, sorry," I say as I reach down to rub my poor toes.

"Are you okay?" Henry says, reaching down to retrieve the book. It had fallen open to a spread of headshots.

My eyes quickly catch a glimpse of some of the photos.

Nora.

I ignore my still-throbbing toes and grab the book out of Henry's hands. I push past him and sit down on his bed. My heart hurts more the longer I look at Nora's picture. She looks so bright and happy, smiling ear to ear.

"Cassie, what's wrong?" Henry sits down beside me. He wraps one arm around me and pulls me close to him, and then notices Nora's photo.

"I miss her, Henry. I miss her so much." Tears threaten to break down the walls that are holding them back.

"She certainly is quite the character,"

I chuckle at a memory of her calling out Lauren for being a bitch. But the thought of Lauren instantly enrages me, and I think back to Cillian's mirror. I glance toward Henry's bathroom and instantly became paranoid.

What if she can come through Henry's mirror?

I debate trying to cover the mirror somehow, but figure it won't accomplish anything, except making me look crazy.

"You know, I've always thought you and Lauren look alike." Henry's statement snaps me out of my own head.

"Excuse me?"

My tone must have made him realize he said something wrong, and he quickly tries to back track.

"I just mean that sometimes, at certain angles, you look like you could be related, is all."

"That's impossible."

"I know, I just…I am sorry for bringing it up." He hangs his head like a sad puppy. I feel horrible for getting on him.

"No, it's okay, you are totally fine. The mention of her just enrages me and I still have so many unanswered questions."

"How about we put the yearbook down, get comfy, and you can tell me all about it? If you want." Henry slides up to the head of his bed and gets under the covers. He pats the spot next to him and smiles at me.

I can't help but smile back and toss the book to the ground. I crawl up to him and wiggle under the covers. Henry pulls me in close to his chest. I feel so snug and secure. He kisses the top of my head and leaves his lips there for several moments.

"I love you, Cassie, and I know you love Cillian, but I also can tell you love me as well, and that…well that is plenty enough for me."

I trace circles onto Henry's chest with my fingertips.

"I do love you, Henry. I love you so naturally," I say softly.

"But?"

I giggle. "There are no buts, not tonight."

I move my fingertips down his sternum toward his stomach. I feel his heartbeat quicken as I travel lower and lower.

I need a release from everything. I need to not have my brain going a thousand miles a minute, racing through all the shit and trying to sort it out. Tonight, there are no excuses, no barriers holding me back.

His breath catches as I teeter at his sweatpants band.

"Cassie," he breathes shakily as I pull them down.

I slide off my panties and guide my leg over him. I pull myself up so I am sitting on top of him. I grab the ends of the baggy shirt of his that I'm wearing, and slowly slide it up and over my head. I look behind me and wave my fingers to flip off the light switch. The moonlight casts in through Henry's window onto us, illuminating us in its glow.

"Are you sure you want to do this?"

I lean down and kiss him gently. His lips are so soft, but apprehensive at first. I take my kisses and travel to his cheek. I trace his jawline with the tip of my tongue up to his earlobe. I can feel him trembling beneath me with desire.

"Enough Mr. Nice Guy. Show me what you got," I breathe into his ear.

This seems to be enough for Henry. He grabs me tightly and flips me onto my back. He pins my wrists against the bed above my head with one hand. His other hand gently squeezes my throat. I can tell he is judging how much pressure to put, so I tilt my head back to bare my neck more. I lick my lips as we both breathe heavily. Henry pauses for a moment and just looks at me, his eyes consuming every inch of me like a bottle of fine wine.

I wrap my legs around his waist, thrusting my hips ever so slightly, encouraging him to proceed. He releases my hands so he can guide himself into me. I moan with pleasure as my body welcomes him. Our markings come alive and glisten brightly as we become one. The world melts away and I let myself be consumed by Henry. I let go of all my worry and dive headfirst into the abyss.

CHAPTER TWENTY-ONE

You know how you can never remember how your dreams begin? You are just sort of thrown into them? Some scientists believe it's because our minds never stay idle, switching from one thought to another quickly, without having any particular direction. Some researchers believe that it's our subconsciousness trying to highlight something important, so that we remember what we need to, and don't get caught up in the extra, unimportant parts.

The warmth of the attic was both cozy and stuffy. The dry air irritated my nose as I looked around. Something about the attic looked very familiar. There were different sized boxes scattered all over with their contents written on them in black marker. They read: home movies, Christmas decorations, Cassandra baby clothes, and other.

Where am I?

"Okay, Sweetie, I'll close my eyes and count to fifty. You hide, and I will find you," a muffled women's voice came up from below me.

"Okay, Mommy!"

"Closing my eyes now! One…Two…Three…Four…"

I heard the hatch to the attic open and the ladder slide down. I walked over to the opening and gasped when I saw a little girl climbing up the stairs. Her silver hair was pulled back into two little pig tails, and she was clutching a small, stuffed elephant.

Oh my God. It's me. I don't remember this at all.

The little girl giggled as she struggled up the stairs to the attic, but she persevered and made it all the way to the top.

I tried to speak, but no sound came out. I was simply a bystander in this memory.

"29…30…31…" the women's voice continued downstairs.

So, if the little girl is me, then that means…Mom?

I tried to walk over to ladder, but something prevented me from travelling down it. Tears swell in my eyes, as I wanted to go down the ladder so badly.

"Uh-oh," my younger self said. I spun around to see she had caused a box to fall and spill out. I walked over to her and observe.

Younger me plopped down onto her butt and rummaged through the box's spilled contents. There were random trinkets and photos.

"49…50…Here I come! Where are you, Cassie?" I could hear my mother laugh as she searched for me.

Why don't I remember any of this?

I remember hide and seek being one of my favorite games to

play with my mother, but the attic had always been off limits.

Younger me hummed a tune and continued to look at the photos. An older-looking book was hidden underneath some of the photos. Younger me pulled it out and opened it.

"Cassandra, where are you?" my mother's voice travelled closer. "Oh, my goodness, Cassandra, are you up in the attic?"

Younger me continued to hum and ignored the franticness building in my mother's tone. I could hear someone coming up the ladder and I could feel anxiety building up inside of me. I held my breath as I glanced over to the opening.

My mother's beautiful silver hair appeared first as she made her way up the stairs, then her crystal blue eyes, and her porcelain skin. She looked concerned.

"Cassandra, how did you even get up here?" Relief and frustration flooded her face as she made her way over to where younger me was sitting.

Younger me shrugged. "I don't know, I saw the string and wanted to pull it and it just came down to me."

My mother was wearing an oversized sweater and high-waisted blue jeans. Her hair was pulled back into a perfect bun, not a single strand of hair out of place. I wantede to run to her, to hug her, to cry in her arms, and tell her everything, but my legs felt frozen in place.

"Ahh, I see. Oh, honey, what are you looking at?" My mother's voice was always so sweet and warm. She really did make every room that she entered brighter.

"Hi, Mommy, I made a mess. I'm sowwy." Younger me stuck out her bottom lip and acted sad.

My mother laughed as she bent down to help clean up the mess. "That's okay, Sweetie. Life gets messy sometimes, doesn't it?"

Younger me nodded and smiled.

"What book is this, Mommy?"

I looked down through teary eyes and noticed it was an old yearbook. I didn't recognize any of the names or pictures on the page.

"Well, that is mommy's yearbook from when she and daddy met. See? Look," she turned the page, "there's Daddy, and that is me."

I looked at their pictures, both smiling, both so young.

"Cool!" younger me squealed.

My mother had gone back to cleaning up the spilled contents and younger me kept flipping through the pages. I couldn't take my eyes off of my mother. It had been so long, I had almost forgotten just how beautiful she was. Pictures just did not do her justice.

"Mommy! Look, it's me!" Younger me squealed again as I held up a picture.

I leaned forward to get a better look, as my legs were still immobile.

"But I don't have black hair?" Younger me grew mad over this detail and pouted.

The little girl in the photo did look almost exactly like me, except for the fact she had black hair. Her eyes were exactly like mine, except reversed, like a mirror image.

What the fuck…That can't be…

"Give me that!" my mother's tone was stern as she ripped the photo from younger me's hand.

Younger me began to cry as my mother held the photo close to her chest.

"Everything okay up there?" My father's voice called from below.

Hearing my father's voice caused my mother to panic, and she frantically tried to clean everything up. I looked down at the page the picture had fallen out of, that younger me still had in her hands. My eyes scoured through the rows of names until one caught my eye.

Victor Holloway

He had olive skin and the blackest hair I had ever seen. His smile was warm, but his eyes were hard and cold.

"Girls, are you up there?" my father's voice called from below.

"Just a minute, John," my mother frantically spit out.

She grabbed the book out of younger me's hands and shoved it into the box, along with the photo. She used her magic to slide the box far away from me and took me into her arms.

"Cassie, shh, look at me," she said, as younger me struggled against her. "Look at Mommy, Cassie."

Younger me stopped crying and looked at her with big, sad eyes. My mother placed a hand on the side of my cheek, and I could see it begin to glow underneath.

"We do not go into the attic. We do not remember a little girl with black hair," my mother whispered.

Younger me's eyes glossed over as I was put into a trance. My mother repeated her words quietly.

"I'm coming up," my father said, as the ladder squeaked beneath his weight.

I stared at my mother, mouth agape as she hurried to get younger me to my feet. She adjusted her pants and composure just as my father popped his head up.

"There's my girls," he said happily.

My mother laughed as she pulled me along. Piggy dragged on the floor as I walked mindlessly.

"What is up with my little Cassie-poo?" my father asked as he bent down and grabbed my small hand.

My father looked so handsome in a flannel and pair of old khakis. There were paint and grease stains all over him. His hair was disheveled, and he wore large, round glasses but they fit his face shape very well. They made him look like Milo from Atlantis.

"She's fine, she's just tired. I think I will put her to bed," my mother said quickly.

My father stood up and kissed my mother swiftly on the lips.

"How did I get so lucky?" he beamed.

She playfully pushed him away. "Down, boy, down."

They laughed together and started to make their way down the stairs. The hatch closed and I was left alone. I looked around the room and spotted a large, antique mirror leaned up against the wall.

My legs were released from their invisible hold and I traveled toward the mirror. I already sensed that she would be waiting for me in the mirror, but I wasn't afraid anymore.

The little girl from the photo was reflected in the mirror. As I came closer, the little girl slowly transformed into Lauren. Except she wasn't angry, she was sad. I could feel her pain and her sadness exuding out of the mirror. I didn't know why, but I felt compelled to reach up and press my palm against the mirror. Lauren looked down at my hand and slowly pulled hers up to meet mine. But just as her hand was about to meet mine, the glass shattered.

My eyes flutter open to see the white brick wall that lines all the rooms. The morning light is harsh and unforgiving as I slowly wake up. I groan and roll over on my other side. I am startled to see Henry in bed, but then I remember this is not mine, nor Cillian's room. Last night's sexcapade flirts its way back into the front of my mind and I sigh. I don't regret it, so I'm not sure why I feel so off about it.

Henry looks so peaceful as he sleeps. He truly is a very handsome man. His features are all proportioned just right and well defined. My stirring must be just enough to pull him from his slumber. He slowly opens his eyes and begins to move around.

"Bloody hell, why is it so bright?" he says groggily.

I giggle, as his accent is much heavier when he has just woken up. He must've forgotten I am there as well, because my giggling causes his eyes to shoot open.

"Good morning, Henry," I say quietly. "How's your head?"

He groans and closes his eyes. "Pounding. Like someone took a jackhammer to it."

"Gotta love alcohol," I say in a joking tone.

Suddenly, Henry's door flings open, and there stands the Headmistress. Her abrupt entrance causes me to jump and clutch the bed sheet tightly to my bare chest.

"Jesus, Mum, ever heard of knocking? Get out!" Henry is just as surprised as I am, and he too jolts upright.

The Headmistress does not seem fazed by the scene before her and continues to stand in the doorway.

"Training in fifteen minutes. I will see you both there."

"I am a grown ass adult, Mum. You cannot just barge in here like this. Plus, it's Saturday, there isn't training on Saturdays," Henry complains.

"You two have training on Saturdays now. Fifteen minutes," she repeats herself.

"Ugh, get out!" Henry shouts in frustration.

The Headmistress glares at Henry, but leaves the room, shutting the door loudly behind her. Henry flops back onto the bed and groans.

"I am so sorry about her."

"No worries," I say, feeling very uncomfortable now.

"She used to not be this bad, but since my dad passed last year, she hasn't really been the same."

I just assumed that Henry's father was somewhere else other

than the Academy. I didn't realize that he was dead. I probably should have, though.

"Henry, I am so sorry. I-I didn't know."

Henry sits back up and looks at me. "No worries. There is no way you would have known otherwise. Car accident. At least it happened quickly, and he didn't have to suffer…"

A car accident? Interesting…

I can see Henry is being burdened by a memory. I place my hand on his back and rub it gently. His skin is smooth, and I can feel all his muscles as my hand travels over them.

"Life is not fair. That thing is certain," I say to break the silence.

Henry sniffles and takes a deep breath in. "Well, enough about that. We should probably get going, yeah?"

I nod and we climb out of bed. We both dress quickly and quietly. I look at my phone to see if I have any messages, but there are just a couple social media notifications. I wonder if Cillian has made it safely or not, but I try not to think about him.

Out of sight, out of mind, right?

I pull my hair up into a ponytail as Henry slips on his exercise shoes. I contemplate bringing up last night, but don't know how to approach it. I have my hand on the doorknob to leave, when Henry's hand at my waist makes me pause.

"Hey, Cassie?"

I turn around to face him. "Yeah?"

"Last night was truly unforgettable, but I can understand if you want to dial things back. We both had been drinking, and I don't want you to feel like I expect anything more from you now because of what we did. I don't want to complicate things more for you." His words are sincere.

I smile at him. "Henry, last night was one of the best nights I have ever had," I say, because it is the truth. It seems Henry always feels like he has to question himself with me, and that isn't fair to him.

He blushes and smiles. "Good, good."

I take a deep breath. "Well, let's go train...with your mother..."

He chuckles. "Hey, by the way, were you having a bad dream last night?" Henry says as we make our way out of his room.

I stop dead in my tracks. Mom, Dad, Lauren, all of it comes rushing back to me, every little detail. Between waking up with Henry and the Headmistress barging in, I have almost completely forgotten about my dream.

"Cassie, you okay?" Henry asks, as I stand frozen in the doorway.

I clear my throat. "Um, yeah, no, yeah, I'm fine. I guess I must've. I don't remember really now."

"You look like you've seen a ghost. Are you sure you're up for training? I can try and tell Mum that you weren't feeling well?"

"No, really, I am fine. Does the school keep archives of its students and events?" I say, changing the subject.

He chuckles. "Yeah, I mean, that's all in the library. Have you not been to the library yet?"

I squint my eyes at him and give him a sarcastic look. "Ha, ha, very funny. I have been busy."

"Well, I can show you after training, if you want?"

"Yeah, that would be great. Thanks."

"Of course. Come on now, Mum is a bit of stickler about being on time," Henry says, putting his arm around my shoulders.

I nod in agreement and we make our way toward the Training Room.

Training with Henry's mom is a huge adjustment. Instead of her normal posh look, she dons a deep plum exercise pants-and-jacket set. However, her graying auburn hair is still pulled back into a perfect bun. She is unforgiving and relentless in her attacks. She is able to successfully hold off both Henry's and my attacks. I am surprised at how well she handles herself, as I have never seen her out of high heels. She is strong and cunning.

"Stop being so obvious with your blows, Miss Rodden, and you, Henry, stop being lazy with your punches. Follow through, people!"

Henry and I exchange frustrated glances as we try to get the upper hand.

He explains to me on one of our breaks that the Headmistress has an affinity for insight.

"It's like she always knows what I am going to do next," I say, and I chug some water from my bottle.

"Yeah, you know how they say that mothers have eyes in the back of their heads? Well, she kind of does."

"Please don't tell me she has actual eyes…"

Henry chuckles. "No, not at all. Her powers allow her to get insight on what may happen in the next couple of seconds when she is close to someone. Or, for example, her powers allow her to get insight into if someone is lying or not." Henry explains everything so nonchalantly.

Hmmm…interesting.

"But, like, can you ever get around it?" I question.

"Yeah, sometimes. Nothing is perfect, and her insight doesn't always work all the time. Just like anything else, there are many factors at play, many paths that something can take."

"Hmm, interesting," I say, seeing the Headmistress in a different way.

"Okay, both of you, get back up," she directs. "Time to work on your joined powers."

I look at the clock on the wall across the room. It reads 1:33 p.m. I groan with impatience. I just want to go to the library already. I repeat the main themes of the dream in my head, so I won't forget anything—Lauren, photo, mirror, attic, Mom, and Victor.

Henry isn't looking too good from being hungover, but he is trying. I place my hand on his shoulder and try to see if my magic can make him feel better, and it does some.

Henry lets out a large sigh.

"Mum, we've been here all morning now, and haven't had

anything to eat yet. Can we please stop soon?"

The Headmistress walks over to where we are sitting. Looking up at her from down below, she looks even more terrifying.

"Couple more hours, then you can go. You have to be strong, Henry. I expect nothing less of you and will not accept anything other than perfection. Do you hear me?" she says harshly.

Henry gulps and nods. I look at both of them in silence. The Headmistress must realize how harsh she is being, so she offers up something to ease the tension.

"How about I ask one of the guards to see if they can go fetch granola bars or something, hmm?"

I wonder how hard it must have been for Henry, growing up with the Headmistress for a mother.

He gives her a halfhearted smile, which seems to make the Headmistress think she has ameliorated the situation and everything is just fine. She walks over to one of the guards nearby and asks them to retrieve snacks and bring them back. I pat Henry's knee for reassurance as she speaks to the guard. He looks embarrassed, but also frustrated. We help each other to our feet and brace ourselves for more training.

The next couple of hours are spent training our joined powers, with another small break for snacks. We are both exhausted and smelly. I can feel my powers being drained as we continue. Henry and I do learn, however, that working together in close contact, our powers are noticeably heightened. We even discover that we can manipulate electricity. It makes sense now when lights have flickered up to this point. I wonder if Cillian and I could do the same, though. I wish I could've had the chance to do more magic with him before he left.

Thankfully, though, it looks like the Headmistress is tiring as well. We finish up one last exercise and she releases us to go about our day.

"Training. Bright and early, tomorrow morning," she tells us as she gathers up her things.

I shoot Henry an "Are you kidding me?" look.

"Headmistress, do we have to train every day? Can we have tomorrow to just relax? I was also thinking about having a little memorial for Yash and Nora, as well as everyone else who passed," I approach her with caution.

Without hesitation she replies, "Absolutely not. We are in a very pivotal time. With Cillian off investigating our tip, we need to be prepared to move at any moment. Which means you must be at your peak; you both must be. You are the Chosen One. You have people who need you to lead them, which is not any easy job."

My attention focuses on Cillian's name the moment she spoke it. "Did Cillian, I mean, Professor Morris make it over there successfully?"

"Yes, he did. Now get some rest, eat up, and recharge for tomorrow."

"I would really like to be able to hold a gathering or something for everyone, Headmistress. I feel that it may be good for not only myself, but the other students. Plus, to see their leader mourning their people is a good thing, right? It shows that I care, and that the peoples' deaths won't be in vain, or have happened for nothing."

Headmistress Ansley ponders my argument and eyes me calculatingly for a moment.

"Very well. I will arrange something for tomorrow evening, but in the meantime, you will do as I say, and train on my schedule. Understood?"

Like making a deal with the devil.

I am elated with my little win, so I overlook her overbearing attitude.

"Thank you, Headmistress."

She nods her head slightly toward me. She turns toward the exit, but stops herself and turns back to Henry and me.

"Another thing… I do not care if you are fucking, but please be smart about it."

My mouth drops open in embarrassment, and my cheeks flush red.

"For the love of all that is holy, Mum, please just…please just go," Henry says, blushing redder than I have ever seen someone blush before.

She cracks a smile and then heads out of the room. I look at Henry, and we both bust out laughing.

"Well, that wasn't absolutely mortifying," I say between laughs.

Henry shakes his head and finishes gathering his things.

"How about you and I go clean up, then food, and then library?"

"Fooood. Yes, yes, and yes. I am absolutely starving." My stomach starts to verbally protest about its hunger.

We make our way out and back to Henry's room. He says that I can shower first, to get the most hot water. I pause in front of the mirror after my shower. I look over every inch, searching for Lauren, but there is nothing. Just a normal mirror. I sigh and make my way out of the bathroom. Henry is on his phone when I exit, but quickly puts it down when he sees me.

"Shower is all yours," I say, holding up one towel around my body with one hand and the using the other to dry my hair with a second towel.

Henry stares at me, smitten.

"Will you stay with me again tonight?" he asks.

I walk over to my bag of clothes and begin to pull out an outfit. I'm not sure what to say to him, and he senses my hesitation.

"Totally okay, if not. I don't want to assume that you'll be staying here."

I smile at him. "Maybe, okay?"

"Good enough for me," Henry says as he grabs a clean towel and heads to shower.

I sit on the edge of Henry's bed for a moment and hear him start the shower. I am tired and sore from training. I finally retrieve a black turtleneck and a pair or black jeans from my bag and pull them on. Once dressed, I check my phone for any new messages, but there are none. I open my text conversation with Cillian and begin to type.

Me: did you make it okay?

My thumb hovers over the Send button as I debate whether or not to send it. I close my eyes, hit Send, and then throw my phone on Henry's bed. I pace around the room for a handful of minutes until I hear it *ding* with a new message. I practically fly over to Henry's bed and scoop up my phone.

Cillian: Yes.

Yes? That's it?

I groan in frustration. I sit back on the edge of the bed and stare at my phone.

Should I reply? Should I say something more?

My brow furrows as I debate.

"Everything okay?" Henry asks.

I look up and see that he has completed his shower and is standing in the doorway looking at me.

"Yeah, no, everything is fine," I say quickly. "Sorry, I didn't hear the water shut off."

"No worries. You just looked really consumed and I wondered if something happened."

"Nope. All good," I say, putting my phone by my thigh.

Henry walks over to where I am sitting. The towel around his waist looks as if it could fall at any moment. My eyes become fixated on his physique. My breathing gets heavier as he gets closer. Moments from last night flash in my head.

Henry is silent as he saunters over and stops directly in front of me. The towel and his pelvic region are at eye level. I clear my throat and look away to be considerate.

Henry leans down and it looks like he's coming in for a kiss. I close my eyes and prepare my lips to embrace his, but instead Henry chuckles softly, and I feel a tug at my thigh.

"Pardon me, love," Henry whispers in my ear.

I open my eyes and look down to see that I am sitting on the clothes Henry had gotten out to wear.

I stand up quickly. "I am so sorry."

Henry continues to chuckle. "No worries, love. I must admit, I like seeing you flustered."

My turtleneck suddenly becomes very warm and I pull it away from my neck to try and get some air.

"Ha, ha, very funny. Don't know if you know this or not, but you are incredibly good looking. I'd be lying if I said I wasn't nervous around you sometimes."

"I could say the exact same about you," Henry says, moving closer to me again. He takes one of my hands in his.

Ding.

My phone breaks the moment and Henry steps back to his bed. He picks up my phone and hands it to me, but the screen flashes on with the movement, and a message pops up across the lock screen.

Cillian: Did you need something?

I try to grab it quickly out of Henry's hand, but he has already seen who it is. His smile fades as he looks away.

"Sorry," he says, as if he was wrong for having noticed who the message is from.

"It's not important." I slide the phone into my back pocket. "Food time?"

Henry nods, but I can tell the mood has been ruined.

Ding.

I purse my lips as my phone sounds off another message alert.

God dammit. I really need to turn it to vibrate.

"I can wait outside while you change?" I offer.

"Yeah, sure. I'll be ready soon."

Henry won't look at me. I scurry out of the room and let out a frustrated sigh, after closing the door behind me. I retrieve my phone from my pocket and immediately switch it to be vibrate mode. Cillian's messages preview on my lock screen. I slide open my phone and read them.

Cillian: Sorry I did not notify you when I made it.
Cillian: I am sorry for the other day.

I decide to leave Cillian on Read as I try to think of ways to smooth things over with Henry. Him knowing I've seen his messages are good enough for right now. Cillian cannot take up more space in my life than I have already allowed. It isn't long before Henry steps out of his room.

"Henry, I'm sorry. I was just checking to make sure he made it and was safe."

He locks his door and sighs. "You don't have to be sorry, Cassie, and you don't have to explain yourself. All I ask is that you be honest with me."

"Of course, I have been."

Mostly.

"Let's not even worry about any of this right now. I am here with you, and I am not going to let anything ruin that."

I smile. "Sounds good to me."

Henry smiles back. "Now, let's go get some food. I texted Chef Tommy and he said he'd have something waiting for us. I just have to stop by my Mum's room really quick, if you don't mind?"

"Not at all. Let's go," I say. I am eager to move away from the awkward situation, both physically and metaphorically.

The awkwardness of Cillian's texts lingers with us as we walk down the hallway. A few other students roam the halls, as well as guards, of course. Every time we pass a student, they stop and stare at me. Some say a few words, others just observe. I try to be warm to everyone. I follow Henry over to the part of the school where Cillian's room is. I remember the shattered mirror in his room that I still have to clean up.

Ugh. I should do that soon.

We pass Cillian's room and travel deeper down the stretch of hallway, until we come to the end. There is a large, distinguished door that looks more secure than the other doors we have passed. A guard is also waiting outside.

"Hey, Phil, is Mum in?" Henry asks.

"Sorry, Henry, she's away for a meeting."

"No worries. Can I pop in really quick and grab something?"

"Of course," Phil says as he moves out of the way.

Henry turns to me and says, "I'll be right back."

"Sure," I reply, and he crosses the threshold. I try to peek around Phil and get a glimpse inside, but Henry closes the door quickly.

I wait in awkward silence for Henry to return. Phil focuses his gaze straight ahead.

"So, uh, Phil, don't think I've met you yet?" I say, trying to make conversation.

"No, ma'am, we have not met, but I have heard all about you. Everyone has." Phil's voice is deep and resonating. His beautiful ebony skin blends seamlessly with his dark attire. "We are all very hopeful now, I must say. I lost my eldest to the Anarchy a few years back. It is comforting to know that we have real hope now. Those bastards will pay," his accent is Nigerian, and it is soothing.

I straighten my posture. "I am so sorry for your loss."

Phil's face is softer than I originally thought. His eyes are big and warm, his beard speckled with gray hair. I can feel the pain in his heart from his loss. I am compelled to reach out to him, and I do so without realizing. I place my hand on his shoulder and let my magic seep into him, replacing his pain with solace. I can feel his pain, and I know exactly what is wrong.

"What are you doing?" he asks nervously.

I pull my hand away quickly, as if I have just been zapped.

"I am sorry, I don't know why…"

A smile slowly spreads across Phil's face. "Thank you," he says quietly.

The door opens and I take a step back. Henry slides something into his pocket and looks at Phil and me.

"See you later, Phil."

"Of course, Henry. Miss Rodden, it was an honor meeting you," he says, and bows slightly.

"You can call me Cassie if you'd like, Phil."

"Well, Cassie, thank you," Phil says once more.

I give him a smile before we turn to head back down the hallway. I think about the magic I have just done and want to test it out. I grab Henry's hand as we walk and intertwine my fingers with his. He seems surprised at first, but goes along with it. I can feel his emotions. He is anxious and nervous, but there is also a hint of sadness. I try to push my magic deeper, but I see our joined hands begin to glow. I withdraw my magic before Henry notices, and the glowing subsides. Henry rubs my hand gently with his thumb as we walk, and I smile. It is nice holding hands with someone.

We travel into the back room of the Dining Hall, where

Tommy is waiting for us, a large wicker basket rests in his hands. Henry takes it from him and looks so happy.

"Thanks again, Chef!"

"Of course, of course. Anything I can do for the Chosen One and you, Henry, I will be more than happy to do it."

It will be a challenge getting used to all this special treatment and attention.

"Thank you," I mumble uncomfortably.

Henry motions for me to follow him out of the Dining Hall.

"Where are we going?" I ask, confused why we aren't just eating with the others already here.

"Just wait and see," Henry says suspiciously.

Stepping carefully up a winding stone staircase, we come to a large metal door. Henry keys in a code and I hear a click as it unlocks. He opens the door, and a rush of light illuminates the staircase. I have to blink my eyes several times before they adjust. Through the door is the roof of the Academy, or at least a portion of the school's roof.

It is chilly up here, and I shiver as I follow Henry further onto the roof. We are up so high, I can see for miles. Some of the trees have beautifully-colored leaves still clinging to them, not wanting to let go just yet. Those trees are further away from the school than we are allowed to venture. I notice as we move closer to the edge, a small table and two chairs are set up. I feel butterflies start to form in my stomach.

"Wow, it's beautiful up here," I say in awe.

Henry sets the basket down on the table and looks at the view.

"Yeah, it really is beautiful. I like to come here when things get heavy and I need a little escape. I've spent most of my life on these grounds."

There is a slight sadness hidden in his words. I take a moment to imagine what that feels like.

It would feel like a prison, almost.

"Sorry, it's not the nicest setup, and it's chillier than I expected," Henry says. It's obvious he is disappointed by the weather.

I look up to the sky as I take a seat at the little table. It is an endless sea of grey clouds. There is a slight breeze and the threat of possible snow looms in the air. I concentrate on picturing the sun bursting through the clouds and the wind subsiding. And sure enough, it happens. The sun's rays peek through the clouds and shine on us.

"I don't know what you're talking about, Henry. I think everything is absolutely perfect." I smile and wink at him as he sits down.

He looks up at the sky, where the sun is beaming through the grey more and more. He chuckles.

"Are you doing this?" he asks, looking back at me.

"I haven't a clue as to whatever you could mean," I say playfully.

Our spot on the roof has warmed up about fifteen U.S.

degrees in mere moments, while the sun kisses our cheeks and plays on the table. Henry opens the basket, and I am anxious for its contents.

"Close your eyes," he says.

I look at him curiously. "Why?"

"Just do it, Cassie. You are so stubborn," he says with a chuckle.

"Fine," I say, and I close my eyes. I hear items being pulled from the basket and set onto the table. I imagine what he could possibly be doing. I try using my sense of smell, but it is no luck.

"Okay, and…open!"

I open my eyes slowly to find a bunch of assorted snacks, drinks, and sandwiches. My heart instantly melts, as I make the realization that these are all things I have been craving from back home.

"Sour belts, peanut butter and jelly sandwiches, licorice twists, spicy pickles, and oh my god, is that movie theater popcorn?!"

"Sure is, I had Chef go run and pick some up at the nearest theater," Henry beams.

"Oh my god, is that Corn Stuff as well! How did you get my grandmother's recipe?" I am so elated, I can hardly control my happiness. My mouth instantly waters with hunger.

Henry chuckles. "I may or may not have gotten your grandmother's contact information and called to ask her some of your favorite things. I hope that's okay. She said you spoke of me when you visited her."

"That is totally okay! Wow, Henry, I am…I don't know what to say." I have no idea why, but tears start to well in my eyes as I look over the picnic he has created for me.

"Why are you crying? Have I upset you?" Henry grows concerned.

"No, not at all. It's just…no one has ever done something like this for me before."

"Well, uh, I've got one more thing for you as well, actually," Henry says as he retrieves a small velvet box from his pocket. "This is why I needed to stop by my Mum's room."

He places the small box on the table and pushes it toward me. I stare at it hesitantly.

"Don't worry, it's not a ring," Henry says with a smirk.

I let out a nervous laugh and pick up the box. The black velvet is soft against my fingertips. I slowly open the hinged top to reveal a beautiful necklace. I can sense Henry's eyes on me, gauging my reaction.

The necklace is simplistically stunning. It is a gold chain with a gold-set, hexagon-shaped black onyx pendant hanging from it. Dead set in the middle of the black hexagon, is a small-but-beautiful diamond gemstone.

"Do you like it?" He asks nervously.

"Henry, I absolutely love it. It's beautiful. Will you help me put it on?"

He practically lunges from his seat and rushes over to assist me. I hand him the box and move my hair to one side. He removes the necklace from the box, secures it around my neck, and lets it fall to its resting place on my chest. I pull my hair through and look down at the pendent.

"Thank you so much, for all of this, Henry."

He shifts back into his seat instead of walking around and it makes me giggle.

"Mum said we should be trying to use magic whenever we can, to build up our stamina."

"Makes sense," I say as I reach over and take his hand in mine. I try to repeat what I did the night at the bar with the crowd, and with Phil earlier. Henry sucks in a breath, and I can feel my magic working through him.

"What are you doing?"

"A little something I realized I could do. I think I will call it an Impression. Sort of similar to influence magic, but it deals with emotions rather than the mind."

"I feel amazing," Henry says, sitting back in his chair.

"Well, now you can feel exactly how you've made me feel right now."

He smiles, and I blush.

"So, why do you call the corn casserole 'Corn Stuff'?" Henry asks, pointing to the yellow dish on the table.

I laugh as I withdraw my hand from his. "Erm, my mother always called it that, so it just kind of stuck."

"Adorable," he says quietly.

"Hmm, what to eat first? I think I will go with the PB and J and popcorn with a spicy pickle."

"Go for it," Henry says, curiosity in his tone.

Henry and I both laugh as we sit, consuming the various fare. Henry judges me for my unique food combinations, but is open to trying them anyway.

"Everything is so sugary in America," Henry says, leaning back and patting his stomach.

"Yes, yes, it is. But isn't it just so delicious?"

He chuckles. After I finish eating, I sit back and just observe Henry. He is looking out at the view. His oatmeal-colored sweater complements his skin tone perfectly. The way the sun cascades down on him bring his emerald eyes alive with colors I haven't noticed before—there are orange tones speckled throughout. Henry soon notices me starring.

"Do I have something on my face?"

I giggle. "No. I am just appreciating the view."

Henry blushes and smiles.

"Want to get headed to the library here soon?"

I sigh deeply and look back out at the trees and the sky. I need to find answers. I need to make sense of it all.

"There you go again, looking far away. Cassie, what's going on?"

I didn't notice that I have begun to fidget with my new necklace.

"I lied earlier, when you asked me if I had a bad dream. I did. Well, it seemed more like a memory that I had forgotten almost, or one that had been taken away from me."

"Do you want to talk about it?"

"Yeah, I think I do."

With Cillian away, I need someone to talk everything out with and think it through. I need to know if I sound crazy or not, and I trust Henry.

"Can a witch have the power to erase memories or make someone forget?"

"I haven't heard of anyone being able to do that, but anything's possible. Why?"

"I think my mom was able to do it. In my dream, I was very young; I think this had to have been right before the accident. I had wandered off to our attic and found an old yearbook of hers, from her time at the Academy." The sun is slowly being consumed by a sea of clouds. "And tucked inside that yearbook, there was a photo of a little girl who looked just like me, only she had black hair. My mom, she, um, she got really upset and took the picture from me and put everything back into the box. She kept repeating to me, 'We do not go into the attic. We do not remember a little girl with black hair,' my eyes went all glazed, and before last night, I have no recollection of that memory."

"So…what does the little girl have to do with anything?" Henry asks, confused.

"I was able to look at the page where the little girl's picture was tucked, and I saw a man named Victor Holloway."

"That's the guy my Mum mentioned earlier, isn't it?"

"Yeah, it is. Um, I guess, let me try and tie this all together. I've been seeing Lauren around...in mirrors and in dreams. I don't know how, and part of me thinks I am going crazy, but I think she's trying to tell me something. The reason I got so mad at you last night for saying she and I look alike, and that we could be related, is because I think you might be right."

"Come on, Cassie, I was just making a drunken observation."

I look at him. "After my mother slid the box away with the picture and yearbook, I saw the little black-haired girl in the mirror in the attic. And when I got closer, she turned into Lauren. She looked a little different than I remember, but I could tell it was her. Her eyes were exactly like mine, except mirrored." I stand up and pace back and forth, fidgeting with my necklace.

"What are you trying to say, Cassie? How does this Victor Holloway guy mix into all of this?" Henry is growing concerned and stands up as well.

The sky darkens. I glance up at it and try to get my emotions under control.

"I don't know yet. But I think..." I stop pacing and look at him. "My mother was pregnant at her Joining Ceremony. I-I think Lauren is my sister. It does and doesn't make sense at the same time, and I know I sound crazy."

It feels like a weight has been lifted off my shoulders as I say the words out loud.

"So, that's why you've been asking all the questions and want to go to the library?"

"Yeah, it is. I need answers, Henry, and I think that sorting this out will make everything better. The Serpents told me to start from the beginning."

"Well, we are in this together, so count me in. Your battles are my battles." Henry walks over and takes me into his arms for a hug.

I welcome his embrace. My muscles relax into him as his aroma fills my senses.

"I didn't mean to ruin this perfect date with all my crap," I say into his chest.

He leans back to look at me, "Oh, so you think this is a date, huh?"

"Oh, shut up."

We giggle and embrace for a few moments more. When we pull away from each other, we gather our feast and head back to the stairs. I glance over my shoulder at the view one last time and descend the stone steps with Henry. This is a moment that I will cherish forever, but it is time to go back to the real world and finally get some answers.

CHAPTER TWENTY-TWO

We drop the basket off back in the kitchen, but I make sure to grab my licorice twists and sour belts out of it before we head to the library. When we arrive, I am greeted with an endless collection. It seems to be filled with every book imaginable. I truly do not know how I haven't stumbled across the library at some point in my time here. To be fair, though, the entrance is tucked away down a hallway that I never have to travel. I am overwhelmed as Henry and I walk past row after row after row of books. Henry tells me that they keep the historical archives in the very back, in a secured room.

"Why do they have to be secured?" I ask, as we plunge deeper into the library.

"Well, for normal reasons, I guess. A lot of very powerful peoples' kids attend the Academy. Many witches hold very influential positions around the world—which helps us stay in the know about the Anarchy. But you wouldn't know it from looking at the students. You can assume here and there, but for the most part, we treat everyone equally around here. We know little about peoples' home lives on purpose, in case any one of us is captured during an attack."

I think about Henry's explanation as we reach the Archives room. The door is surrounded by windows with mesh wiring behind them. Henry mentions that they are bullet proof. The entrance has a lock in which one must insert a special key, next to a keypad to input a code, both of which are necessary for entry. Henry completes steps and the door whines and groans open.

"Couldn't someone just shift in?" I ask.

"This room is equipped with special herbs and hard spells built into the walls and windows. You can even see etchings if you look closely." He points. "They prevent witches from being able to circumvent the key-and-code combo."

"Oh," I say, walking past him into the Archives.

Duh, that makes sense.

The air inside is stale and musty. I wrinkle my nose in an effort to adjust to the odor. There are several shelves with books and files, as well as filing cabinets.

"Where do you think we should start?" Henry asks.

"Hmmm…I guess let's pull everything we can find on the Anarchy and its beginning and put it in one pile. In another pile, let's place everything on Victor Holloway and my mother and father and their time spent here. Finally, I want everything that we can find on Lauren in another stack off to the side."

Henry looks at me apprehensively as he rubs the back of his neck.

"I know, it's going to be a lot, but I think if we pull everything first and then go through it all, it'll be easier to cross reference, maybe?"

"Do you think you have any 'Chosen One' powers to help us?" Henry teases.

I roll my eyes and smile.

"How deep does this room run?"

"You know, I am actually not sure. I think there is also a level below this as well. The staircase is in the back," Henry says.

"Do you know how the literature is arranged?"

"Current students' files are up front and the further back you go in time corresponds with the further you go back in the room, I believe. The bookcases should be labelled with year ranges. The Anarchy will have their own section. I think that is toward the back also."

I let out a small sigh.

This is going to suck.

"Okay, I will start by trying to find stuff on my parents and Victor. Can you work on Lauren and Anarchy?"

"Let's get to it," Henry tries to act excited, but we both know this is going to take time.

And take time, it does. Henry and I work furiously, trying to pull all that we think may be useful from the shelves and filing cabinets. A lot of files have information missing, or they are arranged incorrectly. For being such a fancy school with fancy protocols to protect all this stuff, one would think they would spend the time and effort to organize it properly, so it could be utilized efficiently. Two of the piles grow as we search, the exception being Lauren's. We both discover that there is very little information about her and her family—which makes sense if everything about her has been fabricated.

On the other hand, there is a plethora of articles and records on the Anarchy. I refine our search to anything that has to do with the Anarchy's origin. When it comes to my parents and Victor, I retrieve everything I find about them. I also keep an eye out for anything involving car accidents in which witches have been killed, to see if there are any patterns to be found there. Something deep inside of me tells me this subject deserves more attention. It can't all be coincidence.

Why were my parents in a rush? Who or what were they running from?

I lean against one of the bookcases and munch on some candy. I am getting overwhelmed and lost in all the records. I pull out my phone and glance at the time. It is 6:03 p.m.

"Okay, I think this is everything," Henry says, bringing a few final files over to complete our piles. "Now what?"

I lower another helpless sour belt into my mouth and look at Henry as I chew it.

"You know, candy doesn't count as real food, right?" he says sarcastically.

"Shush," I finish chewing and swallow. "Well, I guess, now we try and connect all the dots. Is there a white board or chalkboard we can use to organize everything? I think the visual will help us sort it out"

"I can certainly look for one, and if I can't find one, I can always have a guard help locate one."

"Okay, yeah, sure, that would be great. Want to grab some 'real' food for us while you're out there? Since my candy isn't good enough?" I tease.

He chuckles. "Yeah, I'll bring back food as well. You sure you'll be okay in here alone?"

"I should be. I have to start working through all of this mess," I say with a smile, gesturing over the piles.

Henry walks over to give me a swift kiss on my cheek before departing. I sit down at the table on which our piles are stacked and debate where to begin.

"Welp, Mom and Dad, guess I will start with you two. You were my beginning, after all."

Their stack includes yearbooks from the years they attended the Academy, so I start with those. I find a pile of sticky notes nearby and flag any and every page that shows my mother, my father, or Victor. With my parents, it is hard seeing all the photos from when they were younger. They look so happy here, like they are thriving. I hold back tears as I continue flagging their pictures.

Victor's background, on the other hand, is just like Lauren's. It seems to be fabricated, with details missing. He came from a family that had long attended Kingshire. He looks happy and—dare I say— normal, just like my parents do. There are a handful of pictures with the three of them together. They look like friends just hanging out. I do notice, though, as the years go on, that Victor's demeanor appears withdrawn and he is in fewer photos. If he is in one, he is often pictured off to the side and looks sullen. A part of me feels bad for him. I try to find anything that would have caused the change in him, but there is too much to go through right now, and the yearbooks aren't offering much insight.

I check my phone to see how long Henry has been gone—about fifteen minutes.

Ugh.

I open my messages and realize that I have still not responded back to Cillian. There is so much I want to tell him, but it seems like too much to discuss via text. I look out through the windows to see if Henry is coming. Nothing.

Me: No. Didn't need anything. Working with Henry to try and find more info on the Anarchy and my parents.

Three little dots almost immediately form on the screen, signaling that he's typing. My body tenses up in anticipation.

Cillian: Good luck

I sigh. I unclench my muscles and slump back into my chair. As I do so, the door's locks click open and its seal releases. My eyes flash up, expecting to see Henry, but there isn't anyone in sight. I stand up, leaving my phone on the table, and proceed toward the door. It slides open slowly as I approach. My heart begins to pound.

The door creaks open to reveal Henry, who is bent down, retrieving something he has dropped on the floor. I clutch my chest and let out a sigh of relief.

"Oh, my goodness, Henry. You scared me. I didn't see you behind the door at first."

He stands up and chuckles.

"Oh, sorry, love. Fruit cup fell off the to-go container," he says, holding up the Styrofoam cartons and a fruit cup. He also has two bottles of Coca-Cola stuffed up into his armpits.

"Here, let me help you."

My heart is still racing as we clear off a spot to eat on the table.

"I have a guard retrieving a whiteboard for us, by the way."

"You are wonderful. Thank you."

I smile at Henry as we open our containers. I am surprised to see a burger and fries. Since being here, I have yet to see the cafeteria serve hamburgers. I eye Henry suspiciously.

"You know, you do not have to keep asking Tommy to make things especially for me." I hide how excited I am to dig in.

"Don't know what you're talking about," Henry says as he swirls around his container to show he has a burger as well. "I may or may not have suggested we incorporate more meals that are popular in other countries. Tomorrow, we are going to have curry."

"Ahh, well, look at you, helping Kingshire be more inclusive.

I am proud."

Henry blushes. "There's no reason why, with all the different people we have at this school, that we should only make meals related to our current geographic location. One thing at a time."

I look at Henry lovingly for a moment, but soon turn my attention back to my burger. I let out a delighted little squeal as I pick it up and begin eating veraciously.

We devour our food and then continue our investigation into the material in front of us. The guard brings in the whiteboard, and we create a timeline of events. We lay out profiles of Lauren, my parents, Victor, and myself. The hours pass, and Henry and I grow tired. We discover that Victor's father had passed away around the time he starts looking sullen in photos. When it comes to the Anarchy, records stretch back ages, but it is only in the past 25 years that they have really revved up their attacks—causing chaos and mass hysteria whenever they can. There is still so much mystery around the head of the Anarchy though, and how power is passed. Is it a group of people? Is it one person?

It is extremely late when we call it. We are both nodding off and our brains cannot process any more information. We sluggishly make our way back to his room. He asks if I want to spend the night, but I know I should get back to Cillian's room and clean up the mirror. Plus, I want to process everything on my own for a while.

Cillian's room is just as I left it. Shards of mirror are scattered all around the bathroom sink and floor. I do my best to clean it up and then shower. It is comforting to step out and not be worried that someone or something will be staring back at me from the mirror.

I slide into Cillian's bed and my head starts throbbing. I am apprehensive of falling asleep. The thought of dreaming about loved ones long lost terrifies me. It also scares me to think that I might have more memories that were hidden away by my mother. I am sure she had her reasons, but I want to know what those reasons are, and what else she hid from me. Another part of me wants to dream. It's possible my dreams hold more keys to the mystery of my beginning.

Ding.

Henry: I miss you already

Henry: I am so happy you like your necklace. Do you want to meet me or me meet you tomorrow?

I smile at Henry's messages. I touch the necklace, gently resting just below my collarbone.

Me: Thank you for everything. I love it.

Me: I'll meet you?

Henry: Sounds good

Henry: Good night

I set my phone down, my muscles ache from training and I know it will only get more intense. I feel myself slowly begin to drift away into unconsciousness. I am prepared for whatever greets me this time.

CHAPTER TWENTY-THREE

I am surprised to wake up to my alarm blaring and no dreams having been dreamt. I slept so hard that my arm is numb. It tingles with a thousand bees as I try to get the blood flowing again.

"Ugh, stupid arm," I say as I swing my legs over the side of the bed and stand up.

Buzz, buzz, buzz.

Who is calling me this early?

My arm finally starts feeling back to normal and I reach over and pick up my phone. My heart flutters when I see Cillian's contact displayed on the screen.

Cillian. Why is he calling?

I slide the accept button over and put the phone to my ear.

"Cillian?"

"Cassandra, I don't have much time, but you need to listen to me." His tone is serious, and he speaks quickly. "You are not safe. I fear that—" His sentence is cut off and I listen in earnest for the cause. I hear some commotion on his end.

"Cillian? Are you there?" My heart starts to race. I stand up and turn on the speakerphone, then hurry to get dressed.

"Cassandra? Are you there?"

My foot is halfway through a legging and I trip trying to get to phone.

"I'm here. What's going on?" I say breathlessly.

"I am so sorry; I didn't know it was going to get this complicated. Don't come for me."

"Cillian what do you mean? Hello? Hello?"

The line clicks dead as I hear shouting and a scream in the background.

"Fuck!"

I throw on a jacket and hop around as I frantically pull on my athletic shoes. I redial Cillian's number, but it goes straight to voicemail.

"Come on, come on, come on," I say, calling once more.

Voicemail.

"Dammit, Cillian, what is going on?"

I jam my other shoe on and shift into Henry's room. I surprise him getting dressed and he jumps into the air.

"Jesus, Cassie, you scared the piss out of me," Henry complains as he pulls a shirt on over his head.

"No time to talk. Cillian is in trouble. We need to get to your mom," I say. I don't wait for him to respond, and simply place my hand on him. I shift us both without effort to the Training Room.

The Headmistress is setting up today's training exercises with some guards when we appear beside her.

"Oh, perfect, on time. Actually, you are a tad early—"

"Cillian is in trouble," I interrupt her in urgency.

"What do you mean?" She looks just confused as Henry.

"Cillian just called me and said things are not good, and then I heard a commotion and screaming in the background," I spit out quickly.

Headmistress Ansley looks almost relieved for the slightest second.

"What do you mean, Cassie? What type of commotion?" Henry asks from beside me.

"I don't know. I heard struggling. Struggling like someone was maybe attacking him."

Neither Henry nor the Headmistress look too terribly concerned. This frustrates me.

"Why does no one else look concerned? I tried calling him back a bunch of times and it goes straight to voicemail."

"Ah, well, I will check in with Cillian if that will ease your mind, but he is a very well-trained operative and witch. I am sure you are just reading more into the situation than is there," the Headmistress says nonchalantly. "Also, if there were truly an issue, I don't think that he'd be calling *you*."

My ears burn with embarrassment as I realize how ridiculous I sound.

Of course, he would call his boss first, not me. I am so stupid.

I want to shrink away and die of embarrassment back in Cillian's room. I look at Henry, who now looks slightly annoyed.

"Sorry, I just was concerned." I look down at my feet, avoiding both of their gazes.

"Well, hey, on the plus side, you shifted us both," Henry tries to save me from the moment, even though he is irritated.

I look up at him, grateful for his rescue attempt.

"Yeah, Mum, I actually need to still brush my teeth. Do you mind checking in with Cillian while I go do that real quick?"

She looks extremely inconvenienced by Henry's request.

"Sure." She huffs. "I will be right back," she says flatly.

"Thank you," I offer, but she ignores it.

The Headmistress shifts away, and I look back to Henry.

"Thank you. I am so sorry."

"No worries. You've had a lot to be stressed out about lately. It's understandable. I'll be back." Henry says shortly.

"Okay."

He shifts away too, and I am left mostly alone in the middle of the Training Room. The guards around me are silent. I sink down to the ground and try calling Cillian one more time. It goes immediately to voicemail again. A pit forms in my stomach, but I try to not think about worst-case scenarios.

"Hey, it's me. Call me or text me and let me know you're all right. I'm worried."

I think it's a sufficient message and hang up. I wait for the others to join me. To distract myself, I stand up and start to stretch, but it doesn't help me stop questioning myself about what I had heard on the phone.

It isn't long before Henry shifts back, followed shortly by the Headmistress. I wait anxiously for her to spill what she's found out.

"Well, looks like this was all a misunderstanding. I spoke with Professor Morris and he sounds just fine."

That doesn't make sense.

"But what about… I mean, I heard a scream?"

"Ah, yes, well, the Professor said that he was…entertaining another operative." She clears her throat. "Looks like the call was an accident."

"But that's wrong. That's-that can't be the case," I protest.

"You told me you haven't been sleeping well, Cassie. Do you think maybe you're letting your mind play tricks on you?" Henry asks.

I look at him in complete shock. I've told him things in confidence, and now he is using them against me. I want to blast him across the room.

"Well, maybe you two need more time to rest. I shouldn't have been pushing you so hard right away. How about we suspend training for today, and you can use the time to rest and prepare for the memorial later. How does that sound?"

I feel like I am going crazy. I try to keep everything controlled and in check internally, but I am losing my hold.

Through clenched teeth, "Sounds great."

I turn and storm away, but Henry keeps up with me.

"Cassie, where are you going? I'm sorry for saying you were having trouble sleeping."

I stop abruptly and look at him hard in his eyes. "Don't you ever question me again or use what I've told you against me. I am stressed and I am tired, but that does not mean I am making this up. You're supposed to have my back."

My tone breaks through Henry's frustration, and he realizes how badly he has messed up. I can see the understanding in his eyes as he works it over.

"I didn't mean to—"

"Just leave me alone for a little bit, okay? I need to be alone."

"But you'll be back for the memorial, right?"

"Of course I will be. Can I have the key to the Archives room?" I hold my hand out.

Henry looks uncomfortable and glances around.

"I'm not really supposed to let go of it. Plus, you'd need the code as well."

"Fine, whatever then. Can you meet me down there when I text you?"

"Of course," Henry says, a little too happily for the mood of the situation.

I turn and leave him behind. I take a few steps and then shift to Cillian's and my spot. It is very cold out today. I can see my breath as I sit with my legs pulled up to my chest. The ground is hard beneath me, as it's slowly beginning to freeze for the season. I retrieve my phone from my pocket and pull up Cillian's contact. I call once more, and once more, voicemail.

"Ugh, come on, Cillian."

I hang up and type up a message.

Me: Please call me when you can. Something doesn't feel right. I want to make sure you are okay.

I sit there for a while, looking at the pond, letting the cold consume me as I wait to hear anything back from him. I lose track of time as I watch birds fruitlessly searching for squiggling worms in the ground.

Poor things.

I am questioning everything about myself.

Maybe I was overreacting. My mind has been so consumed.

Buzz.

I look down at my phone to see a new text message from an unknown number.

Unknown: It's Cillian. I am fine. Had to get a new phone. This is the last contact I can have going forward. Things are not safe right now.

Bullshit.

I contemplate what to say back.

Me: If this is really you…

Me: What did you call me the first night I spent with you?

Unknown: A dove. No more communication. Goodbye.

My heart skips. I am so relieved that I stand up and twirl around. It is ridiculous how quickly my mood changes when I know Cillian is okay. But with this uplifted mood comes the realization of just how cold I have gotten sitting out here. I shiver and decide to shift back into the school, just outside of mine and Nora's room. I know I should go talk to Henry, but I am unsure of how much time I spent outside, and the memorial service might be starting soon.

I stand staring at our door for more than just a few minutes. I haven't been here since everything went down, and I know I need to face it sooner rather than later. The door is locked, but I have no issue bypassing it with my magic. I enter, leaving the door open behind me. I pretend like the bathroom doesn't exist as I walk past it.

The room is just as we had left it, give or take the few things Cillian had to move when he packed my bags for me. I run my hand over Nora's things as I remember her—traces of her quirky, smartass, positive energy cling to her things.

I wonder why her stuff hasn't been collected yet?

With Yash, his things were packed up very quickly and shipped back to his parents in India. I notice Nora's journal, where she kept her lifelong collection of spells and recipes. I thumb through the pages, leaning against the side of her bed. Everything is so beautifully laid out and detailed. I close the journal and hold it close to my chest.

"I miss you, Nora. I miss you so much. You were the best friend I never knew I always needed." A few tears escape as I continue to hug the journal.

A soft knock on the doorjamb causes me to jump and fling my arm out to defend myself. My head snaps up to see Henry in the doorway, looking apprehensive.

"Jesus, Henry, you have got to stop startling me."

"Sorry," he says, shoving his hands into his pockets.

"How did you know where I was?" I ask a little too harshly.

"I could feel our magic get stronger, so I could tell you were back in the building. I kind of came looking for you then," he says sheepishly.

"Oh, yeah, well, you found me."

"Your lips are almost blue," Henry observes and moves closer to inspect my face.

"Yeah, I was outside. It's cold." I murmur.

"It's crazy being back in here, isn't it?" Henry tries to change subject as he looks around the room.

"Yeah, it is. I miss her."

"Look, Cassie, I really am sorry about earlier. I know I should've just trusted you, but I was letting my own feelings get in the way."

"Thank you for apologizing. I know you and Cillian are not on the best of terms because of everything. I would have reacted the same way if it were you on the phone, though—I hope you know that."

My reassurance seems to appease him.

"Yeah, I know," he says, kicking my foot playfully.

I smile and shove him playfully, but he catches my arm and pulls me in for an embrace. I'm still clutching Nora's journal to my chest as I return Henry's hug.

"I am sorry for getting upset, Henry. It is hard a lot of the time for me to control my emotions, and it felt like you and your mom were against me."

"Do not even worry your pretty head about it, okay?"

We release each other and I wipe the remaining tears off my cheeks.

"Memorial is going to start soon. I am going to go a little early to see if they need help setting up."

"Okay, I will be there soon as well. I came back to find something to wear and got consumed by being here."

"Do you need any help? I can stay if you need me?" Henry asks.

I smile. "No, it's fine. Do you know where it's taking place?"

"Mum said outside in the courtyard. Figured since the sun is setting earlier these days, it will be nice to have it going down in the background. I heard it might sleet, though."

"I'll make sure it doesn't." I don't even think about that being a big deal until Henry chuckles. "I won't do anything drastic. I will just make sure the weather is lovely without a hitch. They deserve it."

"Well, I best be going. I'll see you down there, okay?"

"Hey, Henry, before you go—why haven't they come for Nora's things yet? Or do you know when they might?"

Henry looks puzzled by my question. "Erm, I am not sure. I can check with Mum if you'd like?"

I nod and Henry leaves, closing the door behind him. I set Nora's journal down on her bed so I can get changed, but it slides off, onto the floor. A folded piece of paper falls out as I pick the journal up. I curiously retrieve and unfold it. The writing looks as if it was done in a rush—haphazardly scribbled across the paper.

"Concealment spell?"

I try to decipher the words, but a lot of the pencil markings are smudged. I don't think much of it and tuck the paper back into the journal. Nora was always so skilled at spells—it still astonishes me. An idea pops into my head, and I text Henry a list of items that I will need to execute it before I get dressed.

I choose a black dress I think Nora would've loved—black lace at the top of the bodice, up the neck, and down the arms, snug at the waist, but the skirt flows out to the middle of my thighs.

"Don't you think it's a tad short?"

"Nah, girlie, flaunt those gorgeous legs."

"Are you sure?"

"Oh, to be tall and beautiful, such a terrible thing," Nora jokes.

We laughed so much at our height difference. I reach for a pair of low black heels and slip them on. I try to use my phone's camera to see how I look all put together. I still do not want to go into the bathroom. The faintest hint of metallic lingers in the air, emanating from the tiny room—even with the door closed.

I pack a bag with more of my things. I hesitate, looking at Nora's journal. I want to take a piece of her with me. I tuck the book in the side of my bag and shift quickly to Henry's room.

After setting my things down, I tame a few stray hairs before departing for the memorial. I wobble slightly in the heels walking down the hallway. It has been a minute since I wore heels. I could have shifted, but I need some time to think. I am so absorbed in my thoughts, I barely notice other students and guards passing by me. I think back to my parents' funeral. All the sadness and the pain that surrounded it was unbearable. I've avoided funerals like the plague since then, but, then again, haven't had an opportunity to go to one. One good thing about not having friends is never having to mourn their loss—never having to experience a new normal without them.

Dark clouds roll in as I make my way outside to the courtyard. I use my magic to part the clouds around the school, allowing the sun to shine on us. My eyes quickly find Henry setting up the things I asked him to. I smile as he hurries along, making sure everything is perfect. The markings on my arm begin to throb and glow slightly underneath the lace sleeve. Henry's must've too, as he stops what he's doing to look around for me. When his eyes find mine, his face illuminates with a smile. He is dressed in all black as well—black dress shirt with black pants, belt, and shoes. The first couple of buttons of his shirt hang open.

I raise my hand and give a little wave. He nods his

acknowledgment, but goes back to work. I look around to see a few other students helping set everything up. There is a noticeable increase in the number of guards. Instead of one or two standing guard in any one spot, there are now three or four.

"Be on the lookout this evening." The Headmistress appears beside me. I keep my focus forward, though and stand a little straighter.

I clear my throat. "Do you think something will happen tonight?"

My mind spins with horrible possibilities.

"One can never be too cautious. I presume Cillian reached back out to you?"

I shift uncomfortably in my heels. My eyes drop, but I keep my head straight.

"Yes," is all I can muster.

"Good, very good. See? Nothing to worry about at all." She sounds very happy with herself.

I turn to look at her, "One can never be too cautious, Tabitha. Excuse me," I say, departing to join Henry.

Suck it, bitch.

Everything comes together perfectly. There are beautiful flowers all over the courtyard and pictures of the deceased displayed at the front. As the sun begins to set, everyone takes their seats and waits for it to begin. I don't give the Headmistress time to take over—or take credit—and amble up to the front to begin the ceremony. Her eyes shoot daggers my way as I take the podium.

"Don't worry, Headmistress, you can take your seat. I've got this under control," I say confidently.

I see her jaw clench as she debates whether or not to intervene. I grow impatient with how long she chooses to stand, so I use my magic to slowly seat her. She struggles against my grasp, but soon relents. Henry eyes us both suspiciously from his seat beside her.

I feel confident until I look out into the crowd. Everyone's eyes are on me, waiting for me to begin. Anger, sadness, frustration—all their emotions are being thrown at me. I wish I could absorb them all and ease their suffering.

My throat tightens as I search for where to begin. I take a deep breath and one last look behind me at the photos of all the victims. I need to give them justice. I need to prove their lives will not have been lost in vain.

"Thank you, everyone, for being here this evening to celebrate lives taken well before their prime," my voice is shaky and wavers as I begin. "What happened here on the night of our dance was an injustice to us all, but I don't want to focus on that right now. Each and every one of us here lost someone important to us—the hole left by their absence can never be filled. But we must try to go on and find a new normal. Friends, lovers, classmates, sons and daughters, mothers and fathers, everyone meant something to someone." As I speak, it as if I can feel Nora's magical presence. She is giving me strength even from beyond. "Life is not fair—it is cruel and relentless—but it is our friendships that truly make life worth living. Take a moment to look around yourselves at everyone surrounding you."

I pause for a moment as everyone looks to their lefts and their rights.

"We are all different, but that is something we share in common. Lean on each other, and you will realize that even if you feel like you are all alone, you aren't. Your pain and everything that you are feeling right now is valid. Feeling pain is what makes us human—and it can make us stronger if we let it. Pain reminds us that everything we cherish is worth fighting for."

I stop for another moment, as I feel tears start to well in my eyes. I need to be strong for everyone else.

"Trust me, if I could, I would do everything in my power to bring them all back. I would give my life for theirs in a heartbeat. I am no stranger to loss. It never gets easier, and sometimes the easiest thing to do is close up and shy away from others. When I first came here, I was exactly in that mindset. I never expected to find my best friend. I never expected to find people who I connected with so deeply and effortlessly. And now some of them are gone, and I have to figure out how to deal with that—how to live my life without them.

"I know none of you have known me for long, but trust me when I say that I will fight for each and every one of you. I will not back down until these atrocities have been paid for in full and then some. I will not stop until I bring justice to Nora, to Yash, to

Heather, to Karim, to Julio, to Mrs. Alberts, and to everyone else we have lost along the way in our battles. The Anarchy fights to bring destruction, but we fight for everyone—for everyone to have a chance at surviving this cruel world and making it their own—and that is the key difference between us and them. It is what makes us better, stronger. Light will always pierce through the darkest of nights. Light is what will guide us home. Light is what gives us infinite hope."

Tears run down my cheeks, as I can no longer hold them back, but I feel a new type of strong. I feel powerful. I feel dangerous. The sun is setting quickly, the light of day diminishing in the sky.

"My dear friend Nora was a genius when it came to spells, so if you could please look underneath your seats, you will find one of her Light spells. Please, join me as we make all of their lights shine one more time," I say, retrieving the bag Henry had placed at the base of the podium for me.

"Pour the ingredients into your hands. Let your magic seep into them and mix with them."

I step in front of the podium to demonstrate. Everyone stands and copies me. I can feel my magic mix with the powdered ingredients and the concoction warms slightly. I place my palms together in front of me in the prayer position.

"Take some time to think of all the loved ones you have lost. Cry or scream out if you need to. We are told to bottle up our feelings, because feelings make us weak, but that is simply not true.

Emotions unite us," I speak through clenched teeth as my own emotions and those coming at me from the crowd threaten to burst me at my seams.

Sobs and sniffles cascade through the crowd. The lavender powder in my hands increases in warmth and begins to glow. An orb of bright light forms and lifts, hovering over my hands. The courtyard lights up with different-colored orbs as everyone follows suit. A beautiful array of blues, pinks, purples, and greens glow all around.

"One last time," I whisper as I guide the orb upward. "For you, Nora."

The orb floats upward as my arms reach as high as they will go. The yellow light hovers for a moment and then takes off like a bottle rocket, high into the darkening sky, leaving a trail of color in its path.

I hear all sorts of names being whispered to the orbs as they take flight. The sky is illuminated with a sea of color. Once the orbs reach their maximum height, they burst, causing an explosion of color to irradiate the sky. It is so beautiful—more beautiful than any fireworks show I have ever seen.

I am so mesmerized by the sky, I barely feel Henry slip his arm around my waist. We exchange a quick reassuring glance, and both turn our eyes back to the lights. I can feel Nora's presence so strongly, it's like she is here in the courtyard with us. I picture Nora and my parents, wherever they are, out there in the cosmos, and hope that they are be proud of me.

One last time. I will make you all proud…

CHAPTER TWENTY-FOUR

The following days are grueling, as Tabitha takes out her disapproval of my memorial takeover in training. If Henry and I aren't training, we are down in the Archives trying to piece the puzzle together and gather as much information as we can.

I haven't heard anything more from Cillian. I have an inkling that something might be wrong, but I am trying to not let it overtake me.

Most nights, I sleep in Henry's room, but there are a handful I stay alone in Cillian's. Henry and I never really have the chance to be intimate again, due to being so exhausted from training and research, but he goes out of his way to do little things for me. His home in my heart is growing bigger.

I haven't dreamt at all this week, which is a little concerning to me. I know my dreams have scared me lately, but they have also given me more insight than anything else has. I also haven't seen Lauren in anymore mirrors. I struggle with myself internally if the reason I want to see her is to prove she isn't my sister, or to prove that she is.

I am in deep into a paragraph about the possible transitions of Anarchy power when Henry stands up to stretch.

"Cassie, maybe we should go to bed. It's almost midnight, and I am exhausted." Henry groans.

I set the file down and look up at him. I can see the exhaustion taking its toll all over him. His face is pale, and he has purplish bags under his eyes. His curls are disheveled, and his clothes wrinkled from being hunched over files. Training had been extra toiling, today as we tried to practice our shifting with each other and various objects long distances and back—as well as close combat and energy bursts. Henry and I discovered that we can form energy orbs when our hands are joined. Tabitha took full advantage of our joined power and stretched it thin. We both are exhausted, and our magic was spent after training.

"Yeah, you're right. Let me finish reading this and then I will call it a night."

"Are you going to be staying in my room or…"

"I'll stay in yours tonight, if that's okay?"

Henry is so tired, but he still manages to smile in response.

"Perfect. Sorry if I am asleep by the time you get there."

"Don't worry that pretty head of yours if you are," I tease.

Henry chuckles and then takes his leave from the Archives room. I readjust myself in my very uncomfortable chair and get back to reading. The Anarchy is most likely conducted and influenced by one family. For generations, one family has organized and executed the chaos all over the world through various organizations. Most of their recruits are witches who have been burned by the Protector elders in some way, or were exiled. Others are witches who think that chaos is more exciting and better than coexisting.

The file goes on and on about it, but my eyelids are becoming heavier and heavier as the seconds tick by. I rest my head on my arm as I try to keep reading, but sleep washes over me like a huge tidal wave.

I hadn't noticed that the darkness of sleep had consumed me until I appeared in a darkened hallway. Huge doors lined the hallway, but they were all closed. I didn't feel confused, just that I knew I had to go forward.

I tried the first couple doors, which were made of black metal, plain and sturdy-looking, but they were locked. I tried to use my magic, but unfortunately, in dream world, I was powerless. As I made my way down the hallway, the rest of the doors were either locked or when they opened, the rooms were empty and cold.

I had two more doors to try before the hallway ended. The next door that I encountered was very interesting. It had rose quartz growing out of it. I ran my fingers over the quartz stones and admire their rosy colors. The handle was strikingly different. It was a black and jagged. As I placed my hand around it, I felt the edges slice into my hand. I pulled it back and examined the blood spilling.

"Ouch."

I looked back to the handle, though, and my blood had triggered it to alter and become smooth. I was perplexed by the transformation, but reached out to grab the knob once more. This time it was unlocked. It opened without any hesitation to reveal a small pond. I recognized the pond instantly and knew it was mine and Cillian's pond. I stepped over the threshold and out into the scenery. It was warm and bright. The trees were full of dark green leaves and the sun was high in the sky. A butterfly floated past and it made me smile.

Why am I here?

"Try and catch me!" a young woman's voice squealed.

A teenage girl with silver hair ran into view. Just as she was about to reach the tree next to the pond, a teenage boy with black hair appeared out of the sky and dropped onto her.

"Gotcha!" the young man yelled in triumph.

They laughed and tussled around for a few moments.

"Victor, you oaf, get off of me!" she yelled between laughs.

Mom?

I tried to go closer, but my feet were frozen.

Ugh, not this frozen crap again.

My mother and Victor got up and brushed the dirt off their clothes. They looked to be around sixteen.

"Why do you have to be so brilliant at shifting?" Elizbeth asked.

"Because I am Victor Holloway, superior witch!" Victor boasted.

"We should get back, I suppose. Don't want Headmaster Bellweather to have a tiffy over this."

Elizabeth turned to walk back toward the school, but Victor caught her arm.

"Wait, Elizabeth,"

A strong gust of wind blew through us all as Victor held onto her arm.

"Um, never mind," Victor trailed off.

Elizabeth smiled and gave Victor a swift kiss on the cheek.

"Race you back? No cheating this time, okay?"

Victor's face was beet red, and he smiled sheepishly.

"You're on!"

The two turned and raced back toward the school. The scenery around me swirled and warped to a different time. Elizabeth and Victor were back at the pond, only this time, they looked older, and it was cold. The trees were bare, and there was snow on the ground. A few snowflakes fell from the sky and slowly drifted downward to join their fellows on the ground.

"Cassie," a faint voice whispers from behind me, but I am too enveloped in what is going on with my mother to turn.

"Victor, please don't be upset. I am just confused and stressed. I can't lose you, you're my best friend," Elizabeth pleaded.

Victor looked enraged as he paced back and forth.

"I have been there for you through everything, Elizabeth. I love you. You have no idea the things that I would do for you, the things that I would change for you."

My mother sobbed into Victor as she pulled him into an embrace.

"Cassie, you must come back," the voice is louder now, but I can't make out who it belongs to yet.

How am I seeing this? Who do these memories belong to? My mother?

"Cassie, it isn't safe," the voice continues.

"No, I must know," I say.

The scenery changed again, warping to show colors of grey and black. Again, Elizabeth and Victor were at the pond, this time dressed in all black. The leaves were beginning to fall and, in this moment, the world seemed silent.

My mother tried to place her hand on Victor's shoulder, but he shook it off.

"Victor, I am so sorry about your father."

"Why are you even here, Elizabeth? You've made your choice." Victor's voice was filled with disgust and hatred. "I am sure the Joining Ceremony will just solidify everything tomorrow."

"Victor, there is something I need to tell you—"

Victor spun around and began to yell, "I don't want to hear it! Leave me alone!"

My mother took a few steps back and placed her hand on her stomach. She looked like she was about to cry.

"Very well, then," Elizabeth said before she shifted away.

Victor's demeanor instantly changed, realizing how harsh he had been to her. He screamed with frustration.

"Cassie, we must go, now!" the voice is more audible now.

My ears recognize it now.

"Nora?" I try to look back over my shoulder, but as soon as I say Nora's name, Victor's head snaps up and he looks directly at me.

"How did you get here?" he hisses. "No one is supposed to be here!"

My pulse quickens and I can hear the blood pounding in my ears. My skin prickles and my blood runs cold.

"Cassie! Move! Now!" Nora's voice screams behind me. "I can't get to you in there!"

I will with all my might for my legs to move as Victor advances closer—his eyes, burning red with rage.

"No, please, don't!" I scream.

I am finally able to move my legs. I turn and sprint as quickly as I can back to the door, where I can see Nora waiting. I dive through the door and Nora slams it shut, just as Victor is about to reach me. I crash onto the floor, but quickly scramble to my feet. The door reverberates as Victor beats on the other side of it.

Nora grabs my hand and begins to run back down the hallway.

"Nora, what is going on? Is this real?"

She ignores my questions and focuses pointedly forward.

"Nora! Answer me! What is this? These aren't my memories. Whose are they?"

Nora and I approach a lighter-colored grey door that I had not noticed before. It looks translucent, almost like smoke or vapor.

"He knows you're here. I don't know how you got here, but

you must go. These are his memories. You must wake up!" Nora finally says.

"His memories? You mean Victor? How is that possible? Nora, how are you here? I miss you so much."

Nora looks frustrated. "Just call it divine intervention. I don't have time to explain everything. Now wake up, and get out! Wake up, Cassie! Wake up, and get out!"

Nora shoves me through the translucent door, and I begin to fall downwards into nothingness. Everything is black.

"Wake up! Wake up! Wake up!" Nora's voice gets further away as I fall deeper. I feel the veil of unconsciousness being lifted the deeper I plunge.

I slowly open my eyes to the blinding white lights of the Archives room. My head still rests on my arm and my neck is stiff. Nora's voice rings faintly in my ears as I sit up.

What time is it?

Through still-squinted eyes, I look at my phone, which is dead. I groan and look up to the clock on the wall. It reads 4:45 a.m.

4:45 a.m.? Holy crap! No wonder my phone is dead.

Images of my mother and Victor swirl around in my groggy mind. I groan as I start to move about.

Wshh...Click

I hear the mechanisms within the door unlock and release their seal. I look over toward the door, but cannot see anyone.

"Wake up, and get out!"

Nora's words echo their warning once more in my thoughts. My arms tingle as the hair on them prickles up.

"Hello?"

I think back to the scary movies I always watched when I was younger. The girls being hunted by the serial killer always run up the stairs, when they should be running out the front door, or they announce they are around and alone with a 'hello.'

I stand up from my seat, with my dead phone in hand, and I proceed toward the door. It slides open slowly as I approach.

"Henry? Is that you again?" My voice is shaky.

The door slides completely open to reveal nothing. I let out a sigh of relief, but stick my head through the doorway and look around. I still don't see anyone, but as I scan the area, I begin to grow extremely cold. I wrap my arms tightly around myself, and this is when I hear a deep, menacing growl emanating from behind me.

My chest tightens, my senses start to go into overdrive as my muscles prep for fight or flight.

"Hello, Cassandra," the deep voice growls. "I think it is time we finally meet."

No...

I slowly turn around to see the glowing red eyes that have haunted me. The dark apparition is more formed now. It takes the shape of a large, wolf-like beast with horns. Its teeth are bared into a sick grin.

"Oh, silly me, let me change."

The beast morphs into the figure of a man, his eyes slowly

fading from red to black. I have only ever seen this man in pictures—a man who I have been working under the impression of being no longer with us.

"Victor…I thought you were dead?"

"Ah, I see you know my name. Good. Well, yes and no to the dead part. Evil can't ever truly die, now, can it?"

Victor takes a step toward me, and I fling out my arm in front of myself, my magic already charged and glowing at the end of my hand.

"Don't come near me," I hiss.

This seems to amuse Victor, and he chuckles loudly. "I can see why Cillian likes you."

My heart drops. "Cillian?"

A menacing grin slowly spreads across Victor's face.

"Didn't they tell you?"

"Tell me what? Who?" I demand.

"Maybe you'll want to check in with Tabitha and young Henry on that one, my dear. Old Tabitha did always have a way of spinning things in her favor."

Victor chuckles more, but never takes his eyes off me. It is like he is trying to push his way into my head to take control.

Get out, get out, get out!

I wince as a pain begins to form deep inside my forehead.

"What? You can get into my head, but I can't get into yours? That doesn't seem very fair. Strong you are, but I am stronger," Victor growls as he advances toward me.

I scream and feel a blast of light explode from my hand. It hits Victor head on, and he stumbles backward. He dissipates back into his ghostly black form, eyes red once again. This gives me enough time to turn and run down the rows of shelving, but I hear him close behind me.

Before I have the chance to shift, my legs are swiped out from underneath me, and I crash hard onto the floor. I tumble a few feet before coming to a stop. The breath has been knocked out of me and I wheeze desperately for air. Victor morphs back to his human form and jumps on top of me. He holds me down as I try to wriggle my way free.

"Elizbeth, stop. I am not the enemy here! There's so much more you need to learn!"

I freeze at the mix up of my mother's name. Victor hasn't noticed his slip yet, but my sudden change in demeanor makes him loosen his grip.

"I bet it was *you* who killed my parents. Elizabeth and Johnathan. You KILLED them!" I want to spit in his face.

Victor releases me from his grasp and climbs off me. I breathe heavily as I sit up and watch him.

"You know nothing." Victor turns his back to me, so I can no longer see his face. "All of it, I have made sure to put all of it right in front of you, and yet you still do not see. I have your answers. Come find me if you want them." And with that, Victor disappears, leaving me sitting on the floor, trying to catch my breath.

What in the fuck just happened?

I scramble to my feet and shift to Henry's room. I need answers, and I want them now. Rage burns inside of me. To my surprise, Henry's room is empty. I can feel his magic, so I know he is in the school somewhere. I don't know what the inside of Tabitha's room looks like, so I can't shift there, but I remember the hallway.

I shift to the hallway and it is very quiet. Phil still stands guard in front of her door.

"Oh, Cassie, you startled me." Phil chuckles softly. But I am not in the mood to play nice right now.

"Is Henry in there?" I demand sternly.

"Well, yes, yes, he is. I'm sure he'll be out soon though." Phil quickly realizes that now is not the time for pleasantries and he moves to a defensive stance. "Are you all right? Is something wrong?"

"Move out of the way, Phil. I need to get in there."

"You know I can't do that." Phil braces himself.

"I don't want to hurt you, Phil, but I have had it up to here with all of the lies that permeate this place. Now, you see, I have questions that I will get answers for—one way or another. Now move." My body begins to tremble as my patience wears thin.

I see Phil weighing everything out in his mind.

"I am not going to hurt them. I just need answers. I am trying to be the Chosen One here, but I cannot do that if people continue to lie to me," I try to ease it over.

Phil reluctantly nods and moves out of my way. I walk past him and open the door slowly. I peek my head in first and then enter.

I shut the door quietly behind me as I look around.

Her room is huge. That was to be expected, though, for the Headmistress of Kingshire Academy. There is an entryway, and up to the left is a living room, which is completely visible from my current location. Next to the living room, a desk is set up with at least a dozen monitors hanging over it on the wall. I tiptoe over to the monitors and click a key on the keyboard. The screens buzz alive and their glow illuminates the room.

It looks like each screen is dedicated to a different security camera. The one in the middle is the main computer. My eyes drift to the various screens, and I notice that all the cameras are in rooms where I spend most of my time. Mine and Nora's room, the Training Room, hallways leading to those rooms, and finally, Henry and Cillian's rooms. I feel violated, as the cameras are inside rooms I have been intimate in. Cillian's tousled room, Tabitha saying that she would be watching—all of it clicks.

That bitch.

My mouth falls open in disbelief and anger. I click the keyboard and move the mouse around the main screen to see if there are any logs. I look back to the first night I spent with Cillian, and it is all there. Every minute of our time together. The same goes for the night Henry and I spent together. My nails dig so deep into my palms they rip through my skin.

"What are you doing in here, Miss Rodden?" Tabitha's voice comes from behind me. It is soft but stern.

I turn around; my breathing grows heavy once more as I try

to control my anger. To my surprise, Henry is standing right next to her. He looks scared and regretful.

"You knew about this?" I spit out, and motioning to the screens behind me.

The ground tremors slightly. It is getting harder to control my magic. Henry looks down at his feet.

"I only just found out about it," he says sheepishly.

I scoff.

"You still have not answered my question, what are you doing here?" Tabitha repeats herself.

"If you must know, I was just attacked in the Archives room by someone *you* told me was dead."

She looks confused and concern spreads across Henry's face.

"Are you okay? Are you hurt?" Henry asks, taking a step toward me.

"Like you care," I hiss.

"Well, I don't have the faintest idea what you are talking about," Tabitha says.

"Victor. Victor Holloway attacked me."

She throws up her hands. "Victor has been dead for over two decades."

Instead of arguing the issue further, I get to the question I really want answered.

"Where is Cillian?" I demand.

Both of them fall silent. I scoff again and pull my phone out of my pocket. I know it is dead, but I have an idea. I walk over to

Henry and grab his hand. I concentrate on our energy magic to go into the phone and charge it.

"What are you doing?" Henry asks warily.

"Shut up."

It isn't long before the phone screen pops on, displaying a full charge. I release Henry's hand and slide it open to call the new number "Cillian" had texted me from. I hold the phone up to my ear and wait as it rings.

Somewhere off in Tabitha's room, I hear the faintest ringing sound of an incoming call. She looks sour as I drop the phone from my ear.

"You want to tell me why you're pretending to be Cillian?"

She sighs. "Professor Morris was apprehended by the Anarchy earlier this week. To avoid alarming you and having you respond irrationally, I lied."

I fucking knew it.

"It has been days! When were you going to tell me?"

Her nonresponse is enough of an answer.

"Oh, I see. You weren't ever going to. Did you know about this, Henry?" I turn my focus to him.

Henry gulps and fidgets uncomfortably. "Yes, I knew, but there wasn't anything I could do about it."

"Fuck you both."

"Don't be like that, Cassie. Mum said this was just a ploy to get to you, and I couldn't risk you for him."

"That's not the point, Henry! You have both lied to me

repeatedly. I trusted you!"

"Well, you told me you hadn't done anything with Cillian, and that clearly was not the case."

"No, I told you it was none of your business. And here I was the past week, falling more in love with you. Thinking, yeah this could work. I chose you, Henry. I had a choice at the Joining Ceremony. It was either you or Cillian, and clearly I chose wrong."

Henry is taken aback by this piece of knowledge.

"What do you mean you had a choice?" Tabitha steps between Henry and me.

"Doesn't matter anymore. Where is Cillian?"

"The Anarchy has him somewhere in Ireland. We are not sure of his exact whereabouts—"

"Don't give me that bullshit, Tabitha. I know you know exactly where he is. Give it to me."

"I cannot have you chasing after him. This is what the Anarchy wants," she warns.

"You know, I don't really give a damn. I am starting to see why they formed this group in the first place. And you know what? Victor said he has answers for me, and I believe him. Henry, I am almost positive now you told your mother about my suspicions about Lauren."

Henry looks away.

"Yep, knew it. Where are the coordinates?"

Tabitha stands her ground.

"Do not make me repeat myself," I warn, and the tremors

increase. I use my magic to lift Tabitha up in the air by her throat. "Tell me!"

"Cassie, no!" Henry tries to intervene, but I use my other arm to hold him back.

Tabitha gasps for air as my hold on her throat grows tighter. She struggles, but eventually points over to a piece of paper on the desk. I release her from my hold, and she drops to the floor coughing. I swipe up the piece of paper and glance at the coordinates.

I will have to put these into Google Maps…

I tuck the paper away into my pocket and storm past them. Out of everything, Henry's betrayal hurts the most. My heart aches as I try to plan my next move.

I rush out of the room past Phil. I hear someone running to catch up to me.

"Cassie, wait!"

I look back to see Henry reaching out to me. I try to shift away, but he catches my arm and I shift us both. We tumble to the ground outside.

"Leave me alone, Henry! I am going to get Cillian, and I don't want you in my way," I yell at him, getting to my feet.

Henry scrambles upright. "I am going with you."

"Like hell you are. I trusted you, and you broke that."

"I am so sorry, Cassie, but you have to understand that my Mum, she can get a bit intense. I didn't know that you had chosen me."

"It shouldn't have mattered. Saying you're sorry doesn't fix us. I truly opened up to you and tried to give you my heart."

Henry's face turns frustrated. "You couldn't give me something you didn't have."

"Oh, so I am heartless now? Thanks," I say as I turn to walk away.

"No, no, that's not what I mean. Cassie, stop, please," Henry pleads.

I turn back to face him, tears stinging my eyes.

"You couldn't fully give me your heart, because I know that it has been with Cillian all along. I tried so hard for you to love me."

"I do love you, Henry."

Henry's eyes turn red with tears. "But not like how you love him."

"I need to save him, Henry, and I need answers to all my questions. Please, just stay here with your mother."

I don't give Henry a chance to protest. I shift away to the pub where Cillian found me my first night at Kingshire. The bar is closed and dark, as it is still early in the morning. I sit down in one of the booths and sob alone in the darkness.

CHAPTER TWENTY-FIVE

I sob until my eyes run dry. I feel my face grow puffy. I pull out the folded piece of paper from my pocket and type the coordinates into Google Maps. It pops up a beautiful cliff area in Ireland. From the look of the map, though, I don't find anything that looks like it could be a lair, but, of course, they wouldn't just have it out in the open.

Maybe it's below the cliff?

I think back to the dream I had with Lauren and Victor—I was crawling through a crevasse.

That is a possibility, then.

I sigh and put my phone down, looking around the dark, empty bar. My hair feels greasy, and my clothes are no longer comfortable, from having slept in them. I am even more exhausted than before, and not really sure what to do next. I need a game plan. I find a small pencil on the table and write my plan on the back of the scrap of paper. I've always loved making lists, and this is going to be an important one.

Step 1: find a change of clothes/somehow shower or wash up

Step 2: look at a bunch of pictures of these coordinates and try shifting to a place I have never been/seen before, hundreds of miles away

Step 3: infiltrate the Anarchy's lair and find Cillian

Step 4: find answers to my parents, Lauren, and Victor

Step 5: somehow make it out alive…

I sit back and study my list. I groan, as my confidence is fading. My stomach gurgles loudly from hunger.

"Welp, let's get started, I guess," I say out loud to myself. "There's got to be some food in here somewhere, I would think?"

I slide out from the booth and scavenge for any sustenance in the back of the bar. I find some peanuts and a yogurt cup someone left in the breakroom fridge, but that is about it.

Better than nothing, I guess.

I use one of the bar sinks and some paper towel to freshen up and wash my face. Part of step one is complete.

Now, time to find some clothes.

I pull my phone out and look for a store close by to go to. There is an outdoor shop not too far from the bar. I shift outside onto the street, bypassing the doors to avoid any alarms and start walking toward the shop.

The morning light hasn't broken through yet, but I can feel people beginning to stir in their homes as I pass them. I hear more and more car engines starting and traffic making its way from point A to point B. I try to imagine their lives right now as cars pass by me—what they are stressing about, or where they are going. It is amazing how crazy things have gotten in such a short amount of time.

I finally arrive at the outdoor shop, but they are closed. I knew they would be, but if I can see inside, that will suffice. Most of the lights inside are off, but there is a small light in the back, illuminating a small area. I focus on that spot and shift inside. I didn't notice a nearby rack, and shift right into it, causing me and the rack to fall to the ground.

"Ouch."

I do my best to pick everything up and put it back to how it was. I then venture over to their parkas. I am freezing, with just a long-sleeved shirt on, and I need something a little bit heavier duty. I select a black one that isn't too thick, so it won't limit my ability to maneuver quickly, but still thick enough to fend off the cold. Sticking with the black theme, I grab a black knit cap and a pair of black athletic pants. My shoes and long-sleeved shirt will work well enough.

I quickly remove the price tags and throw on the rest of the items, then scroll through pictures of the area at the coordinates that are my only clue to Cillian. A text message from Henry pops up on my screen, which I ignore.

"It's now or never, I guess."

I close my eyes and try my best to visualize the cliff from the photos I had found online. I picture the grass on top, which is well-away from the edge. All I have to do is get there, and if Cillian is close by, I should be able to feel his magical presence.

I can feel my magic having to work harder, as I haven't actually ever been to this place before. The pull into the unknown feels hesitant, but carries on as I continue to will myself to the cliff.

A strong gust of wind blows against me, which startles me and causes me to lose my balance. I open my eyes quickly, for fear of falling off the cliff, but am relieved when I see that I am at least a few feet away. I smell the salt in the air, rolling in on the sea's waves. It is incredibly cloudy and starts to sleet. I am thankful for my jacket and hat as I look around. There isn't much to see, other than grass that has turned brown. The sleet has made the top of the cliff muddy and slippery.

I feel Cillian's magical presence faintly, which increases my heartrate. At least I am going in the right direction.

Okay, if I was an evil organization, and I had a lair, where would I hide that lair?

I cautiously make my way to the edge of the cliff and peek over. Huge waves crash up onto the it.

Yikes.

"Cassie!"

"Jesus Christ!" I yell, spinning around and almost slipping off the edge.

Henry has apparently shifted to the cliff also, and is standing a few feet away. He instantly realizes that him startling me almost made me fall off the cliff. Henry has changed his clothing to all black and added a coat with a knit hat as well.

"I thought I told you to leave me alone, Henry," I say with annoyance. I make sure to take a few steps away from the edge.

"Look, Cassie, I am sorry, okay? I know that doesn't mean much to you right now, but I love you. I don't ever want to see you get hurt, and I am supposed to protect you. I know, I was spineless with my mum, but you've got to understand that she is the only family I have. I feel an allegiance to her, but I know that what I did to you…I betrayed you and your trust. I may never forgive myself for that, but we are joined—and that is an honor. I want to be the man who lives up to that honor, because that is what you deserve."

I can't tell if it is the sleet or actual tears that are irritating his eyes. My heart is quick to forgive, but my mind is having a hard time coming around.

"Is there anything else you want, or anything that you need to tell me?" I ask flatly.

"No," he says confidently, but something inside me knows it's a lie. I don't have time for this charade, so I go along with it. I need to get to Cillian.

"Fine, but don't think I've forgiven you completely. I just don't think I can do this all on my own," I say reluctantly. Henry smiles briefly.

"What's your game plan?" he asks.

"Uh… well, I got clothes, and I made it here, and now I am looking for the lair, I guess."

"You think it's near the cliff somewhere?" Henry looks around apprehensively at the barren cliff and treacherous sea.

"I can feel Cillian's magic, and I had a dream about Lauren and Victor deep inside of a cave. Those are the only two clues I have to go off of. That and the coordinates I got from your mom."

Henry furrows his brow in thought.

"You got any ideas?" I ask.

"It will probably be a spot that you can only get into by shifting, so it would make sense if it were somewhere alongside the cliff."

"But that's the crappy thing though. We can't shift somewhere if we don't know what it looks like. I got lucky with this place, because I was able to find a bunch of photos online." I throw my hands up in frustration. "I'm the 'Chosen One,' all-powerful, but half the time I feel powerless."

"But, Cassie, wait, you have seen the inside." Henry looks as if a bulb has lit up inside his head.

"What are you talking about?"

"Your dream. You've seen the entrance, or at least one of the entrances. You scraped your arm, so you had to have been there in some form."

"Yeah, but how can we even know if that was real or not?"

"I've been thinking recently that Lauren has been giving you clues and insight on where it is. Whether it's because there's a trap set up, or maybe because you might be sisters."

I think about it, and it starts to make some sense.

"And—about Lauren—I don't think she's just your sister...I think she's your twin."

My mouth drops open in shock.

"But we don't look that much alike," I say.

"There's magic that can alter an appearance, or maybe she's a fraternal twin."

Two sides of the same coin.

"Did your father ever take any pictures or a home video while you were being born?"

My ears begin to ring, and Henry's voice is slightly muffled.

"Um, no, there was a really bad outbreak of the flu that year, and my father was sick. They wouldn't let him come in. But why wouldn't she keep both of us then?"

Or my mother could have taken his memories and implanted the whole flu outbreak.

Henry is stumped by this question. "Well, uh, I don't know. But I think this could work. Especially if we do it together."

I shake my head in an effort to get the ringing to stop. I look up at Henry nervously and nod my head. "Together," I say in agreement.

I reach out my hands to Henry. His hands are warm, as he has had them stuffed into his pockets. They feel nice against my skin—my fingertips are iced over from the cold.

"Together," Henry repeats.

We close our eyes as I feel Henry's and my magic begin to mix. Our markings burn slightly as they are activated. I think back to the cave in my dream—the ragged edges that lunged out to grab and pull my skin, the complete darkness, the light slowly piercing through that darkness.

I squeeze Henry's hands tighter as the tingles spread quickly all over.

Focus, focus, focus.

The sound of the ferocious waves fades away, silence stepping into its place.

Not dead, at least. This is good. Time to open my eyes.

I slowly peek open one eye to see the same small opening from my dream. Henry and I exchange thankful glances that it has worked.

"Now where do we go?" Henry whispers as he looks around.

Cillian's presence is much stronger inside the cave.

"I don't know," I whisper back. "There should be another opening down that way, but that is all I know."

Henry nods. We take a few steps down the tunnel, but the swishing of our jackets is louder than I want to be. I pull on Henry's arm to stop him.

"I think we should ditch the jackets and hats?"

It isn't the warmest down in the cave, but if we want to not be suspicious or draw attention to ourselves, we need to make as little noise as possible. Henry agrees, and we slip off our jackets. I take his from him and shove them both back into the crevasse from my dream.

I am nervous, and my palms begin to perspire. Henry must notice, because he takes my hands in his and looks at me.

"We can do this, Cassie. I believe in you."

I am still mad at him, but Henry is here now, helping, and that is what matters.

"Let's do this," I whisper.

We step cautiously down the tunnel so our footsteps won't make much noise. We come to the other area from my dream—the mirror is still hanging there. I try not to stare at it too long as we pass by.

We continue aimlessly, the only thing guiding us is Cillian's magical presence. The tunnels seem never ending and wind all sorts of ways. It's like a maze. Henry and I keep walking for what seems like ages and we never encounter another person.

"Henry, something isn't right about this," I finally say.

"What do you mean?"

"We've been walking for some time. What if this is another precaution they have, in case people make it this far? An entrance within an entrance?"

"It's possible, but how are we going to be able to find the entrance then?"

I search for an answer in my thoughts and dreams to see if anything makes sense. And then I have it.

"Mirrors…"

"Mirrors?" Henry repeats.

"Lauren was able to reach through mirrors and grab me. I think the mirrors are some sort of portal."

"Well, it's worth a shot. Let's shift back to that area and try it out."

Shifting back to the spot is easy, but as we approach the mirror, the hairs on the back of my neck stand up. I can feel the evil leaking out of the mirror.

"Can you feel that?" Henry asks.

"Yeah, I can."

"I've never felt something so...so..." Henry tries to find a word to fit what we are both feeling.

"Pure evil."

I put my arm up to reach through the mirror, but end up jamming my finger.

"Ouch, ugh."

I tap the mirror's glass. It is solid.

"How do you think we activate it?" Henry asks.

Hmm...

"Do you have a knife or anything sharp Henry?"

"I think I have a pocketknife. Would that work?"

"Give it to me," I say, holding my hand out to him.

Henry fishes around in his pockets and pulls out an old pocketknife. I see the rust as he places it in my hand.

Eek. Hmm, do I really want to do this?

"What are you going to do with it?" Henry asks curiously.

I maneuver the blade out and discover more rust and a dull edge.

Fuck. Welp, better just get it over with. My magic will heal it.

Without answering Henry's question, I close my eyes and slice my palm open with the blade. It is indeed dull, so I have to press hard for it to break my sensitive skin.

I wince in pain as I peek with one eye to make sure it is actually cutting my hand.

"Bloody hell, Cassie, what are you doing?" Henry is alarmed.

I wipe the blood from the blade onto my pant leg and hand the knife back to Henry. My magic is already healing the wound, so I have to be quick.

"Hold onto me," I direct Henry. "We have to do this quickly."

Henry stuffs the knife back into his pocket and holds onto my shoulder. I put my bloody hand up to the mirror and press it against the cool surface.

"Come on, work."

The surface of the mirror begins to ripple and my hand slowly sinks through it. I let out a laugh of excitement as I turn to Henry. He looks both shocked and happy.

"Bloody brilliant," he exclaims quietly.

It feels like we are walking through gelatin as we pass through the mirror. My arm struggles less the further in it goes, and my body follows. Henry is right behind me. We look at each other, relieved at having made it through, before we look around to see where we are now.

We are in a dark hallway. The trim is black, and the walls are the darkest plum color I have ever seen. I turn back to the mirror and find that the trim around the large looking glass is black as well. Paintings of some very scary-looking men line the hall. The floor is a black-and-white-checker pattern.

Damn, this place needs a revamp.

Cillian's presence feels stronger now, which does not help my nerves. I take a deep breath in and listen carefully for any other movement before Henry and I trek further.

"If Cillian is indeed here, I am assuming he'll be on the lowest level," Henry whispers into my ear.

"Okay, that sounds about right for any bad-guy lairs. Let's just act like we belong here. I wish I could change my eye color. It's pretty obvious," I whisper back.

"Here, face me," Henry says. "I told you there was magic that could alter appearances."

I turn to face him.

"Blue or brown?"

"Um, blue?"

Henry places his palm over my brown eye, and I feel it grow warm.

"Stay still," he directs.

My eye feels tingly and uncomfortable, but it is done and over with quickly. Henry withdraws his hand and smiles.

"Take a look,"

I peek behind him into the mirror and am surprised to see two eyes that are the same color.

"Wow, how did you do that?"

I touch around the eye to make sure that it is real.

"I told you there was magic that could alter appearances. Just something I noticed I could do the past couple days. It won't last too terribly long, but it should help for right now, at least."

I am impressed. "Very well done, Henry. Let's go be evil, hmm?"

Henry winks at me and we make our way down the hall. The hallway leads to the top of a grand staircase. There are a few other people at the foot of the stairs that Henry and I notice immediately, and we try not to bring attention to ourselves, keeping our heads high and our eyes straightforward. The men at the bottom of the stairs are conversing loudly and chuckling about the latest attack. They seem not to notice us as we slide past them.

"Eh, you two, who are ye? Haven't seen you two before," one of the men calls after us in a thick Scottish accent.

Henry and I stop. Different scenarios run through my head, and my muscles tense.

"You two deaf or just stupid?" the other says in an accent I do not recognize.

We turn around to face the men. They are both dressed in all-black, fitted suits with black turtlenecks underneath. The one who I assume has the Scottish accent has fiery red hair. The other looks pale and ghastly, his eyes are dark and cold. They send a shiver up my spine.

"Sorry, gentlemen, we are new recruits. First time being here," Henry says as I try not to hold their gazes for long.

"Is that so?" the red-haired man says.

They eye us suspiciously and step up extremely close to us.

Their eyes survey our faces for any trace of deceit. I swear I see the pale guy lift a strand of my hair and sniff it.

They both lean back and break out into a chuckle.

"James, do you remember when we were new recruits?" the red-haired man asks, slapping the back of the pale man named James.

"Remember when I set your pants on fire, Alastair?" James chuckles, but it comes out more as a sinister wheeze.

As James laughs, I notice a scar the running along his cheek. Henry and I side-eye each other and chuckle uncomfortably with them.

"Well, welcome to the Anarchy. Do you need help finding where you are going?" Alistair asks.

"Uh, actually, we were supposed to check on the prisoner. Victor wants us to learn interrogation skills and what not," I say, probably a little too quickly.

"Which one? We've got a lot," Alistair asks. This causes him and James to erupt into more laughter.

"Erm, the professor from Kingshire. Think his name is Cillian," I say.

"Well, I know Victor doesn't normally converse with the new recruits…" Alistair says between chuckles. "So, you two must be some hot shots. Anyway, take the elevator over there down to the lowest floor. You'll find the prisoners down there." Alistair points to an elevator just off to the side of the stairs.

"Thank you. I figured that's where, but thank you," Henry said.

We start toward the elevator when James speaks up.

"What did you two say your names were again?"

"Henry and Cassie," Henry says. I jab him in the side for giving our real names.

"Do you guys know where Lauren and Victor are at right now? We are supposed to report to them after this," I try to turn the subject away from our names.

"I am sure they will find you when they are ready for you," James says in an ominous tone.

I fane smile at them and grab Henry's arm for us to leave. We hurry onto the elevator, but I can still feel James and Alistair's eyes on us as the doors close in front of us.

"Really? Our real names, Henry? You couldn't think of anything else?" I chastise.

Henry shrugs. "Sorry, I was caught off guard and, ugh, sorry."

"It's okay, we just need to be more careful."

Henry shakes his head, and I can tell he feels bad. I scan the buttons for the different levels and find D, the lowest button.

"Well, D for dungeon, I bet," I say as I press the button.

The elevator car jolts and *whines* into motion. It seems to take forever to finally reach the lowest level, but it could just be my nerves. The doors slide open to revel a dimly-lit tunnel. It looks like the inside of the cliff. Flood lights flicker on and cast a yellowish glow from above.

Henry and I step off the elevator and make our way down the

tunnel. We hear various noises—water dripping somewhere, distant screams and moans of people being held prisoner. My stomach twists, and I want to vomit at the thought of one of those screams being Cillian's. His presence buzzes inside of me now. We are getting closer.

Henry and I keep our eyes forward as we pass different people cowering in the darkened corners of their cells. It breaks my heart.

"Yeah, I know the guy. He was one of my professors at Kingshire. I can't wait until they let me have my go at him," a familiar voice echoes down the path. The voice is getting closer.

I stop and grab onto Henry's arm. I notice an empty cell left open nearby, and I hurry us both inside, with our backs against the wall—using the darkness to conceal us.

"What the hell, Cassie?" he whispers.

I put my finger up to my lips to motion to Henry to be quiet. I then touch my ear for him to listen. My eyes grow wider as footsteps draw closer. I bite my lip and have to swallow back the bile that has risen into my mouth.

Henry is still confused until the voice speaks again.

"I can't wait to get my hands on that bitch again as well," Nick's voice causes the attack to resurface. I am burning with rage.

"You know Victor won't allow that. Plus, you'll have to get behind Lauren first," the unknown voice snickers.

I look up to Henry and see that he too has made the realization as to who the voice belongs to. Henry's arm tenses and I grab onto his hand. Our eyes concentrate on the opening to the cell, waiting for Nick and the other man to walk by. I hold my breath and prepare for us to be seen, but Nick and his associate stroll by without notice. I wait until the elevator doors close before I let out the breath I've been holding in.

"I'm going to kill him," Henry says.

"Not if I beat you to it. I thought your mom said he was exiled?"

"He was, but he must've joined the Anarchy when he had nowhere to go. His parents disowned him after what he tried to do."

"Or maybe he went back. Something tells me the Anarchy had more than just one spy at the school—not just Lauren. Either way, we need to do this quicker. There's not a guarantee of who we may or may not run into who could recognize us," I say.

"Can you sense if we are close?"

"Very close."

We quicken our pace, continuing deeper down the hall. We pass cell after cell and do not find him. We are approaching the tunnel's dead end, when we finally locate the right one. I run up to the bars and can see Cillian lying on the floor, not moving. His clothes are torn and dirty. He has bruises and scrapes across his face. I want to cry looking at him.

"Cillian?" I whisper as Henry stays behind me, keeping watch in case anyone comes toward us.

He does not stir, and my worry increases.

"Cillian?" I whisper again, a little louder this time.

Still nothing. I look back at Henry, "I am going to try shifting in."

"Don't," Cillian's weak voice is barely a whisper.

My head whips around. Cillian's eyes aren't open yet, but he has begun to slowly stir. I can't help but smile and get a little excited.

"Oh, Cillian, we are here to rescue you."

His eyes are open now, revealing their beauty—eyes I haven't realized just how much I've missed. But they seem upset, when I expect them to show happiness.

"I told you not to come," he says, pulling himself up to a seated position on the floor.

His words send little stabs into my heart.

"To be fair, I was lied to about your current state. I only just found out you had been captured, so somehow that nulls your warning."

That makes sense, right?

Cillian chuckles and shakes his head. "You are such a stubborn arse, aren't you?"

There's something different about Cillian. His normally cold exterior seems to have been broken down, that or he doesn't have enough strength to keep it up.

"I'm going to try shifting in there to get you out, okay?"

"No…" Cillian says. He winces and coughs. I can hear his lungs struggling as he wheezes for air. I can feel his pain and it hurts my heart.

"Cillian, I've come all this way. I am coming in there and

getting you."

"No, you can't. The cells are laced with magic to prevent shifting and any magic inside of them."

Well, that makes sense. Otherwise, prisoners would be able to get out.

"Oh…" I say, a little embarrassed.

"Cassie," Henry taps me on my shoulder. "I hear people coming."

I concentrate my ears and can hear faint footsteps. They seem far off, though. I look back at Cillian in his cell.

There has got to be a way. Probably can't unlock it with magic either.

The bars holding the cell together look rusted and weak.

I wonder…with enough force I could probably break them.

"It'll be too loud," Cillian says.

"How did you…doesn't matter. I have to try."

I step back and grab Henry's hand.

"What are you doing?" Henry asks nervously.

"Cassandra, no. No magic can break the cell," Cillian tries to dissuade me.

I take a deep breath. "Good thing I won't be using magic."

I focus my magic to make the muscles and bones in my leg stronger, so I'm technically not going to use magic against the cell. I lift my leg and slam it as hard as I can against the weakest point.

The door flings open, but it is indeed loud. The impact bounces off the tunnel walls, amplifying the sound. The noise causes the others in their cells to stir and results in even more of a commotion. Alarms begin to sound off and are deafening. I rush into

Between the Shadow and the Soul

Cillian's cell and take him into my arms. I frantically exam him to see how badly he is hurt.

"I can't heal you in here. We have to make it outside!" I scream above the noise.

"Cassie, they are coming!" Henry is frantic, as the footsteps are now barreling toward us.

Cillian writhes in pain as I try to pick him up.

"Come on, Cillian, we have to get out of here! Henry, help me!"

"I can't. My ribs are broken. Just go," Cillian says, defeated.

"You, there! Stop!" a voice shouts from nearby.

"Cassie, it's too late," Henry says. I can hear the fear in his voice.

I set Cillian back down on the floor and try to think quickly.

"Henry, shift away."

"Absolutely not." Henry crosses his arms.

We do not have time for this.

I walk up to him and shove him outside of the cell. He barely catches his footing as he stumbles across the threshold.

"Go! If they have both of us, then we will be shit out of luck. This way, we can have the upper hand."

Henry hesitates, but the Anarchy is closing in.

"GO!" I scream.

Henry takes one last look at us both and then reluctantly shifts away, just as the Anarchy members are about to grab him. I brace myself and step in front of Cillian. The eye that Henry had changed to match the other starts to tingle. The magic blocking the cell is stripping away Henry's magic. I can feel myself growing weaker, but I am prepared to give them hell.

Nick is one of the members who crowds around the opening of the cell. His face turns into a sick grin when he sees it's me. Cillian has made his way to a standing position next to me, but he has to hold onto my shoulder for support. The tension rises with the anticipation of what is going to happen next.

Fuck, there are a lot of them. I don't think I can physically fight my way out. Maybe if I get outside of the cell.

The alarms cease and the other prisoners settle down. They are watching and waiting to see what will happen. With all the other noise gone, I hear them whispering to each other about me.

"It's her...the Chosen One," a few murmur.

The members part, making way for someone walking through the small crowd. She places her hand on Nick's shoulder to move him slightly to the side, revealing herself.

Lauren.

My eyes squint with disgust, but they also search her for answers. She isn't wearing a colored contact now, and I can see that she does have one blue eye and one brown, opposite of my own. I try to swallow, but my throat is tight. Lauren is dressed in all black, with a black laced top running all the way up her neck. Her dark hair cascades down in full curls.

"Well, well, well...welcome home, Cassie," she snickers.

Everyone around her chuckles. I notice James and Alistair in the crowd as well. They try to play menacing, but I can tell they are anxious about not having reported Henry and me.

Cillian wavers out of the corner of my eye. I loop my arm around his waist for more support.

"Please, let me heal him." I don't want to beg, but I Cillian is struggling so hard against me.

Lauren crosses her arms and thinks about my request. Her heeled, shiny black boots are audible against the hard tunnel floor.

"Hmm… let me think about that…No." Lauren grins.

I am having trouble supporting Cillian, and he slumps to the floor. The others laugh. Rage burns inside me. Even though I am weak inside the cell, tremors begin to shake the tunnel slightly. I glare at Lauren, who remains calm as the others fidget uncomfortably.

"Non desistas, non exeris," the other prisoners begin to chant from their individual cells.

"Quiet!" a member yells at the cell next to Cillian's and bangs on the bars.

"Non desistas, non exeris."

Lauren's grin turns to concern as the once-whispered chants grow into a buzz of commotion. She motions for Nick to enter the cell and grab ahold of me. I jab him directly in the throat with my palm. He stumbles backward, clutching his neck. He gasps for air and tries to use magic against me, but because he is inside the cell, he looks like he is just playing with air.

"How does it feel to be powerless, Nick? I don't need to drug you to attack you," I snicker as I watch him struggle.

His eyes grow wide with terror. He retreats quickly out of the cell. Even Cillian is able to muster a chuckle.

"God, Nick, you are such an imbecile," Lauren screeches. "Everyone, shut the fuck up!"

Lauren walks into the cell and stops in front of me. It is eerie looking into her eyes. I can see it now; I can see all of it—the pain beneath the anger that she has worked so hard to cover. The outline of her face begins to quiver.

"I don't understand," I say, still trying to figure out all the answers to my questions.

Without realizing it, I reach up to Lauren's face. She snatches my arm tightly, digging her nails into my skin.

"You will soon," she says through clenched teeth.

I don't notice her retrieve a taser from her pocket. She releases my arm and digs the prongs into my side. I feel the electricity spark through every muscle and nerve in my body. I want to cry out in pain, but every muscle is frozen. I know I will quickly lose consciousness. I don't feel the ground as I hit it. My vision goes splotchy and the voices fade away.

Fuck.

CHAPTER TWENTY-SIX

I have no concept of how long I am unconscious. Everything is black. It is like I don't even exist—that is, until I hear Cillian's voice.

"Cassandra, wake up."

He sounds far away. I try to open my eyes, but something prevents me from doing so. My head feels like it weighs 100 pounds, and my neck is unable to support its weight.

"You tased her too long, Lauren," Victor's voice scolds.

Victor? Why can't I open my eyes?

"She's fine. Not my fault we have to keep her weak with the spells. If she were to heal herself with her magic, she'd be able to escape," Lauren tries to defend herself.

Bitch.

My vision is returning slowly, but I am still groggy. I try to move my arms, but they are restrained.

"See! She's fine. She's coming around," Lauren says.

I focus my eyes and see Cillian sitting across from me in a

very ornate chair. He looks less banged up, thankfully.

"Cillian?"

He looks worried. I try to blink away the rest of the grogginess as I look around the room. We are in the middle of a grand room. Cillian and I are seated at a large table in the center of the room. The ceiling is high, and the walls are adorned with more dark-themed paintings. I look down to see leather straps restraining my arms. They have markings etched into them, to weaken the captive's magic, I'm sure. Victor and Lauren are standing a few feet away at the head of the table. Victor has on a sleek black suit. The black complements his olive skin very well. His hair is slicked back, and his face is clean-shaven.

"Ah, Cassandra, good. Glad you are awake. Now we can begin," Victor says, clapping his hands together.

"Let us go!" I demand.

Victor walks toward me and outstretches the back of his fingertips to touch my cheek softly.

"But, my dear, you've just gotten here, and there is much catching up we must do."

I turn my head away from his touch. I notice two guards standing at every entrance and exit of the room.

"Please, don't make this harder than it has to be, Cassandra."

I stare at him. His eyes are so black. Lauren sits down in the chair next to mine.

"Fine. You told me you could provide me some answers. Let's hear it."

"Don't be pushy. But, yes, I did say that. Where shall I start?" Victor says, taking his seat at the head of the table. "Ah, I know…you see, the Holloways have held the power of the Anarchy for many years, generations even. It goes back as far as the records do. Each generation is brought up and groomed to take over when the older generation dies. We fight for chaos and to make the world realize that we are superior."

"Okay, but what does all that have to do with me?"

Victor is irritated by my interruption.

"As I was saying, the Holloways have always been a strong magical line. We work under a guise so that we can still walk around out in the world without the slightest incarnation of who we truly are. We send our children to schools just like everyone else. We intertwine ourselves into the masses to acquire knowledge, and also to keep an eye out for the Chosen One. My father sent me to attend Kingshire Academy when I was a small boy. I was there to report back any unusually strong witches, so the Anarchy could either recruit or kill them—just like every other Holloway was to do when they attended."

I think back to my parents.

Is that why they were running?

"We were supposed to not draw too much attention to ourselves, which, as you can imagine, makes things very lonely. And for a boy who was already alone, being at that school was miserable—that was, until I met her."

Victor smiles slightly as his eyes drift off into some memory.

I wriggle my arms to try and get more give in the straps, but Lauren slaps my arm.

"Bitch," I say under my breath.

"Elizabeth Townsend. She was lifechanging for me. It was like she always sought me out to make sure I was included. She made me look differently at life. She made me want to change. I could feel us falling in love, until Johnathan came into the picture and ruined everything!" Victor becomes enraged and slams his fist down on the table, causing it to vibrate. He stands up so quickly that his chair falls backward.

"Liar," I say through clenched teeth. "How dare you talk about my parents?"

Victor rushes toward me and spins my chair around so I'm facing him. He leans the chair back, so it is tilted on its back legs.

"You've been inside my head. You have seen it firsthand."

"You still haven't answered my question. What does this have to do with me?"

He lets my chair drop back down onto all fours and smooths out some hair that has moved out of place.

"All of the answers are right in front of you, Cassandra."

I gulp and prepare myself for my next words.

"Did you kill my parents?"

"I would have moved heaven and earth for Elizabeth. I would have cast down my legacy for her. I would never have done anything to hurt her," he says softly.

I can hear the sincerity in his voice.

"But…their accident was no accident. I know it wasn't…" my voice cracks as tears form in my eyes.

"I do not believe it was either. Now, can I finish the rest of my story, please?"

I nod and try to blink back my tears.

"Your mother was truly something special. She lit up any room she walked into. When my father passed, she was there for me. I was ready to renounce my succession to the Anarchy for her, so you can imagine my shock when she told me she was going to be with Johnathan. It made no sense. She and I were so strong together, and I knew the Joining would solidify all of that, but she joined with Johnathan. Maybe she and I were not meant to be together. After that, I saw she was starting to show. I had pushed her away, and I was so blind, I didn't even realize that she was pregnant. Everything began to make sense then—"

"I know Lauren is my sister." I shock myself by how confidently I say these words. Lauren gets up from her seat and comes to stand next to Victor.

"Not just your sister—but your twin sister. Two sides of the same coin. Of course, we had to cover one of her eyes with a colored contact to hide her heterochromia. It was easier than constantly using magic as eyes are the first to change. But we did use magic for a few other adjustments."

Lauren shivers as her body transforms slightly. Her nose becomes a tad less elongated, her eyes change to a slightly more almond shape like mine.

"It's like looking in a mirror now, isn't it?" Victor chuckles. "Her hair, though, has always been black, which I think suits her."

Lauren keeps her eyes averted from mine.

"So, what? You steal one of my mother's children? You kidnap my sister to get back at my mother?"

This lights another fire within him, and his eyes glow red. He squeezes them shut and balls his hands into fists.

"No, no, no! How are you still not seeing what is right in front of you?" he growls. "You mother may have been able to take memories, but I can keep them. Let me show you."

Victor takes my head into his hands and a memory flashes into view.

"Elizabeth, you're pregnant, aren't you?"

Victor and Elizabeth were standing in a room I didn't recognize.

"I tried to tell you before the Joining. The doctor thinks it might even be twins," she sounded tired.

"Well, give Johnathan my congratulations."

Victor hung his head.

"They are ours, Victor," she whispered softly.

Victor's face lit up.

"So, what does this mean?" he said as he took her hands in his.

She withdrew her hands. "I know who you are, Victor...who you truly are. These babies inside of me are strong. I can already feel it.”

“Does Johnathan know yet?”

“No, not yet, but I will have to tell him soon. I’ve been able to hide it so far, but I’m going to start showing.”

“Come away with me, Elizabeth. You and I, we can go far away from here.”

I could feel his longing and his hopefulness. Elizabeth turned away from him as she began to cry.

“No, Victor. There’s something else you need to know.”

“What is it?”

My mother took off the glove she was wearing and turned her hand, revealing a beautiful emerald encircled by diamonds on her left ring finger. Victor saw it right away.

“John has asked me to marry him, and I said yes. We will be going back to the States.”

Victor’s eyes glowed red and my mother took a few steps backward in shock.

“How could you?” he growled.

Frightened, my mother held her stomach.

“I’m so sorry, but it’s for the best. Once we move, I am going to tell him I am pregnant. I can tell that these babies are special, and I know what your family does to witches who could rival their power.”

This diffused Victor and his eyes returned to a chocolate brown.

“I would never let anyone hurt them. What would you like to do, Elizabeth? I want to be in my children’s lives.”

459

"We can each have one. I don't know how we'll work out all the details yet, but when I give birth, you can take one, and I will take the other."

"That is ridiculous, Elizabeth. What sort of asinine idea is this? Separate them?"

"I've made up my mind. Take it or leave it, Victor."

I saw the moment Victor's eyes turned from a chocolate brown to black, as something inside of him hardened and died forever.

Victor withdraws his hands and the memory fades. My cheeks are drenched with tears.

"No, no, that doesn't make any sense," I cry.

The Serpents must have told her the whole prophecy. My mother was smart, she must've figured it all out. One born evil, the other good. What if she knew all along?

"Cassandra, what did he show you?' Cillian asks from across the table.

I am shaking as I look between Lauren and Victor.

"He's...he's my father."

"What? H-how?" Cillian looks just as shocked and confused as I am.

"So, you ask me, how do you come into play? Well, I want you to come and join your family. We will be the strongest family that has ever led the Anarchy."

I start to have a panic attack, and having my arms restrained is not helping. I have to gasp for air. I thrash around in my seat.

"Let me, let me out, let me out!" I scream.

The room begins to shake. Victor laughs like he is enjoying the show.

"See, Cassandra! You are getting so strong. Even with spells to prevent you, your magic is still finding a way."

Another Anarchy member bursts though one of the doors. He is panicked and sweaty.

"Sir, they've found us," he says, almost out of breath. The other members leave their posts at the various doors to encircle Victor.

During the commotion, I feel one of my restraints begin to loosen. I see that Lauren and Victor are preoccupied. Still breathing heavily, I look at Cillian.

Get ready.

He nods.

"I think it was the boy that was with her when she arrived."

"What boy?" Victor demands.

Lauren groans. "Henry."

Henry's back?

I can feel his presence now. In fact, I can feel the presence of a lot of people from the Academy. The last threads of the binding snap. I quickly try to get the other one off before anyone notices. I can feel my power returning, and it feels good.

I get the last one off just as Lauren turns around and notices.

"No!" she screams.

I shift out of my seat to Cillian as they rush toward me. My fingers fumble with the straps, and I panic. I grab onto Cillian's chair and shift without thinking of where to go. We land hard at the base of the grand staircase. Cillian's chair breaks on impact and he is able to slip off his restraints.

Chaos erupts all around us. There are guards and students I recognize from the Academy attacking Anarchy members and vice versa. I help Cillian to his feet.

"FIND HER!" I hear Victor yell from somewhere nearby. The ground shakes as he yells.

"Cassandra, we must get out of here now!" Cillian says, grabbing my arm.

"No, not yet. I need to find Henry."

My eyes frantically search through the chaos. Henry's presence still feels faint.

"We can try and find him, but we need to move away from here." Desperation shows in Cillian's eyes.

I grab Cillian's arm and shift to the hallway where Henry and I came in. The hallway is empty, but Henry feels closer.

"This way," I say, leading Cillian toward Henry's presence.

"No, you don't!" Lauren screams behind me, and I feel a sharp pain in my scalp. She grabs ahold of my hair and rips me back.

She is on top of me before I can react. She holds a knife to my throat, pressing it so it pierces the top layer of my skin. I quickly look to Cillian, who is trying to fend off Nick and another Anarchy member.

"Lauren, please, just let us go."

I struggle against her hold on me. I know there are many ways I could get out of this, but she is my sister. I want to try and reason with her.

"Do you know how awful it was growing up here?" Her teeth are clenched. "How awful it was when he made the realization that he chose the wrong daughter?! I have lived in your shadow my whole life, and you never even knew I existed. I watched you constantly over the years. I watched the love you were given."

I stop resisting against her. Tears are forming and beginning to fall from her eyes onto me.

"Lauren, I am so sorry, but we can change that now. We don't need to be enemies."

"You know, he wants you alive. He wants to take advantage of your powers. His love can only run so deep with how hard his heart has grown over the years. I hate you. I hate all of you."

I see that she has made up her mind. I use my magic to fling her off me. She flies through the air, but she is quicker now. She shifts away before crashing into the tile. I bounce to my feet and try to sense where she went. Cillian has easily handled the smaller Anarchy member and is dealing with Nick now.

A soft *swoosh* of wind alerts me to an impending blow coming from behind. I twirl around and block it just as Lauren's hand is about to make contact with my face. This begins our fight back-and-forth. Lauren had indeed been holding back before. She is fighting to kill, but that's not what I want. I try to block all of her blows with returns to stun.

"Lauren, please, I don't want to hurt you," I say, pinning her against the wall.

"Well, I want to hurt you!"

She punches me right in my ribcage. I gasp for air and quickly heal the cracked rib.

"No, please, don't kill me!" Nick begs.

I look over to see Cillian holding Nick in a headlock.

"Do it, Cillian."

It is seamless how I have accepted the unspoken communication we share. Cillian nods and then rips Nick's head to the side, resulting in an audible snap. Nick instantly goes limp, and satisfaction fills my heart.

I look back to Lauren, who once again holds the knife in her hand. I put up my hand, and she slices right through it.

"Cillian, we need to get through the mirror, now!"

I will my magic for anything non-lethal. A burst of light shoots from my wounded hand and blinds Lauren. She instantly crumples to the ground, clutching her eyes.

"I can't see! I can't see! What did you do to me? I will kill you!" she screams in agony.

I see the blood pooling in her hands, seeping through her fingers. I take a step toward her to help.

"No, Cassandra, she will be fine. She can heal herself."

I look back at Cillian, who is waiting for me. I take a deep breath and know we need to leave. I want so badly to look back at

Lauren, but I force myself instead to jog to Cillian. We stand in front of the mirror. In the reflection, I see Lauren trying to stand, still moaning in pain. I hold my sliced palm up to the mirror, and it quivers.

"We have to go through it," I tell Cillian.

He nods and begins to walk through. I follow right behind him. Once we are through, I look back, and can still see into the hallway from the other side. Lauren has gotten up and is running full-speed toward the mirror. Her eyes are a bloody mess, but she must be healing them already. I slam my fist into the mirror, shattering it just as Lauren is about to reach it. I hear the faint echo of her screams.

"She'll be close behind if she shifts. Let's move it!" Cillian yells.

Henry feels even closer now. I can feel his presence coming toward us as we run down the tunnel.

"Can you shift us out of here?" Cillian asks.

Before I can answer, we collide with Henry coming around a bend.

"There you are!" Henry shouts. "I have been looking everywhere. I brought reinforcements!" He beams.

"We noticed," I say with a smile.

"Cillian, you're looking less like shit now," Henry says.

Cillian is not amused. "Lauren could be right behind us. We need to get out of here."

"But shouldn't we go back and help the others?" I ask. "I

don't want more people to die because of me."

"Our priority is keeping you safe and getting you out of here. We need to rethink everything. With Victor being your father—"

"Wait, Victor is your father?" Henry interrupts Cillian.

"Long story, but, yes. And we were right—Lauren is my twin sister."

"We don't have time for this! We are getting you out of here, Cassandra!" Cillian yells in frustration.

"Finally, Cillian and I agree on something," Henry says.

I want to protest, but I bite my lip and grab onto both of their hands. I picture the Academy and focus on shifting back there. As the three of us are pulled into the unknown, something tugs me back. I can't see anything distinctively, just morphed colors, as I try to push us to our destination.

What is going on?

Henry's and Cillian's hands begin to slip from my grasp.

"Henry? Cillian? What's going on?"

I try to hold on tighter, but my grasps on both of them is broken, and I am sent tumbling. I land hard on my back. I hear waves of the nearby sea crashing and feel sleet stinging my face. I am quickly grabbed by my arms and thrusted upright. My eyes open to see two Anarchy members, one on each side of me. They quickly slip a strap around my neck and pull it tight.

We are on top of the cliff. I struggle against their hold, but it feels like they have another Weakener on me. I notice a handful of other Anarchy members standing around with weapons in hand.

"Bring her over to me," Victor demands.

The two members turn me around and drag me toward Victor, who is standing with his back to the sea. Henry and Cillian are on their knees on either side of Victor. They have straps around their necks to weaken them as well.

"Let them go, Victor!"

"I told you this would get messy if you did not comply, Cassandra."

"I can see why my mother didn't choose you! You may think you had a heart once, but she always saw you for who you truly were. You are a monster! Everything you touch is corrupted. You know, she had a choice, just like I did during the Joining Ceremony."

Victor's eyes begin to turn red as I spew my insults at him.

"What do you mean?" he demands.

"She could have chosen who to join with, just like I did. She had a choice, and yet she did not choose you!" I laugh cynically.

"Enough!" he roars. "Guess you need to be taught a lesson."

He lifts Henry and Cillian into the air by their necks. They both flail their legs as they struggle against his hold. I try to rip my arms away from the two holding me, but they twist the strap around my neck so I can't breathe.

"No," I try to get out, but it is barely audible.

Victor's smile makes me sick. He waves his hand to position Henry and Cillian over the cliff's edge. Even with the strap around my neck weakening my powers, the sleet increases, and the waves crash harder against the side of the cliff as my anger and fear increase.

"Affinity for the weather, I see. Not fully under control, though," Victor taunts, and clicks his tongue in disappointment.

"Please," I wheeze out.

"Now you must choose who lives, and who dies. The one who would die for you, or the one who already has, so I've been told."

Tears swell as I begin to lose consciousness from lack of air. Thunder roars above us.

"Can't...breathe..."

"Farooq, loosen the hold on her neck. We cannot have any fun if she passes out. She is my daughter, after all."

My skin crawls at the word daughter. Farooq follows Victor's order and loosens his hold on my neck. My lungs burn as they inflate rapidly. I cough. Something dark inside me begs to be let loose as I burn with rage.

Lightning flashes above us in the clouds. A single streak jolts down and strikes just a few inches away from Victor. It causes the ground to explode and sizzle, burning the grass.

"Hey! Cut it out! You strike me, they both die."

"How do I know you won't just drop them both anyway?"

"I may be many things, Cassandra, but I am no liar. You choose one, and I promise I won't drop both," he says with another grin.

I look from Henry to Cillian and back. Henry looks terrified, and Cillian is trying to look calm, but I can see the fear in his eyes.

I can't do this.

"My patience is waning, Cassandra, and from the look of it, your magic is making the tide more violent." Victor is annoyed.

Tears streak down my cheeks and into my mouth as I breathe heavily.

Think, you can do this. You can find a way. Bring the tide up more, that way there's less of a drop—choppy could be better than still.

"Let me go, Cassie. I should have died at the dance. We all know that. Having you come into my life was the best thing that could have ever happened to me, and I am so grateful for this past week with you," Henry yells above all the noise.

"Oh, how adorable. Even I can tell you do not love him as much as you do Cillian, and yet, he would still give his life for you…again," Victor taunts.

"Henry, no," I sob.

"Pick, Cassandra," Victor demands.

I close my eyes, because I do not want to see their faces when I say his name. I know what I have to do.

"Henry."

Victor chuckles. "Very well. Open your eyes! Look at them!"

One of the members jabs me in my spine to open my eyes. Henry looks so sad, but he nods to signal to me that it is okay.

"Say goodbye…" Victor says.

But instead of just dropping Henry, both of them are released and plummet into the vicious sea—the Weakener straps still around their necks. They will drown in a matter of seconds.

"No! You promised!" I wail.

"I lied." His eyes glow red as he smiles.

Something breaks free inside me. My body comes alive with fire as the darkness boils to the surface. My whole body glows, light exploding from me, flinging the members holding me backward, and breaking the strap around my neck. I bolt to the edge of the cliff like a bat out of hell. Victor doesn't have time to react before I hurl myself off the side, diving deep into the black waters below.

The choppy waves allow me to plunge into the water without breaking my arms. The murky water is difficult to see through, even with my body glowing.

"Cillian? Where are you? Henry, can you hear me?"

I try to swim around near the surface, but I have to go deeper for the waves to stop thrashing me around. My lungs beg for air, and I try not to panic.

"Where are you two?"

Swimming around proves useless, so I try a different approach.

"Come to me...come to me..."

I close my eyes and will my magic to pull Henry and Cillian toward me—to search the waters and find them. My heart is pounding, and my body tries to force me to breathe.

I will not fail. I will not die here. I am the motherfucking Chosen One, dammit! Fuck this Prophecy. I choose both!

"Come to me!"

I feel a hand grasp one of mine.

Henry.

And then other.

Cillian.

I can sense who is who without looking. I smile in satisfaction. My hands burn and I feel Henry's and my bond come alive. But something is also going on with Cillian's hand and mine. Our hands burn, and the burn slowly slithers its way up my arm. I look over to see the same markings as Henry and I have forming on my other arm and Cillian's as well. His sleeve shreds as the markings burn into his arm.

No way. We are Joining. I knew it. It just had to be the right time.

Cillian and I look at each other in disbelief. I feel more powerful I ever have before. Now it is time to end this for good. I keep my grip on their hands and use my magic to bring us to the surface. We slowly lift out of the water and into the air. Henry coughs up some water as we hover over the waves.

"Time to end this once and for all."

I turn to my left to Henry and he nods. I turn to my right and Cillian smiles.

"Let's fucking do this," I say, and we shoot up through the air.

We soar to the top of the cliff. I see all the Anarchy members' happy faces turn nervous. I fling Henry and Cillian at the other members, and I head straight for Victor. He starts to change into his ghostly form, but I crash into him before he can. We tumble on the ground together before breaking apart and coming to a stop.

I hear Henry and Cillian fighting as I get to my feet. Victor is quick too, as he is already on his. I use my light power to try and burn his eyes, but he shifts out of the way.

"You really think you can beat me?" Victor whispers into my ear from behind me.

"I know I can. You wanna know why, Victor?"

He tries to land a blindside blow, but I quickly spin around and catch his fist just before it smashes into my cheek. I see a flicker of fear as he strains against my hold.

"Because I am the fucking Chosen One." I smirk as I grab onto more of his arm and spin to flip him over my shoulder.

I look to the sky and beckon more lightning to strike down on the cliff as Victor tries to recover on the ground. The electric charges flurry about, causing my hair to swirl around me. Lightning streaks down, hitting some of the Anarchy members. They die instantly.

Victor tries to shift away, but I use my magic to lasso him and prevent him from doing so.

"No, no, Victor. You aren't getting away from this. Bring it on, *Dad*."

He sets his jaw and squints his eyes.

"Okay, fine. But let's make this truly even. No magic."

He is afraid of me. I can smell the fear behind his macho persona.

"Oh, no, is the King of the Anarchy afraid?"

I no longer feel nervous or scared. I feel powerful. I feel new.

"No magic. Promise?" Victor repeats.

"Sure, Victor. Your move."

He unbuttons his suit jacket and tosses it to the side. He rolls his sleeves up to his elbows, exposing intricate tattoos.

"Come on, already!" I yell. I am tired of him stalling.

He lunges toward me. We match well together as we spar, neither of us able to land a blow fully. I keep an eye on Henry and Cillian every chance I can. They have almost completely neutralized all the Anarchy members on the cliff.

One of my blows lands straight into Victor's heart. He stumbles back and picks up a sword that had fallen near the dead Anarchy member who once wielded it. I look around for another sword while trying to avoid his swings but find none. He is growing frustrated, and that opens more opportunities for error.

Henry's screams break my concentration. An Anarchy member has him pinned. Cillian uses his magic to fling the assailant off Henry when he sees. Because of this, my back is turned to Victor for too long. I feel a sharp blade slice through the muscles in my back.

I let out a howl of pain, dropping to my hands and knees.

Cillian and Henry finish off the last Anarchy member and rush toward me. I hold up my hand to stop them. This can only be settled between Victor and me.

Victor laughs behind me. "Silly, girl, love only makes you vulnerable and weak. Just like your mother made me."

I grit my teeth as the pain is almost unbearable.

"Do what you need to do and end this, Cassandra."

Cillian's words in my head are all the encouragement I need. I let out a scream as I spin around and use my magic to hit Victor with the most force I can manage. He isn't expecting this and is knocked onto his back, his sword flying off the edge of the cliff. I shift on top of him.

"Cassandra, here!" Cillian shouts, throwing a sword to me.

I catch it and hold it high above my head, the silver blade pointed down at Victor's chest.

"Love doesn't make you weak. It gives you something worth fighting for. You've taken so much from me!" I yell at him.

Victor looks up at me in shock.

"Please, I am still your father, after all," he tries to dissuade me.

"Johnathan Rodden was my father. You? Well, you are nothing to me."

"You promised, though. No magic," Victor chokes out.

"I lied."

I plunge the sword deep into his heart. Relief flows through me as his body goes limp, and the life leaves his cold, dark eyes.

Finally, it is over.

I slowly stand and look out at the sea, which is slowly calming, but rain and sleet still fall. Henry lets out a victory scream from behind me. I close my eyes and smile, tilting my head upward, letting the rain soothe me.

We did it.

A stabbing pain suddenly rips through my chest and I scream in agony. My eyes fly open, and my hands reach up to my chest to find the source of the pain. I don't see or feel anything visibly wrong on the outside—no blood, no wound—but still, so much pain.

The rain picks up.

"What..." I say, turning around, but my heart already knows what my brain hasn't grasped. My eyes go first to Henry, who is looking to his side, his mouth open in shock. They then dart to Cillian.

His eyes lock onto mine, a sword protruding through his chest. Every muscle in my body freezes.

Cillian falls slowly to his knees as the sword is withdrawn, fear erupting all over his face. Lauren appears behind him. Her eyes are wild and filled with rage. I will my frozen body to move, but it feels like I am walking through quicksand.

I should have killed this bitch when I had the chance.

Lauren shifts, disappearing out of sight, and I launch myself toward Cillian, my brain finally processing. What was drizzle is now a downpour. I catch Cillian in my arms before he collapses.

"She's over there!" Henry screams and points behind me.

I look over my shoulder and see Lauren kneeling by Victor's body. She's holding his hand one second, and they have shifted away the next. But I don't care about them anymore.

I almost don't want to turn my eyes back. I don't know if I can bear it. Blood is pouring out of his chest, his skin going bone pale. Tears well in my eyes.

"I can fix this," I barely whisper, as I try to make sense of my frantic thoughts. "I brought Henry back before. I can fix this."

I can feel that my powers are drained from the fight, but I will be dammed if I don't try.

I close my eyes and hold Cillian tightly.

"I can fix this!" I scream as I will my powers to help me accomplish another miracle.

But nothing happens. The blood does not recede.

"I CAN FIX THIS!" I wail. "Come on! Please, please don't leave me."

Tears are flowing down my cheeks. I peer up through the rain to look at Henry.

"Henry, help me, please!"

Henry bends down and places his hands on Cillian. I close my eyes again and give it my everything, but I know that even though we are all bonded, Henry and I together will never be as strong as Cillian and I were together.

"Cassie," Henry says my name so softly, I almost don't hear him over the rain. Or maybe I just don't want to.

I keep my eyes shut and continue trying as hard as I can.

"Don't you give up, Henry. Don't you dare give up. I can fix this."

"Cassie, stop! We are all drained." I can hear the pain in his voice. Even though he and Cillian haven't been on the best of terms, when a bond is dying, it still hurts. You still are losing a piece of yourself.

Henry stands up and turns his back to Cillian and me. He screams out in frustration.

"No," I sob, "no, you are just weak! We can do this! I can fix this! Help me!" My sobs cause my whole body to shake. I hate Henry for just giving up.

My knees slowly sink further into the mud as rain pools around us. All three of us are completely soaked, but nothing matters anymore. This can't be how this ends.

"Little Dove," Cillian's voice is soft, but it pierces through the thunderous rain. "Look at me, please."

I squeeze my eyes tighter and shake my head. I know this time, I can't bear it. I don't want this to be real. It just can't be real.

"Please, Cassie." His pleas break my heart even more.

I slowly open my eyes and look at him. Fear no longer bleeds through his eyes, in its place, a calmness. I try hard to keep the sobs from breaking through, but when he reaches up to touch my face, the flood gates are broken.

"I am so sorry. I-I can fix this. I promise. P-p-please don't leave me. I can't lose you."

He smiles slightly. "Of course, you can, Little Dove. Cassandra, you are one of the strongest people I have ever had the privilege knowing."

"Stop talking like this is goodbye. I can fix this, Cillian. I can save you."

But we both know it's a lie.

He gives a small laugh. His body feels so weak. "Always have to be stubborn, don't you?"

I can't help but laugh with him. "You don't get to make me laugh right now."

His tone turns serious, "Your smile is one of my favorite things about you, and if it's the last thing I see, then I will die a happy man."

I grab his hand and hold onto it against my cheek.

"But I don't want you to die." I have never felt so weak in my life as I do in this moment. "Everyone leaves me. You can't leave me." Now I am the one begging.

"Cassandra Rodden." Some blood trickles out the side of his mouth. "I have loved you since the moment I first saw you. You have always been my missing piece. There is a letter hidden within our spot. Find it, and read it."

His words sink deep into me—words that I have wanted to hear for so long.

I look into his piercing blue eyes one last time. "I love you, too."

His body goes limp, and the light slowly slips from his eyes. I grip onto his hand tighter, as if holding it tighter will make him stay.

"No!" I wail and collapse onto him. "No! You can't leave me, please! I can fix this! Everyone leaves me! Everyone I love leaves me. I can't lose you too."

The world around me goes muffled, a piercing hum replacing everything.

"Cassie," Henry's voice sounds far way. "Cassie, we have to

go." I feel his hands under my arms, tugging slightly to get me up. I try to shake him off of me, but he just grips tighter. I can't even tell if I am making any sound at this point. I can't feel anything anymore, except an overwhelming emptiness. An emptiness that is swallowing me whole. Darkness consumes my vision, and everything drifts away. It is at this moment that I wonder if—and even hope that it is possible—to die of a broken heart. I now know what it takes to turn someone evil.

CHAPTER TWENTY-SEVEN

Five Months Later

"That was so hot," a man whose name I don't remember exclaims as he falls back in the sheets.

I roll my eyes and swing my legs over the side of his bed.

"Just, wow, like, I get laid a lot, but that was by the far one of the top five," he continues.

I ignore him as I stand up and try to find my clothes, which had been flung off on the way to the bed. Trash and dirty clothes litter his floor. That and me being decently hammered does not aid in the search for my clothes.

It has been months since Cillian's funeral and I have spent nearly every day since then in this same situation. Drinks, drugs, things, and people. I just want to fill the void his death left behind in my heart. I was able to find the letter hidden within our spot back at the Academy. He had buried it just underneath the tree, protected by spells and a plastic baggy, so it would not get ruined. I haven't read it yet. I can't bring myself to.

Anarchy members went into hiding after the Protectors infiltrated their headquarters. There were a lot of losses on both sides. I tried to search for Lauren to exact some revenge, but I couldn't ever sense her magic. One dead end led to another and then another and so on.

I finally find all my clothes and get dressed.

Whatever-his-name-is sits up in bed, "We should go get food sometime, yeah?" He brushes his long golden locks behind his ear.

I side-eye him as I pull up my jeans.

"No, thanks."

"What, so just good for a bang then?" He acts almost as if he is insulted.

I slip on my other shoe and look at him. "Look, whatever your name is—"

"It's Chad," he states proudly.

"Of course, it is. Look, Chad, you're hot, but you're kind of stupid. So, uh, yeah, just the bang." It isn't just the liquor talking. This guy is actually really dumb, and trying to hold a conversation with him is like watching paint dry—slow and boring.

"Whatever, bitch."

I laugh and walk out of his bedroom. I have been called worse by better, and I truly don't think anything can hurt me anymore.

New York City is still alive at 3:00 a.m. as I descend Chad's front steps. Maybe that's why I've stayed here longer than other places. It makes me feel a little less alone, with all the people all of the time. Henry tried to follow me as I had shifted from city to city to make sure I didn't do anything too drastic. But my self-destruction became too much for him. I was so awful to him. I resent him for what happened to Cillian and I wasn't able to hide that. Our bond also felt broken after Cillian died. I usually check in with my grandmother every other week, but even that has started to slip. I resent my magic for not helping me when I had needed it most. Just one more thing to add to the list of things that have betrayed me so far in life.

I sway as I retrieve my phone from my back pocket and try to figure out where I am.

Ding.

1 new message: Unknown

I slide the notification away, and I search for the PickMeUp app.

Great, prices are surging at the moment.

Ding.

2 new message(s): Unknown

"Ugh!"

My drunken anger is fueled by the second notification. Hello, anger issues again.

I am finally able to order my ride and wait for it to show. I could try to shift, but I am in no state to accidentally end up shifting into a body of water, or off the edge of a building. Maybe that wouldn't be so bad though, I often think.

I pull up Tinder and look through the options of men and women, to see who I can fill some time with next. I feel Cillian's letter poking out of the back of my phone case. I keep it with me at all times.

Maybe I should read it now. I am still intoxicated, so maybe that will help.

I hesitantly pull it from the little pocket. I struggle to open it, with my phone still in my hand. I take a deep breath and begin to read.

My Little Dove,

If you are reading this, that means I am no longer here. I knew when Tabitha assigned me this mission, it would be one I may not come back from. There is still so much for you to learn, and I fear things are only becoming more complicated. You aren't safe. I am so sorry I have failed you once again and cannot be there to protect you. Tabitha threatened your safety if I did not leave you alone. I fear she may have had a hand in your parents' death. But I could not let her hurt you. She is afraid of you and your power. She believes you may turn one day, and will stop at nothing to make sure the Anarchy does not get their hands on you. Momentary discomfort, I told myself.

I must say, I was not always truthful with you. For I have known you much longer than you have known me, but you have had my heart since the moment I first saw you. I was assigned years ago to watch over and protect you if needed. I was hoping to tell you all of this in person one day. I never regretted the night we shared together. But I do regret not loving you as fully and openly as I have always wanted to. We all have pasts; we all have pain.

I fear there is much more to your story, and we have only touched the tip of the iceberg. I pray you don't have to read this, even though I am not religious. But I would do anything to protect you and please know that I'll be protecting you even if I am gone. I have things in place so trust me and trust the ones you love. If I cannot bend the will of heaven, I shall move hell for you.

Forever and always yours,

Cillian

Ding.

The notification startles me as my phone buzzes in my hand. Tears roll down my cheeks. Emotions overload my senses, and I am having a hard time handling them all. I am angry and sad and confused. I quickly fold the letter and shove it into my pocket.

I should not have read this while drunk.

I stare at the notification as my PickMeUp stops at the curb. My drunken thoughts grow paranoid. Maybe something has happened to my grandmother.

3 new message(s): Unknown

My driver rolls down his window. "Are you Cassie?" his tone is stern, but his dark face is soft. He has a full black beard and is wearing a brown jacket.

"Yeah, hold up, okay?" I slur as I slide the notification open. He sighs in frustration.

Unknown: Cassie, it's Lauren

Unknown: I think we can help each other. Meet me at Copperstone Diner. 8am.

Unknown: I can help you bring back Cillian

My heart leaps into my throat and I feel like I am going to vomit everywhere.

"Look, lady, are you my rider or not? I gotta get going."

I slowly look up at him, my mouth hanging open.

Cillian.

"Cassie, it's time to come home," a familiar voice says off my side.

My skin prickles and my blood runs cold. A voice I will never forget, but I thought I would never hear again. I am hesitant to turn and confirm if it is really her. I don't trust my mind right now.

The driver gets fed up and drives off, leaving me teetering on the curb, frozen—too scared to look. I take a deep breath and turn my head slowly. And there she is, standing just a few feet away from me.

How can this be? I have to be imagining this, there's no way this is real.

My body begins to shake, and I think my knees might give out at any moment. My head stops turning and her face comes into focus.

"Nora?"

The Prophecy

Good and Evil
Two sides that have fought against each other
Since the Dawn of Time
Battles raged in the Shadows
And prices Paid by lives lost

But Legend speaks of a Witch
With a Lost Soul
There will come a time
From a decision made
That will open a Pathway
For Good and Evil to be born

Two sides of the Same coin
One side basked in Glorious Light
One side drowned in the Darkest Night

For she who carries the weight of Both
Shall give way to the Chosen One
Two paths will Lie before her
One that will lead to her Salvation
The other to Damnation

Challenges will arise
Scales will be tipped
And an Ultimate Sacrifice Reflected in Red
For the Chosen One shall rise only when
Balance is Found
Between the Shadow and the Soul

ABOUT THE AUTHOR

Ciara lives in Michigan with her family and furry, four-legged kids. She spends way too much time consuming all sorts of different books and escaping into different worlds. When not reading or writing, Ciara can be found absorbed in a movie or TV show. Sometimes, you can even find her streaming a video game online.

Made in the USA
Coppell, TX
21 February 2021

50594232R00272